Praise for TITLE 13

"Ferro has given us an insightful, tightly-crafted, and wickedly cutting novel that forces us all to think about the things we don't want to think about. But it's just such a funny story, too. The only times I stopped laughing were to panic and cry a little."

—Brian Boone, *Splitsider*

TITLE 13

A Novel

Michael A. Ferro

Harvard Square Editions
New York
2018

TITLE 13, by Michael A. Ferro

ISBN 978-1-941861-46-2
Printed in the United States of America

Published in the United States by
Harvard Square Editions
www.harvardsquareeditions.org

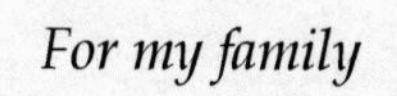

For my family

Chapter One

THIRTY-SEVEN PAGES of highly classified TITLE 13 material were reported missing at the Chicago Regional Census Center on Wednesday morning.

At five p.m. on Tuesday, after the employees of the Windy City's RCC had packed their sensitive data into large, regulated heavyweight folders and filed them neatly away into their sturdy desks under lock and key, and after the keys had been put away into delicate key-sized numbered lock boxes and secured deep within the office behind squinting eyes peering over simple shoulders, and sometime after the government-issued identification badges had been scanned by beeping units fastened to the wall near the single exit, not long before security personnel with no known names and scrupulously molded foreheads had disabled access to the floor, something had gone terribly wrong without anyone in the office seeming to notice a thing.

It was troubling that thirty-seven pages of TITLE 13 information could go missing from the CRCC with no one knowing how or why. Then again, troubling concerns have helped to keep our government funded throughout a number of domestic and international security incidents.

Once even a single page of TITLE 13 paperwork is lost, it is not long before a ripple effect spreads among the populace, targeting the lives of a select poor few and ushering in an enhanced form of absurd chaos only known within the likes of the United States federal government.

* * *

Coincidentally, Heald Brown had been discussing TITLE 13 information with a few of his co-workers before they left the office on Tuesday. Though he did not possess an imposing figure, Heald often let his sarcastic and disputatious nature create a larger image for himself—something that many of his fellow civil servant clerks at the Chicago Regional Census Center had grown accustomed to, or simply ignored for the most part.

Miłosz Pavlenko was a nervous young man who had immigrated to the United States from the Ukraine a few years prior. He had come in search of a better life and a good education; instead he found himself working for the US government alongside Heald. Still, Miłosz poured himself into his work, becoming a source of encyclopedic knowledge on all things relating to the census. Heald rapped his fingers on Miłosz's desk.

"One of the reasons that so many people loathe the United States government is that it is a massive hoarder of personal information—like some jaded recluse stockpiling damning evidence on the world at large," Heald said to Miłosz while he packed away his paperwork for the day. "Every single embarrassing love letter that you've ever written or received, every horrifying account statement or profession of greed, every damning secret you've buried in a shoebox and tucked away in some forgotten closet at home—that is what the federal government embodies to your average cynical tax-paying member of the American public. Too much is known by too many, and our paranoia is enhanced by the simple fact that we can never know just who knows what."

Miłosz scratched his head. "I do not know about this, Heald.

The government created some of the most stringent rules and regulations for censuses concerning the protection of privacy for the public at large. They keep sensitive information in the hands of those who are in the need-to-know category and made one all-encompassing regulation: TITLE 13."

Heald exhaled as if he'd just stepped into a warm sunbeam.

"Ah, good ol' TITLE 13. Like a vigilant nun ready to crack a metaphorical ruler across our hairy knuckles for any malfeasance."

"Erm, I do not know about that, Heald. TITLE 13 contains the type of information that all civil servants employed by the Department of Commerce are sworn to protect under the penalty of incarceration, though *no one* has ever actually been tried or convicted for dispelling or misplacing such classified information." Miłosz smiled.

"You mean, at least not according to any public record," Heald added with a wink.

Miłosz looked at Heald with a note of consternation and gulped hard, as if he'd just swallowed a small water chestnut.

It was then that Janice Torres, another clerk in their department, overheard them and walked over. She was short and slender and about the same age as both Heald and Miłosz—mid-twenties—and, also like them, had settled into a mediocre low-level government career after being out of options during a difficult recession. She casually leaned onto Miłosz's desk.

"It's great when Milo starts reciting rules and regulations like this," she said. "So much better than reading it out of an enormous manual. Perhaps it's your accent, Milo? Like an interesting audiobook. Either way, please go on."

"The United States Code is the codification by subject matter of the general and permanent laws of the United States," Miłosz began. "It is divided by various broad subjects into fifty-one titles and was first published by the Office of the Law Revision Council of the U.S. House of Representatives in 1926. The next main edition was published in 1934, and subsequent main editions have been published every six years since. In the five years between main editions, annual cumulative supplements are published in order to present the most current information."

"Jesus, how did you memorize all that?" asked Heald. He leaned in close to Miłosz. "Tell me the truth: you're a computer, aren't you. You're an android built by the Department of Commerce."

Miłosz was too focused to comment, his eyes now closed in peaceful reassurance as he continued recalling the detailed information.

"Of the fifty-one titles, twenty-six have been enacted into positive statutory law, including TITLE 13. When a title of the code has been enacted into positive law, the very text of the title becomes evidence of the law. Sections 9 and 214 of TITLE 13 look at 'information as confidential; exception' and 'wrongful disclosure of information,' respectively. Government employees handling this sensitive information must take an oath of office never to disclose any of the Personally Identifiable Information, or PII, that they are knowledgeable to while in the service of the government."

"I'm going home, but tomorrow morning I'm looking up how to administer a Turing test for our little foreign *friend* here," said Heald, beginning to walk away.

Janice looked at Miłosz and grinned. "So what are you getting at, Milo?"

"I guess what I am saying is that the TITLE 13 information should be safe. TITLE 13 means we are bound to secrecy… all of us." Miłosz looked around with a cautious eye and began to chew on his fingernail. "Perhaps I should be going home, too. All this secret paperwork is very much making me nervous now."

"Probably a good idea," said Heald from his nearby desk. He was packing away papers and clearing his workstation like much of the rest of the staff preparing to leave. "I hear the deputy director of this office has the many eyes of Argus."

Not long after that, the thirty-seven pages of TITLE 13 information disappeared.

Chapter Two

COMMON BELIEF IS that the traffic is horrendous in Chicago, but after spending most of his life in Detroit, Heald did not mind it all that much. At times, he was grateful that there truly was no reason to own a car here, unlike back in the Motor City.

As he waited for the subway train to pull into the Red Line Lake Station beneath State Street on Tuesday evening, Heald enjoyed the satisfaction of knowing that everything was just fine. Not only did he not mind the cruel heat within the subway tunnel, he also felt an odd, random reassurance that the situation back at the office was just as it was supposed to be: calendars had been properly mismanaged, and project deadlines had been pushed back further into oblivion to accommodate the increasing inanity as actual hard dates for data collection sent from DC grew nearer, and demand for analytics began pouring in alongside thinly veiled threats. It had indeed been another perfect Tuesday at one of the country's largest Department of Commerce's Regional Census Centers.

"Do you know what time it is?" asked a well-dressed man standing along the platform line.

Heald had not worn a watch since middle school, but he still had not bothered to break the natural motion of turning his head down to his wrist and examining it as if one were still there, though there never would be again. He ventured a guess.

"Five twenty-one?"

The man turned squarely toward him and put his arms down firmly against his sides. Heald watched closely.

"No," the man said. "Do you *realize* what time it is that

draws near to us?"

Heald noticed a number of buttons pinned in mishmash fashion across the man's pressed lapels. They were a faint cream color with a yellow cross bearing through them. The man and Heald stood at odds for a moment as the man awaited a response. When he could see that none was forthcoming, due to the nonchalant way that Heald had stuck his finger into his own ear, the man continued.

"What we've arrived at here is the *precipice* of a new dawn, with a new day just ahead," said the man. "We've had ten years since the start of the new millennium to try and set things right, and we've failed. Surely *you* among all people must know that."

Heald looked down and saw that his government ID badge had been hanging loosely out of his suit jacket from the chain around his neck; he innocently tucked it away into his front shirt pocket. The man watched this, then took a step closer toward Heald, who, in turn, took the opportunity to sneeze as loudly and as fraudulently as he could right into the man's face. Unfazed, the man continued.

"It's not like everyone down here doesn't know *exactly* who you are and what it *is* that you *do*," said the man. "Why would you try to hide it?"

Heald stared aimlessly just over the man's shoulder for a moment.

"And just what is it that I do?" asked Heald. The few individuals who had not turned their heads at Heald's incredible sneeze now did so to watch what was developing.

"If you need me to tell you that," the man replied, "then we are all certainly in much more trouble than any of us could have known."

"What?" asked Heald as he stuck his finger back into his ear.

As the gazes of onlookers rose over the rims of their glasses and across the sea of bodies, Heald kept his focus intently upon the man. In the tunnel, the stagnant, swampy air began to billow up and stir around them. It circled slowly around their feet and offered a much-needed reprieve from the warm stillness, signaling that a subway train would soon be approaching the station.

Heald leaned across the yellow markings of the platform that designated safe distance from the tracks and looked far and deep into the darkness of the hollowed tube to see the growing headlights. He noted the deadly electrified third rail, as he often did while staring at these tracks. The man and a number of people stood motionless, anxiously awaiting Heald's response as the situation grew tenser with the approach of the train, the steady metallic hiss growing louder. An onlooker causally loosened his tie while another wiped sweat from his brow with the rolled-up sleeve of his dress shirt, suit coat in his other hand.

The reverberations of an arriving subway train deep underneath the streets of the city above sound very little like anything else. What begins as a low hum grows fuller and more mechanized with each passing moment—as if two enormous brake pads were being scraped along a rusty wall inside a small and circular empty room. While the sound is not deafening, it can make one eye close involuntarily, cause teeth to grit when they otherwise might not.

The man, aching for a response, let his eyes grow wide and bleary with anticipation.

Heald slipped his hands slowly into his pockets, pulling back the front flaps of his suit jacket, and leveled his eyes at the man. "I don't *think* I am who you think I am," he finally replied. "Then again, I *might* think I am similar to who you *think* I am. Who's to say?"

The man and those around him who had been listening to their conversation were forced to quickly move aside as a woman with a baby carriage pushed her way through the crowd in hope of being first to board the arriving train. The train pulled quickly into the station, then began to slow.

"That doesn't mean anything!" cried the man. "If you know something, then for god's sake, say it! We all know you're a *government man*!"

The train came to a stop and its doors opened.

"If you truly think that I'm a government man," said Heald, "then you know that I'm the worst person to ask for information." The man stood on the platform as Heald and those around him began to board after the woman with the carriage had muscled herself in. Heald took two steps backward onto the train without ever turning his back toward his inquisitor.

Two automated bells chimed through the subway car's speakers, and a male voice calmly stated through the sound system that the doors were closing. Heald watched through the grime-covered windows as the man stood with a terrified look on his face and turned his palms skyward, as if drawn up by the pull of two identical magnets on the streets above, while his forearms remained at his sides.

The train began to pull away, and the man was quickly out of sight. Heald glanced around and noticed that everyone had already disregarded the encounter between him and the man and returned to their newspapers and cell phones. Heald didn't mean to, but he grinned.

* * *

Exiting the subway car, Heald felt droplets of sweat fall upon his unbuttoned collar and onto the back of his neck. At this point, his wrinkled white dress shirt was soaked through, and his bright red tie had dampened to a blood-like color. Walking up the urine-soaked stairwell from the station below and into the blasting heat of the outside light, Heald looked down the street past the single row of trees desperate for water and then up at the skyscrapers that seemed content to own the atmosphere. Within their shade was the only respite from the sun's last powerful onslaught before a cooling dusk settled upon the city.

"Boss man," said a smirking, jittery-looking man holding out a cheap newsmagazine. His other hand held extra copies, and a torn, weathered bag sat near his feet. "You gonna buy one a my papers today?"

Heald smiled back and walked over toward the man.

"Depends. What's the news today?"

"Same news as all news, man. It's all bad news. They *still* in recession. They's *still* a war, and I *still* out here, less you buy a paper or two, my man."

"Now why would I buy two of the same paper?" asked Heald. "Tell you what, I'll take *a* paper. A little information never hurt anybody, right?"

"I guess not," said the man. "But what do I know? You the boss, boss man."

Heald took the paper and opened it up, eyeing the man

over the top of the page. The paper shook in his trembling hands. He had to get home.

Heald's key got stuck in the front door of his apartment building. Again. The door unlocked and opened, but he was unable to remove the key after it had performed its one and only function on this earth. Was this a key problem, or a lock problem? After a few moments of fiddling with it, Heald was tempted to jerk his hand and break the key off in the lock, if only to recover the rest of his keys. Finally, he felt it wriggle loose, and he threw open the cast iron door and quickly whisked himself into the air-conditioned lobby.

At a small desk sat a doorman with enormous, dark-rimmed eyeglasses and a snow-white bird's nest of hair upon his pale head. His face was buried deep inside a large book—nose nearly pressed up against the pages. Looking up for a brief moment, he flashed Heald a courteous grin, as might anyone who was on a brisk autumn walk through a park. Heald nodded and walked through the lobby toward the mailboxes.

Sitting within the inner lobby were two young men who appeared to be engaged in a fierce nose-picking competition, though each was oblivious of the other. The one on the left side of the room seemed to be working hard to flick his harvest from the tips of his fingers, yet appeared to be having some difficulty. The other man kept his right hand free to explore the endless depths of his nostrils while the left poked lazily at the screen of his smart phone.

After collecting a few bills and a letter from his mailbox, Heald headed up to his apartment. Once again, this time at his own apartment door, the key got stuck in the lock, and Heald once again fought the powerful urge to break it off, or to perhaps kick his door down (though he knew he was more likely to just hurt his foot). He finally managed to get the door open and walked inside, and slammed the door behind him with his keys still jangling from the lock.

Setting the mail and the letter upon the tiny end table within the four-hundred-square-foot apartment, Heald noted that his hands were still shaking. He turned and looked into the sink for an empty glass. Within the sink was a treasure trove of sickening squalor: plates were piled upon other plates with silverware mixed about, all coated on the corners with dark, bubbled grime; a glass half-filled with a faint, milky liquid topped with foam sat to the side; and two forks missing essential prongs rested, submerged in a bowl atop the mess.

Reaching to grab the glass that contained the mystery milk, Heald accidentally activated an incredible animation: as his hand settled upon the glass, a flock of what seemed like millions of tiny fruit flies took flight in a dizzying array all around the kitchenette. As if drawn by some preternatural force, a rogue group of the fruit flies, likely more wild and adventurous than the others, zipped madly right at Heald's face and into his nostrils.

Frantic and somewhat terrified, he breathed in deeply through his mouth and blew a blast of air out through his nose to expel the miniscule invaders from the warm, soggy comfort of his proboscis. Some of the bugs flew right out, riding on a glob of snot as Slim Pickens rode the bomb. Grabbing a crumpled piece of paper towel from the wastebasket, Heald wiped the mess from his face and watched as the swarm of fruit flies swiftly disappeared into new and uncharted corners of the cabinets and crevices within the room. They disappeared like magic under the hood of the stove and behind the refrigerator; some—the bravest or the stupidest—returned to the sink, right back into the fray.

Heald picked up the dirty glass and tipped it over, and noticed a mass of dead flies in the liquid headed toward the drain. Rinsing it clean, he set the glass on the counter and turned to open the freezer. The cold glass handle of the half-gallon jug of vodka felt wonderful in his hand, and he twisted off the top and poured the glass nearly full, his hand still shaking and beads of sweat forming on his forehead.

Heald drank, emptying the glass in one fluid motion. He opened the refrigerator door and grabbed a carton of orange juice, drinking a hefty amount. While he waited for the shaking to cease and the vodka to take effect, Heald began the arduous process of disassembling his government attire.

First off, always and obviously, the tie had to go. Such a curious thing a tie is, he thought, feeling the burn settle in his stomach. It was almost as if the tie was meant to simulate the sensation of constant strangulation—a phantom grip always around the neck. All day long Heald sat at his desk within the Chicago RCC feeling as if he were hanging in the gallows, yet never allowed to expire, just dangling there helplessly, slowly and silently dying of ennui. He would look around at his male coworkers as they sat, lump-like, wearing their perfectly knotted nooses. A tie, Heald thought, might just be one of the most hilarious existing examples of madness in the modern man. Grab it and yank hard enough, and you could reduce even the biggest brute into a gasping fool at your feet in seconds. As he finished removing his tie, Heald made a mental note to always go for a man's tie should he ever get himself into a brawl at any tie-wearing occasion.

Next up was the lengthy and disgusting procedure of removing his sopping wet dress shirt; a soaked shirt will cling to a man much worse than most other things, like a horny teenager clings to his prom date. Each button undone felt like one small and significant step closer to some second-rate sovereignty.

Standing with his stomach free and waves of heat radiating off his body, Heald began to feel the alcohol settle within his stomach, the coolness of being set free from his office clothes countered by the warm and comforting sensation within the depths of his belly.

It was time for another drink.

The second drink was always better than the first. As his hands and mind grew steadier, he was finally able to assess the happenings of the day.

After the second and third drinks, Heald decided to go out for a jog down bustling Michigan Avenue, known as the Magnificent Mile. With a few hours of sunlight left, it seemed only fitting to go out and exercise away the empty calories from his dinner. In running shorts and a musty old Detroit Tigers T-shirt, Heald headed out of the stifling apartment, opening the window before he left. Outside of his door, he pulled the keys from the lock without much trouble or thought.

Stretching awkwardly and unashamedly as he made his way through the lobby, Heald noted that there still seemed to be no clear winner in the nose-picking battle, though not for lack of trying, as each competitor still flicked away their offerings onto the floor or spread them onto the armrest of the chair. Heald suddenly felt sorry that he might miss the victor being crowned. He also felt bad for the cleaning crew who would soon be forced to clean the floor and those chairs. There were so many people to feel bad for day-to-day—especially in a city that possessed such a complicated infrastructure.

Heading out into the evening's final hurrah, Heald hopped about, alternating feet, as if he knew what he was doing. The cast iron door of the building closed behind him, and he began his jog toward the shore and south down the Mag Mile. The doorman stood outside at the street corner smoking a cigarette and nodded toward Heald, then quickly returned his gaze back up to the sky, looking for something.

Chapter Three

HEALD WOKE UP with a pain in his ass and in his head.

He rolled off his futon and rose to his feet, then set about the arduous task of assembling himself for yet another day at work. Heald had long since ceased folding and unfolding his futon back to its proper sitting position each night, opting instead to nestle himself into the Heald-shaped crater that had formed in the cushion. Gazing at it lovingly now, he wished that he could climb back in, despite it being about as comfortable as a sack of broken hammers. But no: he had important government work to do. Moreover, he needed to earn money. With all the turmoil in the Department of Commerce, Civil servants had been dropping around him like the flies in his sink, but he would strive to avoid their fate.

A stink filled the air that Wednesday morning as Heald walked to the Brown Line L stop. It was just hot enough this time of the morning that each of the city's downtown dumpsters had their putrid contents heated to a slow simmer that allowed for peak offensive smells. The aroma invoked a number of strong feelings and emotions within Heald, many of which were violent and dangerous when coupled with the groggy aftermath of alcohol-induced sleep and a forced to too-early rising. Olfactory molestation should be a crime in Chicago, punishable along the lines of grand larceny, for Heald had certainly been robbed of his joy.

Among the usual suspects, from dirty diapers filled with copious amounts of baby discharge (How does a tiny human make that much feces? Heald wondered), to the plethora of cultural dishes that could only come from a melting pot town such as Chicago—everything from curdled Indian yogurt coated in yeast to spoiled sausages down on Maxwell Street that may or may not have actually already passed through a human to the strange fruits from the Far East that never seemed to ripen yet somehow could catch an unbelievable price at the Treasure Island food market—all of it, while inspiring Heald to clothespin his nose, somehow made him grin. He stepped up the platform to the raised tracks of the Brown Line.

As the train rolled Heald ever closer to his office, he sat among the other riders but felt entirely isolated. He supposed that everyone feels as if they are trapped in a bubble at some point. While in that bubble, sitting and mulling over their precarious situation, the rest of the world keeps on revolving as if it has gone on and forgotten about them entirely, for it has. The individual is left to float above the planet while they watch from high above, delirious, as everything appears to flow along with minimal effort underneath them, like a stream through a low basin after a steady rain, clearing clouds above.

These bubbles can be filled with items of a pecuniary nature. They may also be filled with heartache, poverty, anger, booze, oppression, grief, madness, or perhaps any combination of the like. The helpless passengers inside feel condemned to their bubbles, powerless to influence the individual fate that each one eventually floats toward, regardless of the hope for something else on the inside.

Each of us—each thing crying out and grasping for a

sharp object to pierce our bubble with—knows that deep down, outside of our own little sphere, it is the same existence and circumstance all around the world. We cocoon ourselves in these things, eventually settling within them as our homes, thinking they are singular or perhaps unique to us, but we share them inside and out with everything that surrounds us. We own our bubbles—our hives of emotion—and there are entirely too many of them. If we do break free of them, we could lose them forever, and as much as we implore ourselves to truly believe that this is our sincerest wish, in reality, we are far too terrified of falling and landing within someone else's cocoon...someone else's world that might not share the comfort and familiar anxiety of our own.

There is no parallel universe that we seek, no other way to see or feel something, because forever and now is the only way it can be done in our minds. Our existence is within one large lottery ball machine, our bubbles feverishly blowing around, bouncing comically off one another; the machine is filled to the brim with our individual worlds, and while we pray and we hope for some divine interposition to draw us near the top for selection, what is the prize?

The train screeched to a stop and Heald's bubble popped. His office was in the Jomira Transportation Center, the central travel hub of the city's downtown area, just across the street from the famous Union Station. (Is there a Union Station in the world that isn't famous?) Workers came from Chicago's suburbs and as far as Wisconsin and Indiana, all on the Midwest's largest rail system, the Midway Line. Between Jomira and Union Station, over one hundred of the massive double-decker trains came in every morning from across the land to drop off the droves of businessmen and women to their hives for the day.

The first two floors of Heald's building, along with train platforms themselves, were a monument to American consumerism, with all manner of high-end coffee shops and juice chains and sausage-and-egg-patty pushers who were desperate to feed you the pork while you fed them the bacon. The building also housed two corporate newsstands, both owned by the same company, each even sharing the same name and sign, just one floor apart. The sad state of the world seemed to be suggest that soon everything printed would fade away.

This truly disappointed Heald. How funny it would be, he thought, to have some future alien race come to our unpeopled planet to find that all physical records of man's social life had vanished over a relatively short period, as if we had decided to start covering our tracks for some reason after the turn of the twenty-first century. As if humans had grown so embarrassed, perhaps even disgusted and disheartened with their own actions, that we collectively decided to no longer keep physical evidence and just left everything to drift into the electronic winds—no material proof, no eyewitness to corroborate the mistakes that we made and chose to ignore. Those aliens would find Plato's writings, the great works of Shakespeare and Homer, even the proud documents of the founding fathers, but please, for the love of their alien gods, let them not find evidence of our social media accounts...

The end of man, Heald assured himself, would not go down in history books, because there would be no books in the physical world for it to go down into. It would happen live and through electronic news feeds, stored away into some server warehouse, somewhere that might not make it through the crisis. All of humankind's greatest and most wondrous achievements throughout history will have existed in some form of print or permanence, one way or another, yet, the crux of humanity's slip into non-existence from sheer disregard for thought would likely forever be lost in an electronic grid, some inaccessible data storage container or a server locked away in a chilly warehouse deep in some remote region of Idaho.

Present hard disk drives can store enormous amounts of information and data, but they can only do so for roughly ten years, as their magnetic energy barrier is so low that the information becomes lost soon after. Mankind has been storing information and creations for thousands of years on everything from ink and canvas to marble and cave walls, but like those earlier formats, today's electronic chips will all lose their stored information within a matter of time. There is some chatter about using newly developed disks made from tungsten, which would allow the data to withstand extreme temperature changes in the environment; this would allow for data to be accessible for possibly up to a million years or more. The important question that scientists seem to be forgetting to ask themselves is whether or not we actually want a record of mankind's recent exploits in the modern world to survive for even a fraction of that length of time.

In any case, data in its current form will not last for very long, yet ironically, another nearly outdated form of data preservation was about to change Heald's life. On the forty-ninth floor of the Jomira Transportation building, home of the Chicago Regional Census Center, it would be paper—that ancient and unwavering constant since the Chinese first put ink to pressed pulp—that would now come to alter his world completely. Paper now missing from the very office that Heald took the elevator up to was going to transform life itself. Had the data been a file on a flash drive, it would likely have been encrypted or remotely purgeable, but because the pages were physical things, an entity capable of being held and folded and tucked into a pocket, the CRCC was fated for doom.

* * *

Heald's office was often abuzz by eight o'clock in the morning, but today, the hallways were empty. He swung out his key card from the chain around his neck and entered through the first set of security doors. Behind that and around another corner, an even larger single door had a manual lock that required those wishing to enter to punch in a passcode of three numbers onto a set of dense steel buttons on a console. Heald punched in that week's code and stepped into the office that was now, somehow, thirty-seven pages shy of extremely sensitive and highly classified TITLE 13 material. The air was often thick with a manufactured, recycled quality that can be found in the cabin of an airliner: synthetic air.

Every man was clad in suit and tie, the standard required dress for male government office employees. Even a clerk like Heald had to wear a monkey suit. One afforded freedom was the color of the tie that a man decided to wear. Occasional Fridays offered men the chance to choose a shirt color other than white, and while most men did not partake, those who did went hog wild: you might see off-white, or a slightly-less-than-or-greater-than-white-while-not-straying-too-far-from-plain-white white. Or cream. One man was even so bold as to try wearing a baby blue-colored shirt—but that only happened once.

Women on the other hand were free to wear any type of flowery dress or blouse that they desired, including knee-length skirts, or sometimes just a touch shorter. Men in the office envied this feminine freedom, though they never complained.

Heald was noting a particularly wonderful set of nearby gams when the pensive and tightly wound Ukrainian clerk Miłosz Pavlenko ran up to him with his eyes opened as wide as manhole covers and one large, solitary vein that looked like a small stick underneath the skin of his forehead throbbing fiercely, begging to burst.

"Heald! We have problem," Miłosz said nervously.

"I'm sure it's fine," said Heald, casually walking past Miłosz to his desk to set down his bag.

"No, Heald. No. I am afraid it is very serious. Something terrible seems to have happened. Everyone is running 'round like chicken with no more head. You know?"

"It's Wednesday, Milo," said Heald. "That's as good a day as any to try and look busy when you work for the federal government, don't you know? Points for effort."

"This...this is not something that I like. How do you say? I have *unfortunate* feeling concerning this entire matter."

"That's why they hired you, ya ol' bean. We need strong, good men with unfortunate feelings."

Heald settled into his chair and turned on his computer. As he stood and began to walk to the break room for a cup of coffee, he did notice that something seemed amiss with his coworkers. Walking past the area of representatives from Springfield, Heald could smell something burning, though there was no flame in sight. One man in a corner of the office was speedily filling a massive plastic jug from a water cooler. Another man, tall and extremely slender, was chewing the erasers off all the pencils on his desk and spitting them out into a garbage can. As he did this, he spoke to himself in a calm, cool voice and Heald could clearly hear the man utter something about his tie and using his office chair as a floatation device. Another man was holding up sheets of paper to a lamp on his desk, as if the light or heat would reveal something hidden.

No one other than Miłosz and Heald had come in yet within the ultra-secret Census Coverage Measurement division, but it was clear that something did appear to have the rest of the office in a commotion much earlier than usual. Heald hastily retrieved his coffee and returned to his desk, only now starting to feel a bit anxious. He thought about it, and then turned his attention to Solitaire, which he began to play on his computer.

The Census Coverage Measurement (CCM) division was kept secret and well hidden from the actual census itself, which was secret and hidden in its own right. In an effort to qualify and regulate the data, the Department of Commerce had created the CCM division back in the 1950s, convinced that additional expenditures and bigger budgets were paramount to winning the government horse race. Simply put,

CCM would go out to double-check the work that the Decennial Census was doing, though in much smaller random samples. Keeping this group of CCM folks isolated from the rest of the CRCC ensured that a fair and balanced stance would be maintained during the Decennial Census, or any other number of operations handed down from Washington.

The standards for security couldn't have been higher, and the Chicago branch prided itself on how accurately and perfectly they had followed Washington's directives on these matters. The day-to-day work of the two divisions, the CCM and the regular census, had to maintain an extreme level of privacy and anonymity from each other in order to function. To achieve this, the forty-ninth floor of the Jomira Transportation building was sectioned off into two offices.

On one side (a little smaller than the other), CCM conducted their business, and on the other, the rest of the census conducted their own. The offices were kept apart through the deceptively simple use of large, fuzzy partitions. These two-inch thick aluminum partitions, covered in a gray and squeezeably soft wooly coating and which did not extend all the way to the ceiling, ensured that nothing and no one under six feet tall could accidentally blow across onto the opposite side, should a gust of wind suddenly overtake the office. And though these partitions weren't exactly what a master craftsman might describe as "stable," they would surely keep inquisitive animals from curiously wandering back and forth between sides of the office, if perchance any were to make it into the building, through security, and up to the forty-ninth floor. Then again, if a grown man or woman were to accidentally bump into one of the partitions, the whole wall would likely collapse, and each department's secrets would be revealed to the other; thus a strict no-stumbling policy was enforced in the Department of Commerce's field offices. (Headquarters had their own policies.)

Heald's desk bordered the Quality Control (QC) group within the Census Coverage Measurement division, which was, in turn, instructed to remain even *more* separate and internalized from the CCM division, as if the whole office was one big Russian doll, groups within groups within groups, getting smaller and smaller. The QC group's mission within the CCM department was to test an even smaller sample of the population within the CCM group's own small sample of the whole Decennial Census's complete population sample in order to even further refine and analyze the results pouring in from the tristate area that the regional office covered, providing yet another layer of security and analysis for the already enigmatic organization. The dizzying array of complexity was often enough to confuse even those endowed with the mightiest mental prowess. This third level of ultra-secrecy was maintained by a waist-high wooden border—which could not stop so much as a heavy sneeze or an angry glance—between the two groups.

It was now a quarter to nine, and being alone in his top-secret division's corner of the office with a nervous Ukrainian was not something that sat entirely well with Heald. Hadn't there been some type of conflict between America and Miłosz's country? Was there about to be?

Miłosz sat innocently enough chewing his fingernails down to a bloody nub. All either man could do was wait for someone of authority to come into the office to see about what might have happened that had some workers in the office ready to use their chairs to float off to some theoretical safety.

Heald looked around and began to feel sick as he sat alone at his desk waiting for his coworkers to begin shuffling in. Beside himself and Miłosz, the CCM department was empty. Heald's superior, Martha Leifhat, who sat just behind him, had not yet walked into the office; she was normally the first person in each morning and despite his usual groggy condition, he looked forward to her chipper and sincere Midwestern greetings. Leaning back in his chair, Heald began to wonder if he had missed some mandatory morning meeting, but then remembered Miłosz sitting not far from him at that moment and knew that Milo would be the last person to miss such a meeting. Heald was an excellent follower in a workplace, much like a loyal prairie dog is to its coterie leader.

What could possibly have happened to keep everyone else? What had the folks on the other end of the main partition acting like confused chickens with no more heads? Where, also, was that fancy pumpkin-flavored spiced coffee creamer thing that Heald had stolen out of the fridge yesterday?

Miłosz was holding a slightly bloodied Kleenex against his chewed and mangled fingertips. He rose and walked toward Heald, who was at his own desk, preoccupied with an error message that had popped up on his computer screen.

"Heald, something is wrong. I feel it."

"Yeah, I know. I've got this error message again: 'The operation completed successfully.' I mean, I'm confused. What kind of error message says something was successful?"

"Heald, what could have happened? When we left, everything seemed fine yesterday. All of everything was good, yes?"

"It's got that red circle with the white *x* in it. *That's* an error message. I know that much. But it was successful? And when I click on the *x* to close the window, it opens right back up again!"

"I was not the last one here, Heald, were you?" asked Miłosz, a little more nervous now. "Who left the office last?"

"'The operation completed successfully,'" Heald repeated. "Did I print something?"

Miłosz's hands were resting on Heald's desk now, and he stood directly in front of him.

"Who was the last person to leave the office?" repeated Miłosz.

"Hell if I know, Milo!" Heald barked after finally taking his eyes off his computer screen. "I'm usually the first one out the dang door—five o'clock on the dot! Now look, come here. Come look at this. I click and boom, it pops right back up!"

"Maybe it is a governmental error message," said Miłosz scratching his head. "As in, 'Oops, we have done something right maybe'." Miłosz grinned sheepishly.

"Miłosz...Mil-osz!" Heald jumped up and thrust his arms in the air. "Did you just make a joke!? An *American* joke!? God bless you, sir, and God bless this country!" Miłosz hung his head and a small smile spread across his face as Heald came from around his desk to pat him on the back.

"Honestly though, Heald, do you think they have cameras on us?" asked Miłosz. "They should watch us more often. I feel like things are happening here and no one is noticing."

At that moment, Janice Torres walked into the area and set her things down on her desk, which was across a short aisle from Heald and just in front of Miłosz. She took out a small pink container of lip balm and began to spread it evenly over her lips—not slowly and seductively, but with the limited passion of a person suffering from chapped lips.

The first time Heald met Janice had been a day of many other firsts for him. It was his first formal job interview in a government office, and the level of security that he'd passed through had both excited and concerned him. Another clerk, one who no longer worked in CCM, had been sent down to the lobby of the Jomira Transportation Center to greet him and escort him up to the forty-ninth floor.

There Heald met Gilbert Tabin, his future boss, and was immediately impressed with the way that Gilbert presented himself—professional and prescribed, yet courteous and receptive to a humorous aside in a friendly way that was neither wooden or false. He was a tall man with taut skin that clung tightly to his face and hands despite his age, at least double Heald's own. It was just the two of them in that bleached white corner office that looked out over the northwest side of Chicago. At first, Heald mistook it for an unoccupied office, for there was no formal desk, and most of the room was cluttered with papers and boxes. The interview was succinct, and Gilbert said that they would be in touch. They called not an hour after Heald had left and offered him the job.

Heald was thrilled to learn that he would finally have a job that could support him after his impromptu—even reckless—move from Detroit, especially as his savings nearly were nearly depleted, but there was also something else that excited him. Before he left the office after his interview that day, he knew that he had met the most beautiful woman he had ever seen.

He'd felt ridiculously shy in her presence and of course did not know what to say when he saw her, but he felt compelled to say something. He came up with the brilliant plan to ask her name and what she was doing there. She gave him a look over and told him that her name was Janice and that while she was there for a job interview, she wasn't going to get her hopes up. The comment intrigued Heald, as he was also somewhat pessimistic about the position after months of steady rejections and felt comfortable around people who were open about their own similar feelings of dejection. It didn't hurt that she was small and striking and roughly his own age, but that didn't matter as much as what she'd said.

Growing up, Heald had been labeled a romantic by his high school and college friends for his naïve nature and what many felt was a basic inability to reserve judgment and logic in the presence of a pretty face. As his drinking grew steadily worse, this attribute transformed from a determination to find someone to share his heart with into a quest to find somebody to give it to—it no longer being safe in his own keeping. On that first day in the CCM office, he saw Janice not merely as a solution to his problem, but as someone who could help him find the strength to confront the problem itself head on and motivate him toward a more prudent path.

Two weeks later, on his first day, after a long background check and vetting process, Heald was thrilled to see that the woman who had tickled his fancy was again in the waiting room when he entered, and she smiled at him politely. He told her that it looked like they'd "both gotten what they deserved," and were "doomed to work for the government." She laughed casually, and he was hooked. They sat next to each other during their orientation, where they both took the oath to honor the Code of the United States, including that of TITLE 13.

"Hey, guys," Janice said now, putting the cap on her lip balm. "What's the good word today?" Heald turned back to his computer screen. He had been staring at her.

"This operation completed successfully," he said.

Miłosz looked up to her and quickly tried to lock eyes in a pleading glance. "Something terrible has happened, can you not tell? Everything is wrong."

Janice sat for a moment and looked straight ahead at nothing in particular. She furrowed her eyebrows. "Well, those are two conflicting reports." She turned to Heald, who was already looking at her again. "What's this successful operation, Heald?"

"That's the thing. I have no idea. All I know is whatever it was, it was successful, and that is a problem because it's making an error message pop up on my screen and there's nothing I can do to make it go away. I can't tell you how many times I've tried to close it."

"Thirty-seven," said Miłosz.

"Huh?"

"Thirty-seven. You have clicked on the button to try and close the window thing thirty-seven times."

Janice and Heald looked at each other for a moment and then back to Miłosz.

"How did you know that?" asked Heald. "Have you been watching me click this button and counting, or is this just like an auditory tick you have?"

"I think is mostly a auditory thing. I have this thing since I was a young boy where I can *per-ceive* sound and *interpret* as a number concept."

"Like *Rain Man*?"

"Like who?" asked Miłosz, puzzled. "Who is 'Rain Man'? A man who brings rain? He can do this, too?"

"No, I mean, like, are you slightly autistic or something like that? How could you count all of those tiny clicking noises? I was trying to close this window on my computer like a madman."

"I don't know. I just did it."

"That's incredible," Janice said without inflection. "Lip balm?"

"No, thank you," replied Miłosz. "My lips are abnormally hydrated all of the time. I think it is survival thing from cold Ukrainian boyhood."

"Makes sense," Heald said, nodding in agreement.

"So, where is everyone?" asked Janice looking around. "Our department is empty."

"This is the problem!" Miłosz cried, remembering something other than his soft, pouty lips. "Something terrible has happened, I know it. Do you think they videotape us? I think they should so we can see what has happened."

Heald was back to clicking the error message on his screen again.

"Well, when I tried to get into the main door just a few minutes ago, the passcode had been changed," said Janice. "It was strange. We're normally told when that happens."

"Changed?" asked Miłosz. "It wasn't"—he paused and looked around as if someone could very well be hiding in a nearby potted plant—"five-two-three?"

"No," she replied. "In fact, the only way I was able to get in was by following close to that new guy from the Springfield office. He held the door for me when I flashed him a smile, even though my smiles never come out right. I always end up looking like I'm ready to bite someone."

"The operation...," Heald said aloud while looking at his screen and slowly bringing his two index fingers together and up to his lips, "completed successfully." He stared into the screen for a soundless moment. "It's some type of puzzle!" he shouted. "An error happened successfully! Has anyone in the office undergone any type of planned surgery of any kind recently? Does everyone still have both of their kidneys? Milo?"

Milo panicked as he brought his hand to the side of his back and felt around. He turned to Janice with an anxious look. "So the passcode was changed? But they are supposed to only change those every two weeks and it was just changed on

Monday." The vein in his forehead returned. "Oh dear my. That is no good. That and this is no good at all."

"I'll bet no one else from CCM has been able to get into the office since they changed the codes without warning. How did you two get in, anyway?"

"I just punched in the old code and the door opened when I got here about a half hour ago."

"Same for me," Miłosz said.

"So they changed the code just this morning? Right after you two got here? That's weird. I think Milo is right—something must have happened."

"Yes," Heald said. "Something did happen. Says so right here. An operation happened and it was successful, but apparently, that's also cause for error."

"Should we go back to the main door and let people in?" asked Janice.

"No! That is against protocol!" Milo shouted.

"Oh, crime in Italy, Milo!" said Heald. "It's not a big deal!"

"What? 'Crime in Italy'?" asked Janice. "What's that supposed to mean? Do you mean *criminy*?"

"No," said Heald. "I mean crime in Italy. There's lots of crime in Italy."

"They recoded those doors for a reason," Milo said after a moment. "Oh dear. Oh *hivno*."

"What?" asked Heald.

"Oh dear."

"What did you say there?"

"I swore. In my language."

"Hivno?"

"Yes."

"What's it mean?"

"Oh dear."

"Bullshit. What's it mean?"

"It means that."

"Means what?"

"What you say."

"Bullshit?"

"Yes. Well, the second part."

"Hivno?"

"Yes."

"*Shit?*"

"Yes."

"This is good. Thank you, Milo."

"Oh dear."

Janice and Miłosz sat quiet for a time while Heald causally inserted his newly learned foreign profanity into some very American-sounding insults. Milo massaged the vein in his forehead. Just then, Martha Leifhat came walking down the row of desks followed close behind by the rest of the CCM division. A wave of relief flowed over Miłosz's face, but was quickly replaced by panic, perhaps for no real reason anymore.

Heald swung his chair around to greet his supervisor, who sat directly behind him at her own sprawling desk in the bullpen they all shared.

"Mornin', Martha. Have any trouble with the doors this morning?"

She was hurried and distracted as she dropped her bag and items to the tabletop behind her, which faced a floor-to-ceiling window displaying a gorgeous, high-rise view of the skyline of Chicago's financial district.

"As a matter of fact, I did," Martha said, looking at him with an ominous, pained smile. "They've called an emergency meeting for all of CCM right away in the large conference room, so we've got to get down there now, Heald."

Heald, unfazed by this news, felt disappointed that he hadn't received the customary motherly "hello" from Martha. Miłosz, who was back at his desk across the aisle and out of what could be deemed normal human earshot, apparently heard this, and fell from his chair without a sound.

Chapter Four

THE CONFERENCE ROOM in the CRCC was large enough to stow away a squad of police cruisers, or perhaps even an Apache helicopter, should the need to do so ever arise. The front of the room was punctuated with a small podium bearing the official U.S. Department of Commerce seal. The massive open room was bordered by tables that allowed for roughly 90 percent of the entire office staff to sit, while the other 10 percent were forced to either stand up against the windows behind the seated staff or sit at a lone table at the center of the room. This physical arrangement was rarely altered and often gave the impression of a courtroom with the stragglers left to sit upon their lonely island in the interior like defendants awaiting a verdict. The CCM group, usually the last to be told about these meetings, often ended up along the back glass or pleading their case from the pitiful marrow of the room.

Somehow, due to some modern marvel of architecture, three of the massive walls in the square room were floor-to-ceiling windows, giving the impression that the conference room itself was a peninsula jutting off of the square building. Yet on many days the forty-ninth-floor windows showed nothing but an endless ocean of white, as the Jomira Transportation Center was often swallowed up by the heavy clouds that hung low and slowly ebbed through the towers like the thick smoke from an old man's pipe.

Heald entered the conference room to see many of the CRCC employees already seated and waiting for the meeting to start. Miłosz walked in close on his tail and grabbed the first empty seat he could find along the outer rim of the tables. Heald realized that the Ukrainian had grabbed the last available seat, so he would be forced to sit in the brooding center along with Martha, Janice, two other regional technicians from CCM, and a couple other latecomers.

The room lay in suspended animation as many moved only their eyes from one person to another, hoping to see if they could discern from the look on one another's faces just what was behind this emergency meeting. Miłosz had brought a tiny bag of tissues along with him to continue to dab the specks of blood from his ragged fingertips.

Sterling P. Less, the regional director of the CRCC, was second-in-command only to the national director, who held his office in the country's capitol. Less had only been to this office a total of four times in the last few months, since the commencement of the 2010 Decennial Census, though he kept the largest private office within the building as his own. This may not have been by his own choice, for Less was actually a very fair man. Throughout many of their previous operations, he had frequently been required to attend to matters of publicity and subsequent gatherings to boost the image of and promote the Census Bureau's activities throughout the tristate area of Illinois, Wisconsin, and Indiana. He was a warm and affable man, and many wished that he were in charge of the CRCC itself on a day-to-day basis, but that task was charged to his deputy director, Elina Flohard. For all of the admirable qualities that Sterling P. Less possessed, Ms. Flohard held just as many that elicited an equally opposite reaction.

Elina Flohard was an minuscule woman, standing at less than five feet tall, though she could pass for five foot two if she wore her hair up in a massive, tightly coiled bun, which she often did. Despite her size, she never wore high heels; many speculated that she did not feel she needed them. Round and overweight, Elina carried herself like a bulldog with bulbous balls, and people much taller than she still dodged to get out of her way as she patrolled the hallways. A former clerk had claimed that he saw her smile and laugh while sharing the elevator with her, but a week after the rumor began, the clerk had stopped reporting for work. He was supposedly spotted two months later looking strung out playing the mellotron at a Bucktown jazz club.

Elina's office sat adjacent to Less's, and she made sure to always keep a receptionist stationed outside his door, lest he drop in for a friendly visit or to deliver some fresh baked goods to the CRCC staff, which he had done once after an interview at the nearby Sun-Times building. Elina brought out the very real fears in everyone who worked under her, which was everyone in the office. A day that allowed for not a single encounter with her was counted by many as a small victory in yet another uneventful day, which today, obviously, was not.

The doors in the far corner of the room near the podium opened slightly as the head of Elina's assistant popped through to take a quick scan of the room. The assistant pulled his head back through the doors and closed them softly. Then Elina herself bullied through, swinging the doors open and tottering in.

Everyone in the room remained silent as she stepped behind the podium, which had surely been altered to accommodate her short stature, but could not contain her full figure from side to side. She set down a single sheet of paper on the stand and slowly scanned the room. For nearly two full minutes, she looked carefully upon each person, as if she wanted to look right through their eyes and into their skulls to see what type of secrets might be printed at the back of their minds. Most could not help looking across the room at something else, breaking Elina's gaze, but some stared right back at her, hoping that maybe it was some type of test, and not showing fear meant passing that test. This was most likely not the case.

Heald, meanwhile, sat still in the center of the room and concentrated on the thought of having his first drink of the night once this workday was over. He thought about how he might someday find a way to live in that warm, Christmas-y feeling that resided in his belly with each of those first few drinks. He watched as Miłosz rubbed the vein on his forehead like one might a pet a sensitive chinchilla.

Despite her small frame, Elina's voice could boom through a room like a bullhorn. She finally broke her silence, speaking with a timbre that seemed to come from someone three times her size.

"What I have assembled here before me is a number of parts within a system that has fundamentally broken down. Any number of you might be directly responsible for what transpired last night, or it might be a sole conspirator at work, but make no mistake, a breach of our security has taken place. For those few of you who may not know what it is that I am speaking of here this morning, allow me to illuminate you. At some point yesterday, we had a complete moral and principled disintegration of our very core values, for the very code that we all swore to uphold, that *YOU* swore to uphold, has been heinously violated."

The room remained still until a collective shudder seemed to vibrate the tables and legs of the many chairs.

"I'm speaking, of course, of a TITLE 13 infringement."

Heald looked across the table at Janice, who had been writing something down in the small notebook she kept with her at all times. She always looked busy writing while someone was speaking, and he told himself that he really ought to do the same.

"Our number one priority here at the CRCC, people, is to collect information from the population at large and secure all of that information in a safe place where it can be dissected, prodded, sampled, and quantified. Anything short of that, and we have failed in our role as civil servants." Elina paused to scour the room. "Understand that not only will we find the employee or employees responsible for the disappearance of this information, but that person or persons, he or she, or them, will be thoroughly prosecuted and reprimanded to the fullest extent of the law—the law that every one of us swore to uphold."

Many of the CRCC employees snuck looks out of the corner of their eyes at one another, hoping to see a bead of sweat or two slipping down the face of the person sitting next to them, perhaps to immediately report that person and have them found guilty and tossed into the center of the room for their ruling. Miłosz's own mouth was slightly agape, and his forehead vein had somehow traversed down his face and now pulsated on his neck, just above the collar of his shirt.

Elina took a moment again to scan the room, puffing out her lower jaw like an anglerfish, defying anyone to make a move.

"Many of you will be called into my office individually to detail the last few hours from your tour of duty yesterday. I expect that within no time at all, this precious and pure TITLE 13 information that has gone missing will once again be back within my possession. Now, do any of you have any questions?"

Every individual within the room had a question on the tip of their tongues. Every mind was probing for what could have happened to the missing information and just what the implications of its being lost were. Heald was wondering if he really needed a fancy notebook like Janice, or if he couldn't just use some loose-leaf paper instead.

Gilbert Tabin, the manager and head of CCM, spoke up. As he stood, he towered over those around him. He was tall and thin, and his salt-and-pepper hair was mostly salt, parted neatly down the middle. The top of his chest jutted out like misshapen papier-mâché, so that his dress shirt tightened around his upper torso while it sagged along his sides and back. He wore thin wire-framed glasses like a depression-era politician. Heald realized now, just in that moment, how similar Gilbert Tabin and Woodrow Wilson looked to each other. Now standing, Gilbert almost began to speak, but first raised his hand.

"Yes?" called Elina.

"May I inquire as to where these specific documents went missing from?" Gilbert asked.

"They were reported missing by the data warehouse technicians at approximately six o'clock this morning. The TITLE 13 documents were reportedly from within your very own CCM division, Mr. Tabin."

At this, Heald raised his head. Gilbert Tabin wore a look on his face that implied he was presently experiencing the early stages of an arduous bowel movement.

"CCM?" he repeated. "But that's just not possible."

"Oh, I assure you, Mr. Tabin, not only is it entirely possible, and also conceivable, but I would deem it inevitable. In my opinion, the lack of integrity that your staff has shown has been a concern of mine for some time. Do not think that all members of the Census Coverage Measurement division possess carte blanche within our greater system."

"Ms. Flohard, please, with all due respect, I feel that it is inappropriate to cast blame before all the facts are known."

Elina rested her upper body on her elbow and clicked her tongue against her teeth as if she had just finished a rather large and juicy slab of barbequed ribs. Not a hair on her head was out of place.

"Mr. Tabin, I would like to see you in my office immediately once I have adjourned this meeting. Is that understood?"

Gilbert nodded confidently, sat down, and touched his glasses, leaving a large smudge on the lens. All eyes in the room were on him except for Heald's, whose eyes were on Janice, and Janice's, whose eyes were on her notebook.

"As for the rest of you, meaning everyone not in CCM, you may leave and return to your work areas. If you do happen to come upon any of the missing TITLE 13 information, it is imperative, and of the utmost importance, that you do not touch it. Don't even look at it or breathe in its intoxicating aroma. You are simply to stop where you stand, use one hand to cover your eyes and nose, and the other hand is to be used to point at the TITLE 13 and await further instructions. Is that understood?"

Heads around the room began to nod.

"Good. Now you may leave."

The instant sound of chairs clanging and scraping against the floor filled the room as the women and men collected their belongings and folders and rose to leave. Heald and the rest of the twenty or so CCM staff sat and watched like the players on the losing team as the winners carried off their captain on their shoulders. Martha sat to Mr. Tabin's left and Leeka Johnston to his right. Leeka was one of CCM's rising stars and a top manager—a tenacious woman who was hell-bent on taking Gilbert's place as head of the division. She crossed her hands politely across the desk, smiled up to Ms. Flohard, and waited for the rest of the room to empty.

Heald looked down at his hands and saw how odd and motionless they were as he rested them upon the table. He kept his head down as he picked up his right hand and held out his palm flat and parallel to the tabletop. It trembled ever so slightly, so he quickly pushed both of his hands into his pockets underneath the table.

As the room's last stragglers were finally cleared

out, an older man in the back tripped against the leg of a chair and stumbled forward for a moment before regaining his composure, bracing his hand along the back wall. Those in the room looked back at him and then quickly back to Elina, who nodded over to her assistant. The assistant tapped his ear and left the room in a hurry. As the old man sauntered from the room, he apologized while looking at the ground, then pulled the door shut behind him.

"Please," said Elina, "come together in the middle of the room so I may speak to you all as a whole."

The group looked at each other. Miłosz immediately leaped up, pulled his chair across the room with an annoying squeal of the metal legs against the tile floor, and took a seat next to Heald.

"I blame myself," Elina began. "I've been far too lenient and hands-off in my entire approach with CCM as a whole. What we have here is an abuse of power. We've allowed you a certain level of secrecy and privacy within this office, even from my own self, in order to honor and keep the integrity of the census. But the truth of the matter is that no one division should have so much autonomy. No one entity should have the ability to remain separate but equal from the larger group. This is why I am charging a solitary task force with investigating this heinous occurrence, to be led by and comprised entirely of *me*."

She clicked her tongue.

"Me, myself, and I will be the judge, jury, and executioner for the crime of TITLE 13 infringement. You all know that this is the only fair way to deal with such an occurrence. It would be unjust to complicate these matters with a cluttered committee, and I certainly know that none of you would ever want to hamper a pending investigation as important as this."

Gilbert bit his lower lip.

"We go through an incredible amount of paperwork every day here in this office," Elina continued. "You do, I do, he does, and she does. Within the confines of CCM, we have file cabinets and closets full of TITLE 13 information that amounts to nearly 3,500 individual cases within 178 separate zones comprised of varying locations within Wisconsin, Indiana, and Illinois that you are all responsible for. I don't have to tell you what these thirty-seven pieces of paper mean, but just in case you've forgotten, let me remind you that should it ever become publicly known that the Department of Commerce allowed for this type of extremely sensitive and personal information to simply be removed from an inscrutably secure, high-level facility such as this, and that anyone in the world, nay, the universe, could now have their unauthorized hands upon said information, then we, all of us, including Mr. Sterling P. Less, and quite possibly even the president of the United States himself, would no longer be safe.

"It would be chaos upon the streets. Children would run free with modified weapons of war. School teachers would farm out their responsibilities to rapists and murderers, and farmers could sanction school teachers to burn and destroy their crops for fraudulent insurance claims."

Heald was now focused on what he was hearing, listening intently, though he felt dizzy and somewhere else entirely.

"Even our own personal medical information and private online viewing habits could become public knowledge. Society as we know it would not only break down, it would disassemble and reincarnate into something wholly new and unique and sinister. Imagine a terrorist force composed of high-speed internet thugs declaring cyber warfare upon the violence-happy brutes within the Pentagon. Imagine gas station attendants with our telephone numbers and email passwords. Picture yourself surrounded by librarians armed to the teeth with social security numbers and hand grenades. *This* is a world that I do not want to live in. *This* represents a time and a place that I dream of often and never wish to cast upon the waking world. Every fiber of my being is determined to keep every fiber of my being *exactly* where it belongs within this system."

Heald looked around in a fog and noticed the rest of the group staring intently at Ms. Flohard. His focus was blurry and his head began to ache. He thought about alcohol.

Elina brought her palms down slowly onto the podium and looked directly out the window behind the group in front of her.

"Turn around. All of you."

Heald turned without looking to see if the others did too.

The skyline of Chicago was striking on that exceedingly sunny morning, and the Sears Tower sat just to the south of them. The sun glinted off many of the buildings' windows and repeated flashes of brilliance filled the office whenever the sun's rays broke through the clouds. Mechanical air-filtration and -conditioning units situated atop these buildings billowed smoke and exhaust against the backdrop of other, taller skyscrapers from their gray and black rooftops. A window-cleaning unit of yellow jump-suited men could be seen ascending the 110 floors of the Sears Tower. Heald heard Elina's voice in his head.

"Imagine if you will—and you will—a mushroom cloud bigger than anything that you currently see out that window. Imagine jet planes and bombers the size of apartment complexes dropping technological marvels of deconstruction upon this city, this world, all around the epicenter of a blooming death cloud. Imagine that mushroom coming to a head, knowing that it is filled with unimaginable heat and concrete, dust, papers—human faces, eyes, and brains. Gray matter filling the radioactive cloud with electricity as all that is inside us leaves us and becomes one with the mushroom. Glass will melt and connect with steel, and we will melt and connect with each other as everything that made us whole is criminally dissected and rearranged. Everything below us, from the sewer tunnels to the subway line, will be consumed into the cloud and jettisoned into the stratosphere, where it will become nothing but silken ash, hardened to a black substance, and turned back to a black dust, transfixed into a black nothing. A stinking, glowing crater all that remains of where you had your first kiss and told someone that you loved them. A mess of a world where everything you've ever done quickly becomes all that you'll ever do."

Heald could feel his hands tremble in his pockets.

"The death cloud will rise ever so slowly after time in a lonely solidarity and dare those bombers to return. It knows no shame as it knows no pride but for the pride we had for ourselves within it. It is not happy to see us go, nor is it reminiscent—it just is. *That* is what we are protecting the world from when we say TITLE 13. It isn't what is actually on those thirty-seven individual pieces of paper that are now out and roaming free somewhere—it's that cloud. We're in a battle with intelligence, and that mushroom cloud is never far from what you can see out that window at this moment. Every book you've ever read or movie you've ever seen or dream that you've dreamt concerning the end by the bomb has been wrong. You won't be playing innocently with your children in your yards when it happens, and you won't be reading the newspaper on the subway when you feel the tunnels suddenly swell with incomprehensible heat—you'll be here, within this office, looking for that inestimable information that we seek, because that cloud can only come down upon us while that TITLE 13 information is lost out there."

The room sat silent for a moment as Heald waited for her to continue. His eyes nictitated and he swallowed hard—then suddenly the waves were gone and his head no longer ached. His heartbeat returned to normal. He focused on Elina Flohard, who had not moved a muscle, and a distinct feeling of time having come back on course after total derailment settled over him. Elina clicked her tongue.

"So, to repeat, I will be meeting with each of you one-on-one in my office to go over your final hours here during yesterday's tour of duty. Let it be known now, I will find out who is responsible for this leak and I will hold them responsible. Until you are called upon, please return to your work areas and begin a complete and comprehensive search for the missing documents. I expect no stone to be left unturned and no cranny nor nook to be left uninspected. This will be a thorough and unequivocally swift investigation that will yield results. I appreciate your cooperation and very much look forward to speaking to each and every one of you personally. Thank you, and you are dismissed."

With that, Elina collected the single sheet of paper that had rested on the podium and walked through the center of the CCM group, who remained motionless and silent, to the exit whence she first came. Miłosz looked back and forth from Heald to Janice repeatedly and dabbed his bleeding fingertips.

The CCM group finally rose and began to file out of the room led by Gilbert Tabin and Martha Leifhat, who were followed quickly by Leeka Johnston and her team of four employees chiefly responsible for the Indiana and Southern Illinois regions. Heald, meanwhile, remained sitting and looked over toward Janice, who was still writing in her notebook, and asked her what time it was.

"It's ten past ten," she said.

Janice then finished her writing, stood, and walked out of the cleared room, leaving Heald by himself. He walked to the massive window, joined his hands behind his back, and looked out over the city, feeling extraordinarily perplexed. He licked his lips, which were cracked and dry.

Chapter Five

HEALD'S EXTREMITIES were slow to respond as he wandered back to his workspace. The workers within the CCM department had begun to collect personal items from their desks, trivial things that were usually overlooked. Every desk in the office had to be emptied before an adequate and proper search for the missing TITLE 13 papers could begin. Heald's desk had only one personal item on it: a photograph of a beagle standing in a messy kitchen, the floor covered in garbage, and a banana peel hanging from its mouth. In the background of the photo, a young Heald was standing near a cabinet wearing dishwashing gloves and holding his hands together in praise. He took the photo off his desk and walked over to Janice, placing it inside a box already half-filled with her own items.

"I'm just going to put this in your box if you don't mind," Heald told her. "It's the only personal item I have here. Isn't that sad? I'm such a sad guy. You know what would cheer a sad guy up? Taking me out to a nice dinner."

Janice was transfixed by her computer screen. "Isn't the guy supposed to offer to take the woman out for dinner?" she asked.

"I'm much too sad for that. I need to be coddled. Coddling would help."

"Hmm. Too bad. And I really hate having student loans. We all have problems."

Heald began to reach back into her box for his photo.

"Isn't it weird that the TITLE 13 information disappeared

after you, me, and Milo were just talking about that yesterday before we left?" asked Heald. "It's like we willed it into non-existence."

"Yeah, I was just thinking about that. Pretty creepy," said Janice.

"So where do you think the lost documents are? I'll bet it's from your region, because I don't think you're very good at your job."

Janice finally looked at him, taking mock offense. "I'm actually quite good at my job. In fact, I'm amazing. See this award I got?" she said, pointing to her pay stub, which was now out on the desk. "I'm going to get it framed and hang it on the wall of my parents' house out in Cicero because that's where I live because I am so successful and good at my job."

"Well, my apartment is about four hundred square feet and I pay nearly a thousand dollars a month for it, Jan, so who's the bigger dipstick here?" He smiled at her.

"You are. You are an incredible dipstick." She wasn't smiling, but nor was she frowning, which Heald noted. He smiled widely so that his teeth could be seen.

"But look at my teeth. These are some *goooood* teeth! I've got all of 'em and they're pretty straight, too. They wouldn't rent an apartment to just any ol' Toothless Joe, now would they?"

Finally, a slight grin crept across her face as he brought his hands up and displayed his teeth with the gusto of a showcase model. "I've been blessed with immaculate incisors as well. I can chew through even the toughest cut of meat. And that's something genetically rare these days. Most guys couldn't chew a wet leaf of spinach, but me? Oh boy. These teeth. I once got locked out of my car and got back inside using only my teeth."

Janice looked back at him again, this time with an actual interest.

"You had a car? What kind of car did you have?"

For the first time since he had walked over to Janice's desk, Heald stopped smiling.

"I had a 1983 Buick LeSabre," he said while looking at the floor. "That car was a boat."

"A boat?"

"It was big, that's all. Really big."

"I never learned how to drive. It terrifies me."

"Well, in Detroit, it's pretty much required."

"Why?"

"Because it's the *Motor City*."

"Oh, right." She crossed her hands on her lap. "You don't talk about Detroit much, Heald."

"No one asks about it much," he said, his eyes focused on the floor. He exhaled a little too strongly and was afraid his breath might carry over to her. She turned back to her computer.

"Well, go use your magic teeth to find the TITLE 13 information already, would you? Your teeth aren't that amazing and you smell like a distillery. Were you out drinking with someone last night?"

Heald had already closed his mouth, and now he turned sideways to her and began to walk away. "No, don't be crazy. You're being crazy."

"Stop drinking on a Tuesday night, Heald," she said as he

walked off.

"Lady, you just missed out on the most incredible set of chompers you'll ever come across in this crummy town. And it's mouthwash," he added softly.

"Bye, Heald."

"Bye, Jan," he said through closed teeth, grinning back at her.

At his desk, Martha was looking through some papers in a drawer and organizing folders into neat little stacks. She saw Heald and flashed him a warm smile, nodding toward the piles she was making.

"Sorry to bother you Heald, but could you give me a hand sorting through these papers? I figured that we'd just start with your desk and then we could go through mine. I don't see how any of the missing information could pertain to our team in Wisconsin, but we've got to be diligent and cover all the bases. All of the files went out to the enumerators on time last week, right?"

"Of course," Heald said confidently. "In fact, I stayed late just to make sure we could get all the papers packed into the boxes and out the door by the last FedEx pickup."

"Oh good. Thanks!"

Heald swirled his tongue around his mouth and tasted the stale, industrial flavor of the last night's vodka.

"I'll be right back," he told Martha. "I'm just going to grab a donut and some coffee from the break room."

When Heald turned the corner into the rest of the Department of Commerce's main office, he saw numerous people standing perfectly still, each of them holding one hand over their eyes and the other pointing off randomly.

Heald stopped dead in his tracks, as if he had accidentally walked into a room full of chimpanzees discussing politics. Slowly he began to tiptoe past the ominous, statuesque bodies, which remained motionless, like monoliths, awaiting further instruction from someone or something. One man was pointing straight up toward a ceiling tile that was a bit off-kilter, and Heald supposed that it was perhaps as good as any other place to suspect the TITLE 13 information might be. Another woman was pointing straight out the window toward a cloud on the horizon.

One man was simply pointing straight toward another man who stood just a few feet in front of him, pointing right back at him. The two were facing each other with one hand over their eyes and the tips of their index fingers nearly touching. Each man's hand was shaking.

Heald continued to carefully meander through the crowd of pointing, blinded individuals, cautious not to disturb any of them or make a sound. He knew what had to be done.

Grabbing a few donuts from the break room (and a few peppermint candies which he quickly chewed up), along with a small cup of coffee, he hurried back out the door and stood silently in front of this peculiar collection of frozen individuals, like some public art exhibit. None of them made any significant movement, though a few could be seen quivering in their extremities.

Heald slowly snuck up behind a gentleman who had been pointing toward the copy machine, a tall, round man with a hint of rouge on his cheeks and a small, trimmed moustache. His large eyeglasses rested over his long, pudgy fingers, which were covering his eyes at the moment. Heald brought the pastry up to the man's nose from behind him, still careful not to make a sound. Heald's hand was shaking steadily, and the pastry was now just underneath the man's nose—the icing atop it nearly grazing the gray bristles of his mustache. The man's nose started to wiggle and his eyebrows began to dance behind his large hand. Heald brought the pastry even closer, allowing it to lightly touch the man's lips as a butterfly would impress upon a flower, then eased it back off an inch, leaving a small white dab of frosting upon his mouth and moustache. The man began to salivate and licked his lips very quickly, like a gecko licking its own eye. Sweat began to bead on the man's forehead, and he breathed in steadily through his nostrils. Heald now very nearly had the entire pastry set to be crammed up into the man's nasal canal. The man slowly began to ball the hand pointing toward the copy machine into a fist, repeating this motion over and over. The crooked corner of his mouth opened and a glistening, purplish tongue covered in thousands of tiny taste buds and pulsating veins eased its way out like an eel, and, like an eel, began to poke about. At that moment, Heald let out an ear-piercing scream, threw the pastry at the copier as hard as he could, and sprinted toward the CCM department, dropping his coffee and flailing his arms wildly as he ran.

He watched from around a corner as the men and women who had been standing motionless finally pulled their hands away from their eyes, stunned to see the terrified man, now on his knees, trembling and pointing at the copy machine covered in bits of exploded pastry. Heald watched as the man shook his head and began to sob uncontrollably and pounded his fists upon the floor as large men with dark sunglasses and pressed black suits entered the room and each took hold of one of his arms.

"I swear to God, it wasn't me!" cried the desperate man. "I'm innocent! That pastry! It's what you want! It had it in for me! I wouldn't let that salacious cretin anywhere near my olfactory system! I've been framed! Whisked, mixed, and baked into a patsy by a pastry! I've nothing to do with this affront to our national security! Stop!"

One of the men in dark sunglasses used a small camera to take a photo of the copier.

"It's not a private pastry! There's no title against an assault with baked goods! It was deemed fit for service along with eleven others of its kind! I've got kids, a wife!"

They dragged the hysterical man, who was no longer willing to walk, toward a long hallway in the back of the room.

"I can fix this!"

His cries were carried off along with him down the long, dark hallway, and another large man in mirrored sunglasses entered the room (though how he had entered the room Heald could not discern). The man took a few more photographs of the scene as the other individuals in the room continued to stand, pointing and covering their eyes. The man in sunglasses took out a yellow tarp and draped it over the copier and told everyone in a plain, emotionless voice that there would be "no more copier services for the day at this station" and to "remain where they stand pending a full investigation."

"No!" came a final, feral cry from down the long hallway. "Anything but that!" And suddenly it was silent. The staff slightly lowered their heads. Heald turned away and blinked a few times, then walked back to the CCM office. Is this really happening? he thought.

* * *

"Does anyone else see that building across the river smiling at us with that wide grin across its face?" asked Ramone Fiddle, a CCM regional technician, as he sat and looked out of the massive window overlooking the Chicago skyline. "It's just, you know, looking right at us, like it's all ready to give a wink."

Ramone wasn't expecting anyone to answer him. A few years back he had suffered vision loss in his right eye after a traffic accident that left his optic nerve damaged. Since then, Ramone sometimes had vivid recurrent hallucinations—fictive visual precepts, as his neurologist called them. At times, for no reason at all, Ramone would see faces or people that did not actually exist. He was an otherwise perfectly healthy fifty-four-year-old man with no mental illness whatsoever, but ever since the day of the accident, he had begun to see things. It was suspected that Ramone suffered from what the doctors at Northwestern Memorial Hospital diagnosed as Charles Bonnet syndrome, or CBS. Though there was no known cure, there was also no immediate danger to Ramone's health other than the occasional vivid hallucination that could last anywhere from a few seconds to an entire day—which became its own sort of hellish amusement. Blinking repeatedly would sometimes interrupt the visions, returning things to normal.

Ramone was a quiet, solid, slightly overweight man who wore large 1980s-style reading glasses. He combed back his curly black hair and sideburns that he had never trimmed above his earlobes since his early twenties. A lifelong ailment led him to favor one side while walking, as if he'd had a long metal rod inserted up his left foot and through to his torso. Despite a childhood in Chicago's south side, he had a charming southern disposition and spoke with calm, measured words. A crisp white shirt always popped between his dark brown skin and one of his many earth-toned double-breasted suits, which he never wore buttoned, and the same pair of dark brown penny loafers.

When his hallucinations first began, Ramone was sure that he had gone batty, thinking that perhaps the accident had jarred lose some frail element of his psyche like a tall glass vase tipping off an unsteady table. His wife was less certain of this. Sometimes during dinner, Ramone would ask why there was a family of Native Americans sitting at a dining table over in their living room. The CBS hallucinations only provided visual indicators—the images had no other sensory components.

Sometimes the hallucinations were comparatively Lilliputian, which had startled Ramone at first. For nearly three weeks one summer after the accident, Ramone avoided swimming pools entirely after he claimed to have seen tiny faces down in the deep end of one. When he peered down at them, he could see that they were trying to talk to him, all without so much as a single sound or bubble rising to the surface. Soon after, a shimmering assortment of Picassoesque figures that watched him construct a birdhouse in his garage finally convinced him to confront his mounting fears and visit a doctor. Now Ramone's visions were just another one of those small things around the CCM office that kept time ticking until five o'clock.

"It looks like it wants to wink at us, smack a kiss—that building there," he said again, this time a little louder. "I know I ain't gonna hear it, but I kinda want to."

Heald was seated at his desk and turned to face the massive window, hoping to see whatever it was that Ramone was talking about, though he could see nothing. Regardless, Heald winked and blew a kiss out to the nearest building.

* * *

Gilbert Tabin had the only office in the CCM division with four walls and a door that could close, allowing for privacy. The rest of the staff sat huddled close to one another in the 1,500-square-foot bullpen of assorted desks and tables with no real barriers or partitions to separate them, save for the short wall that set QC apart.

Gilbert walked out of his office and went to the head of the bullpen, standing in front of the numerous metal filing cabinets that were usually closed and locked at all times, but were now wide open. Bulging manila folders crammed with far too much information and paperwork, held closed by overexerted rubber bands, were now strewn across the floor. He turned to the employees of his division and anchored his hands at his sides.

"Folks, now I know that we all work very hard here to maintain the utmost level of security and scrutiny in what we do, but until this crisis passes, we're going to be under a pretty large magnifying glass sitting under the enormous eye of Ms. Elina Flohard, so we're just going to have to accept that and work with the utmost fortitude and responsibility the best that we know how. I've personally never doubted any of you, and I'm proud to be working with such an incredible set of fine and upstanding individuals."

Woodrow Wilson, thought Heald.

"As of now it is thought that our division is responsible for the loss of thirty-seven pages of TITLE 13 information. While we can't necessarily prove Ms. Flohard wrong at the moment, we can do everything and anything to make sure that the missing information is not anywhere within the confines of our secure location." He took a moment to look around and clear his throat. "I see that many of you have begun to investigate your work areas, and I thank you for that. At this time, I've been called to speak with Ms. Flohard in her office to discuss some items, and when I return, we will talk about our next plan of action. Ms. Flohard will then likely begin to call you into her office for one-on-one meetings to assist her in understanding the situation that took place here last night. Thank you."

With that, Gilbert buttoned the lower button on his suit jacket, so that it billowed out at the top and gave the impression that his chest was that much larger, like a robin's feathered breast, then he picked up his leather portfolio and headed to the deputy director's office on the other side of the floor. Heald and Janice looked at each other, and then they both looked over to Miłosz, who was struggling with a small key trying to unlock a drawer in his desk. Heald looked at the clock on the wall: not even eleven o'clock.

"It's incredible that they still use such mediocre and dull colors for all the new skyscrapers that they're constructing around the city these days," said Ramone, who had turned back toward the window. "When I was in China six months ago, all their cities seemed to be constructing these beautiful buildings covered top to bottom in these wonderful lights that would twinkle and shine day and night. A whole range of colors across the spectrum with God knows what types of advertisements flowing across 'em in Chinese—wasn't important. Here it's just the same old dull, metallic colors: the blacks, browns, and grays of old. Shame."

He continued to look out the window at the skyscrapers, but did not wink.

Chapter Six

TRANSCRIPT OF MEETING BETWEEN MS. ELINA FLOHARD AND MR. GILBERT TABIN

JULY 14, 2010

FLOHARD: Gilbert, thank you for coming here today.

TABIN: My pleasure. I want you to know that I'm as interested as you are when it comes to locating the missing TITLE 13 documents. We've begun the process...

FLOHARD: Oh, I know where the missing information is, Mr. Tabin.

TABIN: You do?

FLOHARD: Of course. You see, it isn't here—I know that much, and that's the problem, because it should be here.

TABIN: Right. But you say you know where it is, then?

FLOHARD: Correct.

TABIN: And if you don't mind my asking, just where is it?

FLOHARD: I've already told you, Gilbert.

TABIN: (pausing) I'm sorry, I seem to have missed that. Would you mind telling me again, please?

FLOHARD: It isn't here, where it's supposed to be.

TABIN: I'm afraid I'm still confused, Ms. Flohard.

FLOHARD: Of course you are. Allow me to illuminate you. You see, there are just two places that the missing TITLE 13 information could be. It could be here, where it is supposed to be, or it could be elsewhere.

TABIN: Right. So you're saying that it's...

FLOHARD: By simple process of elimination, the documents are deemed elsewhere, since they are, in fact, not here. Here is where we would like them to be, need them to be, but unfortunately, they are not. So the only other viable conclusion to make is that the information is elsewhere.

TABIN: Ms. Flohard, you must understand my confusion when I ask how you claim to know where the TITLE 13 information is and you—

FLOHARD: Oh, I understand quite well that you are confused, Gilbert. What I'm rightly trying to fathom is your failure to comprehend the nature of what it is that I am speaking about presently. We've nailed it down now, Gilbert. The nature of it all is perfectly clear to me.

TABIN: Elina—

FLOHARD: Ms. Flohard.

TABIN: Right. Ms. Flohard. Are you certain that the missing TITLE 13 information isn't actually just somewhere in the office as we speak? Perhaps just misplaced or even filed in the wrong location? May I also ask how you are so certain that my team over in CCM lost it? I've got my entire team combing the area for any trace of it, though I admit that the task is daunting considering the size and space and amount of information and sheer quantity of paperwork that we have contained on this floor. We'll find—

FLOHARD: Gilbert, I don't know if I can make this any clearer in that head of yours. Let me try again. There are exactly two places on this entire planet that the missing information could be at this moment: either here or there. It is not here, on my desk, sitting right in front of me in my tender care, keeping it safe from all harm. No, it is not here, so it must be there. Out there. Either lost in your division, or out there alone in the world through carelessness and, dare I even suggest it—theft. What good is confidential information once it's lost its purpose? I aim to rectify this.

TABIN: Pardon my saying so, Ms. Flohard, but that information doesn't belong directly to you. In fact, it cannot belong to any of us. Its very nature is that of secrecy and independence from sole alliance. Our job is to keep it neutral within the parameters of the TITLE 13 code. The fact that thirty-seven pages of this information has gone missing is something that must shake each of us at our cores, but not for loss of something personal, like a set of keys or a cell phone, but rather more so because of the larger group. The public at large has been affected here, ma'am, and not any one individual within the Department of Commerce.

FLOHARD: [silence]

TABIN: Ms. Flohard?

FLOHARD: [silence]

TABIN: You must know I only speak out of concern.

FLOHARD: Gilbert, I'll have to ask you to come with me for a moment.

TABIN: Of course. Anything. My top priority is—

FLOHARD: Just through this door over here, Gilbert.

(END OF TRANSCRIPT)

* * *

Ramone Fiddle was still looking out the window when Leeka Johnston walked to the front of the office and asked for everyone's attention. It was a poorly kept secret that Leeka had been hoping to take Tabin's job, and at that moment, with confidence in her stride and strength in her voice, anything seemed likely and possible. The CCM workers looked up from their tasks as she cleared her throat.

"As you are all well aware, Mr. Tabin has been called to Ms. Flohard's office to discuss the disappearance of the missing TITLE 13 information. In his stead, I am in control of the office and solely responsible for our actions here," Leeka said. "I expect the same amount of respect that you would afford to Gilbert. Now, where are we with the missing information?"

The CCM employees looked around at one another. Heald took a long sip from his coffee mug, grimacing a bit at its bitter taste.

"Have we any idea where the papers could be?" she asked again.

Sensing an awkward silence brewing, Martha decided to speak first. She was quite good at that—filling awkward silences. It was an admirable trait and one that Heald believed fell largely upon the backs of the women of the Midwest.

"Well, Ms. Johnston," Martha began, "I'm fairly certain that the missing information could not be from the Wisconsin region. Heald and I have been going through our notes and data since Ms. Flohard's meeting this morning, and nothing appears to be missing." She nodded toward Leeka with a smile and neatly bowed in her direction like a courteous Asian woman. Heald froze with his mug pressed to his lips and a half-grimace upon his face. Eyes around the room focused on him and Martha.

"So you're telling me that you have already gone through all 298 case files from within each of your twelve collection areas within the Wisconsin territory and found no trace of the missing information?"

Martha began to chew her lower lip and looked nervously from Leeka to her peers.

"Well, no, but we've already deduced that it couldn't have—"

Leeka waved her hand, and Martha immediately stopped speaking.

"Please, Ms. Leifhat, don't assume to know things that you cannot possibly know and report it as concrete truth until all of the facts are known. Would you have come to Gilbert with such shoddy information? Or just to me?"

"Ms. Johnston, all I meant was that we've begun our search and it would seem that—"

"Keep looking, please," Leeka said cutting Martha off once again. "All of you."

At that moment, Leeka sneezed. She looked at those around her and waited for someone to bless her. No one made a sound. They merely watched her hold her fists at her side, standing solid as a sculpture. Leeka began to shudder in the anticipatory silence. Then, all at once, the whole group exploded with a massive chorus of "gesundheit!"

Leeka smiled slyly and turned toward the file cabinets behind her.

"Gesundheit to us all," she said under her breath. "And to all a good night."

Heald sat in his chair and rubbed his eyes for a full

minute. He was exhausted and worn thin. Could things really be this strange? he wondered. He thought about the bottle of vodka in the back of his freezer.

Janice walked up to Heald's desk.

"It's almost lunch, Heald. Wanna head downstairs and get something to eat?"

Heald had packed his lunch that morning—peanut butter and onions on white bread and two granny smith apples along with a grapefruit. It was waiting in the break room's refrigerator.

"I'd love to," he said.

* * *

After a quick lunch together that featured, as customary, Heald sarcastically jabbering at Janice, they arrived back at the CCM office. Gilbert Tabin's office door was still open, and he was nowhere in sight. Heald made a move to return to his desk, but Janice reached for his forearm to stop him.

"Hey, Heel, where do you think Gil is? He didn't come back from Ms. Flohard's office before we left for lunch, right?"

Heald stuck out his lower lip and shook his head.

"Well, that's weird, don't you think?" she asked. "He was gone for nearly an hour before lunch, and he's still not back. What do you think they were talking about for so long?"

"I'm pretty sure they were probably just talking about the missing information."

"Do you think this is *serious*?" she asked. "I mean, the TITLE 13 papers being gone and all."

Heald put his hands in his pockets. "Well, it's obviously not a good thing, no, but I don't think we have anything in particular to be worried about, right? I mean, it's not like *we* lost any of the info. The missing papers didn't have anything particular about us in in them, so, it isn't, like, you know...that we have any, um..."

Janice looked at Heald's eyes, which she rarely did with any individual.

"Are you okay, Heald?"

"Yeah."

"You don't seem right."

"Bad crêpe," he said at first, averting his eyes, then looking back and flashing a minute grin.

Janice looked back at her desk. "Something bad is going to happen, isn't it?"

"Depends on your definition of 'bad,' Jan," he replied. "I mean, do I think we'll be seeing any mushroom clouds outside of the windows here anytime soon—clouds that billow and swallow up our dreams? I'm going to go out on a limb and say that was probably all hogwash." Heald laughed but never took his eyes off Janice. She looked back at him, perplexed.

"What?" she asked.

"Never mind. I'm sure everything will turn out just fine. All I mean is that at least we're not responsible."

"But how can you be so sure? There's so much frickin' paper in this place that it almost seems impossible to fathom that we're combing this whole floor for thirty-seven individual pieces of it that are so horribly important. And for that matter, why would Gilbert disappear?"

"Who said he disappeared?" said Heald, looking uncomfortable for the first time in the conversation. "All we know is that he went to Ms. Flohard's office. They're probably just discussing the next logical steps to remedy the missing-information problem. Cheer up. Nothing really matters."

Janice sat down at her desk and put her purse down at her side. "I don't like it, Heald."

He went to put his hand on her shoulder, but hesitated when he noticed his hand trembling. He held it just above her shoulder, expecting to feel her warmth, but felt nothing.

"I mean, all is well. Everything is dandy," he said.

She ignored him, lost in thought, and brought her computer screen back to life. Heald walked back to his desk to help Martha look through the Wisconsin files. Ramone Fiddle was still busy searching the skyline when Heald walked past him. Heald thought he might ask him what he saw at that moment, but decided not to.

Chapter Seven

HEALD CAREFULLY REPLACED the photo of his beagle onto his desk. He had retrieved it from Janice's box after it had failed to make her laugh. The photo itself, taken at his childhood home in Detroit, was a bittersweet one, as the dog in the photo had died just a few years prior. He pulled off the flimsy cardboard backing to take the photo out of its worn wooden frame and turned it around so that he could read the inscription on the back. It had been written not long after the dog had died and Heald had moved to Chicago to try to start a new life. The handwriting—his own—was sloppy.

Respice post te! Hominem te esse memento! Memento mori!

(Look around you! Remember that you are man! Remember that you will die!)

Heald had briefly studied the classics in college and had always adored the story from Tertullian's *Apologeticus*, in which a Roman general had assigned a servant to stand behind him at public gatherings to shout these phrases as the masses praised his exploits. Juxtaposed onto Heald's comical photo, the sage advice might have appeared lost, but for him, keeping mortality close and remembering that death lies at the end of every scenario was extremely important. To live is to always remember death, Heald thought.

In this world, Heald knew that everyone is tasked with choices to be made, and consequences must follow from each and every one of them. Youth is often used to exercise poor decision-making and as a flippant precursor to the pure wisdom that many assume will come with age. But sadly, so many never have the opportunity to achieve that sagacity due to the unfortunate intrusion of death into the timeline. Too much is put off for that which can be done later, which sometimes never comes to pass thanks to the indifferent infliction of the reaper's touch. To always remember death is a concept much bigger than merely keeping an eye on one's own future.

One must look back upon their past and recount where they have been, as well as where all others have been (and where they ended up). One must understand that everything they do, have done, and will do in the future will have some recourse not only for themselves, but for those who will follow. Youth cloaks this in a guise of immortality, a moment-to-moment existence, yet for naught, since the naked truth is that death comes for everyone and all things alike. Death itself is uninteresting, though, even to those who would obsess over it. The fascination lies in the stock of the time between birth and death. Like a fire in a pit that rises from a small flame and roils through a high inferno, it casts its brilliance upon everything, sometimes burning objects around it, giving warmth and life to some and becoming the beacon of doom for others, powerful and peaceful all at once. For that fire in the pit and the man tending it alike, death is no more interesting than the bucket of water dumped over the smoldering coals once the night is spent.

For Heald, remembering death was not morbid; it was merely something that helped to bring a certain authenticity into each and every day, every moment—which he would then squander and douse in alcohol.

It was nearing two thirty in the afternoon when Heald had finished looking at the photo and its inscription on the back. Sitting at his desk, he placed the photo back into its frame, though he noticed that he could hardly keep his hands still. It was about that time of the day when his spells of dizziness would worsen. He sat on his hands and tried to get a solid swallow of spit down his throat, but felt a certain resistance from deep down in his throat. The spit would pool at the back of his mouth as he tried several times to get that one decent swallow to 'reset' his facilities, but it was an arduous and sometimes terrifying task. With each failed attempt, Heald felt as if he was losing oxygen; a smaller inhale followed by a smaller inhale, each growing exponentially smaller as his throat would not clear. Each futile breath clutched something inside his chest and squeezed it. It was simple: just swallow. Take what you have in your mouth and swallow it down your throat. Take that breath that your body is craving and move on. As his heart began to race, he was not surprised that he was suddenly terrified of death. He would grit his teeth and silently grip the sides of his desk, making sure not to draw any overt attention to himself, and do everything physically possible just to get that desperate grasp of air. He then took his right hand and began to anxiously squeeze his neck where he swore that he could feel something inside of his throat.

Despite conscious attempts to make it not so, Heald knew how crazy this must have looked to someone who might have been watching him. Here was a man sitting in his three-piece suit in the middle of a busy office on an otherwise seemingly unidentifiable Wednesday at two-thirty in the afternoon, and he was pretty sure that he was dying because he was suddenly unable to breathe and swallow the pool of spit at the back of his throat and his now-shaking hand tried desperately to poke and prod at his neck in a feeble attempt to find some type of release button or valve switch to free him from the possibility of death and yet he would never cry out once for help nor seek any attention whatsoever. Moreover, no one ever really seemed to notice Heald going through this routine each and every day around this time—or so he thought.

As usual, Heald finally summoned the ability to swallow and took in the lungful of sweet oxygen that he'd been fighting for in silence. Afterward, he would disguise the whole ordeal with a loud, fake cough and brush it off as if nothing had happened, returning his shaking hands back underneath his thighs, continuing to count down the moments until the clock struck five and he could leave for the day to join the madness down on the streets of Chicago. Another otherwise seemingly unidentifiable Wednesday.

Heald cleared his throat and turned to Martha, who had been looking through one of the drawers in her desk. He thought that right as he had first turned his chair he had seen her eyes on him just over the top of her desk, as if she had been watching all along, but he couldn't be sure.

"So Martha," Heald said, "Did you hear about that poor woman and her young daughter who were walking alongside the Sears Tower last week during that horrible wind storm?"

Martha's eyes met Heald's and grew wide.

"My goodness, no," she said cautiously. "What

happened?"

"Well, it was on the news and I happened to catch an update on the story last night," he began. "Apparently, this lady was walking along Wacker right at about two o'clock when that bad storm struck last Thursday. You remember it?"

She nodded. Miłosz, who had been walking by to deliver an already examined box of files to the "been-checked" pile, stopped and set the box down on the floor near Heald's desk to listen.

"Well, she was walking with her little girl, who was about six years old, I think they said, and they were trying to get to the Brown Line stop on Wells when the worst part of the storm hit the tower. That wind was really blowing up there near the top, as you can imagine." Heald pointed to their own windows.

Miłosz was next to Martha and they both stood erect with a tempered intensity on their faces. The vein in Miłosz's forehead began to emerge like a worm after a cool rain.

"Thing is, those glass windows at the top are really only able to withstand so much pressure from sudden gusts. Internally and outwardly...that pressure. I mean, sure, they can take a lot of wind—something like a thousand-somethings-per-square-something, but, you know, everything has a limit to how far it can be pushed."

"So, what happened, Heald?" insisted Martha.

"Well, unfortunately, the wind was just too much I guess, and the panes at the top buckled and seven sheets of that heavy glass from the ninety-seventh floor broke out and began to fall."

Martha gasped and brought her hand over her mouth.

She turned around after a moment and squeezed her eyes shut.

"Yeah, well, the wind carried those window panes all the way over to Wacker and Wells, just across the river and outside the Merchandise Mart where this lady was walking, or running actually, to get to the Brown Line stop and out of that rain and wind...with her little girl."

Heald stopped speaking and began to wonder why he had even thought about the story. Why had he decided to share it? What difference—large or small—was the telling of this tale going to do for this small group of people surrounding him?

"Oh god," said Martha, cringing.

"What?" asked Miłosz. "What did happen?"

"She was killed," Heald said without inflection. "She died immediately, but the little girl lived."

"But how?" insisted Miłosz.

Heald now felt quite reluctant to continue, but at the same time obligated by his carelessness in bringing up the story in the first place. Perhaps it would be best to say no more, he thought—better to leave it to their imaginations...or perhaps it might not be.

"She was sliced in half when one of the window panes came crashing down on her just outside of the station. She'd almost made it, too. It came down and split her perpendicularly with the street. Right in two. Down the middle."

Miłosz and Martha both gasped and brought their hands to their faces, Miłosz applying quick pressure to his forehead vein. Heald thought about all the gory details that he had read on the internet concerning the accident, but decided that he had said plenty.

"And the little girl?" asked Miłosz.

"She survived fine. Not a scratch. I mean, she was physically uninjured, but after that, you know...who knows. She was just holding her mom's hand running down the street when it happened. Nightmare fuel, that's for sure."

"Oh Lord, how could I not have heard about that?" said Martha. "That's just down the street from us!"

Heald leaned forward and looked down at the floor, still feeling ashamed. "They said they got the scene cleaned up pretty quickly, just covered everything up before rush hour and the foot traffic. But that girl...they didn't have her on the news or anything, thank goodness, but you just know she's never going to be the same. Poor thing. Nothing will ever be normal for her again."

"My goodness, I should think not," said Martha. She shook her head and let her jowls sag. "Tragic."

Miłosz was stunned and unable to move, other than the subtle petting of his vein.

Heald continued to look down and saw that his hands were now shaking badly in his lap. He placed them into his pockets. "She had to be there right at that moment. Had to be running—if she'd only been walking, or briskly walking, the glass would have missed her. She had to be running right at that certain speed right at that moment with that specific momentum."

Heald turned to the window.

"I'm sorry I even mentioned it. I really am. I didn't know that you hadn't heard about it. I don't even know why I brought it up. I mean, it's clear that we've got our own concerns right now with the missing TITLE 13 information and all, but it's just something that I've been thinking about, I guess. About the asininities of life."

He raised his head to see his co-workers studying him.

"Or something. I don't know...that poor girl, huh?"

They all nodded, returning their glances elsewhere.

"Oh, Heald, that's such a horrible thing—no wonder you've been thinking about it," said Martha. "Anything that terrible would pull anyone right out of reality."

Heald looked at the photo of the dog on his desk.

"If anything, I'd say it pulls us right back into reality, Martha. Don'tcha think?"

She paused for a moment, looking fatigued from the whole exchange.

"Yes, I suppose that's true."

They sat in silence together for a few moments before Miłosz bent over to lift up his box and walked away. Martha disappeared behind her desk once more and Heald sat still, looking at the photo of the happy beagle. He brought his hands out from his pockets and picked up the frame, holding it in his quivering hands. He reached into his desk and took out a notebook, ripping a sheet from it. With as steady of a hand as he could manage, he wrote:

Respice post te! Hominem te esse memento! Memento mori!

He folded up the paper and put it in the inside pocket of his suit jacket and patted it to make sure it was secure.

* * *

It was nearing the end of the day, and Gilbert Tabin had yet to be seen by anyone in the CCM department. No one else had been called in to speak with Ms. Flohard, and she herself had not been seen since calling Gilbert into her office that morning either, though it was not entirely strange (or unwelcome) to have a whole day go by and catch no sight of Ms. Flohard. Since the disappearance, an unsettling sense of confusion had begun to spread among the quarantined CCM employees, like those in the frantic first days of a virus outbreak. The rumors would spread quickly and prove difficult to control before long.

"I heard Gil fell down the building's laundry chute," said Bobert Roberts, a team supervisor in QC. Bobert was his actual birth name, but nearly everyone called him Bob, except for Heald, who insisted on calling him Bobert. He was a very tall man with a beer gut that looked out-of-place on his otherwise slender frame. He had a full head of lustrous light brown hair, which made the other middle-aged men in the office quite jealous. He always wore the same teal dress shirt on Fridays and never allowed a lunch to go by without consuming some type of meat—usually smoked in his smoker that spoke of fondly and frequently, as if it were a promising child.

"The what?" asked Wendy, a QC clerk. "Did you say 'laundry chute'? Like a little door you drop your clothes into and they fall down to the laundry room below?"

"Yep, that's the thing."

Wendy brought the tips of her fingers up to her temples and made a small high-pitched wheezing noise. She was young, about the same age as Janice, Miłosz, and Heald, but stood out as the most all-American looking of the group. She had long blond hair, a twang of Valleyspeak (despite being born in Wisconsin), and always seemed to have a perfect, chipper attitude that could only be broken down by complete and utter nonsense. Heald and Bobert reveled in this fact.

"How could a building of this size have a laundry chute?" she asked. "And more importantly, *why* would a building of this size have a laundry chute? We're on the forty-ninth floor, ya know? You're saying to me that you think there could be a chute like that running through all sixty-eight floors of this building and that somebody's doing laundry? Where? In the basement?"

"That is exactly what I am saying," said Bobert without a hint of emotion.

"And Ms. Flohard had Gil dropped down that chute because...?"

Bobert turned his head sideways at Wendy.

"Who said anything about Ms. Flohard dropping him down there? I said he fell, but that does make sense, what you said—dropping him down there. That would make sense if he lost the TITLE 13 info."

"Gil didn't lose the TITLE 13 information," Wendy said defensively. "In fact, it's, like, more likely that one of us had something to do with it rather than him. Think about it, okay? How often does he even bother working with the day-to-day paperwork? No, it was probably one of us."

"Oh god...," said Bobert, wearing a look of dread. "Are you saying what I think you're saying?"

"Yeah, Bobert. She's saying it's clear that we're the next

ones to be tossed down the building's laundry chute," said Heald.

Bobert put his palms down calmly onto his desk and closed his eyes.

"I knew it," he said in a resigned manner. He took a shiny metal pen out of his shirt pocket and placed it carefully onto his desk in front of him, all without opening his eyes.

Across the office, Leeka Johnston was speaking on the phone to someone, nodding in time with the rhythm of her conversation, actually saying very little into the mouthpiece. Miłosz was standing next to Janice and Heald, and as the three of them watched Leeka through the corners of their eyes, they simultaneously began to bite their nails. Janice had long, painted nails, and it was clear the polish had a horrible taste to it because she scrunched her face each time she drew her fingers away from her mouth. Miłosz had very little left to chew on.

"He is gone," said Miłosz. "I know this. They've disappeared him, and we will never be seeing him again."

Heald kept his corner glance on Leeka, who kept nodding and had not spoken in her conversation for nearly two minutes. "I'll bet some goons beat him up."

Janice looked over at each of the two men standing next to her. "But why? He didn't do anything. I mean, literally, he didn't *do* anything—he couldn't have. He wasn't even in the office yesterday afternoon, was he?"

Both men paused to think back just twenty-four hours.

"No, he wasn't!" she insisted. "He was at a field office all yesterday afternoon in Elgin. Hell, I should know—I helped plan the frickin' meeting for him."

"The goons got him for sure," said Heald. "They beat him up real good."

"Stop it," said Janice.

But Heald wasn't listening. He had centered his focus on Leeka. He was watching her with a torrid intensity, and he kept his hands deep within his pockets as he spoke.

"Those goon bastards...they probably tossed him over the side of the rooftop. I'll bet they lured him to the top with promises of a promotion and grade raises and absolution from the TITLE 13 debacle. How could any career government man refuse? Yeah, I'll bet they waited until he had his back turned, his proud and strange enormous chest faced outward overlooking the beautiful skyline of our fair city, looking for that harbinger of doom somewhere far off and never suspecting it was right behind him, happy as a salaried clam, until they slowly crept up behind him—soft tar up on those rooftops, mind you—and they gave him an easy push over the side and watched him fall sixty-eight floors to the cement below. I'll bet it was the easiest thing they ever did."

Miłosz and Janice both looked over at Heald.

"Those rotten goons," muttered Heald.

"Heald, are you okay, my friend?" asked Miłosz, putting his hand on Heald's shoulder. Heald rapidly turned his eyes to Miłosz's hand and they grew wide with terror and his mouth opened wide. He stared at the hand as if it were a tarantula. Then he turned back toward Leeka.

"Maybe they just cubed him," Heald said. "Yeah, I'll bet they cubed him is what happened." Both Janice and Milo appeared confused by this expression. "It's where they take a man and put him into a large metal box and start moving the walls in, two at a time, so that all four walls come together, and then they bring the ceiling and floor together at the same time, until you're left with a meat cube that used to be a man. You get a perfect cube, one foot by one foot by one foot. Cubed. A cube. Or it could be smaller, depending on the man, of course. Or woman. But to cube a *woman*? Jeez, that's ridiculous."

Heald was beginning to feel quite dizzy.

"You think they made Gilbert into a cube man?" asked Miłosz. "But, how would they do that? Why? Mass is mass and shall not, *cannot*, be created or destroyed. You'd have such a mess of Gilbert all over the place." Miłosz brought his fingers up to his mouth. "Oh my goodness. No. Imagine it. No. No!" He was shaking his head back and forth. *"NI! Ya ne rozumiyu!"* he shouted to Janice's surprise, startling her, though Heald was unfazed. Miłosz looked at Janice and walked out of their area and off somewhere alone.

"The goons cubed him," said Heald once more to himself. "Or tossed him off the top of the building. Or cubed him and *then* threw him off the top of the building."

Leeka Johnston smiled and thanked the person on the other end of the phone line and hung up. Heald quickly turned to a nearby cabinet, pretending that he was sorting through papers, but he instead just looked out-of-place. Janice watched him.

"I have to hand it to Ms. Flohard," Heald said quietly, whispering to Janice out of the side of his mouth. "It's the perfect plan. *Flawless*. You cube the man and then toss him off the top of a building. By the time the meat hits the streets below, it's just a block of fat and goop and fragmented bones, like it might have just fallen off a butcher's truck." Heald took a handful of papers and counted them out one by one for no real reason, his brain working double-time on his new theory. "Or, *OR*, you take all the cubes from all the men that you've cubed and you build a giant cube box, of all the meat cubes, in some secret room here right in this building. Yeah, I'll bet there's some halfway-constructed cube of red slop in here somewhere comprised of all the Census Bureau's 'problems.' What's on the floor above us?" he asked aloud, turning to Janice. She wasn't paying attention to him. She stood looking down at her long fingernails. "But where could they get a cubing machine installed on this floor? Or even the floor above us? The thing would have to be huge." He looked around nervously and leaned in closer to Janice. "Has anyone ever really been *inside* of Director Less's office? Is it a real office? Doesn't he have some girl who sits outside his office all day? Like a receptionist? What's her name? Her *real* name...has anyone ever heard anything that could even remotely be considered a cubing coming from his office?"

* * *

At quarter to five Heald had just finished sorting through a large file of TITLE 13 information pertaining to the Green Bay field office when he noticed the time. It was at this point of the day that Heald's jangled nerves were completely worn thin, twisting like live wires throughout his body, and his shaking grew quite noticeable. He rubbed his forehead and steadied his hands and began to pack up the papers and folders on his desk for the day.

The ritual went something like this: all sensitive information that was out in the open for the day's use would have to be cataloged back into the original files and locked away into each team's cabinets. The Wisconsin team that Heald and Martha covered had six main regions: Milwaukee, Madison, Eau Claire, Green Bay, Superior, and Wausau. Each of these files had countless amounts of PII (Personally Identifiable Information) and it all went back into the master cabinets, which were locked and secured. Then each key was logged and placed into a master key file, which was itself placed into a safe accessible by only three people in the entire office: Gilbert Tabin, Leeka Johnston, and Ms. Flohard herself. Ms. Johnston's access was restricted only to times when Mr. Tabin was out of the office or out of contact.

What sounds like an incredibly complicated procedure for securing the TITLE 13 information within the office had actually been boiled down at that point to something that took no more than ten minutes to complete. At quarter to five, Heald knew the time had come to start the process.

As he took the key to the Wisconsin cabinets out of his pocket, Heald closed his eyes and tried to insert the key into its socket without looking. After about twenty seconds, he decided that he was bored of pretending to be blind, and he just wanted to leave. Nothing could stop him now—not the heat, not the thought of the physically arduous commute back to his apartment, not the silly homeless folks barking strange comments, and not even the missing TITLE 13 information. At this point, it became a game that Heald played each evening and one that felt like he was winning without fault. He locked the cabinet with the PII inside and headed over to the area of the CCM office by Gilbert's door where the keys were kept.

Wendy, the QC clerk, was filling out the sign-in sheet for the QC set of keys that she was returning when Heald walked up behind her. She smiled at him in a way that was meant to clearly demonstrate that she was smiling, not frowning or anything else that could possibly be misconstrued as unfriendly.

"And how are *you* doing?"

"I'm fine," said Heald, hoping to make his way around her as quickly as possible. She watched him gripping the handle to the safe.

"Heald, um, why are you shaking?" she asked, giggling uncomfortably.

Heald's eyes ballooned as he looked at the safe.

"Are you scared?" she asked. "Don't worry, Heel. The papers are probably around here someplace, and, ya know, as soon as they find them everyone will realize just how crazy everything is and I'm sure that, like, everything will be fine. It'll all be good." She was a terribly pleasant person at times.

Heald relaxed his eyebrows, which was no easy task, since they acted almost independently from the rest of his face. He also unclenched his buttocks.

"Yeah, I gotta admit it's been stressing me all day," he said. "I mean, I just don't see how any of us is going to get any rest until that information comes back or until they at least find out who was responsible for losing it. Then, you know, they'll just cube 'em and move on. Get back to business."

"Cube?" Wendy asked.

Heald hesitated. "Oh, ha!" he guffawed. "I meant to say yelled at. I'm sure they'll, you know, yell at that person."

She smiled politely and continued to fill out the sheet.

"You know, I used to have an uncle who was stressed out all the time, like, just jittery and kinda bounced off things," she said. "He used to tell everyone to take long baths with, um, Epson salt, or something like that. You should probably try taking a salt bath."

"Yes, you are entirely right, and that is something I plan to try out tonight just as soon as I get home."

"I'm serious! I don't know what it was about putting salt in his bath, but it seemed to help him. You could tell when he'd done it. He'd come over and be steady as a rock. Just soaking in the salty water."

"Like a turkey."

"Yes, just like a turkey!"

Heald turned to her and grinned widely.

"I am going to go home and fill the bathtub in my apartment with water that is as hot as I can stand and pour as much Epsom salt into that water as I physically can, and I will soak into this mixture like a piece of meat accepting a relaxing and invigorating brine."

"Yes! You gotta do it! Just Epsom salt, or whatever, and you'll feel good as new." She burst out laughing and Heald joined her, trying to mechanically match her tone and pitch. At the same time, he slipped the Wisconsin key back into its place in the safe and scribbled his name and the time (4:56 p.m.) onto the docket.

Janice walked up with the key to the Central and Northern Illinois regions and tried to make sense of the ridiculous scene between the Heald and Wendy.

"What's so funny here?"

"Epsom salt. Brining myself. Gonna feel like a real good turkey," replied Heald.

Before Janice could respond, he headed back toward his desk. He grabbed his suit jacket and tossed it over his shoulder, all the while keeping a grin on his face like a pale shield, and made a beeline for the door. There was no code to punch into the doors to leave the office, but he made a mental note that the code would probably be changed again by the time he got to the office the next morning. Then he mentally scratched off the note because he didn't care.

"Brine the meat. Cube the meat," Heald said quietly to himself as he put on his sunglasses. Between the black suit, black tie, white shirt, and shades that hid his eyes, Heald looked every inch the government working man. He tucked his Department of Commerce ID badge into his shirt pocket as he left. Sometimes he would have some fun and tap his ear occasionally while out on the street, looking around with a stern and menacing impression. Today however, he was flat-out exhausted and uncoordinated. The walk to the subway station would test his equilibrium as by this hour, his dizzy spells usually got the best of him and he had to rest on the concrete islands along the street, propping himself up...just so long as he could keep his breath and focus on swallowing. He needed to breathe.

"Brine the meat. Cube the meat."

Chapter Eight

THE SMELL OF SMOKE hit Heald the moment he entered his apartment building. Since the air-conditioning inside the building was not functioning, it was impossible to differentiate whether the heat within the building was due to a fire or to the nearly 101-degree temperature outside. Everything was hot to the touch. His damp wool suit and dress shirt clung to his chest like a magnet. His inner thighs and boxers were swampy. It was all terrible and very disgusting.

As the scent of something burning grew stronger, Heald cared less and less about walking into a wall of flames within his apartment; his main concern was vodka. When the elevator doors opened on the second floor, he stepped out and looked in both directions, half-expecting to see a raging fire, and surprised to find he felt a little disappointed when he did not. Heald dragged his heavy feet, bogged down by sweat-soaked socks and soggy shoes, toward his apartment door.

Inside, the smell of booze was overwhelming. The hellish perfume of alcohol, body odor, and smoke was pungent. Anyone else might have gone running, but for Heald, it was just another sensory signal that he was back within his element. He shook off his suit jacket and flung it over the window air-conditioning unit, which he switched on, to cool and dry the garment. The standing water among the dishes in the sink had a putrid, organic smell that reminded him of the slop under dumpsters. He pulled the bottle of vodka from the freezer and gagged. Looking at the casserole dish in the sink, he saw the foam had become discolored, sitting atop the water with wild hues of rust and sunset among the hardened, crusty grime.

The bottle was painfully cold in his hand. In the hot, sticky air, the bottle was instantly coated in frost; it felt dangerous, like a volatile chemical. Heald removed the cap and knocked back a massive slug, taking a moment to swallow, followed quickly by three large successive gulps. After making sure that he was not going to retch it back up, he looked down to his cell phone. He had missed a text message while he was in the subway out of cell service.

It was from the woman who lived in the large one-bedroom apartment on the third floor above him. Since moving to Chicago, Heald had only managed to make one friend, and that was merely because of their mutual friend, booze. Her name was Alice, and her hair was that incredible shade of dark brown that absolutely encompassed and absorbed everything around it: her eyes, ears, nose, lips...all faint monuments to her gorgeous hair. Her hairstyle reminded him of Jackie Onassis, the way the bob kind of curled up just at the base of her shoulders and allowed for her whole neck to be seen, if you could sneak a proper glance. Perhaps the Jackie O connection was what had drawn Heald to her, the elegance of her presence, but whatever it was, he did like seeing her. Her message on his phone read:

ALICE: movie tonight? drinks? :)

He had been in Chicago for nearly two years and had known this woman for about as long. Each Wednesday, they would get together with her two cats to watch a movie in her apartment. They would sit close on her silk-lined, floral-patterned couch and the cats would meander about, eventually resting atop his head, chewing on his hair. The cats also settled their furry bodies right on his face when they appeared especially bored or felt particularly neglected. He replied:

HEALD: As always it shall be

Then he worried that that sounded stupid.

Alice Harold was a couple years older than Heald, pushing thirty, but could have been mistaken for younger. She had one of those small, ageless faces that other women envied. She was a little taller than most women, which probably intimidated possible suitors as much as her beauty did, and she was lean, with tanned skin, and amazingly smooth elbows, which he always noticed.

And that hair. My god, that hair, Heald thought as he felt the warm calm of the vodka flowing through him. He took another swig and placed the bottle back in the freezer before he walked into his tiny bathroom in the corner and turned on the water to take a shower.

Pulling down his wet boxers, Heald gazed into the mirror as it began to fog, slowly obscuring him more and more. After college, he had taken pretty good physical care of himself for a while, but that was a few years ago. He was developing a paunch in the front and soft rises of back fat were apparent above his rear. He watched his reflection as he sucked in his gut, thrust out his chest, and bobbed his hips around to make his penis flop. He did this until he felt the contents of his stomach rolling around, then flipped off the light and stepped into the shower.

Heald was already buzzed. It hadn't taken long, perhaps rushed by the heat or his fatigued state, but regardless, it was the perfect moment for him, there in the dark with the water raining down. The physical symptoms of withdrawal—shaking, dizziness, headache, confusion, rapid pulse—all began to subside. The warm water from the showerhead felt incredible as he concentrated on the heat that flowed outward from his belly and into his veins.

He closed his eyes and washed his body in the dark, but he was not alone. The TITLE 13 information was with him. As he scrubbed his crotch maniacally, he tried to push the thought of the missing papers clear from his mind. Less and less he cared about the TITLE 13 information and more and more he focused on washing his junk.

As he turned the rusted metal knobs and the pipes let out an angry whine that vibrated the bathroom walls, the water flow slowed to a drip. Heald reached for a towel and dried his hair while still standing in the tub, then stepped out and put one foot up on the toilet seat in a pirate stance so he could vigorously towel off his privates. He knew he was wasting his time down there, as Alice had always kept things strictly platonic.

Still naked, he ambled over to one of the two side-by-side windows in the cramped apartment, thrust his arms high above his head, spread his legs, and shook his penis in front of the window. He hoped that somebody might be watching, laughing, perhaps getting some type of joy out of this sad display. He headed over to the freezer to get another drink before considering clothes.

Although they were routine, Heald always tried to dress well for his get-togethers with Alice and her awful cats. Every clean piece of clothing that he wore over to her place came back coated in a thin layer of impossible-to-remove feline fur. No matter how many times he rolled those cheap lint removers over the hair, or strained to pick out each one with his fingers, he could never seem to get it all off. Sometimes he wondered if the futility of the cat hair removal would somehow set him down a path of slovenly abandon. Despite knowing this was not the case, he preferred to think that it might be.

Heald was allergic to cats, though he'd never mentioned this to Alice in all their time together, afraid that she might feel bad about inviting him over and stop, or worse, ask to watch a movie at his place. He could tell that Alice noticed when he started sniffling and wiping his eyes, but she rarely brought it up. She was funny like that, he thought, and by funny, he meant inconsiderate. In the end, Heald had no one to blame but himself for the wheezing and sneezing, but it wasn't often an issue, because by the time he arrived at her place, he was buzzed or drunk and the dander in the air had little noticeable effect on him.

Heald did have to make sure that he didn't go too far too quickly with his drinking. Nights that he planned on being alone were different, but when he knew that he was going to be spending time around company, he tried—*tried*—to pace himself. He thought of himself as the world's greatest functioning alcoholic (though he would never boast about it, as this would defy the very concept). Most alcoholics feel this way about themselves, that is, until they spill their drink or knock their glass onto the floor or accidentally drop a microwave out the window at a party.

Heald saw no limit to the amount that he could drink before entering a social setting, but there certainly was a limit as to what was considered socially acceptable. He took another quick pull from the bottle before settling on his nicest sweater, a half-cashmere thing he'd received from a relative last Christmas, which still had remnants of cat fur on it from previous nights. Besides, he said to himself, putting the bottle back in the freezer, she'd already be drinking, too. He reasoned that she'd never really notice if he arrived half in the bag, and most of the time, he was right.

He brushed off his pants the best as he could, examined them for stains, and headed out the door knowing that he would be back soon.

* * *

Heald entered the staircase at the end of the hallway and started up the stairs. After missing his footing on the third step and grabbing the railing to keep from falling, he reached into his pocket for a piece of gum. He stood there chewing vigorously for a few moments, spreading the minty wad around his gums and pushing his tongue through it, spreading it thin. He continued up to the third-floor entrance. When he walked into Alice's hallway, the smell of ethnic cooking woke his senses. It wasn't a disagreeable smell, he thought, just unusual. Before the door closed behind him, he leaned back in and spit his gum down the center of the stairwell.

Ever since moving into a large apartment building, Heald was paranoid that people were constantly sitting on the other side of their peepholes, looking through them, waiting for something nefarious or sexy to happen in the hallways. This thought was perpetuated by the fact that he did this himself from his own apartment when he was bored and/or drunk. His resulting phobia made him feel self-conscious, causing him to walk a little too peculiarly. But on Wednesdays, he reminded himself that he was walking to the apartment of a beautiful woman and that anyone spying on him would know this. The thought filled him with a momentary empty pride. If the only sex he was having was the hot, imaginary sex within the minds of curious tenants in his building, then he wanted to enjoy it.

When he arrived at Alice's door, he looked closely at the number: 301. In the center of the zero was the peephole that he feared. Her apartment was double the size of the rest on the floor, the only one at this end of the hallway. He could not help but think that she was on the other side of that door, staring through that peephole, giggling to herself. He tried to appear cool and relaxed, hoping to prove to that person on the other side that she was crazy for not sleeping with him and for giving herself up only to broad-shouldered, statuesque men. He smoothed his short hair and instinctively exhaled into his cupped palm to check for any trace of vodka on his breath, though he wasn't sure he could smell anything over the strange cooking smells. His head was good and light, and it was time to knock.

Alice opened the door wearing her pajamas—pajamas spattered with something that looked like cake batter. He felt his heart and his penis sink in unison.

"Heald!" she cried. "How many times do I have to tell you

that you don't have to knock! Just come in." She was smiling, and her voice was excessively high-pitched; it might have been the most annoying thing that he had ever heard in the entire world. Still, Heald was immensely happy to see her in that moment.

"You don't think it would be weird to just have me walk into your apartment? I mean, I could be anybody," he said. "I could be a murderer, or even a rapist."

"Well, you're not those things," she said flatly. Heald noticed that there was a nearly empty wine glass on her end table. Good.

"Can I ask you again why you leave your door unlocked all the time? I mean, just what the hell are you waitin' for here, Alice? This isn't Canada. Sooner or later, someone you don't want to come in here is going to come in here because you don't lock that door."

She was piling baking utensils into her sink; the smell of sugar and spice and everything nice hung in the air. "I just don't see the point in locking it, you know? I mean, we have a doorman. Who's gonna come in here?"

Heald moved into the kitchen, but slowly, as he could feel the lightheadedness coming on strong. "I don't know who, Ally. In all honesty, you don't either. It's just a bad idea. You think that doorman—that old guy buried in books—is going to do anything to stop a common thug? He doesn't give a shit. He *can't* give a shit."

She winced when he cursed and he immediately regretted it. She had grown up in a very strict Baptist household, and she'd told him that she rarely cursed. In truth, he knew very little else about her past, and she didn't speak much about her childhood or family life. All he knew was she lived away from all her family and hardly ever went home. If it pertained to her life before she came to the city, Heald knew very little about it. He knew she was close to thirty, and that she had some type of history on the outskirts of Indianapolis from before he met her. Whether that history was a good or a bad one, or whether her religion or childhood factored into her drinking, he had no clue.

"Listen, this is Chicago for cryin' out loud, Alice. It's not like we live in the ghetto or Lawndale or something, but it's still a violent city. In fact, it's the most violent city in America!"

"I thought that was Detroit," she said without looking up from the sink.

"Detroit is perfectly safe," he said.

"Well, either way, we live in the Gold Coast, Heel. It's not like the *bad guys* are gonna get us here." She watched him as she licked the batter off a whisk. His demeanor changed—the way thunder can have an immediate effect on an excited dog.

"They're not 'bad guys' like the jerks you meet online, Alice. I'm talking about killers and thieves and rapists. Gold Coast or not, this is a dangerous town. End of discussion." He feigned a smile. "Just tell me you'll start locking your door, okay?"

She dropped the whisk into the sink and hopped over to the couch. "Okay."

"It's very easy to worry about people here," he said.

"O*kay*," she repeated and picked up her wine glass. Her living room smelled so much like cats and cat food and cat urine and cat crap and other pernicious cat things that he wanted to vomit. He was horny, annoyed, and wanted to throw up. "Do you want something to drink?" she asked.

"Yes, please," he said. "Are you drinking wine?"

"Well, Darnell did give me that bottle of rum last week. We could polish off what's left in that bottle."

Heald watched her. "Which one was Darnell? Was he at your party?" He scanned the room for her cats. Normally at about this time they would pounce out from some unseen crevice onto his head. Perhaps if he could lock eyes with them while they lurked, he could spoil their premeditated attack.

"He wasn't at the party until later," she replied from the other room. "Like, way later. At the end. Anyway, the rum's good! Raspberry something."

"Did I meet him there?"

She was back in the kitchen now. How nice it must be to be able to get lost in different rooms to avoid conversations within your own apartment, Heald thought.

"Well, he didn't come until it was pretty late, you know? So you were, er...already pretty gone by that point," she said.

It embarrassed him when people brought up his drunken escapades from previous nights or at past events. In truth, Heald really could not stand parties unless there was a woman there that he was engaged in some level of infatuation with or plenty of alcohol that he could stick close to, or both. He tried to maintain a level of control at these events, but between the things he thought he saw and the things he told himself were happening, and his man-child personality—well, he was something of a perfect storm of irresponsibility.

His drunkenness often played out in one of two common scenarios: he would either drink too much, starting out as a good-humored and good-natured guest before getting carried away and often carried out, or he would suddenly become sullen and withdrawn, seeking an empty room or heading outdoors, looking up at the buildings around him. When he thought about it, Heald couldn't actually remember getting back to his apartment from a party in a long time. Everything just seemed to happen—day after day after day.

Alice walked back into the living room holding two glasses filled to the brim.

"How's work going—and that girl you keep mentioning?" she asked.

Heald's thoughts drifted from the missing TITLE 13 information to Janice to the alcohol that he was holding in his hand. Before he could take a drink, he also thought of Alice's cats. He was certain that they were nearby, like tightly coiled springs.

"Work?" Heald said. "Work was good. Great. All is well." He took a long drink. She had made it quite strong, and Heald gritted his teeth and drew his lips back. Whether or not she knew what she was doing, he thought, he might have loved her in that moment.

"I recorded a great movie last night," she said from the kitchen. "It's Bette Midler, from the eighties! She's this brash actress, alongside Shelley Long, who's prim and proper, and they each want to study with this famous acting coach, but they end up dating the same guy, so..."

Just then, a cat leaped from the top of the wall unit next to the television and landed right on top of Heald's head, sinking its claws into his scalp and onto the back of his neck. He shrieked and cried out ("Mother of God!") as the cat planted itself onto his chest and used its sharp claws to pull at his cashmere sweater. Heald had spilled his drink.

"Dinky!" cried Alice. "Dinks, there you are! How are you, my baby girl?" She was smiling as Heald sat pinned to the couch by the feline. Women and cats, he thought.

"How sweet of you, Dinky," Heald said, "but you managed to spill my drink, you adorable little fuzz ball." He looked over to Alice, hoping she would either remove the cat from him like a tick, or at least refill his drink. Without a word, she walked over, took the glass from Heald, and went back into the kitchen.

"You should know better than to spill Mr. Brown's drink," Alice said.

Heald did not understand cats. All his life he had been a dog person, naturally averse to cats due to his allergies. Many of the women that he knew in the city had cats. It couldn't be as simple as men being "dog people" and women being "cat people"; he knew that was too one-dimensional. Maybe something about cats' apprehensive and complicated nature drew women to adore them, sensing a mirrored personality that had to be appreciated, or at the very least, respected. Dogs, with their fanatical, uncomplicated, and singular devotion, were everything a man could ever ask for.

Alice returned with the refilled glass and watched as the cat climbed up onto Heald's chin, batting at his face with its paws. Heald was now stroking the cat's head, though only moments before, while Alice's back was turned, he had been trying to shove it away. The cat pushed its head toward Heald's hair and began to chew on it.

"Aw, she likes you!"

"Yes. I love this cat so much."

After handing Heald the drink, Alice sat down on the couch next to him. He moved the cat to one side of his face and reached his lips out from behind the furry stomach to take a drink. Now was a measured time—a time when balance was key. The shakes were gone. Contentment flowed over him, and his head grew light. Alice leaned forward to pick up the remote, and as she did, she rested her hand on his leg.

"So anyway, Bette Midler and Shelley Long want to be famous actresses. The guy that they're both dating ends up getting killed, but they think he may have faked his own death and—"

"Oh, right," said Heald, interrupting her. "You already told me. Sounds amazing. You can go ahead and put it on now." Another reason Heald felt he had to be good and drunk whenever he came over to Alice's apartment: Bette Midler movies.

As they both settled, the alcohol took a grip on Heald and he began to think.

"Can I ask you a question, Alice?"

"Sure," she replied, only half paying attention as she struggled with the remote.

"Do you believe in evil?"

Alice stopped and looked over at Heald. She knew instantly that this was not a playful exchange.

"Yes, of course I do. Absolutely. I know you claim not to believe in God, Heald, but He is real and so is evil. It's just as real as this glass of rum and the Devil is, too."

Heald looked out her window and saw that the street lamps had come on, and the city grew speckled with the tantalizing lights that drew so many from so far. He took another drink and gently moved the cat off him and over to her lap.

"I don't so much as mean in a religious sense," he replied. "What I mean is more so in a sense of we. Us. Humans. Here on Earth. Are *we* capable of inherent evil as a people, and not just, like, in some philosophical struggle between religious right and wrong?"

Alice looked frustrated. She took a long sip from her own glass. "The Devil is real, Heald, and there is evil on the earth. Everyone knows that. Demons can enter our hearts at any moment and we become puppets to sinister incarnations." Heald detected an unexpected rural sociolect in her speech, as if she kept it ready in her handbag at all times, her sole possession brought from Indiana.

"Yeah, I guess that's what I wanted to hear," Heald said. He leaned back and took another long drink.

"Can I start the movie now?" she asked, "Or should I go get dressed so we can go to a late-night mass somewhere?" He couldn't tell if she was serious or not. When it came to religion, it was always hard for Heald to differentiate.

"Ha," he tried casually. "Yes, please start the movie. I'm just dying to see it."

She eyed him for another moment and moved the cat onto the couch cushion between them, then folded her arms.

"You don't have to watch the movie if you don't want to, Heald. Just say so. We don't have to do anything."

"No, no. Don't do that. I'm sorry. I just really had a long day at work, and I'm a little tired is all. That's all." He smiled.

"And maybe a little drunk, too," she said, then turned away without waiting for his reaction. "I'll just turn the movie on."

"Please do."

* * *

About a half hour or so into the movie, Heald felt like he was going to do one of three things: get up and kick his foot through the TV screen, grab Dinky the cat and kick *her* through the screen, or find some excuse to get up and head back downstairs to his vodka.

He knew that he had to make his move, one way or another. He had not been watching the movie, so he couldn't quite tell if this was a good time to tell Alice that he was briefly heading back downstairs. As Dinky purred and used her sandpaper-like tongue on his chin, he gently moved the cat over toward Alice.

"I'll be right back," he said getting up and inching his way to the end of the cushion. Engrossed in the movie, she had no reaction at first, then fumbled for the remote when she sensed his movement.

"Is everything all right? Here, wait, let me pause this."

"No!" he shouted, holding up his hands. "No, that's fine. You can keep going. I've got a firm grasp of what's going on in my head. I won't miss anything. I'm just gonna run downstairs real quick and check my phone. I left it down there, and I'm expecting a call from my parents."

She hesitated to not pause the movie then turned on the lamp on the table beside her. "Ugh, you always leave your phone downstairs. You should just put it in your pocket before you come up here."

He was halfway to the door by the time he responded. "Yeah, that's a peach of an idea. I really should. I'll be right back. I'm gonna just grab it now. I won't miss anything. That sheriff is one crazy character!"

"The sheriff isn't in it yet!" she called back after him. "They're only in Iowa!"

Heald was closing the door. "Oh, right. I mean that other guy. That thing he does. With the thing. Hilarious! Be right back." He closed her door and inhaled the not-cat-piss air. It felt like stepping out from behind a truck's exhaust pipe.

In his apartment, he went to the freezer and poured a large glass roughly halfway full of vodka. He drank it back fast and quickly exhaled, clearing his throat. The warmth that flowed through him was not quite like that of the first glass of the day, but it sufficed. A comfort flowed over him, like watching his father barbeque as a kid back at his parent's house. Or something like that. Something nostalgic like that.

The urge to urinate came on strong and fast. Feeling confident, Heald decided to attempt peeing into the toilet from across the living room. He failed.

After he went into the bathroom and dropped a towel to the floor, he turned off the air conditioner and headed back upstairs, locking the door behind him—"Because I'm not an idiot," he said to himself. He wanted to get back up to Alice as soon as possible. That drink would get him through the rest of the movie, or at least until she offered him something else.

For a moment, he stopped and wondered if she might be doing the exact same thing that he was—sneaking around and hastily drinking while he was gone. He sincerely doubted it, but the thought comforted him.

Walking up the staircase, he began to realize that little patches of time were starting to elude him. He could not remember exactly what he'd done in his apartment other than get the drink. At the top of the steps, he opened the heavy door with too much force, and its rebound nearly knocked him back toward the stairwell.

When he got to her door, he didn't knock. Instead, he opened it suddenly and took a forceful step into the darkness and yelled out, "You crazy broad! This door was unlocked, so now I'm here to rape you!"

The moment after he said it, he was filled with shame, terrified in a way that someone backing out of their driveway might be when they hit something and hear a yelp. He wondered if he should just turn around and crawl into a ball somewhere in his apartment.

"Could you just hurry back here already?" he heard her say quietly. "You've already missed, like, half of the movie." For a moment there was nothing but the sound of Bette Midler. "And that wasn't funny," Alice added.

Heald swallowed and walked in. He used his hand to steady himself against the hallway wall before he turned into the living room.

"Sorry," he said softly. "I am evil."

Chapter Nine

SITTING UPRIGHT against the side of his bathtub, Heald woke promptly at six thirty in the morning. He was not wearing pants.

His legs felt heavy, their many dark hairs pressed down, clinging to the skin, like a field of grain flatted by a wide thresher; an unpleasant film of dried sweat stuck everything in place. He reached down and pulled up a few hairs from the skin and they were as brittle as dead leaves, his fingertips now soiled with the film. He was still wearing his half-cashmere sweater and it was covered in cat fur.

He remembered that it was a Thursday and the swift mental lurch into the real world brought with it a torrent of disquieting realities concerning his job, getting to the office, and other misfortunes ahead. Heald sometimes wished that his internal clock wasn't so finely tuned to a nine-to-five working schedule. He wished that he could oversleep like any other irresponsible alcoholic and be fired. Then again, he would still have bills to pay, and rent was due. To hell with this world, Heald thought as he rose and tried to gain his footing through the fog in his mind and the rubber limbs he sprouted each morning.

Heald could not remember leaving Alice's apartment after making that awful rape comment. There was nothing so lonely and miserable as the memory of making an inappropriate comment to someone he desired during the throes of a binge. He removed the soiled sweater and thought about a shower, but knew if he took one, there would be no way for him to reach the subway to make the train that he needed to catch in order to get to work in time. He ran a comb through his short, wild hair and swiped some deodorant under each arm.

Contrary to most functioning alcoholics, Heald never once drank before he was scheduled to work in the morning. The urge to do so was always present, but it stood for him as the last barrier between whatever he was now and the edge: something even more dark, solitary, and irreconcilable. Everyone has an edge, and Heald knew that he would stand on his each and every morning and look down, but he dared not to lean too far.

Sometimes the unsolved mysteries of a drunken night's progression could be traced by looking at his phone to see if he received or sent any ominous messages. He had Janice's phone number, and that thought always terrified him—the dreadful possibilities concerning what could be done with it. Heald was a shy and reclusive man by nature when not at work or obliged to be social, but he was impervious to the soul-charging effects of alcohol and loneliness. Picking up his cell phone, Heald saw that there had been no incoming or outgoing messages, and while that momentarily saddened him, he ultimately felt relieved. He often wondered why he didn't receive more of a response—good or bad—from Alice for his actions, for she had undoubtedly witnessed his debauchery more than most. Immunity, he thought. Or perhaps she possessed some great and secret physical strength and looked forward to the exercise of picking him up stinking drunk from her couch, tossing him over her shoulder like a bag of wheat germ, carrying him down to his apartment, and placing him in the bathtub at his belligerent insistence.

It was nearing seven a.m. and Heald still had to throw on his rumpled suit and make it downstairs, out into the sun and up onto the Brown Line station a few blocks away to catch his train. It would be close.

* * *

These warm mornings are simply wonderful, thought Heald. Just down the street from his apartment building, there was a small park named Washington Square, filled with trees and a fountain and grass and bushes that very nearly made you forget that you were smack dab in the middle of one of the country's largest monopolies of concrete, brimming with enormous steel monoliths. It was a beautiful place to stop and allow his brain to realign with his body. Sometimes, when he reached the massive fountain in the center of the park, he felt like dunking his head into the water and drinking until his stomach pushed through his shirt. Usually right when this urge arose, he would see a few pigeons standing along the outer rim of the fountain, carelessly depositing their stool into the water, and the yearning within him would suffer a swift death.

This Thursday morning the air was dry and still somewhat cool. Heald knew that he would miss his train, so instead of rushing to the station, he opted to sit on one of the metal benches and take a moment to himself. There was now a direct correlation between how long he sat and how late he would be to the office. He figured that if he was signed in by 8:44, he'd be fine. He felt the need to savor this moment on the bench.

Sometimes it was just too much.

If you sat at the west end of the fountain, the sun would rise over the skyscrapers at just the right angle and you could watch as beams of sunlight moved like glistening caterpillars across the branches of the large trees that left shocking impressions through the vibrant green. The Gold Coast was filled to the brim with people at opposite ends of the spectrum of life. Well-to-do older couples and elderly singles would doll themselves up in their finest fashions and meander about with little to no care for anything. Long, darkly colored blouses atop the aged, well-cared for skin of some former debutante dotted the park like a chess board. Not a soul under forty was in sight, but in a way, Heald was comfortable with that. His generation harbored far too many pressures and binding conformities under the guise of individualism. Better to mingle among those who had a collective consciousness of shunning individuality, he thought.

Heald did not think it would be accurate to call himself a neo-luddite, now that he thought about it, as he had certainly come to embrace some of his generation's most prized conveniences, including the internet, portable music players, and other certain technologies. On the other hand, it would be easy to label him as a declinist. He felt fully prepared to embrace an abrupt removal of the floor beneath society, like some effortlessly entertaining parlor trick.

Perhaps Heald's true contentment stemmed from the peace of mind that resulted from being a self-absorbed farcical solipsist. Everything good and bad, evil and honorable, real and unreal—right down to the stain of spaghetti sauce that he now noticed on the crotch of his pants—was just for him, merely a product of the inner workings of each neuron firing within his brain. In a way, it gave him solace to believe that all the nonsense in each new day might all just be something that he could undo through sheer force of will once he had had his fill—like the way a child is convinced that he can explode an airplane flying miles in the air, just by staring at it and concentrating hard enough.

The only other option for rectifying the wrongs of this world was through death, he thought, and with each new disappointment in his physical condition or mental health, he resigned himself to not think about invoking this resolve, opting instead to lie down and submit himself to the cosmic gag reel.

At that moment, a bird passing overhead relieved itself midflight and its droppings landed neatly, without a splatter, next to the spaghetti sauce stain on his pants. Heald looked back up through the trees and again at the beams of light coming down that touched his face and warmed and opened his pores and felt that a certain equilibrium had been restored and that this new karmic medium was just enough for him to get up and head to work.

* * *

Nothing at all about this subway ride is good, thought Heald.

When he first moved to Chicago from the suburbs of Detroit, he was excited by the prospect of using public transportation. Like so many others, he had seen movies where the main characters would ride around in subways and meet all kinds of interesting people and see all types of fascinating things—from beautiful strangers and exciting sights to the seemingly impromptu sessions of jazz and classical music played on ragged old instruments by men who looked like antediluvian wizards. Yet these things, so evocative of life in the big city on the screen, were far and away from commonplace in much of the Chicago public transit system. The average symphony of sounds that one could actually expect to encounter was more likely to consist of a young couple arguing over the care of a fussy child, a lone man shouting violently and endlessly to no one in particular, and a group of young adults joyously farting and screaming over the outcome of a Cubs game. A sea of odor and upraised arms, grasping onto the high rails along the ceiling of the car, the hot miasma that enveloped the subway, people vacuum-packed like coffee grounds—this was the reality. And in the face of this, if Heald heard even one musician playing any type of instrument, no matter what they played or how well they played it, he was delighted. His commute was no longer a burden—it became an experience.

The front of the Jomira Transportation building hung over Madison Street like an enormous sundial, cutting through the sunlight. The dazzling rays that Heald had admired not long ago in the park now cast their brilliance on the buildings opposite his and reminded Heald of the actual time; he had less than ten minutes to make his way through the intense crowd. People exiting the trains that arrived from the suburbs into the Jomira building poured into a steady stream of bodies that matured into a river, leaving the unfortunate few, like Heald, who actually worked in the building to struggle against their current like spawning salmon.

Before he entered the building, he stopped to relish one of the last aspects of his morning commute that he truly enjoyed: crossing the bridge over the great Chicago River, taking one final glance at the tranquil water. He held the palms of his hands against the sides of his head near his eyes much like horse blinders, concentrating on something in the water—perhaps a seagull bobbing up and down—for the final seconds before he plunged into the world of government office life.

A water taxi was dropping off a load of passengers at the dock near the foot of the bridge. He looked farther down the river and saw the sun gleam off the water and admired the blinding fine light upon the shallow waves. A single individual in a kayak made his way down the river, seemingly unaware that he was within a jungle of glass and steel, and not lost in some outdoor wilderness in Michigan's Upper Peninsula.

Chapter Ten

THE SNAKE MADE ITS WAY along the bank of the river while the water flowed effortlessly through the dense foliage of the trees. It was a small snake of some garden variety, covered in tiny, dark-toned, shiny scales, as though wet, slithering through the tall grass at the edge of the water. The snake turned its head toward the river that rolled along rapidly, and it looked across for a moment, then continued along its path. It did this every few feet, weaving through the thick blades of grass as heavy pipe smoke laces through a hanging chandelier in a quiet study.

The snake came to a stop once more and put its head out just over the water, though this time it kept focus on the opposite side of the river. It lowered its head and slipped into the water like a noodle sliding off a fork, quickly poking its head back up, then began undulating its long body in the water. From the bank it looked like nothing more than the curved end of a stick protruding from the surface.

Voices came from upstream. On the water, sounds carry far beyond their ordinary reach and it was soon apparent, if not to the snake, that people were coming. Unaware, the snake continued downstream, progressing slowly toward the other side.

Around the bend upstream, a young boy appeared sitting in a kayak, engaged in a feverish attempt to out-paddle the rest of the group behind. As he widened the distance between them, he laughed and struck a pose of victory and turned to see if those following had noticed. He looked like a strong child, brimming with confidence. His small hand reached over the side and dipped into the cold water, creating a tiny wake. The child's smile was infectious. More people came around the bend.

"Paul!" cried a woman to the man in the boat next to hers, both well behind the child. "Can he tip his boat over if he leans over like that? What if he falls in?" She had her long blond hair in a ponytail and wore padded gloves on her hands. The life vest strapped to her chest was at least one size too big. Next to her, the man, burly and much larger than the woman, took a relaxed pose. His short black hair was echoed by a rough five o'clock shadow. Despite his intimidating appearance, there was a consoling calm and rational presence about him, perhaps a practiced intensity of level-headedness, like that of a police officer.

"He's fine," said Paul. "Don't worry about him. If he tips, the water here is no more than two feet deep. He's twelve now, you know." The man dipped his paddle into the water and stuck it into the riverbed so that he could turn his kayak and look behind him. After a moment, another kayak with a young girl rounded the bend. She appeared older than the boy, features more matured. She paddled haphazardly, trying in vain to produce a balanced momentum. "I'm more worried about Lynn, to be honest." Facing upstream toward the girl and her craft, the man motioned to her with his own paddle. "Alternate, Lynn! Alternate, honey!"

Up ahead, the boy was drawing close to the snake, which had noticed the kayaks and lowered its head, increasing its pace to the left bank. In an instant, the boy knew what it was. That tiny serpentine head poking out over the water, encircled by little ripples from the frantic motion, was all too familiar to a boy who had spent plenty of time in the woods behind his parents' suburban home.

"Snake," the boy said under his breath. "Look at that thing. Where's it going?" He quickly turned back to the rest of the group and opened his mouth to alert them. Then he took a moment to look back at the waterborne snake. Cocking his head just a bit, the boy could see that the snake was desperately trying to avoid him. The boy looked back to the adults briefly and then back to the snake and silently began to cheer it on, seeing that it was headed toward the water's edge. He put his paddle into the water behind the snake and lightly pushed to propel the water holding it, though that only served to frighten the snake. What a strange world for this thing, the boy thought.

Seeing that he would be unable to coax the snake along, he turned back and called out, "Careful! We got a snake in the water up here! Don't kill it! It's just trying to get across! Don't kill it!"

Instantly the man stiffened up and displayed a cold, alert stare. He brought up both ends of his paddle from the water and held it parallel to the surface.

"Heald. What do you mean 'snake'? A snake? In the water? What kind of snake? How big is it?" The man floated helplessly as he refused to return his paddle to the water. He comically began to float downstream next to the woman, slowly drifting sideways. Nothing about this sight seemed right at all. The man had his hands nearly straight up in the air, the double-sided paddled like some sort of trophy over his head. A man, nearly one thousand times larger than the snake, and nearly double the size of his children and wife, was seemingly inconsolable and paralyzed with fear at the thought of a snake in his vicinity. It was hard not to smile at the sight, and the boy did.

Heald kept watch on the snake and surmised that the only thing on the creature's mind was getting across the river and as far away from these people as it possibly could. Malice isn't always easy to spot in someone or something, but if you aim to find it, you look into its eyes. As the boy looked at the snake, hardly able to see its tiny eyes for it fleeing, he knew that there was nothing to fear. The only threat that existed here would be one they made for themselves, he thought. The boy smiled and looked back toward his father.

"Dad, it's completely fine. It's just a small snake. He's only trying to get to the other side. Twenty bucks says that he was already in the water and on his way when we showed up and scared the pants off him."

"Snakes don't wear pants!" yelled the girl from the back of the group.

The woman, seeing a rare opportunity for some fun at the expense of the man's insecurity, decided to join in. "In this circumstance, neither does your father!"

Unaccustomed to the group poking fun at him, Paul sat snugly in his kayak and kept his sarcasm to himself, though he was usually ready with his quick wit to jab back at opponents. Heald wondered if something inside of his father's brain made him unable to respond in any form other than a quiet survival instinct. At that moment, the man and the snake were just two creatures sharing the same mindset and capabilities. Apart, they were formidable in their own rights, but brought together, they shared a set of systematic brain patterns that had existed for millions of years and had kept both their species alive.

"Fear isn't a joke," the man began. "It's something that has kept me—us—all of everything alive forever. Every living thing feels fear! Right now, I do, because it's a friggin' snake." He adjusted himself in the seat, hands still over his head, and scanned the water around his craft for any small movements. The woman and children were still laughing. "How is this a funny thing? You dumb people actually have the gall to laugh at someone who is experiencing fear? What are you—schoolyard bullies?"

The boy still had his eyes on the snake, which had nearly made it to the water's edge, jostling through the crystal clear rolling liquid as quickly as a snake its size could.

"How is fear funny?" the man continued in a stentorian tone. "If people didn't fear things, they wouldn't be around very long, I can assure you that! You think if my ancestors hadn't been afraid of a giant snake or python or whatever back throughout history and saved themselves or their families from that danger that they would have survived and that I'd be here now, having created you dumb kids?"

The group continued to chuckle at the man's exasperation.

"Oh, yes, that would be rich," he continued. "My great, great, great, great, great grandfather is stumbling around some jungle and comes across an enormous snake poised to eat him, but instead of running, he pats it on the head like a puppy and dances around it. Well, he's dead; everyone else down the lineage is dead too. I'm dead, and you kids are dead. I guess that's hilarious!"

"I'd still be here regardless of what you or your ancestors did, honey," the woman added with a joker's smile.

"It's a friggin' miracle you'd survived for as long as you had before you met me!" the man barked, now nearly smiling himself. His kayak still spun around, rudderless. "Without my fear and instincts, you, the kids, and not a few other people on this planet would be long gone!"

The boy listened intently to his father, still smiling and keeping one eye on the snake, letting no one know where it was. "It's almost gone now," he called out.

"Yes, Paul, I don't have enough fingers to count on to name all the times that you have saved this family by utilizing your justifiable fear against tiny, garden-variety snakes," the woman said. "You are truly our hero."

The man now returned his paddle to the water and straightened out his kayak, though he still kept watch over the ends of the paddle.

"Fear," he said. "Get to know it. Learn it. Live it. Accept it. You never know when listening to your gut might actually save your life. And if you're too proud to listen to it, you won't ever know it because you'll be dead."

"Snake's gone," said Heald, turning to his father.

"For now!" said the man. "You never know when fear can strike. It's never wise to let your guard down for even a minute. Remember that."

"Okay," said the woman. "That's quite enough there, honey. It was a stirring lecture, but I think we're all safe now. Heally said it's gone."

"This has very little to do with the snake itself, you know," the man said to the group. The boy had returned to the small huddle of kayaks, and the girl was finally was able to point her craft in the direction that she wanted, though she was still lagging behind. The man looked keenly at the boy. "Fear, Heald," he said. "It could save your life. Could also save the people you love. It doesn't matter how big you turn out to be in the end. If you can respect your mind and appreciate your fear, you've got a chance, bucko."

"But dad, it was just a tiny snake."

The man righted himself and paddled into the front of the group. He now spoke as he looked farther down the river with his family close behind.

"Size has very little to do with it. Very little. It's not going to always make sense, Heel. You'll see. My father told me the same thing. Listen if you know what's good for you."

It was incredibly rare to see his father afraid, but perhaps that made Heald appreciate it all the more. Most important was the fact that he knew his father could admit fear, despite his considerable size and power. He let his mother pass him as he waited near the back for his sister to catch up.

As the group continued to paddle down the river and eventually out of sight, the snake made its way through the brush along the edge of the water. The ground was cool and moist, and the snake spotted a large, flat rock in the sun. It slithered over to the rock and up onto its hot, dry surface, drawing strength from the warm rays after its ordeal. It coiled itself tightly and remained still until a hawk swooped down without a sound, like a child stealing a cookie, and grasped the snake in its talons. It returned quickly up toward the clouds, dangling its prize below it.

Chapter Eleven

TRANSCRIPT OF 8:30 AM MEETING BETWEEN MS. ELINA FLOHARD AND MS. LEEKA JOHNSTON IN MS. FLOHARD'S OFFICE

JULY 15, 2010

FLOHARD: Ms. Johnston, I want to thank you for agreeing to meet with me so soon on this Thursday morning. I'm quite sure that you have a lot to do.

JOHNSTON: Oh, that's no problem, Ms. Flohard, ma'am! I'm happy to be of service! Anything that I can do, really. I–

FLOHARD: Do you have any news concerning the missing TITLE 13 information?

JOHNSTON: Well, not yet, but I'm sure that it will come up soon. You'll find that the party responsible for losing it is no one under my supervision. Regardless, I'm confident that one of my people will turn it up. My goodness, what a stunning brooch you have there! Might I just–

FLOHARD: You say that you don't think that the leak was from within your department?

JOHNSTON: No, ma'am. Not with one of my people directly.

FLOHARD: And just why is that your conclusion?

JOHNSTON: Well, you see, I don't run a ship so loose into the wind. My ship is tight. I have a ship-shape ship. My sails are–

FLOHARD: Are you implicating Mr. Tabin in this breach, or someone within his team?

JOHNSTON: [silence]

FLOHARD: Ms. Johnson, I'm afraid I don't have

time for games or a free moment to lollygag around anyone's own feelings concerning this matter, and neither do you. The information is out there. Lost out there. It's unsecured. It's just waiting for someone to find it and do it wrong. Thirty-seven whole pages of enticing and quantified knowledge spending its time out there in the great foreboding dark. It's possibly growing even more powerful in each moment that it is out of my grasp. Now you see, feelings and emotions are nothing when compared to this, regardless of whom they belong to. I'd gladly sacrifice anything in order for the immediate and unconditional return of the TITLE 13 information. I would like it now. NOW!

JOHNSTON: [silence]

FLOHARD: I'm sorry, Ms. Johnston, but as you can see, this missing information means quite a lot to me and to my superiors. Now, once again, do you have reason—good reason—to implicate Mr. Tabin in the egregious breach of the TITLE 13 code?

JOHNSTON: Yes.

FLOHARD: And why is that?

JOHNSTON: Because, quite simply, it could not have been any of my people, Ms. Flohard. I've personally trained each and every one of my subordinates, down to our team clerk, Ms. Janice...er, Ms. Janice, ma'am.

FLOHARD: Ms. Janice what? What is her name?

JOHNSTON: I beg your pardon, but her name escapes me at the moment.

FLOHARD: You are missing information?

JOHNSTON: The leak or source of the breach is with Mr. Tabin and his team. That you can be sure of.

FLOHARD: [silence]

JOHNSTON: Ma'am.

FLOHARD: You know Mr. Tabin was called into my office here yesterday to speak with me, correct?

JOHNSTON: Yes, I do.

FLOHARD: [silence]

JOHNSTON: Ma'am. Did he admit that he was responsible for the security breach?

FLOHARD: No. No he did not. In fact, he claimed neither he nor anyone on his team could have been responsible.

JOHNSTON: Well, that's just simply not the case. I hope that you were able to see that he was not being entirely honest with you. I'm sure that someone in your position, with your level of intelligence, knows when they are being fed anything but the truth, or anything less than that. I'm sure of it.

FLOHARD: [silence]

JOHNSTON: Ma'am.

FLOHARD: But of course.

JOHNSTON: My, that brooch is just so lovely I can hardly stand it. Could I perhaps just for a moment—

FLOHARD: Were the teams aware that Mr. Tabin did not report back to the CCM office after he met with me yesterday mid-morning?

JOHNSTON: I think that they were aware, yes, Ms. Flohard. Were they supposed to be aware?

FLOHARD: [silence]

JOHNSTON: I'm sure it's for the best.

FLOHARD: That what is for the best?

JOHNSTON: Oh, just that Mr. Tabin, you know, didn't return.

FLOHARD: And why is that?

JOHNSTON: Because now I'll be able to have my team quickly locate the missing TITLE 13 information without any further distraction. Of course, I'll need security access to all of Mr. Tabin's files and authority to delegate work and responsibilities to his team personally.

FLOHARD: [silence]

JOHNSTON: That brooch!

FLOHARD: Please continue to do everything within your power to locate the missing information as soon as possible and keep me informed of your progress along the way. When you need to know, I'll let you know of the things known that you need to know.

JOHNSTON: Of course, ma'am. I've never lost any TITLE 13 information before.

FLOHARD: Yet.

JOHNSTON: Yet, or ever. Rest assured that it will be found.

FLOHARD: Good.

JOHNSTON: And...Mr. Tabin?

FLOHARD: Do not concern yourself with Mr. Tabin right now, Ms. Johnston.

JOHNSTON: And if members of his team ask anything concerning his whereabouts?

FLOHARD: Ms. Johnston, neither you, NOR ANYONE, is to concern themselves with the location of Mr. Tabin right now. There are more pressing matters at hand.

JOHNSTON: Of course, Ms. Flohard. Of course. By the way, your hair is simply spectacular. The way it shines on your head. You can see a glimmer on your magnificent brooch, which I may add—

FLOHARD: Good day, Ms. Johnston.

JOHNSTON: Good day, Ms. Flohard.

(END OF TRANSCRIPT)

* * *

The striking new building now in focus next to the Sears Tower had been ornately adorned along the entire exterior with alternating black and white tiles. It appeared as if a giant kitchen floor, sprawling up thousands of feet, had somehow taken root and stood like some enormous chess board against the sky. Completely devoid of windows, the building sparkled as if it had been newly polished by an obsessive-compulsive homemaker. Circling the top of the building was a beautiful, gothic limestone border. At dead center in the middle of the building, probably around the fiftieth floor, was a slowly expanding hole, drawing in upon itself, yet growing larger as if someone had fired a gun into the center of the building and the exterior were made from tightly woven fibers that were pulled inward by force of the bullet driving through it. It continued to grow in size from the bullet's original point of entry. Not a single brick or steel beam was noticeable—just a vibrant alternating black-and-white tile design, constantly drawing in upon itself and replenishing along the outer edges—an illogical whirlpool powered by some infernal machine that would ensure the building was to never fall within its own self, like some unflappable curse.

Ramone knew it was not a real building. Usually a not-so-subtle hint alerted him when his CBS had kicked in and something he was seeing just wasn't there. For others, the fact that this particular building was covered in smooth black and white tiles (not to mention seeming to have appeared at a moment's notice) would have been the first dead giveaway that they were seeing something unnatural. But Ramone had witnessed a lifetime of Chicago architecture. Newer and more modern buildings—some with very unusual designs—were popping up each year. When his vision played tricks on him involving the city's urban landscape, as it so often did, it reminded him of the retirement home that he had been constructing in his mind. A simple place where so many coconuts were strewn about like the staplers, tape dispensers, and pencil holders scattered around the office. His wife could look upon the tropical waters and he could go back to treating each and every crab that he saw scuttling along the ground like it was real and substantial, whether it was or not.

Now up on the forty-ninth floor of the Jomira Transportation building in the U.S. Department of Commerce's office suite, where he sat inside the top-secret CCM office constructed with a number of hardly-there partitions and mismatched, massive file cabinets, Ramone waited for another day to begin.

Turnover of personnel within the office had increased recently as operations were speeding up for the Decennial Census. Many of the younger, more technologically knowledgeable workers within the office, fresh out of college, were busy looking for other employment, or just flat out quitting their jobs to be free to do as they pleased. Despite the recession, young folks just did not seem content to toil away in a government office day after day. Unemployment was high, and yet the younger generation was walking willingly into the ether. It seemed to not matter whether you brought a decent paycheck home, but only that you were *fulfilled*, and sometimes that thought just flat-out terrified Ramone; someone needed to pay his social security. He had no children of his own, but he had heard stories from friends and acquaintances of how children were returning home after college entirely unsatisfied with what the world was willing to offer them. Entitlement and privilege had done away with a necessary fear, Ramone thought. Then he stopped worrying, because he knew that he would soon be at his retirement home with his coconuts and crabs and wild hallucinations with not a care in the world.

Ramone giggled like a little girl. He watched as a man from the Springfield office—a man of considerable build and perceived masculinity—half-opened a large pink umbrella and gave it a quick twirl as he walked through the security doors by the front of the office. The umbrella had a smiling face complete with big, twinkling eyes adorned with full, luscious lashes and a set of pouty red lips. The face spun as the man twirled the umbrella again and again, looking at Ramone as he did, and Ramone, as he always did, smiled and winked back at the face of the umbrella. The Springfield man shot over a stern glance and continued on his way, though he no longer carried an umbrella.

* * *

Heald sauntered into the office nursing a fake limp. As he walked past the bin of umbrellas near the entrance, he cursed himself for having forgotten his own. He bemoaned the thought of possible rain on his walk home, but he also regretted not being able to use a sturdy umbrella as a cane or a walking prop as he made his way around with the limp.

Every now and then, Heald liked to pretend that he had some type of physical ailment. One time, he came into the office and favored his right side throughout the day, hoping that Janice might ask him what was wrong, but she never did. Eventually Martha asked him with genuine concern what had happened. Heald saw that Janice was close by, filing some papers into a cabinet, so he quickly recounted an amazing story of how the night before he had gone out jogging down the Magnificent Mile, as he did most every weeknight, and was running through a crosswalk—for which he had the proper signal, he noted—and was nearly across the street when a speeding taxi came barreling down the road and smashed into him. As Martha gasped and Janice's ears perked up to listen in, Heald told Martha about how his survival instinct had kicked in and he remembered that if you were about to be hit by a car, the best thing to do was to jump straight up into the air the moment before the impact, hopefully saving your vital parts. As Martha's eyes grew wide and Janice turned to face them, Heald noted that the quick thinking likely saved his life, but that he came down hard upon the car's hood with his right side just before he was ejected toward the sidewalk. He was able to leap right up, but the cab had barely slowed at all and took off south down Michigan Avenue before he was able to "throw a shoe or something" after the taxi. Martha was left speechless, her soft, pink palms pressed against her open lips. Janice, on the other hand, went right back to her desk without so much as a sound, and Heald soon felt like an idiot.

There were several times that Heald had come into the office nursing such faux maladies on different occasions. One Monday morning he wore an ace bandage on his wrist, claiming that he had injured it while snowboarding back home in Michigan. In actuality, he had burned it against the hot coils on the stove while drunk. Heald had never been snowboarding before, but anything sounded better than burning yourself on hot stove coils after a long and drunken weekend alone riding the Red Line back and forth from the northernmost stop of Howard to the southernmost of 95th/Dan Ryan for no discernible reason.

Heald now decided to nix the whole fake-limp idea. Janice wasn't in yet, and he didn't feel like committing to a whole day of this charade. On days in the past when he'd feigned a condition, he didn't usually have much to do in terms of actual work, but when he remembered the missing TITLE 13 information, he decided that a ruse on this day would be wasted.

Heald thought about how Gilbert Tabin had not returned the previous afternoon from his meeting with Elina Flohard. Looking over at Gilbert's office, Heald could see that he was not in. He began to think of cube steak and hoped that perhaps there was just an obstruction on the Midway Line, or perhaps a jumper, and that Mr. Tabin would soon be walking through those large double security doors at any moment. Then Heald began to wonder why Janice hadn't arrived at work yet either. Was he even supposed to be here? What day was it?

A voice from behind startled him, and he spun around to

see Martha sitting at her desk.

"I said good morning, Heald!"

"Morning, Martha!" he said. "What a pleasant day, huh? Sun's hitting the building just right out there to make everything sparkle and shine like the waters of Lake Michigan just before a sailboat race or something, am I right?"

"Sure, absolutely," she said, grinning. "You didn't happen to see Gilbert on your way in this morning, did you?"

"Nope, unfortunately I didn't. I was just thinking about him. I hope everything's all right." Heald turned to his computer and turned it on.

"Me too. Did you hurt your leg? I thought I saw you limping."

"Cramp."

* * *

A single, massive cloud was rolling in, overtaking the city from the northwest section of the sky. Heald had spun his chair around, and, since Martha was off at a meeting somewhere, his view of the big, bold azure surrounding the enormous fluffy specter was unencumbered. The floor-to-ceiling windows gave him a rattling view. On days when the wind was strong, the large glass panes would buckle and shimmy, and some within the office would occasionally glance over with an anxious pause. There would be sporadic moments on those windy days when it felt like any of the countless windows that circled the building's many floors might pop free, and everything from the papers to the desks, computers, chairs, and their nervous occupants would all be sucked out and away through random, unbiased chance. Crucial and elemental TITLE 13 information would rain down to the streets, where every unsworn nobody would be free to feast their prying eyes on the information with glee and total abandon. The mangled and exploded bodies littering the sidewalks would stain the confidential data and remain untouched until the proper authorities could come and scoop it all up with shovels.

But on this day there was no wind. All the windows were motionless and silent as an array of spindly spiders made their intricate webs along the metal support beams running on the side of the building. On windless days like this, the spiders made their webs as if they would be there forever—never to be touched and free from all foreign influence—a world solely of their making.

Along skyscrapers, the wind blows up toward the sky, which can produce some mindboggling sights. People are often stunned to see so many spiders creeping and crawling along the glass and in nooks and crannies just outside skyscraper windows. Heald, normally bored by whatever he was working on, often spent long periods of time staring out the window. His coworkers thought that as a relative newcomer to Chicago, he was just enamored with the skyline and unable to pull his eyes away from such a smorgasbord of concrete, steel, and awe-inspiring construction. In reality though, Heald was often just ogling the spiders. On calm days such as this one, they worked as hard as ever and were just as determined to do something as they might be anywhere else in the world at that moment.

When the wind picked up hard, the gales would race up along the sides of the buildings and gather all the spiders like a basket full of berries. As the gust of wind reached the top, the cluster of creatures snowballed. If a human will pay outrageous prices for a higher and more unobstructed view of the city, imagine how slighted they must feel to have to drag themselves through ten to twelve hours of annoying and grueling labor in the financial district only to see some spoiled arachnid get whisked up among the elites just outside the glass window in the executive lounge. Heald figured that many of the most well-to-do folks in Chicago found their way to the top just as easily as the spiders had.

Regardless, the spiders that Heald now gawked at worked just as hard as anyone to create their dream home among the higher levels of the buildings, and yet they somehow remained blissfully unaware that as soon as a hearty breeze approached, they could be cast away from their homes and flung elsewhere. Sometimes, if the wind was right, that elsewhere could be hundreds of feet below on the pavement. Heald couldn't help but wonder if a spider would perish from such a descent. Insects seemed impervious to damage from a fall, no matter the height. He thought of the incredible of distance of the fall in human terms. Take for instance the fall of a human from ten feet—the height of a regulation basketball net. Certain factors would have to come into play to estimate the possible damage to a human from such a fall, but in all likelihood it would cause some type of injury, be it a bruise or a broken neck. A bug, with a solid exoskeleton, could fall from a distance of ten feet—relative to size, thousands of feet for a human—and land safely without effect. Heald tried to extrapolate this concept to a bug falling from the side of a building fifty stories above the sidewalk below, but soon he began to feel exhausted, shaky, and sick. He tried to decide on a comparable fall for a human—perhaps from a spacecraft or high-altitude airplane. As soon as the craft began to skip along the atmosphere, a human would jump from it and fall to the surface far below. Of course the human would be annihilated by the intense heat of re-entry depending on the height...In any case, the spider would be completely unaware that anything was about to happen to it—good or bad. Would it even know that all of its skillful labor had been for naught, or would it just keep spinning?

Perhaps the fact that the spider was unaware of its fate was the best thing about being the spider, thought Heald. He imagined falling to earth from space.

As a rather large, black, and hairless spider continued working along the window just outside the glass near Martha's desk, the prodigious, silent cloud, white as a cotton sheet and as puffy as a bulging bed pillow, slowly stole along the outer edge of the city's north side. The cloud, if Heald looked at it from just the right angle, leaning back and peeking through the lower slits of his eyelids, seemed to stretch as high as the heavens and as far north as Wisconsin. There it sat, looming nefariously, as clouds often do. Yet, at this moment, no one in the CRCC seemed to even know that it was there.

Ramone walked slowly back to his desk just as Janice entered and walked toward the window. Ramone sat as Janice stopped in front of Heald, who was unaware of her presence due to his continued fascination with the spiders the cloud. She paused, almost as if holding her thought out in front of her within her hands, and tried to concentrate on whatever it was that Heald seemed to be transfixed by.

"Did you ever work in downtown Detroit when you lived back there?"

Heald spun his seat and planted his forearms on his desk to stop the motion.

"Actually, I did, yeah, briefly. Downtown and in some of the worse-off areas. But wait, do you mean, like, in a skyscraper?"

She nodded.

"Nah. A lot of the skyscrapers in Detroit are empty. Not many of 'em are anywhere near this tall anyway. Especially none as tall as that guy." Heald was pointing behind him and off toward the Sears Tower, of which only the colossal black midriff could be seen.

"That is a big one," Janice said.

"*Too* big," he replied.

She reached across his desk in front of him and took hold of the photo of his dog and turned it around.

"Do you ever miss this dog? Your family?"

"Of course."

She turned the photo back so that it was facing Heald.

"What do you think you'll do when you retire, Heel?"

He couldn't help bursting out with a horrible-sounding cackle. "Are you kidding me, Jan? Who says we'll *ever* retire? You're joking, right?"

Her face was stern.

"What are you, a masochist?" he added with a grin.

She loosened up. "No, come on, Heald. Seriously. I know it might not be the retirement of our dreams, given the eventual crumbling of social welfare and whatnot, yada

yada yada, but just say you could retire right now, or you know, guarantee that you could retire at the age you wanted to, with money, what would you do? Where would you go?"

Heald brought his smile back inward and put forth his own cold expression. Without any inflection, he replied, "I would retire to Easter Island."

"Easter Island?" she said. "With the big stone heads?" Her face had scrunched up as if she had placed a sour candy on her tongue.

"Yeah. The heads."

"Why?"

"I'm not sure," Heald replied. "Something about the heads being around everywhere would have a palliative effect on me, I guess."

"That doesn't make any sense."

"Why not? Sure it does. Think of it like this: if the heads are always out there watching, then there's never a need to be mindful of myself. We spend so much time watching over our shoulders—literally and figuratively—that we never have a moment's peace. There's always something to do!" Heald raised his hands high above him to emphasize this point. "With all those heads around, I'd finally have a chance to just enjoy life and bask in the serenity of the void."

"They're stone heads, Heald. They're not real."

"You don't know that."

"Yeah, I kinda do. They're rocks."

"Well, obviously they're not *human* heads."

"Then what do you mean?"

Heald sat still for a moment and admired her perfectly shaped eyebrows. Then he edged his glance up to her widow's peak, which brought his line of sight cascading like a rollercoaster down that long, shiny black hair of hers, like water on a full moon night. He reluctantly brought his eyes back toward hers.

"Never mind. What would you do, Janice?" he asked her.

"I don't know," she said, still perplexed and examining her fingernails. "I guess I'd find somewhere to go and something to do. Something *real,* and not some damn ridiculous thing like whatever it is you're trying to say." She looked back at him.

"Well, I'm sorry," he replied. "But I just don't think it matters. Why not dream the absurd? I don't see people in our generation ever being fortunate enough to retire. I know I won't be able to." Heald wore his flat expression like a shy child dons a cheap plastic Halloween mask. "Maybe you *should* come up with something nonsensical to do with your time in your *pseudo*-retirement."

Janice made a not-so-feminine grunting noise and turned to Ramone, who looked particularly old at that moment. "What will you do, Ramone? You know, well, when you retire..." She hesitated as if she'd just said a dirty word. Ramone slowly turned his chair and looked vaguely confused, as if he had not been listening. He had definitely not been listening. "Are you planning to retire anytime soon?" she asked.

Ramone laughed in short, calculated giggles that had a strong element of the deep south in them, perhaps due to the way Ramone's words seemed to be sewn ever so slightly together in a long strand. It was a laugh that you half expected to come from behind the mouthpiece of a trumpet.

The sound came out as a perfect "ah-heh-ah-heh-ah-heh-ah-heh," and Heald realized that it could go on and on unbroken forever if Ramone so desired.

"Retire? Soon? Well, I hope so, but I don't have any concrete plans set just yet."

"But *when* you do, what that you want to do?" she asked.

"Well, I suppose I'll follow my dream like they all say we should do and do what I've always dreamed of doing."

"And what is that?" Janice added, almost motioning him along with her hands.

"If, of course, you don't mind us asking," Heald interjected, looking quickly at Janice and then turning his focus onto Ramone, noticing that Ramone's large eyeglass lenses were covered with greasy fingerprints.

"Well, I suppose I'll finally open that SeaWorld I've always wanted to open here," he said with a resolute smile, closed eyes, and a thrust of his chest.

"Here...as in here in Chicago?" asked Heald.

"Yep," said Ramone, turning back a bit in his chair and folding his arms across his chest. "Right here in good ol' Chicago. We can bring the palm trees in and give 'em special food and light so that they can live year-round, and I'll set up the park right off Lakeshore Drive, maybe down 'long the south side somewhere."

Neither Heald nor Janice needed to say anything. They looked at each other for a moment, and Heald instinctively put his hands into his pockets and leaned back. Janice glanced at Ramone while Heald looked up at a ceiling tile and what looked to be a red stain along the corner where two tiles met. Janice was studying Ramone's profile for any body language that might indicate that he was joking. Ramone was content to not say another word about anything.

As if she hadn't missed a beat, Janice said, "But you realize that can't be done. I mean, the winters. The fish could never survive the winters. They'd never..."

"They're not all fish. Lots are mammals," Ramone said without opening his eyes.

"Right, *I know,* but still, they just couldn't thrive in an environment like this...it's impossible. Right?" She looked over to Heald, who had been looking up at the ceiling but now returned her look and nodded at her discreetly. "They'd die."

"Well, naturally, maybe they'd die. But no, they would not," said Ramone now opening his eyes and turning back to the two of them. "Now I'm not saying that it's gonna be easy to get all those beautiful creatures here, but I'll be retired. I'll have time and I'll have money."

"What about the corporate side of things? SeaWorld isn't going to make this an easy thing to do," said Heald.

"There's money to be made. Corporations love money. We all love money, Heald."

"That's a fact!" shouted Heald, jumping forward and pointing one finger toward the ceiling.

"Are you going to have killer whales there, Ramone? You know, orcas?" asked Janice. "Will you have orcas?"

"Oh, of course."

"Well, you know those animals just can't live in captivity. It destroys their minds."

"Sure they can. It's good for their minds. Toughens 'em

up. Think about it like this: we're creatures living in the wild. This city, these streets, and every machine and living thing that roams 'em—we're among those things and they drive us to do horrible things all of the time. People jumping out of windows and landing on children. A rail car conductor deciding that he's had enough of it and speeding up the train till it derails and takes out the lower section of some low-income housing development. Prophets and whatever in commercial airline planes who've had it with the Western world and are promised something better in the life just beyond that's all too tempting to pass up, so they slam the nose into a building—just like this one here. The wild is just that, little lady: wild. Too wild. There's too much at stake. Best to be in a tank."

Ramone took a long sip of his coffee and looked off past Heald and Janice. Then he appeared to come back to life like a wound-up toy. "Now, I mean, really think about it, okay? Even for something like an orca, the world is just too overproduced and manufactured. It's like a bad song, with all the jibber noise mixed in there. Makes it no good. That's what the world is now. It's not the world of two hundred or three hundred or even a thousand years ago. This ain't the world the orca came to be in. The game has changed for 'em all. We're just sparing them of having to make the decision of whether or not they want to play. The things I'm talking 'bout—this is the new austerity."

"A brand-new SeaWorld Chicago with penned Orcas is the new austerity? And you think that the government would sponsor this facility?" asked Heald.

"Preeeecisely," said Ramone, pointing at Heald. The

corner of his mouth turned up.

"And the government—the very same government that we work for, I must remind you—thinks of this as a viable thing? A solution?"

"Most definitely." Ramone leaned back in his chair and crossed his fingers together on his lap.

Heald did the same thing and they both looked over to Janice, sitting in exactly the same pose perpendicular to each other. "Well, Janice, I have to say, this does all seem to make a lot of sense. I'm sold. I mean, orcas are pretty important, and a lot of people seem to feel strongly about them, as you yourself have indicated. Don't you think that Ramone might be on to something here? With unemployment rising to record levels and debt-to-GDP ratios all grim and such, I don't think we have any choice other than to support Ramone in this decision." Heald motioned to the window behind him with his hand. "I mean, he's right! This is certainly not the wild unknown that our forefathers would have wanted for any old species of whale!"

Janice's mouth creeped open a crack; just enough perhaps to slide a coin through as she looked at Heald with disbelief in her eyes. Her hands formed into fists.

"Heald, stop it," she said without looking at anyone and then quickly turned to Ramone. "And Ramone, you can't possibly think that orcas are the new austerity, let alone think that it is a good idea to plunge these animals into a tank and show them off while they suffer mentally and physically inside a clear glass box with people being paraded through dimly lit tunnels to inspect and gawk at them from all sides and point their grubby fingers at them!

Most people don't even like looking at themselves in a mirror, let alone having some stranger poke their eyeballs out at them from all angles. And just how, how is a SeaWorld Chicago supposed to help with the country's crumbling economy?"

"Advance ticket sales into over-capacity and night shows," answered Ramone. "We'll sell far too many tickets in advance and keep the fish performing day and night, which will help because it will keep the animals lean and in shape. We can more than offset the cost of additional lighting. We'll keep the trainers and entertainers working around the clock, too. Less corporate input into animal-based healthcare."

"That's just stupid," said Janice.

"Orcas are important," Heald added flatly.

"Heald, I said *stop*." Janice held her index finger up to his face, just a few inches away, but never looked over at him. Heald was pleased to think that she knew exactly where his mouth was at all times.

"Do you even know how smart an orca is?" she asked Ramone, squinting at him. "They happen to be even more emotionally advanced than humans. Did you know that?" Another pause. Ramone and Heald sat motionless. "Inside of a modern orca brain, there is a more highly advanced center for emotional development than in our own. Oh, yes. Orcas have more sense and can feel more than we're even capable of knowing...*literally*!" She smiled while nodding. "It's not just that, either! There's an actual lobe in the brain, both human and orca, and theirs is more complex than ours. I saw a movie about it. You know what it controls? Emotional intelligence. Did you know that? Do you even care? You'd be willfully torturing animals."

Ramone continued to sit with a sly smile on his face, his dark hands covered in blackish liver spots interlocked like a row of worms taking turns lying down next to one another on wet pavement.

"It's a whale," said Ramone. "I'd be doing it a favor. The wild ain't the same place that these whale's ancestors grew up in. It's an ugly wild out there now. *I'd* have heated tanks."

"Did you ever see *Free Willy*?" asked Janice.

"A free morpheme," Heald whispered.

"What?"

"It's a free morpheme. 'Whale' is. It's a completely free *morpheme*."

"It's a killer whale," said Ramone. "That's why people will still come to see it. That's why it's the new austerity."

"Well, if it's a killer whale, then it's no longer a free morpheme. At that point, it becomes a bound morpheme. Or, maybe, perhaps not. Perhaps it can appear with a lexeme, like killer." Heald could feel his hands shaking and his mind becoming clouded.

"What the hell are you two talking about?" yelled Janice.

"Well, of course the whale will be bound," said Ramone. "We'll have to keep them tethered to the bottom of the pool, otherwise they would just swim away. Or leap out...we could charge to see that, come to think of it."

"Sure. They could just swim south down the Mississippi, head on down through the Chicago River," Heald added.

"Like that invasive species fish...those, uh..."

"Asian Carp."

"Yeah! Like the Asian Carp."

"Asian Carp in reverse!"

"I could put those in tanks, too. People'd pay to see that."

"Yes they would. Those orcas are smart. They could swim down to the Gulf of Mexico. They're real smart. Very smart. She said so," Heald said, pointing over to Janice and winking at her. Janice was at her wits end. Her shoulders slumped. "What do you think, hon?" asked Heald.

"You know exactly what I'm thinking, Heald, and don't ever start calling me 'hon' or 'honey.' I hate that term."

"What should I call you, then?"

"You can call me Janice."

Heald leaned back in his chair again and waved off something in front of his face with his hand. "That's confusing," he said.

At this point Janice looked ready to leave, despite Ramone's own look of renewed interest. This was certainly the longest that either Heald or Janice had ever spoken to Ramone in all their time working for the Department of Commerce.

"Just what do you aim to do with this park?" asked Janice. "What is its purpose?"

"I aim to build and establish my legacy," Ramone said matter-of-factly.

"Your legacy?"

"That's right. I know you both young, so you may not understand the concept, but I want to leave something behind. I want my name to mean something after I'm gone. I clearly ain't gonna do that around here," Ramone said, motioning around the room while continuing to look at Janice.

"You want to achieve immortality," said Heald.

"Preeeecisely. Once you know you're gonna die and there ain't nothing you can do about it, the next logical thing you got to do is live in each fragment of time like it's the one that's gonna be remembered forever. I want to go down in history as being completely compliant with the new austerity."

"Like Marcus Brutus? The Ides of March?" asked Heald.

"Maybe more like Caesar himself," said Ramone. "I want to inflict change."

"That's more like Brutus," Heald said under his breath.

Ramone slipped his shoes off and brought his right foot up and tucked it under his bulbous left thigh. "It isn't fair that past figures got to make their mark, got to make their names famous hundreds and thousands of years ago. Those names have all gone down in the annals of time and been resurrected constantly throughout history since then, for good and bad, giving them a level of immortality that people in our day in age will never know."

Heald brought the knuckle of his index finger up to his chin and leaned forward toward Ramone.

"And you feel this isn't fair because history itself is coming to a close."

"*Preee*-cisely."

"I see," said Heald.

"And I'm sorry, 'cause I know that implies that there will be nothing left by the time your generation comes up. I'm afraid we went ahead and botched it all up good for you, and for that, someone ought to be very sorry."

"That's quite all right," Heald said, waving him off. "We'll close up the shop, but someone else will have to hit the lights."

Janice put her hands on her hips. "Well, I refuse to believe that civilization is coming to an end. There's just no evidence. Every generation says that theirs will be the last at some point."

"Ramone," said Heald, "if the goal of achieving immortality is a lost cause, then why do you want to bother to even pursue this dream of your whale park?"

"Immortality is only as valuable as time is itself, relative to a culture. I suppose I can just go on and hope that I'm wrong."

"But you don't think you're wrong."

"No, I ain't wrong."

"So we've come to the edge, the precipice of what is possible and what can be achieved...of what can be left behind as a whole then, huh?"

"Most likely," said Ramone. "Again, I apologize."

Heald flicked his response away once more. "So why would young people, like Janice and myself, ever even bother getting together? Why would we ever care to start the whole microprocess of perpetuating life on a small scale if it's all for naught?"

Ramone looked straight out the window. At that moment, he was watching as the Sears Tower sprouted an enormous, spiteful-looking face, furrowing its eyebrows at him and pulling back its lips to show two horrible sets of glimmering teeth.

"What else you gonna do, kiddos?" said Ramone. He began his perfect staccato laugh again just as Miłosz walked by carrying a box of papers. The Ukrainian was so startled by the jarring joviality that he let out a terrified, emasculating gasp, though Ramone continued laughing, oblivious to those around him.

The massive white cloud had finally settled over part of their building, and its broad, dark shadow was creeping over other parts of the city. As Ramone looked back to see the face on the Sears Tower, the cloud cast a shadow over the entire north side of the building, and the face disappeared into the long, drawn darkness.

Chapter Twelve

THE LUNCHROOM at the CRCC was large enough to accommodate roughly twenty people at a time, though it had gone largely unused since yesterday's disappearance of the TITLE 13 information, as management and high-level supervisors tried to keep their teams working around the clock to locate the missing data. Though it was only CCM that had been accused of losing the incriminating documents, the entire staff of the CRCC had been tasked with its retrieval. And though nothing had been found yet, the search continued, much to the indignation of the staff as a whole.

Random employees were still sporadically turning up purported clues to the whereabouts of the TITLE 13 papers, and Heald occasionally spotted people standing motionless and silent, peppered throughout the office like stone obelisks from a doomed age that had seen more time in ruin than in prosperity. He watched as they stood randomly with their eyes tightly covered by one hand and the other pointing with purpose toward some indiscriminate object of interest, or perhaps at some other poor fool. The recovery task force would then flood into the area like sewage through a grate and begin a full investigation, yielding nothing and saying nothing. On rare occasions, the lead investigator would tap his ear and the pointing individual would be escorted away for hours at a time, only to return later drained of all emotion and energy, disheveled and blank. They said nothing after the fact.

With fewer employees using the lunchroom to take their regulated thirty-minute breaks—opting instead to eat at their desks or simply go without—the room had quickly become a mausoleum. When the younger employees of CCM gathered there to eat, still able to sneak away for their lunches, they opened the blinds and let in the light from the city outside. No matter how often he saw it, Heald could not help but look out with awe into that concrete jungle below. He also watched for spiders.

On any regular day, Heald would sit for lunch with Miłosz, Janice, and sometimes Wendy or even Martha. Though Martha was much older than the rest of them, they enjoyed her company because she was such a kind and sweet presence—it was like having a friend's mother around. With her soft-spoken nature and Midwestern warmth, she could fit into any group. But today, Martha was off at a meeting of the department heads covering for Gilbert, who was still missing. Wendy, ever diligent, was also likely off somewhere shuffling through stacks of documents. Today, it would just be Miłosz, Janice, and Heald eating together, and that suited Heald just fine.

"Could you please pass the salt, Janice?" asked Heald while motioning over to the cheap white silo-shaped saltshaker near her. Janice just stared into her large ceramic mug of cold, beany-looking soup.

"Do you think they fired Gilbert? Could that be what happened?" Janice asked her soup. Miłosz immediately raised his head.

"Fired?" Miłosz replied. "As in gone for good? But why would they do this?"

"I told you, he's most probably been cubed," said Heald, still gesturing toward the salt. "I'm still gesturing toward the salt, Janice."

"Stop it, Heald. I told you I don't like that. I didn't like it when you first said it, and I don't like it now. It's just weird."

"Salt's not weird."

"Don't try to be funny. It's not cute."

"But we work for the government," said Heald. "Something fishy must have happened. Something incredibly fishy is always swimming about."

"Again, not cute," she said. "And who cares who we work for? You know, it's so damn hard to tell what the hell is a joke with you and what you're actually trying to insinuate or if you're even insinuating anything at all. Where did you even come up with the concept of 'cubing'? Okay, let's say you're right. Let's say they cube everyone. What kind of organization just goes around cubing their whole staff? It's ridiculous."

"Ridiculous doesn't mean impossible. It's a finely tuned system, and you can't have people shitting on it. Gotta get them out and forgotten. Cube or be cubed. I would love some of that salt right there." Heald's hand was beginning to shake as he held it outstretched over the table.

"I still have trouble with this," said Miłosz. "So, you are saying, for essence, some person would be put into a room with machine walls that would...squeeze in from the sides and squish him into cube?"

"That's about it. He'd be dead, of course."

"I would be hoping so!"

"Ugh," Janice grunted. "Would both of you just shut up?"

"I might stop if I had some salt."

"What the hell does salt have to do with anything?"

"Because then I could salt my food and eat it, and I would have food in my mouth so it would be difficult for me to continue talking."

"Difficult, but not impossible," she said, and looked toward the floor. "Are you wearing different-colored socks, Heald?" She finally slid the saltshaker across the table.

"Thank you."

Janice picked up a spoonful of her soup then let it fall back into the cup.

"Seriously, though, you guys, where could Gil have gone? I mean, is he out because he wants to be out, or was he asked to leave? Or maybe he's sick at home."

"Okay, so the last anyone saw of him was when he went into Ms. Flohard's office, right?" said Heald while waving the saltshaker over the top of his sandwich, an unseemly amount of tiny white crystals falling into the porous, seed-filled bread. Miłosz could not help but stare at Heald's sandwich.

"You know, Heald," Miłosz said, "I hate to say anything bad about your food but you know that shaking of all that salt is really a not good thing for you."

Heald paused a moment and looked at his sandwich. Janice finally took notice of this now too and displayed an abhorred reaction.

"It's whole wheat bread," said Heald. "And it's got all kinds of nuts and grains and seeds and some kind of flax thing, too. Eating like this, I'll live forever. Plus, it's low-sodium bread." He resumed salting.

Janice let out another grunt, like a tennis player.

"Why do you buy low-sodium bread if you're just going

to put that much salt on it?"

"I don't let the bread companies dictate my sodium intake. I am the despot of my bread fate."

"But why not just buy regular bread?"

"I have an autocratic method to bread-buying. I do as I please."

"Knock it off with all the high-minded bullshit, Heald," said Janice. "You're wearing two different-colored socks."

Janice let out a grunt to end all grunts. If Heald knew her for the rest of his life, he was quite sure there would never be a grunt that could top it, so he savored that grunt and tucked it away in his mental box of curiosities.

Heald set down the saltshaker, finished with his task but horrified to find that his hand was not finished shaking. Worst of all, all attention was now on his hands. He watched them shake for a moment and brought them under the table onto his lap and sat looking at his sandwich.

"That's really not healthy, Heald," said Janice, stirring her soup. Heald was looking out through the glass, hoping to gather the attention he'd drawn from them and beam it out the window.

"I know. I know you're right. I just can't seem to stop." He wouldn't look at them.

"It's simple," Janice said, now in a calm and collected voice. "Just don't do it anymore. Be healthier."

"I really should. I wish I could."

"It's sad, Heald."

"It's a sad thing," he replied.

Miłosz leaned in over the table and brushed his upper lip with his finger.

"It leads to number of health complications," he said. "At the end, could be the problem that ends up killing you."

Heald looked back at Janice and she returned the gaze.

"Most likely you're right," said Heald. "But where's Gilbert?"

Janice dropped her spoon into her cup and it clanked loudly. "Maybe he knew something that we didn't. Maybe Gil was more involved with the TITLE 13 information than the higher-ups are letting on," she said. "Could it be a cover-up?"

"But was not the fact that the information went missing at all leading to a sort of cover-up of some sorts?" asked Miłosz.

"A *cover-up* cover-up!" said Heald. "It's ingenious! Though it does only perpetuate my cubing theory. It would, in fact, necessitate it, without a doubt."

Janice picked up her cup of soup and looked at her tiny wristwatch.

"Time to go. I'm done with this conversation anyway." She glanced at Heald and he could almost, just almost, sense a smile upon her face. "You're hopeless, Heel."

"You called me Heel," said Heald through a smile.

She picked up her lunch bag and headed for the door leading back into the office. "See you back in there, Milo," she said, and then added, without looking back, "I called Miłosz Milo." Then she was gone, and Heald sat alone at the table next to Miłosz. Heald still had his hands at his sides.

"The salt," Miłosz said while looking at Heald's ear, since Heald was still looking at the door that Janice had disappeared through. "It's not good for you, my friend."

"I know."

* * *

Summer had only just begun, or perhaps had been going on for months, for he never knew when the official seasonal line had been crossed; it was nothing like transitioning from night to day. Somehow Heald got the sensation that the days were shorter—perhaps not everyone's days, but certainly his, as if he lived in some hemisphere all his own.

As he sat at his desk after lunch, Heald thought only of one thing. Though there were usually two things at the forefront of Heald's mind, one would always succeed in overwhelming the other. In reality, while Heald thought his current situation in life was the result of these two sources of frustration and pleasure sieging warfare on one another, caught in a ferocious battle within his mind, there were several factors that permitted this line of thinking. While we sometimes feel that our current mental state is the result of the two polar sides of our needs and desires doing combat, the truth is much more complicated. None of the worries and fears that people like Heald fill their minds with ever *actually* abate or leave them, but rather they take a permanent place in some cerebral Rolodex. There those suspicions and paranoias await their turn to be called up at some point in the future. The brain forgets *nothing*.

The problem with people like Heald and so many other compulsive individuals is that they never find a constructive way to cast off their compounding anxieties. The thoughts remain within their internal index, festering and fermenting, growing more potent while the user remains ignorant of internal efforts to neutralize the stress. As time goes on, these individuals collect further examples of these harmful parasitic thoughts, and soon their existence feels as if it is composed solely of those things. From the tallest hair on their head to the chafed bottom of their heel, they become a mere transport for an entire system of fatalistic leanings. With the space inside of them for that which is good and healthy and positive growing smaller, those like Heald think of solace as a rare commodity. For any creature presented with few options for escape, the desire to lash out and be a brash is a vicious one; sometimes it comes in the form of a bottle of vodka stashed in the back of a freezer. Catastrophic damage is costly but relative; the barrel of a gun can be pointed out at the world or directly at one's self. Negativity, like mass, can neither be created nor destroyed—it exists in everything.

As Heald shuffled through the papers on his desk, he began to think of all the responsibilities that would consume his days from that point on. It wasn't just the growing pile of work on his desk that worried him, but also the endless banal tasks of everyday life that filled him with dread. The thought of having to take his suit to the dry cleaners terrified him. He also had to drop off of his rent check under the door of the leasing office within his building—a check that was already three days late. Then there was the task of stopping at a small specialty shop on the way home to pick up that one type of horrible cheese that Alice enjoyed. He would also need to stop at a cobbler to see if they could fix the soles of his dress shoes for work, since he only had the one pair, then he remembered that cobblers were probably not a real thing anymore.

There was also the task of taking the time to sit and pay the rest of his bills, all of which were past due. His only motivation to complete this task was to keep the freezer running. In addition, he still had to buy a birthday gift for Janice. Her birthday was that weekend, and he hoped to ask her to join him downtown, perhaps with friends if she preferred (but they would have to be her friends, for he had none other than Alice, and she wasn't invited). Then there was the never-ending trove of promises that he made to himself but would never keep: to work out more and find more time to run and jog through the lively streets of the city.

The list of things to do grew larger as each new hour passed. To Heald, the truth of the matter was that there was really only one thing that he *needed* to get done in order for him to maintain himself through each new day and new task: to never—*ever*—run out of alcohol at his apartment. As a seasoned drunk with a steady income, this was never more than a slight possibility; he knew where his priorities were. A good drunk, like a wise highway driver, never lets the tank get too low.

* * *

By the end of the workday, Heald was still trying to summon up the courage to ask Janice to do something together over the weekend. He went over all the possible conversational approaches within his head as he tried harder and harder to fight the unsteadiness in his hands and in his heart. Most of all, he was battling with his mind in an effort to convince himself that he was worthy of being happy.

Heald had never had a steady girlfriend, though there had been some flings and late-night encounters. In the past he'd blamed this on foolishness, immaturity, and a dearth of self-esteem. Now, all of that was compounded by his current dependence on drink, so he blamed his habit for his inability to find a mate. He thought, if only he could find someone to settle down with, he wouldn't have to settle down with the bottle. When he pleaded his case within his own mind, even he knew that it sounded clichéd and broken. The way he was now, in life, and quite physically at that moment at his desk, he found it hard to ponder a life without alcohol. The need—the pure physical and emotional necessity of it—was more powerful than anything he had ever felt, save for the love of his family. That was the one other thing he could not do without, he thought. It would not be reasonable to say that he *needed* the love of a woman, for he had never had that before, and he was still alive.

Heald looked down at his hands and felt his heart begin to race. It was impossible at that moment to tell if the shaking was caused by the thought of asking Janice to join him for dinner or from withdrawal. Frustrated by this loss of control, he took the rare stance of tackling the issue head-on, and before he knew it, it was actually happening: he was walking over toward Janice's desk.

She was putting all sorts of things into her purse: lip balm, some type of makeup tube, a few pens, something he guessed was a sort of ear makeup, and lastly, her cell phone, which she had been staring at before placing it into her bag. She looked up and Heald was standing in front of her desk, his hands in the tiny pockets of the vest that completed his three-piece suit. It was such a dark brown color that it almost appeared black unless you were right up close to it like Janice now was. She looked at the vest and briefly thought of their first-ever real conversation, which was regarding the color of this particular suit—a rather lackluster conversation all around.

"So, how's things?" he said taking his hands from the vest and pushing them into his pants pockets.

"About the same as they were at lunch," she said.

"Yeah, I'll bet," he said, laughing and watching her closely. She appeared nervous and out of sorts. Her eyes darted around the floor by her feet. Then she abruptly spoke.

"I was kind of hoping that maybe we could get some of us together for drinks after work today," she said.

Heald could hardly believe what he had just heard. He felt his heart bang twice within his chest and then he felt nothing above his belt. His immediate concern was that he couldn't be sure whether the cause of his erection was the thought of seeing Janice for drinks or the drinks themselves.

"Drinks? Today?" he said, attempting to remain calm, then blurted, "That'd be great!" He pursed his lips a bit, slouched, and said, "I mean, sure. Whatever. That'd be cool, I guess. I don't care. You know."

Janice did not appear to take notice of his response. Instead, with her face directed toward the floor, she spoke softly. Heald crouched over to hear her.

"Do you think you could ask Miłosz to come along?" she said.

Heald was still feeling the flood of joy rushing through him as he responded. "Miłosz? Sure! I adore Miłosz. Let's get that adorable S.O.B. to join us, why not, huh? Janice looked up now and grinned at Heald, who motioned over to the area where Miłosz sat in the row behind her. "I'll go ask him now," he said, and playfully rapped his knuckles on her desk in two short taps before heading over to Miłosz's desk.

Miłosz was studiously collecting the items on his desktop and arranging them neatly, organizing the last of his pencils so that they would be parallel with the front and back of the desk and perfectly centered. Nearby were seven perfectly arranged paper clips. Heald tapped his knuckle twice onto Miłosz's desk as he had done moments earlier. Miłosz looked directly at the intruding hand like a squirrel eyeing his last acorn.

"Miłosz, my boy! How are ya? It's nearly quittin' time, ol' sport!" Miłosz flashed Heald a nervous smile.

"Yes, it is. This day of work is almost over."

"Sure is. In fact, I got little after four thirty by my estimation," Heald said tapping his wrist, though there was no watch there. "Have you got any big plans for tonight?" He only let the question hang out there in the open air for a moment. "Because I think you should join Janice and myself for some wonderful company and a few drinks at a local establishment after we get out of here today. It'll be great! Whaddaya say, ol' bean-head?"

Miłosz raised his eyebrows with a quick flash of concern. "Just the three of us? Are you sure you would want me there with you and Janice? I had kind of thought you two were, perhaps, maybe...something like, togeth—"

Heald quickly shook his palms in Miłosz's face, waving them back and forth in an effort to cut off Miłosz's speech.

"Wellwellwell, I don't know about any of that, but no, no, no, that's not an issue for you to think about, ya ol' sport-bean, so just no, no—please, won't you please join us, won't you?" Heald was still waving his palms in Miłosz's face.

With a blank look, Miłosz sat up and shrugged his shoulders. "In that case, yes. I will go and be happy."

"Now that's an ol' bean-face for ya! We'll meet you by the bus platform outside in front of the building right after we get out. We'll all walk somewhere together. I'm not actually sure where we're planning on going yet...I guess I never asked Janice. Whoops. Well, we'll figure something out. The hard part's over with."

Miłosz nodded, and Heald once again tapped his knuckle on the desk and Miłosz once again looked directly at the surface that he had touched. Heald walked back over to Janice. She was looking down into her purse but he could see the corners of her eyes watching him as he approached.

"Miłosz," she said plainly. "What did he say?"

"He said sure and that he'd meet us down by the stop in front of the building. Where are we going, anyway?" Heald asked. He began to make mental plans for a surprise romantic dinner for her (perhaps that weekend) on the rooftop of his apartment building.

Janice had said the name of a place to him but he was lost in thought and had to ask her to repeat it.

"The Fontz Club. It's nice and low-lit and we can actually talk to one another."

* * *

As Heald rode the escalator down to the bottom floor of the Jomira Transportation Center, he found it hard to comprehend the two different sets of emotions rising within him. At his side was a beautiful woman, and soon he would be drinking. Janice appeared anxious, wanting to force her way along the left side of the escalator, past the people holding onto the railing. Heald stood still and grinned as he looked over toward her and wished that he could see himself and her from the second-floor platform just above them as they made their slow trip down side by side. He began to rock back and forth on his feet.

Most everyone around them appeared tense in an effort to begin their voyage home by way of bus, train, or cab, but Heald was finally in no hurry. His heart was racing and a numbness came over the crown of his head, little spasms causing his neck and arms to twitch, but he knew these subtle tics would be hidden within the sea of humanity.

They reached the ground floor and slowly walked in the condensed line of people to the front doors. Heald jutted in front of Janice when their turn to exit came, and he held the door open for her.

"Thanks," said Janice looking around nervously. "Do you see Miłosz down here yet?" Heald didn't bother to look around.

"Nope. Maybe we should head along without him. He'll find us. He's smart. Everyone is always saying how much downtown Chicago looks just like any old town in Ukraine."

"Stop it."

They stood while people swarmed in and out of the building all around them. They were two ants with a death wish who had stepped out of the work line. Heald began to think about the drinks that he would order. Normally, when he got home, he went for a quick half-full glass of chilled vodka to steady his nerves, stop the shakes, and quiet his head from churning inward. His top priority now, he told himself, was to not appear to be an alcoholic. He did not want to walk into the bar and order two double whiskeys and a beer kicker, as he had done so many times in the past with old college friends. Normally, to avoid anyone noticing his excessive early consumption, he would offer to purchase the first round of drinks for a table and go to the bar by himself. Then he'd order a quick large drink or two (depending on how much they cost and how fast they were poured) while the others in his party would look for a table or wait to be seated. He'd wink at the bartender, make a quick joke, like "this oughta help," pointing over to the group while rolling his eyes, then pay for the drinks and bring them back to his party, as if nothing had happened. Every drunk has his or her ways. He would try to do just that when they got to the Fontz Club.

Before too long, Heald noticed Miłosz standing across the street at the bus stop looking helpless. For a brief instant he thought about telling Janice that Miłosz had said he might have to change his plans at the last minute and that if he was not outside, they should leave without him. Janice was looking down at her cell phone and never once lifted her head, leaving the responsibility of finding Miłosz solely upon Heald. He thought about how easy it would be for the two of them to just take off and go straight to his apartment rooftop and spend the evening together under the stars. Just leave Miłosz behind and make their way together hand-in-hand down the busy street, skipping the whole way while falling into deep and passionate love, laughing like senseless hyenas the entire time. The thought was so ridiculous that

Heald let out a guffaw right then and there, though the sound of it was lost in the chaos.

Heald contemplated the Miłosz predicament while staring at him across the street. Look at him there, he thought, with no clue what's really going on here. Heald could not help but to feel bad for the guy. All alone in a strange new country, in a giant city filled with noises and brutes and horrible smells. Heald suddenly felt guilty. If he left poor Miłosz on that corner while he walked to the bar with Janice, at some point a renegade bus would careen off the road, whether by deranged driver or mechanical failure, and plow right into his sorry eastern European hide and spread him onto the walls and streets in a fine red Pollockesque mess.

Heald clenched his left hand into a fist and raised his right hand high and waved it around so that Miłosz might see him. After a moment, Miłosz acknowledged him and waved back, flashing what Heald told himself was a very stupid grin. Miłosz was now motioning for the two of them to join him on his side of the street. Heald used the clenched fist to nudge Janice on the arm, and even through his tight fist, he could feel the softness of her skin. She looked up, and he pointed toward the other side of the street.

"Miłosz is over there."

She looked across the street and sheepishly smiled and looked back at Heald.

"Hurry, let's cross and meet him."

They walked to the crosswalk and waited for the signal to change. Heald saw Miłosz anxiously waiting on the other side.

"Want me to take your hand?" asked Heald. "To cross?" He immediately regretted saying it.

She looked at Heald as if he had just pulled off his pants, bent over, and laid an egg. "No, Heald. I spoke to my mom and she said that it's okay for me to cross the street on my own now. But, uh, thanks."

Heald let out a small laugh of surrender to the sad moment. He had been too excited, but he would calm down once he had a drink. Now he had to wonder: What if she had said yes?

Over the last few years, Heald had become resistant to the thought of another person touching him. He feared that somehow, in some way, all his transgressions and ineptitudes would become evident at first contact with someone else, as if his failings could seep through his skin. This was especially true when it concerned someone he wished to care for deeply. It was an anxiety that he had hoped would dissipate over time, or prove to be hollow and perhaps even silly once he had met the right person, but up to this point, that was just a working theory. He had had regular physical contact with girls in his younger days, but over the last few years, as his addiction had taken hold, he'd come to find this concept intimidating. Still, he would have reached over and taken Janice's hand in a heartbeat if she'd said yes.

The light changed, and they began to cross. Miłosz extended his hands, welcoming them over to the other side of the street like a child would.

"Friends!" he cried. "Where are we going?"

"Tell him," said Janice to Heald.

"The Fontz Club," he said and turned to Janice. "Wait, is it really called the Fontz Club? What the hell kind of name is that for a bar? It sounds like some place a teenager in a leather jacket might tell me to get lost."

Janice was looking at Miłosz now.

"It's nice! And it's upscale and usually not too crowded so we can actually hear each other and have some space to ourselves."

Heald shrugged. "Works for me."

Miłosz eagerly agreed.

They walked with Janice in the middle. Heald always took the side of a woman facing the street when walking on the sidewalk to protect them from any possible danger. It was something that his father taught him to do when he was little. Yet as they walked down the street now, Heald thought that he wasn't quite sure he was actually protecting anyone. Should a taxi driver decide to lose his mind and swerve into the wall of bodies on the sidewalk, there was little that Heald's body could do to alter any impact—especially for someone as small as Janice. In fact, he figured that by just standing there next to her, he was somehow enticing fate to deal them a horrendous blow, if only to test this theory. He glanced over and turned back to see the cars speeding by. Heald assured himself that it was the mere gesture of pitting himself between a woman and a car that was meant to be the crux of it.

After careful consideration, factoring in his nervousness and withdrawal, Heald figured it would be best to at least get a double vodka at the bar as soon as he got there and to drink it fast. Maybe two. He thought he might be walking strangely, as he was normally unsteady on his feet this late into the day without a drink, but it was too hard to tell. His head was still dizzy and he could feel the tremors.

* * *

The Fontz Club wasn't busy. In fact, it was completely empty, save for a lone man in a suit who had an open briefcase on his table in the back with a spread of important-looking papers scattered out in front of him. Also in front of the man was a full bottle of beer, sopping wet, obviously left untouched and allowed to sweat in the room for some time. The napkin below the bottle was soaked.

Heald was the first to walk through the door and held it open for Janice as she walked in looking straight ahead, followed closely by Miłosz. Heald couldn't decide at first if he was pleased to see the bar so barren. As the sunlight came through the street-level windows, it appeared that the room was filled with a still smoke, only slightly moving, like a fog along the highway. The businessman in the back didn't bother to look up as they entered. Heald looked over at Janice, who was now looking at Miłosz, who was himself looking up at the ceiling and making crude movements with his eyebrows. The first thing Heald considered was the level of difficulty he would face in order to get drunk in this place; ordering side drinks and going up to the bar alone without either of the other two noticing would be a challenge. For a brief moment, Heald thought about suggesting that they should leave to find a place that was a little more sociable.

"I like it," said Janice. Heald touched his tie with his trembling hand. As he tried to swallow, he caught an immense lump at the back of his tongue and felt like he might choke. In that moment, more than anything in the world, he just wanted Miłosz to open his mouth and say something. Anything. Or perhaps just throw himself out the door into the path of oncoming traffic.

"Have either of you ever been here before?" asked Miłosz.

"No, but I've heard of it," said Janice. "There was a little write-up about it in the *Red Eye*." At this point, they both turned to Heald, who had finally conquered the lump and made a few casual swallows. He was breathing a little heavily from the exercise.

"Never heard of it." he said. "Love it."

As they scanned for a booth, Heald watched a bartender setting up glasses along the back wall. Then he saw the waitress walking toward them, and his heart began to race. Like all addicts, Heald began to piece together, scene by scene, how this whole evening would play itself out and how he could best satisfy his need to drink while maintaining a public façade of control. He knew that he needed to organize his compulsions accordingly, and for anyone but an addict, this would be an incredibly arduous ordeal, but for someone looking for a fix, it was just another aspect of day-to-day life. First: the waitress would seat them and take their orders, making it impossible for Heald to order himself two side drinks to gulp down as quickly as possible without anyone else knowing. Second: his companions would monitor his overall drinking at the table, since the bar was empty and there would be a natural curiosity as this was a new experience for them to share; he would need to find a way to achieve the heavy drinking in the shadows. Third: in such an atmosphere, any deviation from standard casual drinking in a social, post-work setting would raise some type of alarm, so he would need to remain focused. Heald could almost feel the lump returning in his throat.

The waitress was coming closer. She was dressed in that pseudo-upper-class service uniform that most of the fancy downtown bars used to maintain an aura of luxury accommodation. Her white dress shirt, which was completely buttoned to the top and covered with a slightly slanted clip-on bow tie, was one size too large. The black dress slacks she was wearing looked just a bit too tight, producing a muffin-top effect, though Heald would certainly not categorize her as overweight; hers was a pants problem. When she was about ten feet away, she slowed and began to turn, raising her arm.

"Please, you can sit anywhere you like," she said, waving her arm in an effort to display that the place was obviously empty. "I'll go grab you some water and come take your orders."

Heald could tell that this was the type of place that was going to charge at least fifteen dollars for a decent-sized drink. It was robbery, though he knew that he was powerless to stop it or protest it—just bad luck of the draw. They walked to the opposite corner from the businessman, and Heald's mind began planning how he could get the seat next to Janice, leaving Miłosz to sit all alone on the other side of the booth. He came up with a plan to walk to the table and offer Janice a seat on one side of the booth while they were all still standing and then casually slip himself into the space next to her. Genius.

As they approached the table, Heald set his plan into motion and extended his hand to offer Janice the seat. She paused for a moment and appeared uneasy.

"I think there's something on that seat," she said. "Let's sit over here instead." She made her way over to a table by the window. "Miłosz, could you sit on the inside by the window?"

"Not a problem," Miłosz replied, easing his way into the booth. Before anything else could happen, Janice sat down next to him, pushing her flowing dress under her thighs with her hands. Heald stood and pretended, perhaps only to protect his own shattered confidence, that this had all gone exactly as he had planned it. He smiled as he sat down on his side of the booth facing the two of them. As disappointed as he was, he could only think of one thing.

"Mother of pearl, this place is great!" Heald said unexpectedly, startling even himself.

"Oh, yes," said Miłosz. "It is very pleasant. Pearly. Very swankish."

"Oh, God, it's swankish as hell. The swankishest."

"I like it," said Janice. The waitress then seemed to materialize from nothingness and set down three glasses of ice water onto the table in front of them. The glasses were already covered in condensation, as if they had been poured some time ago, waiting for them.

Heald wanted to vomit suddenly. His urge was to grab the glass of water, chug it down, and then hurl it right back up onto the table—anything that might settle his stomach in that very instant. Instead, the waitress spoke.

"So what will you folks be drinking tonight?"

Heald instantly pointed to Janice, as if to signal to the waitress that she should be the first to order and that she'd best talk to her. It was an old alcoholic's trick—let the rest of the table order their drinks first, hope that someone else would be ordering a large drink or hard liquor, and then order that and possibly more for yourself, because "hey, if you're going to have one, I might as well, too!" It was a lame trick, and not much of a trick at all, but built itself well into the whole construction of the drinker's compulsive mindset.

"Ma'am?" asked the waitress.

"What are you having?" Janice asked looking over at Miłosz, who was startled at being called to attention.

"Errm, I will have an IPA beer if you have one."

"Sure do," said the waitress scratching her head. "You want the sixteen-ounce?"

"Errm, yes. Yes, sure please."

"Ma'am?" the waitress asked again.

"The same."

Miłosz now looked straight ahead as if he were an android set to standby mode. Heald couldn't believe what he was seeing...what he was hearing. Was he just that desperate for a drink? Or was this all playing out in front of him just like it appeared? He tightened his thumb and index finger around his kneecap under the table and tried to hold it like a large, flat stone. He moved it and it floated freely from side to side. The waitress was looking at him, as was Janice. Heald decided that this had all happened too fast.

"I'll have a double bourbon, neat," he said. "And let me try one of those IPAs, as well."

"Be back in a bit."

Janice looked down at the tabletop in front of her.

"Are you celebrating something, Heald?" asked Miłosz.

"Yes," said Heald, immediately looking somber. "This drink is to good ol' Gil...a fine manager whom we shall all miss."

"Don't do that," said Janice.

"Suit yourself," said Heald, instantly annoyed with the whole situation. He leaned back in his booth, uncomfortably aware of all the extra space around him, and put his arms up on the seatback behind him. "I drink to good men."

"Can we not talk about this right now?" asked Janice. She turned to Miłosz. "Milo, what were your plans for tonight before you decided to come out?"

"Well, I am still working on my graduate school applications. Right now, I am working on one for a good school in Milwaukee. That's in Wisconsin. Minneapolis is in Minnesota."

"No shittin'?" Heald said sarcastically. "Are you shittin' on me?"

"Stop it," said Janice. "He's joking, Miłosz. We know those two cities is all."

"Oh, sorry," said Miłosz, genuinely apologetic. "I always get those two messed. I think I say things like those out loud on accident sometimes when I am trying to do a reinforcement in my head."

"That makes sense," said Janice smiling at Miłosz.

Heald hated Miłosz. He wanted to take his trembling hands and use them to rain down blows upon him. Heald thought that he had never loathed someone in this world as much as he loathed Miłosz at that very moment, which made him feel somewhat ashamed. Regardless, he wished for all of Miłosz's stupid hair to fall out right onto the table in massive clumps, leaving as bald as a penis. He wanted a perfect two-foot-by-two-foot chunk of the ceiling to collapse and fall right onto his ridiculous head then and there. If a hole opened up in the floor and swallowed only Miłosz, that would be ideal, he thought. Heald smiled at both of them.

"Can you hand me that menu?" Janice asked Miłosz, pointing to the paper menu that was sitting along the wall of the booth. Miłosz brought his hand out from under the table (WHY WAS HIS HAND UNDER THE TABLE? screamed a voice in Heald's head) and reached for the menu. Miłosz had taken off his suit jacket and rolled up his sleeves at some point. For the first time in his knowing him, Heald saw Miłosz's forearms, and they were rather muscular. Heald instantly loathed those, too. He wanted to rip those well-built arms off at the sockets and beat Miłosz over the head with them.

The waitress finally returned with the drinks. She set them down and asked if anyone would like to order food. Heald picked up the glass of bourbon (which was hardly a double, he noted) and downed it before anyone could say anything. He plopped the glass down with a loud clank onto the table and cried out "To Gil!" and all eyes centered upon him.

"I'll have another," said Heald, pointing to the now-empty glass. "And I think these two will be sharing something together."

Chapter Thirteen

IN THE REAR OF THE YARD, just behind the long chain-link fence, there was an overabundance of massive spruce and pine trees. They stretched as far back as one could fathom—or so as far as the mind of a six-year-old boy could fathom, which was quite a distance. It was an awe-inspiring sight for the child, paradisiacal with its lush greens and shady wood tones, timber pillars forever anchoring the brilliant colors to sway and twist from their perch as the wind willed.

The stark contrast between his parents' well-manicured yard and the untouched sylvan world beyond it, separated only by a thin line of chain-link metal, charmed Heald. It was incredible, he thought, that people could stop nature right where it stood—keep it from progressing. It was not a thought of conservationism at that age, just marvel. Then again, he thought that perhaps it hadn't been men who trimmed and plowed the earth flat and reconstituted the ground, making way for homes and streets and sidewalks and wide, short lawns, but rather that these things had always been so, since he had never known it any other way. Perhaps nature—the tall pines and black, coarse dirt coated with leaves—was the thing encroaching into the world of his parents and neighbors. Maybe the subdivision was gradually being swallowed by these wild natural elements that lawn mowers and weed whackers could only hold at bay for so long. If so, he thought, nature's assault was a gentle one and not at all alarming, as the homes just stood there awaiting the trees' placid advance.

Heald's innate curiosity often drove him into those woods

for long walks filled with plenty of pauses to pull a strip of bark from a birch trunk to find what was beneath and many a hand stuck into a strange crevasse to see what was inside. He surmised that one day all this burgeoning wilderness might overwhelm and become everything.

The mind of a child.

Each afternoon, after what felt like an eternity at school, Heald would blow like a dandelion seed through the front door and weave throughout the house, shedding his bag and his nice school shirt, then run out the sliding back door to those behemoths draped in green furs, protecting a world that he saw few enter. That was the primary appeal to him, for there was this canopy of life that held no other sights or sounds of people, and he felt compelled to interact with only that which had no other motive than to simply exist. He once heard his father tell his mother that they were raising a "nemophilist," and while he did not know what that meant, he took kindly to the label, for he saw his father smile as he said it.

Before too long, Heald realized that the woods behind his family home were actually home to a plethora of wild living things. Where he had first ventured to find isolation, he now discovered something new. From large creatures—or what could be considered to be large by suburban Detroit standards, including raccoons, deer, rabbit, and foxes—to the tiniest insects that marched their way across a single fallen leaf upon the moist ground, all things great and small seemed to be right there beside him, in that place he had thought of only as dark and terrifying when he peered at it from his window at night. The whole entity had taken Heald's young heart by storm like a great idea that required careful planning and consideration to yield exceptional results.

It was on one of these little excursions into the "back woods" as he called them that Heald soon came across something he had never come that close to before. There, at the base of a stump surrounded by rainwater, was a large bullfrog. It was like any other he had seen in a book or on television, but in this moment, here, it was new. As he approached it, he could see the frog sitting perfectly still, save for its ballooning throat, which had caught his eye. Getting closer, he stepped upon a twig, and the resulting snap sent the frog leaping, but it was not alone. A host of frogs, at first hidden to the eye, began moving every which way. He lunged for one and cupped it in his hands as the others made their way off under leaves and into a small pool of still water. Heald had acted so fully on instinct that when he realized that it was indeed within his hands, peeking out at him through a small opening between his thumbs, a momentary sense of panic struck him.

Right then, he knew he wanted that frog. He wanted it to be his and wanted to take it home with him, back to his world.

Not knowing what else to do, he ran back toward the house. He had no plan as he ran other than to see what his mother would think. He only knew that he didn't want to let it go.

Heald smashed his nose up against the black mesh of the screen door, allowing him to see inside. He called out to his mother, who came quickly and scolded him for pressing his face against the screen. It only took a second for her to realize that her son was holding something in his hands that was capable of escaping. She put her arms out in front of her.

"What is it?"

"It's amazing. I want to keep it."

"What *is* it?"

He refused to open his hands, adding that it would need a home, and fast.

"Is it slimy...or crawly?" she said, slowly sliding open the screen door, pushing him back and closing the door quickly before heading toward the shed.

"It feels wet. And bouncy."

"God."

She came back carrying a tall white bucket they used for washing cars. She sprayed the inside clean with the hose.

"It's not a spider, is it? Or, like, a cockroach-type thing?"

"Nope."

She set the bucket down at his feet and noted his outsized grin.

"Heally, are you telling the truth?" she asked, her hands on her hips.

"Yep."

"Well, let it down. Let's see what it is."

Heald lowered his hands into the bucket and released the frog. It blinked by drawing its eyes down into its head, inflated its throat, then jumped up against the side. His mother sighed with relief.

"Oh, it's a little frog!"

"It's not little!" exclaimed Heald.

His mother leaned back and replaced her hands on her hips, this time with her fingers pointed back toward her spine. "Well, he's cute. I think he's adorable. You can keep him—for now."

Heald looked up at his mother with a quick, stoic glance.

"For now? Why only for now?"

"Because you can't keep a frog forever, honey. I'm sorry, but it just doesn't work that way. Why don't you go get some bark and leaves and stuff from out there and put it in the bucket to make it nice for him."

Heald ran back to the woods to gather supplies. He didn't care about what his mother had just said; he wanted to keep that frog and he aimed to do so. It would be a battle he would fight later. He returned and placed the items inside the bucket, trying to replicate piece by piece the area where he had found the frog, though it looked nothing like it when he was done. For the remainder of that evening he sat next to the bucket and occasionally touched the frog but always found himself staring at it. He had wanted it and now he had it.

The next day, he returned home from school in a rush and ran through the house, tossing his bag to the floor. His mother was sitting in the living room, and before she had a chance to open her mouth, Heald was out the back door. Heald looked around the area where he had left the bucket the night before but found it nowhere in sight.

Something was wrong, he thought.

It was a large bucket, completely white and hard to miss. Still, it was nowhere to be seen. His mother opened the sliding door and Heald raised his head at the squeak of the metal rollers. She was looking off in the back by the shed; Heald followed her gaze to the rear of the yard and saw the bucket near the unwound hose. It was turned upside down. Heald looked back at his mother with the same stoic gaze he had shown her the day before.

"It's not dead, Heally," she said with a small smile. He

said nothing and continued to look at her eyes, as if he could ascertain the real answer from them before her lips said anything more.

"It's not dead, honey," his mother repeated. "It just had to go." She stopped and turned her head a bit and raised her eyebrows, trying to display some empathy for the boy. "Heally, I looked in on the frog this morning after you had left for school and the poor thing was just not happy. He was hiding from me under one of the pieces of bark and breathing slowly. He didn't move much anymore and he didn't hop around a bunch like he did last night. Besides, honey, we don't have anything to feed him, and we don't even know what he would like."

She could see no reaction from her child.

"I don't think he would like what people eat and you know he would hate what I make. Just think about how much your father complains about it," she said with a smile and a small laugh, though the boy did not reciprocate. Heald never lowered his head. He never took his eyes off his mother.

"But I wanted him," he said, not sounding hurt, but mostly confused. "I wanted to *keep* him. I would have taken care of him. I would have made him happy. I would have kept him safe."

"Oh, honey, I know. I do. But that's the thing—the hard thing. Sometimes it isn't about what we *want* or what we would like. Sometimes it's not up to us at all."

"But I thought he would have been happy."

"Sometimes when we want something and when we feel like we can make something better, or feel more happy, we forget that these things have a will of their own. And that sometimes it isn't up to us how these things go. Sometimes, we just have to let things be."

"But *I* was happy."

His mother raised her eyebrows at him as she had done before and crossed her arms in front of her chest. "Oh, I know, Heally. But you'll be happy again. And just know that we made this thing *very* happy just by letting it go. We got a chance to have it be with us for a bit, and we got to see that things would be better a different way. I know it's not the way you wanted. I know that you would rather have it here right now, but this is for the best. It may not feel like it right now, but trust me—this is the way it has to be. You may see him again someday out there, and then you might see what I mean."

She held her arms out for him. "Come on. I'll make you some macaroni."

Heald didn't say anything. After a moment, she brought her hands back in and smiled, turning back inside and sliding the door shut behind her.

Heald put his hands behind his back and began to walk toward the shed. Without breaking his stride, he brought his foot back and lightly kicked the bucket on the ground in front of him, knocking it over onto its side. He turned back and began to walk toward the house but stopped and bent down next to the bucket to look inside of it.

It had been wiped clean.

* * *

There was a noise from above.

Heald's eyes opened in a flash and focused on the textured ceiling with its strange ability to look wet and fresh and old and worn all at the same time, like a meringue under glass. He did not know why he had woken. At least he was on the futon, he thought. His eyes quickly darted from the ceiling to the small digital clock that sat on a high wooden cabinet. It read 6:27, a.m. inferred, as the sunlight was weak making its way from the east through the grime-covered window. Plus, 6:27 would be too early for the sun to be setting if it were in the evening. Today was Friday, he reminded himself, and he was ready to be done with clocks for a few days.

There was another loud noise above him.

Heald sat up gradually and as he did, felt sick to his stomach. Before he could comprehend that thought, he heard another bang from somewhere above him. He looked up at the whipped cream ceiling and wondered if perhaps someone might be pushing a large cabinet against a wall in the apartment above him. Over and over, just pushing their wooden cabinet up against the wall to make sure that it was right up against it and that not an inch of the square footage (which should actually be thought of as "square inchage" in apartments this small) was wasted. As he heard another jarring thud, Heald began to wonder if perhaps it wouldn't be best for the tenant above to use their own head to bang against their cabinet to make sure it was even to the wall.

Then Heald knew that there was someone just outside his door.

There is a strange and unsettling feeling that one can get when they live alone in a tiny studio apartment. It allows them to know when someone is standing just outside their door, and it is not unlike the feeling that people describe when they stay in a home that is haunted and claim to have been watched by something in the night. Heald sat motionless.

Every muscle froze—as if to move would be the same as to be seen. It is a perplexing thing to be in this predicament; make a sound and you could be given away, the assurance of stealth lost. He knew that he could not have been detected yet, having done so little since opening his eyes. Adjusting himself from stealth to detection mode, Heald turned his ear toward the door. Squinting, as if that might help somehow, he was able to hear what he thought might be the sound of paper rustling, as if someone were handling paper with great care just outside his door. Heald thought of the TITLE 13 information and nearly sprang to his feet.

Just then a folded piece of white paper slid quickly into the room from under the door. Vindication! I knew I wasn't alone! he thought. Then it looked almost as if the piece of paper were being drawn back out to the hallway by the small corner that was still under the door. Heald leaped from the futon, only then realizing that he was still wearing his white dress shirt and tie, and looking down, saw that he had slept on his suit jacket, which now more closely resembled a trampled Pomeranian. As he leaped, the posts on the bottom of the futon gave off a loud squeal with the weight shift and he knew the element of surprise had been lost.

Stepping over to the door and swinging it wide open, he saw the folded note below him and stuck his head out to see the back of a young woman walking briskly toward the stairwell. He wanted to call out to her, but didn't know what to say.

"I'm sorry," the woman said as she stopped.

"I...er, can I help you?" Heald replied.

She turned toward him. She had cropped brown hair that went just to her neckline and a shapely, attractive figure. She looked past him down the hall for a moment, as if he wasn't there at all, and then lowered her eyes.

"I'm sorry," she repeated. "I just wanted to drop off that note, but I didn't know that you would be awake, or up, rather." She looked now at Heald's eyes for just a split second and then turned her wary gaze down the long hallway just over his shoulder. He looked down at the note and noticed that he had been standing on it with his socked foot, which was moist for some reason. He picked up the note.

"Oh, well, would you like me to read it now, or should I wait until you're gone? Perhaps you'd like to just tell me what it says? I think I'm awake now." He smiled at her and thought back to many years ago and being in grade school, watching as other children passed notes back and forth to one another that asked questions like *Do you like me?* and *Want to hang out sometime?* Almost always, there would be two drawn boxes below the question labeled *Yes* and *No.* Sometimes there was a *Maybe,* but that was risky and could lead to more notes and a greater chance of being caught. But what pre-teen doesn't secretly enjoy indecisiveness? Besides, children have the luxury of being blunt if they so wish.

"It's okay," she said, holding out her hand as if to urge him not to open it. "And I'm sorry, but there was just so much noise when you came back late last night. I had no idea what was going on. I live right there," she said while pointing to the door across from Heald's. She lowered her head again.

"Oh," he said with a noticeable tone of deflation. He again realized he had no idea what had happened the night before. "About what time was that?"

"Maybe a quarter to one? Or one o'clock?"

"Was I alone?"

"I couldn't tell at first. I only heard you through my door. I thought that I'd heard a couple of voices, but actually, I think it was just you. You were talking to yourself quite loudly in the hallway for a while. Then, once you got inside your door, I'm pretty sure I heard you singing. *That* was when I was sure you had to be alone."

Heald grinned. "That bad, huh?"

She looked stunned. "No! I didn't mean that, it's just..."

"Come on, admit it. There's alley cats out back that can croon better than me." He was smiling, and she reluctantly returned the grin.

"Okay, it was pretty bad. But nobody sings that well when they're drunk."

"Who says I was drunk?"

"If you weren't drunk, you should probably say that you were." Now her grin was complete.

"Oh, I was bombed. Tanked. Completely snockered," he said. "But I'm also really sorry."

"I suspected so."

Heald held the note in front of him and her delicate grin vanished.

"Oh, please! Can I have that back?" she said, taking a few steps toward him with her arm outstretched. Heald held the note now like it was a volatile mixture of chemicals.

"Did you write bad words in this?"

She smiled again, quickly, but only politely, with her eyes on the note in his hands and nothing else.

"I'm sorry, I just..." she began. "I didn't get a lot of sleep last night, and not just because of you, and I'm afraid I may have been a little too grumpy when I wrote that." She stopped just in front of him with her arm still hanging out in front of her. Heald instinctively turned his head to the side a bit so that the smell from his breath wouldn't hit her.

"Listen, I'm sure I deserve to be subjected to everything this letter has to say, but if you want it back, that's your decision." He held the note out and she took it and placed it into her handbag. "Feel free to chastise me in person, though. I deserve some rebuke for this."

"I think I wrote the word 'foolish,' so let's just say that it was that. Foolish."

"That's it? Too easy."

"Well, it's Friday."

"That's no excuse for me."

Heald kept his head turned to the side. The woman began to look around uneasily.

"Well, I have to get to work," Heald said sullenly. "I am sorry if I made too much noise, though. I can be pretty inconsiderate."

"That's okay," she said, clutching her bag. "It happens sometimes."

She turned and walked away, and as she did, Heald felt compelled to say one last thing.

"Feel free to leave me angry notes under my door anytime." She turned and gave him a half smile, but he felt any connection that might have been there had already been courteously severed, like a fleeting glimpse at a comet's tail out of the corner of your eye. He put his hands behind his back and stepped into his apartment.

It was quarter to seven now. Did she have a ring on? he asked himself. I'm a fool! I didn't even look to see if she was wearing a ring! But why would she be? She lives in a studio apartment alone. Heald began to debate himself. I suppose she could be involved with someone, though, he thought. She's probably engaged to some guy and they're looking at condos in Streeterville or Wicker Park. She's just dying to get away from hopeless idiots like me, cavorting around an old building in the Gold Coast in the early hours of the morning. I'll bet she's engaged to an astronaut. Probably a weightlifting astronaut. Well a weightlifting astronaut isn't so impressive, because there's no gravity in space, so to hell with that guy.

The warm feeling that Heald had felt while speaking to the woman morphed into a hot flash of resentment, and he felt guilty because of it. At the same moment, in his right side just below his ribs, he felt a familiar dull pain.

My liver, he said silently to no one.

Heald began to think about the night before for the first time. What exactly had happened? He hated this part—the slow, scattered return of memories from the night before. He remembered going out for drinks with Janice and Miłosz. He remembered that there seemed to be a sense of flirtation or interest directed from Janice toward Miłosz. He remembered that he had, in a moment of blind jealousy and self-loathing, decided not to conceal his plans to drink to excess and ordered plenty of booze. But other than those things, he couldn't recollect what might have happened after that. Thanks to the woman with the note, he knew that he had come home alone and drunk (no surprise there) and began to sing aloud while having trouble opening his apartment door. Was he happy when he was walking home? Why would any of what he remembered have made him feel happy? What the hell could possibly be so freaking wonderful about finding out that the woman you covet is herself in love with someone else? Had perhaps Miłosz accidentally fallen under the wheels of a passing bus? Had she leaped into Heald's own arms for safety and security? These little exercises as a pseudo-detective after daily binges were getting tiresome.

It wasn't fair to be delighted at the thought of Miłosz being smashed under the wheels of a bus. Miłosz wasn't such a bad guy. Just ridiculously lucky and completely unaware of it—the worst kind of luck to be witness to. Miłosz probably had no idea how Janice felt, at least not up until that night. For that matter, though, neither had Heald. Maybe Janice didn't feel anything, and Heald had just gone from bone dry to bombed too quickly and misinterpreted the whole interaction. Enough questions, he said to himself. It was time to get ready for work.

Just then, Heald's clock radio alarm went off and he slammed his hand down onto it. Perhaps this was the day that Miłosz would get himself cubed at the CRCC.

After a quick shower, he looked at himself in the mirror. His shirt was new, his hair was combed, and his teeth had been brushed, but he could still feel the alcohol ebb and weave through him, no longer potent, but toxic all the same. The shakes were just around the bend.

Heald wanted desperately to rip off his tie, reach into the freezer, and fill up an entire glass of vodka. Instead, he opened the apartment door and turned to close it, then saw his cell phone on the hardwood floor beneath the futon. He had not even considered the phone until that moment. With his jacket over his arm, he walked over and reached down to retrieve the phone. Looking at the screen, he saw that he had two unread messages waiting for him.

Chapter Fourteen

HEALD WOULD NEED to hail a cab in order to get to work on time. Finding an available taxi in the Gold Coast at this time of the morning could get tricky. He stood under the awning of his building, watching as an array of luxury cars and taxis boomed up the one-way North Dearborn Avenue. Available cabs were not hard to spot for someone living in the city because they behaved differently than the other cars. It was a science much like studying animal behavior in the wild. Available taxis traveled in the lanes closest to the sidewalk at a slightly reduced speed compared to the other traffic. They were ready to break and pounce on a waiting fare at a moment's notice. Cabs with occupants stuck to the center lanes and weaved through traffic like horses jockeying for position.

Heald began walking with the direction of traffic and thought about the messages waiting on his phone. It was an older model, with caller ID for calls but nothing else, so it only displayed that he had messages, not whom they were from. He was hoping that one of them was from Janice, and at the same time, hoping he was wrong. If one was from her, what did she say? he thought. How would he respond? Did he say something inappropriate at the bar about her and Miłosz? Then again, it might also be a positive message. Maybe she messaged him to confess her plan to make him jealous by feigning an interest in Miłosz. Perhaps once she saw him start to derail, she realized what a cruel trick it was.

More than likely it was not that.

He decided not to look at the messages for the moment

and instead concentrated on finding a ride. Heald was now a block to the west of Dearborn on Clark heading farther downtown. He had turned himself around, walking backward with his suit jacket over his left arm and his right arm free, ready to wave down the next taxi that displayed predatory behavior.

As he was trotting backward, his eyes caught a glimpse of the backside of a building painted with a large, colorful mural. Having no luck at the moment with any cabs, he abandoned his backward trot and turned toward the alley, where he could get a better look at the painting.

Even though it was still early in the morning, the heat had already begun to lower itself like a too-thick comforter over the city; the sun creeping over the tops of the skyscrapers made it worse. Despite the shower and fresh clothes, Heald could already feel the effects of the soupy humidity on his skin. As he walked into the alley, the pungent smells from the dumpsters left a sensation like backwash in his throat. He approached the mural and stood in front of it, scanning it—trying to make sure that he was seeing everything. It had been done with a mixture of spray paints and other amateur supplies, though he couldn't be sure of what, since he had no knowledge of street art.

The mural featured a woman at the center, pulchritudinous and powerful. She was wearing some type of golden vestment and a curious smile upon her face. Both arms had a long section of the cloth flowing over them. Her left hand was at her chest, cupped over her heart, and her right hand was raised to her face, covering her right eye with a flat palm, like some ancient hieroglyphic.

* * *

Heald was in a taxi when his cell phone began to ring. He felt his insides tighten and he dared not to look down at the phone for fear of seeing who was calling. When it stopped, he waited to see if the phone would vibrate with a voice mail. It did.

Heald looked up at the cab driver and noticed something in the man's ear. It was a wireless device with a little flashing blue LED light. The driver was speaking aloud, albeit softly and in a different language. Heald could not help but to think about the incredible amount of concentration needed to drive in such a manner—speeding and weaving between other cars—all while casually talking to someone on the phone. Then Heald realized that he was trying to avoid thinking about the missed call and voice mail; of course, this realization meant that he had failed.

"Up here is fine," Heald told the driver. "Just by that corner with the man standing near that white dog taking a dump on that newsstand."

"De dog?" the driver asked while looking over at his side mirror. "De pooping dog?"

"Yes, de pooping dog. Just pull up past the poop if you can." He wondered if the driver would have to explain "de pooping dog" to whomever he was also speaking to once Heald got out. Most likely not.

Heald paid the driver and stepped from the taxi. The man with the dog was using a small blue plastic bag placed over his hand like a glove to pick up the dog's waste. This made Heald smile. He looked up at the Jomira Transportation building with its 1980s-colored blue and green pastels and curved windows widening toward the ground floor.

Before entering, and despite being very close to being late, Heald felt a compulsion to go over the morning's events involving his phone; he needed to organize his thoughts before proceeding any further. He stepped over to the side as swells of people brushed past him in either direction. Before he'd left home, he known that he had two unread messages; both of these messages were left on his phone sometime between when he had gotten very drunk with Janice and Miłosz and when he had awoken that morning. It was conceivable to think that the person who had called that morning in the taxi might also be one of the people who had left a message, meaning that they would have sent a late-night text message *and* made an early morning call, enhancing the importance of the caller/message-sender's need to communicate with him. It was also possible that all three items were non-related and also possibly entirely unimportant. Heald was consumed with the astonishing mixture of simultaneous anxiety and boredom that had become the crux of his life. How he envied those people who could breeze through phone calls and text messages without so much as a casual fart.

Knowing that it could be embarrassing to face Janice without having read the messages, especially if one was from her, he decided to take the plunge and look at his phone while he rode the escalator.

The first unread message was sent at 10:53 p.m. and was from Alice. She asked why he hadn't contacted her about their plans to watch a movie at her place the previous night. It was safe to assume that he would have likely still been out with Janice and Miłosz at that time and never saw it. Alice may have even come down to his apartment and knocked on his door only to be met with silence and left wondering as to his whereabouts, since it was no secret that Heald had little social life. Alice did know that Heald liked to wander around the city at night, though. Heald had no recollection of having plans with Alice the night before; most likely he agreed to something while he was drinking at her place on Wednesday. He studied the message for a moment, realized it was an easy fix, but decided to reply later in the day. One message down.

The other message, which he'd purposely ignored, now loomed larger than before. Nothing was this easy, he thought. He was sure it had to be from Janice, and the more he thought about it, the worse he felt. He exited the elevator and stepped into the CRCC hallway. He wanted to make sure Janice wasn't in the office yet before he looked at the unopened message. Heald gradually peeked around the corner into the CCM area to see if she was at her desk. Her workspace was empty and untouched, and she was nowhere in sight, which was odd, since he was five minutes late. Heald walked over to his desk and set his stuff down, saying hello to Martha as he did so. He looked down at his phone and decided to listen to the new voice mail first.

"Heally, hi, it's your mother." Heald could already sense that something was amiss in his mother's voice; it sounded distant and uncertain. "Can you please call me back as soon as you get this? It's very important...I love you."

In that short voicemail, Heald noted two aspects of his mother's speech that alarmed him. First was the obvious inclusion of it being "very important" that he call her right away. While Heald's mother, like all mothers, knew the power of the word *important* when it came to alerting their children to the need for a return call, it was the inflection that struck Heald as frightening. She had said it rather quietly and in a tone someone might use when they understood that they had lost something and knew it was never coming back. The second aspect was the inclusion of the "I love you." His mother had always said it during their calls, but this time, she said it with the same sentiment and resolution of someone standing upon the edge of a great precipice. Someone wanting to share one last true thing with the world before they made their next move.

Without any hesitation, Heald hit the button to call his mother back and sat with his one hand pressed against the desk, as if it needed to be held down, while the phone rang on the other end. When his mother picked up, Heald stood and walked over to an empty corner of the office so he could speak in private.

"Mom, is everything all right?" There was a long pause and Heald felt his own anxiety ballooning.

"Hi, Heally honey. How are you? Are you at work?"

"Yes, Mom, I'm at work, is everything alright?"

Another pause.

"No. There's something I need to tell you."

Heald began to panic and turned to look out the window, daylight burning onto his face like a hot iron.

"Mom, please, what is it? Is everyone okay?"

"Your father and I are fine. Your sister is fine. It's grandma, Heely. She's...she's very, very sick." Heald could hear his mother crying now. Soft at first, but then unguarded once a few seconds had passed. He could say nothing. Heald had not been prepared to hear that. He didn't know why, though, because when a young adult is expecting bad news about a family member, the most likely culprit would be someone elderly, but he'd just never considered his grandmother, someone he had been so close to, as a person who could ever be sick.

"I know it's sudden, and we're all in a bit of a shock, but you have to come home...this weekend. It really can't wait." Heald's mind raced and he thought about how his own mother's mind was probably doing the same. "There's really no more time, Heally."

He looked out the window at the spiders making their webs just a few feet from him. The sky was clearing now.

"I'll leave work as soon as I can and get on the first flight or bus home. Whatever is faster in the end. And Mom...I'm sorry."

"Oh, I'm sorry, too, Heald. We just want to be sure you get to see her. I'm sorry this is so sudden."

See her? he thought. Heald realized that he didn't even know what had happened.

"Is she awake? What happened?"

"She's awake and completely mentally sound, but she was in a car accident just a mile from home. Someone T-boned her at an intersection. She's not in any pain, but it's hard to explain over the phone."

"I understand. Let me leave work and get ready and I'll be home as soon as I can. Please keep me updated, mom."

There was another momentary silence and he realized

now how rare these pauses were in his ordinary conversations with his mother.

"I love you, Heald."

She said it from far away.

Heald hung up the phone and walked back to his desk and explained the situation to Martha. She told him to leave immediately and that she would be fine without him for the day. Martha also expressed a look of sincere sorrow and reminded him that there was nothing more important than family and that it was just a Friday and they would only be looking for the missing TITLE 13 information anyway. He thanked her went to gather his things. He saw that Janice was still not in and that Miłosz hadn't arrived either. Heald wanted to think about his grandmother, but it didn't seem quite real—at least not yet—so his thoughts were invaded by Janice and Miłosz.

Inside, Heald could feel his heart thump heavily. He felt guilty and tried to think of his grandmother. There was so much there—more than he could comprehend at the moment. But he couldn't shake the growing suspicions concerning Janice and Miłosz's absence. Where could they be? And were they together? Was his grandmother really dying so suddenly? Heald closed his eyes and shamefully thought of the bottle in the back of his freezer and felt worse. It was at that moment that he remembered the still-unread text message on his phone. He quickly pulled it out and opened the message, sent at 12:31 a.m. He read it aloud in a soft voice.

JANICE: Are you okay?

Chapter Fifteen

HEALD DIDN'T BOTHER to check the price of a ticket home by train. Not only was it usually about the same cost as an airline ticket, thanks to low airfare rates after 9/11 and the recent recession, but trains themselves seemed to have lost their all-important sense of nostalgia over the years. Also, although Heald enjoyed train travel, it did not always suit the purpose of the trip, which in this case was expediency. Trains were a luxury for which America was no longer willing to grant patience—another symbol of a bygone era.

After using his desktop to browse available flights, Heald purchased a bus ticket. It was just after nine o'clock by the time he'd finished making his arrangements, and he looked over to see if either Janice or Miłosz had come in yet. They hadn't.

Heald decided to put off answering Janice's text from the previous night. He figured that it would be rude to wake both her and Miłosz as they were lying in bed together, spooning after a long and exhausting night of rigorous lovemaking. But Heald was in no mood to placate himself with sarcasm. His thoughts went to an image of the two of them lying together in bed, naked and carefree. A wave of paranoia crept over him as he wondered if perhaps he had cosmically induced his grandmother into illness just to have a physical excuse for running from the city, but that thought was easy enough to dismiss. It felt as if the worlds of his past and present were conspiring to collide and implode.

Heald knew that he needed a change of scenery—a breather of sorts. Perhaps a weekend out of this urban isolation would help to set the car back on the tracks. This injection of mortality into Heald's everyday life was a necessity. Throughout the inner city of Chicago where he lived, it felt like death was much more present—more real than at home in the suburbs. Maybe it was the sheer size of things—the bigger buildings and bigger alleys and bigger personalities—all ready to do their inflated part within the playbook of chaos and uncertainty. Death was preoccupied here, unlike in the suburban neighborhood of his home in Michigan. Death took notice and precedent there, while in Chicago, it was prosaic at best.

* * *

Traffic was nominal as the bus pulled away from Union Station, heading south onto the Dan Ryan just after lunch. Heald was hoping for a quick trip as cars began to speed alongside the bus.

Packing for the trip, he'd grabbed a few items of clothing and then begun to think about alcohol. He decided it would be easiest to take the half-gallon of vodka out of the freezer, use it to fill a large plastic water bottle, then wrap the bottle inside a T-shirt and pack it along with the other items in his bag. After he had rolled the plastic bottle up and packed it, he took the half-gallon and drank what was left. His hands had been shaking, but that would soon be gone.

The bus passed underneath the large sign that welcomed travelers to Chicago. Heald remembered seeing it when he first came to the city, feeling pleased that the honorable Richard M. Daley was pleased to receive him. It felt like it had taken some time just to get to the city limits, but with Chicago safely behind him and growing smaller by the second, Heald finally felt as if he could close his eyes and rest, like an off-duty cop. He could feel the booze in his system helping to sedate him. He thought about how he might be able to take one more drink from the plastic bottle without anyone noticing. Looking around at the various people on the bus, Heald spotted an older lady sitting alone and he was reminded of his grandmother. He did not want to think about her yet; he told himself that he was not ready for it.

Growing up, Heald never felt a proclivity toward any religion, and his parents respected that. They rarely asked about it and never insisted that he make any decisions, instead leaving the door open for him to come to them with questions. By the time he was six, his family had quit going to church altogether, though his father had never gone and Heald had only been a few times with his mother and his sister, who had been baptized though he had not. In the end, it came down to a simple question posed by his mother: "Do you want to go to church, Heald?" Heald replied that he didn't. The case was settled, and everyone moved on. It was one of the most thoughtful and considerate gifts that he could ever remember receiving from his mother.

Heald's grandmother was an intensely spiritual person. Despite this, she had never forced so much as a stick of gum on anyone. If a loved one or dear friend asked for her thoughts on the meaning of life or what came after death, she would converse with them for hours—and she was a woman with plenty of loved ones and dear friends. As a lifelong atheist, Heald knew better than to bring up the topic of religion with strangers in the Midwest, but his grandmother was different; he felt comfortable with her. She had an unwavering ability to reserve judgment and simply listen to people, appreciating what they had to say. His grandmother's faith was one based primarily upon the spirit, and if she were hard-pressed to give a definition to her beliefs, or to put a name on them, she would sometimes say it fell somewhere within the grand spectrum of Buddhism, though she was also drawn closely to the beliefs of some Native American tribes as well. A few times she had mentioned how so many of the world's popular religions sprouted bouts of violence and war, while Buddhism professed peace and admonished fighting, though she was quick to admit that many native tribes engaged in war as an almost religious experience in itself.

Heald wanted desperately to talk to her in that moment.

The bus was rolling along through the afternoon sunlight when it came upon the outskirts of Gary, Indiana. The amber tint of a rusty fender could have been the city's calling color. There seemed to be little that remained of the post-war industrial steel city. Gary had seen its fortunes rise and fall throughout the twentieth century at the south end of Lake Michigan. There were a number of factories and warehouses that from the highway appeared derelict and rundown, yet the smoke stacks that lined the tops of these buildings still belched some type of harsh gas into the air.

It was never the smoke that caught Heald's eye, but the fire. Some of the stacks billowed out pure flame, burning off excess fumes, but to a passerby, it only made it seem all the more post-apocalyptic. The fires burned day and night—never ceasing to fill the sky above the factories. From the bus, it looked like the forgotten remnants of a ghost world.

If Heald had been from any other part of the country, he might have been surprised by the landscape in Gary. But throughout the Midwest, ghost towns had become commonplace, just as they had in the wild west over a century prior. The small communities often didn't last long once the resources dried up or railroads left. These days in the heartland, when the resources went, an entire industrial landscape became a haunted arena. There were still plenty of people in Gary, but they were overshadowed by the sheer vacuum. On the highway, you could see cars with people in them alongside you, but looking off into Gary at those massive fire-spewing pillars, there was scarcely a sign of human life, not even a sound. It was not fair, but it was now, more or less, a wasteland—a decomposing reminder of the Midwest's position in the Rust Belt, its flaming hopes monument to a ghost crew of laborers still tending to the aging machines and furnaces, waiting like birds on a wire, for something, anything, to happen.

When Heald was three years old, his grandmother took him to a local Michigan tribe's powwow ceremony. He watched, blissfully unaware of the ritual's symbolism or deeper meaning, entranced by the wild dancing and manic drum banging. His grandmother may have tried to explain some of it to him, but Heald couldn't remember it now. What he did remember was that at some point, she leaned over and handed him a small wooden trinket. It was round and smooth, and as he held it close, he could see that it was painted like a turtle and had a number of holes in it. It was lightweight and hollow. His grandmother told him to bring it to his mouth and blow into it, and when he did, he felt the air escape through the holes as it made a whistling sound. While he was blowing, she put her finger over one of the holes and Heald heard the pitch of the sound change. Rather than explain what she was doing, his grandmother watched as he figured out the meaning of the holes in the turtle, exploring it now as an instrument. The turtle fascinated Heald, and she encouraged him to make as much noise as he wanted while the loud ceremony was taking place in front of them. Suddenly he felt like he was a part of the whole experience and not a mere spectator.

It was a memory that he would never lose, but for the life of him he could not understand why he recalled it now, on this long and cracked road through the heart of timeworn America. He was acutely aware then that he was closer to his future than he was with the memories of his past.

* * *

Coming from Detroit, Heald was no stranger to the ruin and decay in the Rust Belt. Though his family had relocated to the suburbs before he was born, the 1980s were a less-than-fruitful time for the Motor City. For an age, the tall and powerful buildings downtown were matched only by the equally tall and powerful Detroiters in the factories that had helped to mold, shape, and drive the backbone of industry and build the machines that put a halt to fascism, asserting the United States as the dominant economy in the world. But it was not meant to be, for it did not last. By the Reagan administration, when Heald was very young, most of the damage had already been done to the city, and residents were adjusting to their city's new role as a home of despot criminals, forgotten legacies, and ruined promise. The pride of the city never left, but the residents began to assume the shapes of their once tall and powerful buildings: broken and falling into disrepair.

This was when the aging smokestacks atop the monumental factories began to shut off one by one. There were still plenty left running to keep the air over the city filled with that choking industrial aptitude, but you were never far from a hollowed-out factory, massive steel tubes on the roofs pointing up toward the sky with nothing left inside but dust and cobwebs. These giant pillars of concrete and metal now jutted high like extended index fingers from broken and casted hands, pointing toward something they would never touch.

Gary and Detroit had suffered similar fates, though Gary had the debatable advantage of being cast in Chicago's mighty shadow. These days, a decade after the turn of the millennium, the Motor City had been pinpointed by media outlets and popular culture as one that had perhaps suffered long enough. But Detroit would need help to rise from what it presently was to what it could be. Tired of the so-called "ruin porn," America tapped Motown as a land of renaissance—a place ready to be reborn, ready to rise from the ashes, as was foretold by the city's longstanding motto: *Speramus meliora; resurget cineribus* (We Hope for Better Things; It Shall Rise from the Ashes).

Heald left the city with no prospects or hope of a new deal. The resurgence had begun recently and Heald had felt a stab of guilt ever since leaving, feeling that perhaps he had abandoned his hometown too early. What might have become of his life had he stayed and been witness to the consummate change? Would his world still be as it now was?

As Heald sat there on the bus ride back, he looked around at the riders holding computers on their laps and headphones over their ears, those lost in a paperback novel. He reached into his satchel and pulled out the bottle and took a casual pull from it as if he was merely taking a refreshing drink of water. He looked across the aisle toward the people sitting near him to see if they had noticed, but they hadn't. Pushing the bottle back into his bag, Heald looked out the window at the industrial landscape that whirred by through the dirty glass.

* * *

As they crossed the state boundary into Michigan, Heald felt buzzed. He knew that he had to be careful not to get drunk. There were meticulous situations like this one where his objective was just to maintain control and feel better—to keep any panic and withdrawal subdued. More often than not, this level of control was much more difficult than he cared to admit. Keeping a drunk focused on anything other than drinking could be an unreasonable task, like trying to tame a lion with a rolled-up magazine. To distract himself, Heald thought about sitting at his desk at the CRCC, where he would have normally been during this time of the day. He thought of the one photo on his desk of his family's first dog.

The dog's name had been Alan and was a mixed-breed Labrador hound. Alan had different-colored eyes, which was the first thing that the family had noticed when they went to pick her up from a questionable breeder in Flushing, Michigan. The house was so run-down that the concrete steps leading up to the front door had partially collapsed. The door itself was stripped of most of its paint. Heald's mother was alarmed, no doubt for the safety of her two young children, but their father persisted. He ignored these things and walked right up to the door and knocked.

A large woman opened the door and simply asked if they were there for a dog. Inside, it smelled of urine, and dark stains seemed to have made their way from the carpets to up along the walls. She sat down in an easy chair near children lying on the floor in front of an enormous old television set turned to a show about narcotics officers in a beach community. A jigsaw puzzle sat untouched on the floor near the far wall.

A man entered the room from somewhere in the back of the house and wiped his hand on the back of his jeans a few times before he extended it out to Heald's father. His father shook the hand without hesitation. The man grinned in a friendly fashion, highlighting teeth that looked like pinto beans. He offered Heald's father a beer, which his father declined, though he did so with a gregarious grin, saying that he was interested in buying a dog. The man extended his hand out toward another doorway behind him, where he said the litter was waiting, and told them he'd be happy to let them "view the wares." The family stuck close together and followed Heald's father as a single mobile unit.

The area of the home that housed the dogs had a smell similar to the previous room, only it was much more intense—nearly unbearable. Young Heald, only four at the time, was so taken aback that he instantly coughed upon entering this new room. His sister, then six years old, made a feigned gagging noise and stuck her tongue out. Neither gesture was noticed by the man, or perhaps neither drew a reaction out of him due to some good grace. Their mother put a hand on each of their shoulders and held tightly, but Heald's fathered glowered at them.

The yellow-and-tan puppies were in the back of a makeshift pen all barking and mad with excitement at the first sign of this new life entering the room. They formed a small pyramid at the base of the plastic gate, each hoping to be the first to climb up and out of the mess. Heald's father instantly locked eyes with one of the pups and asked to hold it. The man reached his bulky arms over the pen and picked it up, handing it over father. His mother remarked at the different-colored eyes that the puppy had, and his father said that it was the first thing that he had noticed. He turned the dog to face the children and its tail began to wag back and forth gradually, as if for its first time. The seller claimed the pup to be the best of the bunch. Heald's father said he would take it and paid the man.

As they walked down the driveway, Heald's sister looked back at the house and began to say something disparaging but their father abruptly cut her off.

"Be nice to people, Lynn."

In the car, Heald's sister said she wanted to name the dog Alan. His mother quickly pointed out that they hadn't bothered to ask what the sex of the dog was. Heald's father, now angling the car back out of the driveway into the street, said that he wasn't as concerned about the dog's gender as he was about other things, though he added that it was a female. His sister was upset, her heart clearly set on the name Alan, but their father just said, "That'll do fine, honey."

As the puppy sat between the children and nosed its surroundings, Heald said that he liked its two different-colored eyes. His mother looked back at her children and at the puppy and said, "You know, your grandmother once told me something that the Native Americans say about dogs with different-colored eyes: they are extraordinary, for they have the ability to look upon both heaven and hell."

* * *

The bus made a pit stop along I-94 at a gas station convenience store outside of Jackson to give the riders a chance to rest and stretch their legs. Heald was the last passenger off the bus. His thoughts were flooded with memories of the dog and his grandmother. He would have no more to drink during the bus ride. He wanted to face his family with a clear and conscious mind, and he'd already had enough to keep him from shaking. Plus, he reasoned, it would leave him some to drink once night came and he was sleeping in his own bed for the first time in a long while.

Since his senior year of college, though it pained him to admit it even to himself, Heald could scarcely remember a night where he had gone to bed without drinking a generous amount of booze. Since childhood, he'd suffered from chronic insomnia. Thoughts of doom, dread, and despair swelled up inside of him and crept out from the dark corners of his bedroom when he was young.

Heald had made it through high school a staunch advocate of sobriety. Going into college he had only ever had one drink, but a few weeks after moving away to school, he knew he would have to set his teetotalism aside in order to fit in with the rest of the crowd.

His insomnia worsened in the university atmosphere. The pressures and stimuli all around exacerbated his sleepless nights and led him to seek a release, which he soon found in alcohol. The booze not only made the transition to sleep a seamless one, but filled his mind with an intoxicating sense of calm and well-being beforehand. He began to look forward to going to bed each night knowing that his anxieties and fears would soon be gone.

The drinking also had other beneficial properties. Heald found himself enjoying social gatherings on campus and became more talkative at parties, even finding the courage to talk to women. It rarely led to much romance because just below the surface he was still the shy, awkward guy that he'd always been. On the whole, though, he sensed that something was different; he could accept people and situations without the relentless nagging sensation that something was wrong or askew and that he was to blame. But above all, Heald found himself being able to drink and fall right asleep.

Within a couple of years, Heald found it difficult to limit his drinking to just the evening hours. He had become less concerned with alcohol's beneficial effects in curing insomnia and more enamored by its ability to help challenge his enduring anxiety and depression. Over the course of his undergraduate studies, Heald gradually began drinking earlier and earlier in the day until he experienced the urge to start as soon as he woke up. More often than not, he would still wait to drink until he had returned from classes or his part-time job as a clerk at the university library. The classes eventually fell from his list of priorities and he began to attend only sparingly to take the tests, opting instead to stay home to read his textbooks or to watch television and drink. Despite this, Heald never missed a shift at work and never drank before he had to report in. Even in these early stages, one message rang clear from the start: never mess with your livelihood.

When it came time to graduate, Heald was naturally flabbergasted at how fast the whole experience had flown by. After graduation came the next logical step: a career. The job market seemed fine, so he returned home to begin his search.

Heald languished for months without any real work, but the Great Recession had not yet hit, and prospects were rumored to still be promising for those in his graduating class. Heald focused his energy on becoming an adept alcoholic – something he found he took to quite intuitively. His full-time job now consisted of living at home, reading random noise on the internet, taking odd jobs down in the city, mowing his parents' lawn, and securing enough booze throughout the day to ensure a nighttime free of worry, dread, and anxiety. Meanwhile, most of his other friends had moved away or found stable careers soon after college and proceeded to get on with their lives before the fall of 2008, when the real blow to the economy hit.

And my, how it hit.

Nowhere did it seem that more went wrong than in

Detroit. Two of the Big Three automakers collapsed and went into bankruptcy, and factories soon closed their doors. Blue-collar workers who had been elemental in contributing to the great industrial machine suddenly found themselves out of work with bills to pay. The new focus was survival, the tightening of belts, and the parting of ways with things of little inherent value that had become mainstays in modern everyday life within the middle class. The mortgage bubble burst, and no one was more surprised as to how high that bubble had risen into the air than the people who were inside of it and now saw how far they had to fall.

A few months after the crash, Heald was well aware that the job market in his hometown was becoming oversaturated with laid-off workers looking to stay afloat by seizing up what few jobs there were. And with many of the companies that would normally have been hiring entry-level college graduates putting a freeze on hiring, the situation grew bleaker by the day. Many nights, after he had started drinking but before he had settled into a full-blown stupor, Heald couldn't help but curse himself for his years of indolence.

Around this time, Heald decided to take a trip to Chicago. He had never been to the Windy City but had heard plenty about it. Chicago and Detroit are inextricably tied to each other as capitals of the Rust Belt. Heald knew that somewhere west of him at any time was this massive Mecca of the Midwest; like so many Americans in tough times before him, there was a growing sense within Heald that if he just stood at the top of a high peak and looked westward, he would see golden pastures that marked a new beginning. He felt like some old prospector infected by a sense of manifest destiny, with westward expansion being the only option for some semblance of success in his life. It's the age-old reaction to an age-old problem: pick up, move yourself elsewhere, and see if your problems follow you like a lonely dog. The hope is that they stay back and attach themselves to some other unfortunate soul. With that in mind, Heald set forth to explore.

As the bus made its way west along I-90 during that first trip to Chicago, Heald felt a rush of excitement and optimism that he had not experienced in a long time. Along the massive multilane expressway that leads into the city, there is a bridge over the Calumet River that gives the first glimpse of the incredible skyline. Heald wasn't expecting it to appear so soon after crossing the state border from Indiana into Illinois, but as the bus drove over the bridge Heald leaned close to his window and got his first look at the awe-inspiring row of dynamic steel edifices rising from the earth.

He remembered sunlight everywhere, and as he gazed at the glint off the vibrant mirrored structures, he thought he had spotted a glowing golden nugget. Few young people have come across this sight and not been taken aback. The buildings looked new, the city expanding by the moment as the bus drew closer. They rounded the lake and made their way north up the Dan Ryan, the immense, monolithic Sears Tower guiding them in like a beacon on some intellectual shoreline.

Before the weekend was over, Heald had viewed a number of apartments in the downtown area and lined up a place in the Gold Coast. He called his parents to tell them the news and was met with a curbed enthusiasm. Heald pooled together his savings from the string of perpetual jobs he had held since he was fourteen and prepped his meager belongings for the move, convinced that he had uncovered the long-awaited remedy to the fatalistic life that he'd regretfully settled into in Detroit. He would waste no time finding a job and a girl in Chicago, and most importantly, he would finally discover happiness in a life that he realized was rapidly slipping out of his control.

Money would produce stability. A job would dictate routine. With these things would come the inspiration to find love, to meet the woman of his dreams and share it all with her. Arrogant and simple? Sure, he thought, but it was also too tempting to pass up when compared to the inimical alternative.

And with the move he could once again look forward to complete independence—freedom from that isolated room in the back of his childhood home. It would be a chance to prove to himself that he didn't really need alcohol—that it had merely been a crutch to get him past the insufferably depressing and anxious times of his late youth.

Heald knew he was young to be looking to start over, but this was rapidly becoming a new world.

* * *

Heald leaned his head against the window of the bus as it entered the Metro Detroit area. He opened his eyes. The bus was silent, and he looked at the land whirring by around them. He had arranged to have his parents pick him up at the bus terminal in downtown Detroit. His mother said that his grandmother had decided not to stay in the hospital and wanted to be at home. His mother had given few details when he'd called from the road, but time was short and they had made her comfortable. Heald still didn't know the specifics of what had happened, but that wasn't important right then. His thoughts had wandered throughout the ride back, but the big picture was finally going to need to be examined: his grandmother, someone he loved so deeply and thought so highly of, almost as his own personal deity, would soon be gone.

Just over a break on the horizon, Heald could see the telltale skyline of Detroit emerging.

Chapter Sixteen

"THEY FOUND SOMETHING in the test results while she was in the emergency room that made them nervous," said Heald's mother. Heald was in the backseat; his father was driving. His mother's voice was soft and somewhat rehearsed, as if she'd repeated that statement throughout the day. "The results were abnormal, so they tested a few other things."

Heald stared ahead with an absent expression and then furrowed his brow.

"How'd they get her results back already?" he asked. "And why is she at home and not still at the hospital?"

His mother looked across to his father, who was watching the road in front of him.

"Well," she began, "don't be upset, but the accident actually happened earlier in the week. The crash itself wasn't terribly serious, just a few sprains and bruises, and we know how busy you are with work and how difficult it can be for you to get away from that city and we didn't want you rushing home and having to miss all that time. We know how much you love her, how much we all love and care for her, and we wanted to know for sure what we were dealing with before we tripped any alarms. There was little you could do from Chicago for a minor accident."

Heald always enjoyed hearing his mother say *Chicago*. "Shi-*caw*-go."

He realized he hadn't told his parents about the crisis at work and the missing TITLE 13 information. For the last few hours he'd completely forgotten about it, too. At least, he didn't think he'd told them about it. Days were beginning to meld together like a linked chain, somehow separate things, but indecipherable at the joints.

"It was after she'd gotten back home and we got the diagnosis this morning that we knew we had to call. She refused to stay in the hospital the way that she was. Perhaps she suspected something and didn't want to be there when it was confirmed."

"When what was confirmed?"

His mother paused and took a gasp of air. His father was probably listening, but showed no sign of it.

"Cancer. Stage IV. It's terminal," she said closing her eyes as her lips gently flattened and began to droop at the corners.

He had prepared for the news since his mother first called that morning, and he expected to hear this, but hearing his mother say it in person, a heaviness that had built up within his chest sank down somewhere deep inside of him. His heart beat, but it simultaneously felt as if it had no real function; nothing right then to pulse and churn throughout his body but thin air—his veins like empty subway tunnels. He placed his thumb into the center of his opposing palm and closed a fist around it.

Terminal, he thought. The end stage marking the defined boundary from one thing to another, should there be another. A place where a long-distance bus might make its last stop before gassing up, checking under the hood, and heading back out on the road—the terminus being the only location where things actually came to a halt, unless the bus was deemed no longer fit for travel and had finally reached its *terminal* terminus.

He looked at his mother now.

"I'm so sorry, Mom." After a pause, he added, "When can I see her?"

She turned back to him for the first time since embracing him on the platform at the bus station. "I'm sure that she'd like to see you as soon as possible." She put her hand out to Heald, and he let go of his thumb and took her hand from underneath and held it. He felt his heart once again pump something tangible through his chest.

His father merged into the next lane on the right as the car carried the Brown Family north along I-75 through Detroit, past the dilapidated warehouses, ghostly factories, and boarded-up homes that lined the expressway.

* * *

Heald's parents had gotten a new dog after Heald had moved to Chicago. With both of their children moved out, and the grief from the loss of Alan several years before having subsided, Heald's parents decided it was time for a new family pooch.

Heald had only met the dog on a few occasions during the infrequent times that he visited home over the last few years, but he was quick to pal around with the new dog, and the two seemed to take to each other naturally. At times Heald did feel guilty when he thought of Alan. This new dog was a mixed-breed hound they had rescued from a local humane society hosting a sponsorship event at a pet store. In the Brown Family's collective opinion, rescued dogs were more grateful for everything: every moment on the couch, every squirrel running along the top of a picket fence, and every kernel of food in their bowl. An indestructible kinship developed between the dogs and the Browns. No canine ever spoils a second chance at a good life.

And yet, despite the idolatry displayed by their new dog, Arnold (an actual male dog this time), there were random times when Heald found himself withholding his affection. With no real clue as to why, he would sit there and let the dog nuzzle and paw at him while he would fixate on something minute, keep his hands tucked under his arms, and become lost in a thought. Heald was frightened by his own behavior, as he felt certain that he had much love to give. In his mind, he often thought about releasing this unbridled wellspring of love, unclasping and allowing the hysteria of tender emotion to pour from him...but there he would sit, slighting a dog for no apparent reason. Why did he do this? he wondered.

Their car traveled down the placid neighborhood street, and near the end, his family's house came into view. It sat at the dead end bordering the tree-lined woods. So many of the homes looked the same with their familiar designs and outlying yards, each populated by the same people tending to the same lawns and shrubs throughout the years. It was a place where rhyme and reason dispersed a natural calming agent throughout the streets that wove between the fences and through the bushes and allowed for an orderly American middle-class existence where safety and tranquility were paramount, a promising shelter from the confusion of the outside world.

They pulled into the driveway and Heald could see his sister Lynn and her fiancé standing in the garage. Her face displayed that melancholy smile that always comes out on good people when they see or feel something that makes them pleased despite it being a sad or remorseful time. The thought of their grandmother that weighed down on the corners of his sister's smile, preventing it from being as full and wonderful as he remembered. Her fiancé, Richard, was standing beside her with his hand on her shoulder. At their feet stood Arnold, whose tail began to wag as the car pulled into the drive and came to a stop.

"Heald," Lynn said, opening her arms to embrace her brother. He dropped his satchel and overnight bag of clothes and hugged her, turning his face away, noting how warm she felt, but his thoughts right then went to the bag at his feet and the water bottle inside it filled with vodka. What if one of them discovered it? Heald went into a conditioned state of protection and hyper-awareness that had become second nature when it concerned hiding and protecting his family from his addiction. It was almost as if somehow his parents and sister, perhaps even Richard, knew exactly what he had in the bag—what he was hiding at that moment. Years went into creating the perfect façade. Some alcoholics are better at this dual life than others, and the more you love your family, the harder you fight to shield them from what you have become.

His sister held him a bit longer then pulled herself back to get a better look at him. He told himself that he wasn't shaking, but he wasn't sure, as it had been a few hours since his last drink on the bus. She could peer deep into his eyes—deeper than anyone else in his immediate family—and he hid them from her as he had done since he was a kid, for she could spot anything. He looked down at the dog to turn his mouth and breath away from her. She kept her hands on his shoulders, sizing him up, then gave the them a gentle squeeze, to which he displayed no response. For a brief moment, her expression grew serious. She squeezed him lightly again.

"Are you okay?" she asked. "You seem different. Are you sick?"

Heald took a step back from her grasp and kept his eyes centered on the garage door behind her.

"I'm fine," he said. "Just worried. About grandma."

She looked at his neck briefly and he could feel his pulse quicken. Why didn't she work for the police? he thought.

"You don't look well, Heel."

"I'm just tired. Long trip and rather sudden."

He finally looked back into her eyes and held his breath, concentrating with all his might to shield anything that might be hidden. He blinked a few times. Then Richard stepped up and extended out his hand in front of him.

"Good to see you, Heald."

Heald didn't enjoy touching anyone, especially strangers, though labeling Richard as a stranger at this point was just cruel. But something about shaking Richard's hand still felt like he was making a new acquaintance. Richard bent over toward Heald's bag.

"Let me get that bag of yours for you, buddy."

As if it were a reflex, Heald stepped between Richard and the bag and grabbed Richard's wrist. Then loosened his grip and grabbed the bag himself.

"No, no," Heald said while picking up the bag and tossing the strap over his shoulder. "I got it, no worries. Thanks though, Richard."

Richard stepped back, likely afraid that he had crossed some strange personal boundary with Heald. He had dated Lynn for many years and had come to know her brother as a very shy and painfully reserved guy, but he still looked surprised at every odd fluctuation in Heald's behavior. Heald bent close to the ground over his bags to pet the dog, making cooing baby noises at the excited pooch. Heald was never reserved around other people in his love of dogs and was always happy to push the attention toward an animal. It was the difference between night and day when it came to people vs. animals.

"This guy!" Heald shouted as he rubbed his hands over the dog's coarse hair and clasped its ears, rolling them over and over in his hands like little balls of dough. He continued to talk to the dog as his parents came up from behind and said hello to his sister and Richard. Heald stood up and readjusted the weight of the bag on his shoulder, though it wasn't heavy. "I'm going to drop these off in my room."

As Heald walked into the house he was struck by an unfamiliar smell. He breathed deeply and was startled to realize that the scent was not unfamiliar but forgotten: he had been gone so long that he smelled his family's home as a stranger might. That signature scent undetectable to a home's residents was now overwhelming to Heald in the house he still thought of as his."

* * *

Heald's parents had spent the two previous nights at his grandmother's condo and had organized the hospice care that would allow her to be comfortable until the end. He asked if it would be all right for him to visit his grandmother alone that evening, which he realized was a lot to ask for considering the circumstances, but his family was happy to oblige. They knew how close the two were, and, despite Heald's move to Chicago and infrequent trips back home, he always made an effort to see his grandmother when he was back in Detroit. The family sometimes discussed how much time alone the two had spent throughout Heald's childhood, meeting at her home for long discussions and spending time out and about when she was younger and abler. He would drive to the rural northwest area outside the city where she lived and they would set aside hours of the day to just sit and talk, stopping only to eat a meal that she had specially prepared before his arrival.

Heald's grandmother helped him foster a keen, respectful love of nature. After the divorce of his grandparents before Heald was born, his grandmother had decided to travel the world. She visited the Japanese archipelago, the Great Plains of the American West, and so many of the places in between. She'd left her indelible mark upon the world that had in return given her such strength and knowledge, and she met many people and earned the right to call several of them her good friends. She was the only grandmother that he knew who was so often busy visiting friends, not only in her own home, but across the states and around the world—visiting them for children's weddings, exploratory trips, and existential escapades. It was a major point of pride and inspiration to him as a young man to have such a "worldly grandma," as he used to put it.

His grandmother's heart was deeply rooted within the

spiritual realm that stretched across the tangled gentile fibers of Eastern philosophy and Native American mythology. And while Heald sometimes found himself disagreeing with her beliefs, he never once regretted a moment of a conversation with her—such was the affection and care she had for the inviolability of all individuals. Never once had she forced a single thought upon Heald, even when he told her as a very young boy that he had no personal belief in a higher power. She merely smiled, took his hand, and told him what a wonderful person he was. In that moment, he remembered his chest swelling up as he gripped her hand tightly.

To his grandmother, each living creature had a soul. This concept had stuck with him when he thought about her. When he was little, he watched her pick up a large spider without a hint of hesitation and carry it to her sliding glass door to release it outside. Heald had found himself attempting to do the same with bugs that he found in all the places that he'd lived, but when it came to spiders, he often had to settle for finding some apparatus to pick them up to carry out. Sometimes, if they were particularly menacing, they still met with the boot. He wasn't trying to save the souls of the spiders, but he did so as a testament to her, hoping that a bit of what made her so extraordinary might somehow awaken within him.

There were so many things that he felt like he had to discuss with her now. His hands trembled on the steering wheel of his parents' car driving along the back roads near her home. Soon he would be seeing her for the last time.

Heald rolled down the windows, and cool air rushed into

the car. Feeling the breeze on his neck through his unbuttoned shirt, he thought about the sopping mess he usually was at this point in the day walking off the subway line near his city apartment.

For as long as he could remember, Heald had wondered what it would be like to say good-bye to someone he loved; it was one of those things everybody knows they will someday face, but also one of those things that you rarely feel adequately prepared for.

Heald's grandfather had been a severe alcoholic. The disease eventually led to his grandparents' divorce and served as the motivation for his grandmother to travel the globe looking for answers and understanding. His grandfather had died when he was very young, only four or five years old, but in the many years since his death, Heald's mother and grandmother had occasionally opened up about the type of man he was and their recollections of him as a person, father, and husband, as well as what others had said about him while he was alive. All had agreed that when he was sober, you'd be hard-pressed to find a kinder, more noble man. But the drink brought out something rotten from within him. He was a mean drunk, plain and simple.

In the last few years, as Heald had sensed his own drinking spinning wildly out of his control, he'd begun to ask his grandmother more and more about the man he'd known so briefly and had now nearly forgotten. It was clear through her recollections that in life, his grandfather had been a force impossible to ignore, though for many different reasons. When he was quite young, Heald's mother and grandmother both hesitated to talk about him, his influence all too real and raw within their minds, but as Heald grew older, they softened as the fond memories emerged to the forefront.

"The pain and the hurt are gone now," his grandmother said once when the subject had been broached. "All that's left is the love we shared for each other. He was a man of such brutal affliction, tortured by things he would never speak of, including the war. I know that war changed him. Yet, his capacity for love and learning was boundless, and he was a self-educated man—something that he prided himself on immensely—though he rarely talked about it. The only thing that could curtail or rein in his wild sense of wonder was the drink, though it eventually robbed him of everything, including his gift of compassion. After a certain point, he was too far gone, and the love just dwindled down to a pile of gray, shapeless clay deep within him that could no longer serve as much of anything. I've never stopped loving him, and I never will, but it was such a sad thing, Heald. Only now, long after he's been gone for some time, do I feel like I can truly begin to understand the torment and sadness that he went through—so much of it his own doing—so much of it beyond his control. I couldn't rationalize anything until many years after he'd passed."

In his final years, Heald's grandfather had successfully quit drinking and attempted to repair the broken relationships with his family, though, as is the case with most alcoholics, the trust was gone and the wicked memories were fresh and absolute. There were a few nice gatherings, including a family Christmas at his uncle's house that Heald could vaguely remember.

At the party, Heald's father told the three-year-old Heald to go and sit on his grandfather's lap so he could take a photograph. Heald could remember nothing before or after that photo, but that split-second image—the fleeting moment of being seated on his grandfather's lap, looking around at a big group of people gazing back at him and smiling, his father at the center holding a camera pointed at the two of them—he could remember that moment so vividly. Like a photograph that his own mind had taken of that photo, his could see his mother sitting across the room on the couch next to his grandmother, his father on one knee in front of them trying to frame the shot. He remembered how cold and bony his grandfather's knee felt as he sat on it. There was no sound associated with the image frozen in his mind, though Heald wished that there had been. He had no memory of his grandfather's voice whatsoever. They were two individuals, tied through blood and lineage, having only crossed paths briefly in this world, and yet they seemed to share a common bond of something real, something dark. The thing about blood, Heald told himself as he was driving, was that while it was in your veins, it also held the particles of your past.

Clearly there are differences between him and me, thought Heald, the most obvious and fundamental being Heald's tendency to slip into bouts of catatonic depression and futile thinking while drinking, as opposed to any inclination toward anger or rage like his grandfather. Undoubtedly there are psychological and sociological factors that go into shaping an addict's behaviors. They told Heald that his grandfather had died at the age of fifty-eight from complications of cirrhosis of the liver and a massive heart attack, the latter doing the job quickly, according to coroner. He had died alone one morning in his shabby apartment not far from Heald's parents' house (his grandfather had tried to slowly inch his way closer to his children). He was putting on a necktie when it happened and was found next to his bed, already cold to the touch, with the knot in his tie loose.

As the car wound through the trees along the road, Heald arrived at the thought that was always on his mind, the thought that he dreaded above all else: while he might not be fifty-eight or have lived through a lifetime of shame and sorrow brought on by his disease, it was ostensible that he was drawing closer to his own sort of despondent conclusion of life.

Heald finally arrived and parked the car in front of his grandmother's condo and walked to the side of her building. In the back, facing the floor-to-ceiling windows of her living room where she was likely resting, sat a large, beautiful lake surrounded by tall trees and hollowed-out logs. He could remember fishing for bluegills off the small wooden dock and trying to catch a glimpse of the snapping turtle that lived underneath it. The sun shone down upon the lake and gave a blinding glimpse of another world, somewhere hidden.

Heald walked up to the plain white door, looked at the wind chimes with a ceramic bird at their center, and drew in a heavy breath.

* * *

Heald knocked and took a step back on the small concrete stoop. In the petite garden a row of healthy tulips dipped forward and back in the calm wind. He looked at the door and examined its exterior closely; he had seen this door so many times in so many different shades of light since he was a child. It had always been some off-white, eggshell or vanilla cream, but Heald could no longer remember if the shallow cracks that he saw in the paint like wrinkles on aged skin had always been there, too. There seemed to be so many now, making their way along the molding of the door and around the knob, small and consistent, like little ranges thrust upward between two tectonic plates of paint that had been exposed to the elements for too long.

Heald knocked again and began to feel anxious. Why was no one answering? He reasoned that there should have been someone there with her, maybe his aunt, who would leave once he'd arrived. Had he not knocked loud enough? Could she be asleep? His mind began to race and his heart beat wildly in his chest like those ceremonial drums in his past.

What if?

There was a panel of small windows on the upper half of the door, and he remembered not being able to see through them when he was younger and smaller, always looking up at them. Despite being tall enough now, he dared not look in. A paralyzing fear held him back, but Heald decided to do something that he had never done before at his grandmother's house (knowing their shared penchant for privacy) and let himself in.

As the door opened with a less-than-subtle push, he felt a warm aura and the scent of his grandmother's home came rushing at him like an excited dog. It was one of the most intense and welcoming home scents that he had ever encountered, and one that always filled him with a sense of excitement as it signaled the beginning of something wonderful and interesting. As he stepped in, Heald reassessed his surroundings and there, lying on the simple, cream-colored couch, propped up against a stack of hand-knit pillows, was his grandmother. Heald froze in his tracks, standing with the door still ajar behind him. Her hands rested at their opposite shoulders and her head had slightly listed to the side. The look on her face was irenic.

Heald couldn't help but notice how small and withered she appeared; her eyes had sunk back into her skull. Her glasses were on the table and Heald studied her face, realizing now how rare it was for him to see her without those spectacles resting on her nose. She wore a plain teal sweater that he had seen her wear many times before, though now it looked far too large for her. She had always been quite small and frail for as long as he could remember, but her size had been consistent in his mind. At this moment, though, he felt as if he might be looking at what little remained, like seeing the last remnant of a spilled glass of water gradually evaporating on hot pavement in the sun.

Then she opened her eyes.

She was staring ahead at the large and open floor-to-ceiling windows wearing no discernable expression on her face. Heald rested his feet, realizing only then that he had been standing motionless with the balls of each foot lifted. He eased the door closed, having to give it a slight shove at the end. She turned her head toward him and stared directly at him for a few moments, blinking, with no sign of recognition. Reaching over, she delicately picked up her glasses off the table and pushed the arms back over her ears with care. Then she looked back at Heald and smiled.

"Oh, Heald," she said in a weak tone. "Heald." She attempted to sit up. Heald moved to step into the living room but stopped to quickly kick off his shoes, then rushed to her side.

"Grandma, wait. Let me help." He put his hand on her bony shoulder through the bulky sweater she wore, expecting her to refuse his offer of help, as she'd often done in the past. Despite her small stature, she prided herself on her independence, but at this moment, she put up no resistance.

"Thank you, Heald," she said, easing into a sitting position. She righted herself and then brought her head up to look at him squarely and smiled once more. "It is so wonderful to see you, Heald. It really is. I sent Diane away so we could talk alone but I must've fallen asleep."

When he was certain she was comfortable, Heald smiled back at her and avoided looking into her eyes for a moment, but was drawn back into them almost immediately. They were a pale brown with hints of faint green and light blue; they had always reminded him of the colors of the earth—thousands of miles in two tiny spheres. But now they were faded and graying, like a light morning fog.

She was weak, there was no doubt about it, and Heald suddenly felt extremely sensitive to the elements of time all around him, terrified of its snail-paced but irrefutable effects. He didn't know what to say at this exact moment to this person who meant so much to him; someone he understood would be gone soon.

"I love you," he said, surprised at his own candor.

Her eyelids relaxed as her cheeks filled, and her grin morphed all the lines on her face. "Heald, my dear. I love you, too, sweet boy. So much." She gripped his wrists. "So much."

He held her hands in his palms for a moment and then he eased back into the wicker chair next to the couch and pulled it close to her. There they sat and silently enjoyed the pleasure of each other's company in the brightly lit room, as they had done so many times before. She'd always been one of the few to know what he was thinking at any given moment, even when it felt like he himself didn't know exactly what is was. She had a wonderful way of articulating those thoughts that he had not been wise enough or old enough to understand. There was a fantastical realism about her mindset—something that he had always hoped might pass to him—but was beginning to understand that such a worldview could only come from experience and maturity, the interweaving of time and moral reasoning.

"Can I get you anything?" he asked. "Would you like some water?"

She just kept smiling. "No, I'm fine, dear. Thank you."

"How are you feeling?"

She leaned back into the pillow that Heald had propped up behind her, and though her smile receded slightly, her expression did not change. "Well, I'm not going to fib, Heald. My body is shutting down." He felt his chest instantly swell up and his heart began to race once more. He wanted to take action, but what could he do? His grandmother just looked at him with that full row of teeth exposed. "It's okay," she added. "It's natural. This is just how it happens sometimes."

Heald lowered his head instinctively. "I know, but are you in any pain at all?"

"No, I'm all right. Thank you. The only suffering is on the outside of it." She reached out for his hand again and he gave it to her. "I want you to be able to ask me anything. We both know that I'm going to pass soon, and that's okay, but I want you to feel free to talk to me about anything that you'd like. Anything that's on your mind or that you may be wondering." She squeezed his hand. "Really, anything at all."

Heald had often thought about death and dying. From times when he was a child lying in bed in sheets soaked through with his own sweat, shaking and crippled with fear, to days when he could think only of the fast-approaching night and restless dread. He had been petrified by the thought of dying—slipping noiselessly into a thinning nonexistence.

When he first had started drinking, so many of his overbearing anxieties and fears had been pushed back into his subconscious. But as his drinking grew steadily worse, he found those dark thoughts growing more extant once again in his everyday life. Now he sensed the fears were out of his control; he felt a loss of command over his body, powerless to the alcohol that fueled his emotions, but also kept him functioning. Death and dying were becoming more prominent in his reflections—concepts that clung to every consideration, no matter how mundane. Death was everywhere, and it had its hand in everything that he did. Now, confronted with someone he cared for, someone so close to that unescapable end—so close that Death might have been right there sharing the room with them—he could only think of one question to ask her right off the bat. It was a question he was sure she had known he would ask.

"Are you afraid?"

There was no hesitation in her voice.

"Not at all. Heald, I'm ready." She squeezed tight again, likely as tight as she could. "It's all right, because I'm ready."

The hard part was over—he'd opened the jar.

"You don't fear the end of everything? All of this coming to a close?"

"No," she said. She appeared to be choosing her words now with great consideration. "I welcome the peace, dear. It's a matter of coming to terms with the understanding that your time here on this earth has drawn to a close. That's all. Quite simple. It's not a frightening thing, because it's just the next step...the next logical thing that I have to do."

She took a moment to gather her thoughts.

"You see, this is no longer how I would wish to live. My strength is leaving me, what little that I had left," she said with a small laugh. "And I am not comfortable anymore. My body has begun to shut down, but my soul still carries with it all the love from everyone and everything that I've encountered. I am very lucky for that. This is how I want to pass over, Heald."

He carefully examined her eyes, sunken into the dark recesses under her pencil-thin eyebrows.

"What does it feel like to lose control of your body and still hold the soundness of your mind? I mean, how do you know?"

"It's a frustrating thing to be unable to have your body keep pace with an active mind, but you learn quite quickly as you grow older that the more you learn, the less the body responds to you. I knew recently when they made the diagnosis that my body had finally come to a point where it could go no further and that I would be foolish to deny that fact for one moment longer. I do not wish to become entombed within myself. I would rather allow my body to die so that I can be released, so I can find the peace I've been trying to understand my whole life. I believe I'm finally just one step away from something splendid."

Heald thought about his shaking and the spasms involving his inability to swallow and the growing number of what he had come to accept were alcohol-induced seizures that he had experienced in the middle of some nights. He thought about how he had tried to go to sleep without drinking two weeks prior for the first time in years. He thought about that night and how his mind felt as if it were filled with electricity and live wires and he shook, sometimes violently, while rolling back and forth over and over like a perfect metronome for hours on end. He finally gave in and made his way across the tiny apartment to the freezer and filled a large glass with vodka and quickly drank it. After his nerves had settled and the power was cut to all the downed wires within his mind, he felt exhausted and slipped into a drunken blackout as the night lights of Chicago filled the streets, reflecting off his window.

Now he looked back at what was left of the body of his grandmother, someone who still overflowed with spirit, but was burdened by the husk of what was left. Somewhere between her and him, between the couch and the chair, he imagined the faceless and shapeless figure of a Death between them. His hands trembled, and an uneasy feeling washed over him.

But what if she had lost her mind and not her body? he thought. What if she'd been robbed of her self-awareness but still had a working vessel to move about in?

"Is there nothing that you fear?" he asked. "What about after you've gone?"

"That is what I am *sad* about, but not what I *fear*," she replied. "I'm sad about the people I love and the inevitable unhappiness that will arrive in my wake. I wish I could explain this to everyone that I love as well as I can with you, Heald—especially your mother—but they will see that the sadness is only temporary. I'll miss being with them and you in the here and now, but soon the sadness will be lifted, and a better understanding of what is and will be will follow. It always does, no matter what the grief." She gave a gentle tug on his hand. "Do you mind if I ask what you're thinking, Heald?"

He was silent for a moment, noting how cold her hand felt, and put his other hand on top of it, as if to warm it.

"I was thinking that young people must fear death because we have so little experience with it—such a poor working relationship with it. We fear the unknown, and for the young, there are so many unknowns, but none greater than death—not sorrow or worry or anger or poverty or contentment. For us, we who are young in body, death always seems so far away...to most."

And with that, for the first time in a very long time,

Heald felt like he was about to cry. Pools of moisture formed on his lower eyelids, and he knew that if he blinked, a tear would fall. For some reason, he wanted to hold back those tears, to be as strong as she was being. He realized how rare this opportunity was: to talk to someone he loved so much about something that had haunted him so personally and so intimately, all without the reservation of fear. But indeed, he was filled with grief and fear, for in his mind death was not another door into a new world or plane of existence, or just a "next step," but rather the final step into the eternity of some black pane. A natural thing, though one without recourse or consideration for circumstance or scrutiny.

The tears fell from his eyes. In his heart he knew that they both would never truly know if she was right or wrong about death. Once she was gone, that would be it, and there would be no report from the other side—no telegraph or wire call from an ocean liner on the other side of world to let the others back at port know it had safely made passage. All fact would be lost and only circumstance and love would prevail. Heald cried now because he knew that there would be no relief for him and that in his final moments, he would be no more certain that he was right about anything. He looked into her tremendous earth-colored eyes and saw the dead certainty in them and the inscrutable comfort that they held. Her faith in the good and the natural guiding her mind to the ultimate place of effortless harmony. So badly he wanted to just hold her and have whatever it was that settled her mind pass into him.

She watched now as a tear slid down his cheek, and her eyebrows turned up as she cocked her head to the side. "Oh, my dear Heald."

He pulled his hands away carefully and wiped his eyes.

"It's fine," he said. "I'm just thinking about something."

"Do you want to share it with me?"

"It's just, I feel that the worst fear of all is the fear of the unknown, because that's the fear that truly cannot be shared or easily explained to others."

He looked back at her with his eyes still watering, ready to fill once more. Her cheeks billowed with a grin.

"Heald, you sweetheart, I hope you don't think that about me. I don't feel that way. In fact, I feel quite the opposite. This is why I want to share this experience with you and talk to you about anything that you might want to talk about. This is not a scary time for me."

Heald sat back and took a deep breath, wiped his eyes, and clasped his hands in front of him on his lap to steady them.

Her cheeks fell flat against the bone. "But that's not what you're worried about in this moment."

He smiled. "What you said does make me feel better, Grandma."

She leaned forward as far as she could and reached across the table for a small notebook.

"Let me tell you something, Heald," she said, opening the notebook and thumbing through the pages. "I want to share something with you that I've noticed these past two days while I've been here in this condition." She settled on a page with a great deal written upon it. "I've begun to see deer just outside that window." She pointed over to the massive sliding door wall. "They come right up to the house, and I tell you they are looking in right at me. I've seen a number of them, or perhaps the same one, and I can tell you that they've never come that close before, and I'll tell you something else: I've also seen a cardinal each of these last few mornings and again at dusk, sitting right outside that window on the post of that deck. And they're all just looking in at me."

She stopped for a moment, lost deep within the mental image she'd constructed. Then she closed her eyes and continued.

"I don't look at these things as mere animals curiously nosing about. I look at them for what I believe they truly are. They are signs—signs of my time coming. The American Indians believe in spirit animals, Heald, and the tribes that I've studied with talk about the importance of each person's guiding spirit animal. Your mother or I may have told you before, but we believe the spirit of your grandfather is a cardinal. I believe mine is a deer. And the fact that those two animals have been showing up at my window, just outside my home and peering into it, well, it just fills me with such a feeling of solidarity. The cardinal is a pretty rare sight in this area, and that one returning day after day tells me that your grandfather is watching over me and that he loves us and he's ready to help me make this transition now. He may have failed at a lot of things in life, but his love was certainly eternal and it's these small signs we get from the other side that let us know that everything is going to be okay. That this, and all that goes with it, will be all right."

She closed the notebook and placed it back on the table.

"That really is quite beautiful, grandma," he said. "Such an amazing thought."

She took his hand again.

"There's something else, Heald. I feel that when someone passes, they can sometimes show those still living that they're still there with them. That they're now at that place where they feel an all-encompassing peace. If I can, I'm going to try to do this with you and the ones that I love. I'm going to do this with a scent."

Heald let out a hearty laugh, and she quickly joined in.

"Now, I know this sounds strange, I know, but those who have passed can share their presence in many forms, like with your grandfather, but I've often noticed that sometimes I will be sitting alone in a room and I'll suddenly smell something that I shouldn't be able to smell. Like in this room here, I will sometimes get an unexpected whiff of a certain flower—one that I neither physically have in this home or in any form of perfume or fragrance. The windows will all be closed and it can be the middle of winter, yet I'll smell it out of the blue. I can't help but to be led to believe that that may actually be someone I knew and cared about or loved trying to make a connection with me, trying to show that they are still there in some form and watching over me. It's a comforting thought, to be sure."

She reached out for her grandson's other hand.

"I want you to know that if you're ever in a room and suddenly smell something that should not be naturally occurring, like lavender, that that will be me, Heald. That'll be me reaching out to you to let you know that I've made it and that I'll always love you." She squeezed. "Promise me you'll keep your senses aware for that."

"I promise, grandma."

She squeezed gently again and then lay back down across the couch, and Heald helped to get her settled. As he did, he considered the courage and strength it took to be in his grandmother's current situation. To have lived her whole life one way and followed in so many beliefs, and to have the fortitude to still honor that faith even to the end, eliminating all trace of doubt. Never once did a single tear come to her eyes throughout the whole conversation, so strong was her love and conviction. When she was ready to rest, Heald knew he had one last thing to ask her before their time was up, knowing that it might be the last thing he ever asked her.

"Grandma," he said quietly, "what do you do as the last thing before you go to bed knowing that any moment, perhaps right after you close your eyes, you could expire?"

She only needed to pause for a moment to collect her strength, for her thoughts were still clear.

"I count all the things that I am grateful for that happened on that day. Anything, Heald. Even something as simple as a good meal."

Heald thought about how he had begun to drink more and more each night over the last few years, eventually leading to what he now did, which was to drink himself unconscious whenever possible, effectively halting all thoughts, anxieties, and fears that he might have.

Heald put his hand on his grandmother's shoulder as she was beginning to fade off into sleep. He turned and looked out the window, wondering what he might see there and thinking about what she'd said.

"What a lovely thing to do."

Chapter Seventeen

HEALD WAS DRIVING HOME, recalling how just before he left he had leaned over and kissed his grandmother softly on the forehead as she closed her eyes to sleep. For all she knew she could have been closing her eyes forever, and the look upon her face told him that she needed nothing more. When he had kissed her forehead it had been like pressing his lips against a warm piece of wax paper, and as he turned to walk out of the room he stopped to look back at her timeworn features resting on the sun-bleached pillow, coated in brilliant light shining in through those expansive, clean windows that held nothing back. Her clothes and skin and eyes were as faded as the cushions she lay upon, and Heald realized that though her features were small and delicate, they had indeed been toughened through her long life. She was truly a woman who had earned each crease and slight imperfection that she now wore.

He left her then, and as he backed out the door, he peeked through her great windows and saw neither cardinal nor doe, but instead her resplendent view onto the glimmering pond and thought once more of the snapping turtle, looming slow in the dark somewhere just beneath the glass surface of the water.

Heald was surprised that he had cried, and in truth he felt like he could cry again, but the tears no longer came, instead replaced by a muted melancholy that felt like it would never leave. Heald felt exhausted, and though it made him guilty, he was also keenly aware of how badly he wanted a drink. After psychologically taxing episodes, he often reasoned that the reward of drink was appropriate. The same was also true of anything physically demanding, or really any type of inconvenience or unpleasant experience; his culpability had tapered over time as his intake had increasingly become a necessity, but it was always there nonetheless.

He wanted a clear head to process the conversation he had shared with his grandmother—the last one that they were likely to ever have. He wanted to find a dark and solitary spot to ruminate over their conversation. When he thought of the cardinal, he told himself to watch the road. When he imagined a future spent seeking her esoteric scent, he commanded himself to keep an eye out for his exit. And all the while the involuntary part of his mind knew that he was going to stop at the first liquor store he saw off of the expressway, for he was fully aware that the contents of the plastic water bottle in the bag he'd brought from Chicago would not be enough for that evening.

* * *

"In the plastic fifth, please," Heald told the clerk at the counter.

The clerk had already taken the glass bottle of low-quality vodka off the shelf.

"You want the plastic bottle?"

"Yes. Please."

"Why?"

Heald gave a blank expression as he stood still with both hands holding an open wallet over the counter.

"Why do you sell it?" he asked, then he shrugged. "If you

gotta know, I plan to bang the bottle against my head a few times before I drink it and a plastic bottle tends to serve better for this."

"Excuse me?" the clerk said. Her face showcased her plain and bored confusion, as if she didn't really care to know why he wanted to bounce the bottle on his head, but needed to know for some form of posterity.

"Nothing. I'm only kidding. I'd just prefer the plastic bottle, please."

The clerk said nothing and took the plastic bottle off the shelf.

"Thirteen dollars and twenty-four cents."

Heald thumbed through the few bills that he had in his wallet while his hands shook, and he was sure that the clerk must have noticed it. He took out fifteen dollars and handed it over while she counted out his change.

"Can I please get a small paper bag for this, too?"

She kept her eyes on her counting.

"I was gonna give you a bag, honey, don't worry. Law says I have to anyway."

"Thanks."

She handed him his change, and he stuffed it into his pocket. She bagged the plastic bottle, which was much slimmer than a regular glass bottle, and pushed it toward him along with the receipt. He grabbed the bottle by the neck through the paper bag and twisted the bag to conform to the bottle's shape, then he pushed the receipt back toward her. She took it nonchalantly and dropped it into a waste bin near her feet.

"You have a nice day," she said.

"We'll see," he replied. "You too."

* * *

Heald no longer kept in regular contact with the friends he'd had throughout high school and college. It wasn't a decision made as much by choice as it was by circumstance, for after he had moved to Chicago the sheer proximity of the distance proved cumbersome, and Heald was not much of a fan of phones or emails or social media. Many of his friends still lived in the Metro Detroit area, and he visited them occasionally. They used to go out drinking regularly before his drinking became a solitary habit. Other friends had moved to different parts of the country, and when that happened, a hearty good-bye was said, and promises to meet and visit were made but never kept.

These days, trips home meant a day or two spent with family during the daytime and a bottle in his childhood bedroom at night, which suited him fine. Deep down, though, Heald always held hope that a rekindling of certain friendships was never more than a sincere phone call away. In truth, many of Heald's old friends had grown tired of him, exhausted by his incessant lamentations of never finding "the right girl" and, eventually, any girl. When he used to drink with friends, he would envisage the perfect woman and interrupt other people's stories to speak about her. He told his pals that he was convinced that if he could just find someone right for him, his problems would dry up. As time went on, even as he spoke it aloud, mostly in drunken moments, he began to wonder if it was actually true.

It had also become apparent to his friends that Heald's

drinking was no longer just a byproduct of being young and having fun, but more likely evocative of some unseen leviathan that dwelled beneath his surface. Being young themselves, many opted to focus instead on their own developing lives.

As he turned down his parents' street for the second time that day, he thought it wouldn't hurt to have a friend to talk to at this point. Then he wondered if he would still know how—how to share and confide in a positive way that would encourage helpful advice, instead of just bombarding someone with negativity.

As he pulled the car into the driveway, he prepared for his ritual of somehow getting his newly purchased bottle of vodka into the house without his family's knowledge. There was an old tennis racket in the backseat of the car with a vinyl and cloth case. Noting the extra bit of room inside the case, Heald managed to slip the bottle, paper bag and all, in with the racket and force the zipper closed.

As he opened the front door, his father was standing by the sofa in the living room in plain sight, clearly looking around for something he had misplaced, moving certain trinkets and photo frames around on the sofa table. Heald stopped briefly, then closed the door and started for his bedroom.

"Everything go all right, Heald?"

"Yeah," Heald said, casually bringing the racket behind his back, making sure that the side with the bulge from the vodka bottle was facing away from his father. "As well as can be expected, I guess."

"Mmm. It's not an easy thing."

Heald lowered his head and nodded.

"No. No, I suppose not." Heald turned to continue toward his room but halted and looked back at his father, who had resumed his search. "What's not an easy thing?"

His father looked at him again. "What's that?"

"You said, 'It's not an easy thing.' What isn't?"

His father glanced around the room briefly. "You know, this situation going on."

"Grandma dying?"

Silence.

"Yes."

Heald nodded in agreement and turned to head toward his room. As he did, his father spoke.

"You going to be playing some tennis while you're home?"

Heald froze. He turned back and held the racket outstretched a bit, looking down at it, with the bulge again facing away, hidden from his father.

"Yeah. In fact, I was probably going to maybe give a few friends a call and go play a bit to get my mind off things. Figure maybe it could help."

His father turned back to the items on the table.

"Sounds like a plan, Heald. Couldn't hurt."

* * *

It was near eight o'clock in the evening when Heald began to feel truly terrible. He hadn't want to crack open the bottle as soon as he'd gotten home, but dizziness and nausea were washing over him, and the shaking was worse. His mother would be home from his aunt's house soon, and he was sure that she would want to talk to him about his visit with his grandmother. The talk would not be strictly for his benefit though, so he rationalized an obligation to take action for his mother's sake. He knew that his sister and her fiancé would still be looming about as well and that he needed to self-medicate in order to face any of them. A strange sense of duty overtook him as Heald reached into the tennis racket cover and pulled out the plastic bottle. He twisted the cap, cracking the seal with that all-too-familiar sense of anticipation that he'd grown to secretly adore. The cap slipped from his moist palm.

In the privacy of his childhood room, Heald was a king. His parents had always granted him a wide and respectful berth, which he had cherished since he was a boy. He thought fleetingly about how wonderful they really were and how he had squandered their trust in return.

He would need something to chase the alcohol with in order to mask his breath, he thought, and he decided to make a brisk trip to the kitchen to pour a glass of orange juice. Before he could second-guess himself, Heald exited his room in a hurry, past the living room where his father sat focused on the television, quickening his steps to blur his compromised condition. The orange liquid sputtered out of the carafe as his hands shook while he poured the juice, then he darted back to his room. After closing the bedroom door, he stood silent for a moment to ensure there was no sound of following footsteps or interest in his activities. Satisfied, he lifted the plastic bottle and tilted it into his mouth, taking a long pull that was comprised of three large gulps. Savoring the burn, he swallowed with great difficulty and took a small sip of the orange juice, making sure to wash it around the inside of his mouth, though he nearly choked.

The trick here was not to make a cocktail out of the two drinks, but to keep the vodka and orange juice separate so he could drink one, then the other, both in pure form, with the pure juice able to somewhat mask the strong alcohol scent after. The concoction mixed within his stomach and he bounced up and down on the balls of his feet, tossing the liquids inside as if his body were the shaker. Heald knew that it would have him feeling more stable within a short period of time.

It felt like ages since he had been in Chicago, since he had seen Janice. With all that had happened since that morning, he'd nearly forgotten that she hadn't come in to work before he'd left. He resumed his thoughts from early that morning, back to when he had first woken in his apartment, wondering just what had happened to her and Miłosz and why they had both not shown up for work. With one problem taken care of as he closed the cap back on the bottle, he decided to contact her before his imagination got the better of him once again.

He returned her text and was surprised when she responded immediately:

HEALD: Hey. I noticed you weren't at work today. I'm fine. Is everything okay with you?

JANICE: Yes, I'm okay, just had some important stuff to take care of today that couldn't wait. How was work?

Heald decided not to mention that he had traveled back home to Detroit.

HEALD: It was great. Wonderful, really. Ramone saw a new face on the Sun Times building that apparently nodded at him in appreciation for his dedication in resolving the TITLE 13 fiasco. I made googly eyes at it and teased a few of the new spiders who made a home outside of the window near Martha's desk. They were none too impressed.

Janice was slow to respond. Then:

JANICE: Okay.

Panic filled Heald. "Okay?" He felt it was time to lay a few of his cards on the table.

HEALD: So I was wondering if it would be possible for us to meet after work on Monday. Maybe we could go to the Art Institute to talk or even grab a bite to eat?

He sent the message and felt his chest fill like a balloon. Was it as bold as he thought it had seemed? At this point, did it even matter? He took another quick drink from the bottle, surprising himself. He drank the rest of the orange juice and nervously cradled the phone waiting for a response.

JANICE: I'm not sure. Maybe.

Dread. But it wasn't flat-out refusal. He would have to work for this, he thought.

HEALD: I just thought it would be nice to get out of the office so we could talk and escape the TITLE 13 nightmare for a while. Just you and me.

He sent the message. Then added:

HEALD: No spiders.

Another agonizing wait. Heald could visualize her staring at her phone, biting the tip of her index finger as she considered his proposal. He began to plan his next move once she refused.

JANICE: All right.

Relief!

HEALD: Wonderful! I think it'll be great. Really looking forward to it.

He sent the message and leaned back into the old gray rolling chair that had been in his bedroom since his days in elementary school. There was no further response from Janice, but perhaps she was busy.

Then he thought that perhaps she was not alone.

Before he could sour his mood, now that he was riding on the first wave of euphoria from the vodka, he decided to reply to Alice's text message from earlier in the day, which he figured would be a pretty non-taxing ordeal, since his 'date' with Janice had been set.

HEALD: Sorry I missed your text earlier. I can't hang out this weekend unfortunately. I'm making plans to try to meet up with a girl from work.

Perhaps he could invoke a twinge of jealousy from Alice since this was such a rare occurrence for him. Alice responded right away.

ALICE: YAY! I'm meeting up with a guy I met online this weekend too! WE GETTIN LAID! ☺

Or perhaps not, Heald thought.

* * *

The rumble of the garage door sounded like an advancing Panzer division and Heald knew that his mother must have arrived (and that his father was not using the lithium-based garage door spray he'd bought for him as a gag gift). Assessing himself, Heald could sense that he had drunk neither too much nor too little. He tucked the plastic bottle into a dresser drawer underneath some of his underwear and an old city league baseball uniform and headed out to address his family in the living room.

Heald was surprised to see his sister seated next to their father on the couch. She offered the same muted smile that she'd shown him when he first arrived. Heald returned it.

"Hey, Heally," she said. "How ya doing?"

They each heard the back door close and the sound of keys being set on the counter. His mother appeared from around the corner of the kitchen. Her expression was unguarded at first, looking straight ahead at the wall. Suddenly aware of her surroundings, she locked eyes with Heald and forced a grin. Heald's father muted the television and asked how she was.

"It's all right," she said. "Diane is, well...we're..." She surveyed the room. "Where's Richard?"

"Oh, he's gotta go to Cleveland early tomorrow to visit his brother and for a work thing, so he couldn't stay. I told him he didn't have to stay. I hope you don't mind."

"No, that's fine," said his mother, waving a hand. "He should be with his family."

She didn't say anything more for a moment as the family awkwardly acknowledged the silence in the room. Heald embraced it, though it was short-lived.

"Besides, it's kind of nice that we get to be together here alone as a family for a bit. I mean, our old family...Richard is of course soon to be family."

His sister waved back at his mother. "No, of course. I understand what you mean."

"It feels like so long since we were all together under one roof, just the four of us. It's nothing against him. It's just...nice," his mother added. She looked ready to cry, her emotions teetering on a delicate edge inside of her. His sister stood up, quickly flattening her blouse with her hands as she rose, and reached out to her mother above her father, who was seated between them and looked as if he didn't know whether he should move or not, so he elected to remain perfectly still, one hand on the remote.

"No!" his sister cried out. "Oh, no, Mom, no...I know. I didn't think that. He felt bad about going but I'm sure he also thought it would be nice for us all to be alone and talk. It does feel nice to have us all here again."

Heald looked at his father as Lynn mentioned having time to talk. Heald knew there was a warm, compassionate element to his father and always felt equally apprehensive and anxious to see it. On most occasions, his father regulated himself to merely observe the scene while a situation unfolded in front of him—something that Heald now found himself doing in similar circumstances—but on exceptional occasions, his father could offer an incredibly generous and succinct thought that had the ability to bring a conversation or situation to an immaculate and satisfying conclusion, leaving Heald in complete awe. Heald aspired to be as collected and precise with his own interjections, but all too often his drinking or lack of self-awareness robbed him of that valuable candor. He watched his father now and tried to mimic his sagacious demeanor while his sister and mother reasoned with one another.

Eventually his mother and sister finished their embrace

and his mother changed the subject, turning to Heald.

"Heally, how was Grandma? How did everything go? Do you mind if I ask?" She hesitated, unsure if she had just crossed some delicate barrier of privacy that had long stood around Heald and his grandmother.

Heald instinctively began nodding, unsure what to say. He had hardly given himself the time to reflect on the weighty conversation he'd shared with his grandmother and realized he had forced it out of his mind, unable to face it until he'd had a drink. But he'd had the drink, and he could feel the rush of sentiment coming at him like the growing headlights of an approaching subway car. With the alcohol slackening some of the wild nerve endings in his mind, a part of him felt like professing a boatload of copacetic revelations, and still another part of him felt a hushed call for reason as he regarded his father.

"It was nice. Very pleasant actually." He was still nodding and thought of the lake behind his grandmother's condo and the trees that lined it and how he might never see them again in the same light. "The whole thing was cathartic. Very pastoral."

The family looked at him curiously.

"I see she taught you another word," his sister said with a wink.

"She's an amazing teacher."

His mother smiled, satisfied with his response. Arnold the dog entered the room then, emerging from somewhere deep within the house, and walked up to Heald's mother. He looked up at her from her feet as his tail wagged.

"Arnold was thinking about you," said Heald's father to

his wife. "He loves you. We all do."

She knelt and pet the dog and put a hand on her husband's knee. Heald watched as his mother made her way past his father and sister to the open seat on the couch, settling between the two and taking a spare pillow to place on her lap. The dog meandered over to the rug in front of the fireplace and made two quick circles, sniffed the ground, then collapsed, curling into a ball and tucking his nose under his tail. Heald looked at the sight of his family nestled together on the couch and felt the balloon in his chest again. He wrestled with the urge to take a seat next to his family, but instead gave a small wave, followed by a slap on the thigh, and turned to make his way back into his bedroom. Walking back down the hallway, he was overwhelmed with guilt, and he wondered how he could ever have allowed himself to be brought to such a sorry state as to turn his back on such an incredible group of magnanimous people.

* * *

The stars are so pronounced, thought Heald as he looked up into the sky on that moonless night. It was one of those nights that you could scan the entire canopy of heavens above and not see a single cloud—a rare and shockingly picturesque view out into the universe. It was cool now in the dark, mysterious hours after midnight, and the faint breeze pushed aside the throngs of worries from a troublesome day.

He was drunk now, but not so much so that he'd moved past carrying the full weight of his thoughts on each shoulder. Now they were spread apart in the forefront of his mind like a great, burdensome list of responsibilities, each more daunting than the last—a dictatorial row of bricks waiting to be hauled to some mental worksite. He looked back up at the stars. On nights like this in Chicago, when his wild emotions were mixed with just the right amount of alcohol, Heald left his apartment and went for a walk or for a ride on the L. His favorite trip on cloudy or rainy nights was taking the Brown Line from the stop near his apartment south to the Loop, watching the rain wipe across the train's windows with the buildings in full view. On nights when it was clear and beautiful, he would ride the Red Line underground from Clark/Division to Harrison and get out to stroll among the headless and armless iron giants of the *Agora* art installation.

Being drunk gave Heald enough confidence to ignore the risk of being caught outside in his parents' backyard. As he looked up now, he was happy he had left the house. Heald had nearly forgotten how clear the night sky was in the silent blackness outside of the city. In Chicago, when you looked out into the chasm of space, all you could see was a dull haze of city light that permanently obscured anything past the high reach of the metropolis's glowing towers—a thin lace curtain drawn over the entire expanse of the universe. Here though, Heald was able to fondly remember all those aimless twilights of his childhood.

As a kid, particularly when he was feeling especially bored or despondent, Heald would try to count the stars that filled the sky on any given night, but would rapidly be vexed by their sheer numbers, so he instead became lost in their presence and nothing more—a wonderful sense of being adrift in a sea of glimmering treasures. The true gift of a starry night sky was being able to send off all your importunate fears into the abyss where they could dissolve amid all that nothing and return as some more manageable entity, transferred back to their owner with a trace of the heavens upon them.

It is true that being confronted with a void as voluminous as space, one can become lost in it all, Heald thought, but he also realized *that* was very much the advantage of it—the most frightening aspect being its most providential thrill: the surrender to it, the feeling of negligibility becoming the all-redeeming power. Some people do give themselves to a higher power, while others capitulate to the cosmic amphitheater and the absurd implausibility of it all.

In his drunken state, it was hard for Heald to tell how long he had been in the backyard. He thought about his grandmother and wondered if she had counted her grateful blessings before going to sleep tonight and whether she had thought of him. He was confident that she had. The disparaging thought of this possibly being the night that died in her sleep made him wistful, and he tried to cast the thought out into the sea of stars that stretched in front of him, hoping it would come back anew, but he couldn't. Like a God above, the stars could use their indifference to their advantage. What felt like a billion burning eyes watching down on him were really nothing more than giant balls of boiling gas set so far away that to fathom their proximity to this world was to invite a fresh madness into an already crumbling consciousness.

It was easy to turn on an emotion or a conviction within a

drunken state, and Heald began to feel himself drifting into unconsciousness as his head nodded lightly. He took one long final glance up at the sky before he decided to go back to his room to finish off the bottle. Regardless of the vast apathy of the stars above, he still liked being able to go outside to see them high and vivid up there, rather than shielded behind some perverse haze like they were in Chicago.

He turned and stumbled inside, trying to close the sliding door ever so gently, so as to not make a sound.

Chapter Eighteen

WHEN HE AWOKE, Heald was relieved to find that he was lying in his own bed. Lifting his head, he saw that he was still wearing the clothes that he'd worn the day before, and despite it being a warm night, he had neither turned on the overhead fan nor cracked the window to allow in the breeze. He'd perspired quite a bit; he felt the booze-tainted dampness that had settled in his socks and around his neck, and he drew his fingers across the wet skin. He knew his clothes would be permeated with the stench of alcohol, so he rose to change.

As he dug through his overnight bag for the balled-up socks he had packed, Heald remembered that he had spent some time in the backyard the previous night and hoped that he had not awoken any of his family members. He was parched and reached for the glass of orange juice he'd refilled in the night. There was a little liquid left, but he noticed a small moth-like insect floating dead in dark contrast upon the top of the bright orange juice. He swirled the glass in a circular motion and watched as the bug disappeared. Lifting the glass above his head, he peered through the bottom but saw no sign of it. He set the glass down on the desk and noticed that he had hidden the empty vodka bottle under a magazine. He quickly took the shirt he'd worn the night before and wrapped it around the bottle and tucked it away into the bottom of his bag. Still quite thirsty, he went to the kitchen to greet his family and to get a glass of water.

His father and sister were seated on the couch almost in

the same position that Heald had left them in the night before. They both smiled and wished him a good morning, which he reciprocated, also with a smile. Heald had become aware through his years of drinking that if a drunk ever did something that upset or alarmed those he shared living quarters with, the evidence of it would be readily available upon the face or faces of those individuals when they first took notice of each other in the morning. There would be a calm yet concerned or inquisitive look in their eyes that would then study his own, searching for some clue as to the whereabouts or doings of that drunk from the evening before. But there was no such look from his father or sister, and Heald felt no small measure of relief pour over him. They returned their focus to the television, and he headed toward the kitchen, giving a small pat on Arnold's head as he went by.

His mother was pouring grinds into the coffee filter when Heald entered the sunlit kitchen. She didn't raise her head as he walked to the refrigerator, which was a little suspicious, he thought. He took a bottle of water from the fridge and set it on the counter. His mother placed the grinds into the basket, and he realized that she must have been making a second pot, for he saw some used coffee mugs near the sink. Taking a drink, Heald noticed that his hands were relatively still, meaning he had been up drinking rather late.

"Coffee?" she asked, still pushing the buttons on the machine.

He thought for a moment, not usually being a coffee drinker outside the early morning hours at CRCC, but decided that a slight change couldn't hurt.

"Sure."

She took another mug down from the cabinet and placed it next to hers on the counter then looked deeply at his eyes. And there, in her gaze, Heald saw the sense of concern and inquiry that he so dreaded. She did not smile, instead keeping her lips taut as she studied his face. He looked away, glancing around at the microwave and porcelain figures on the windowsill, but continued to feel her eyes observing him. He instinctively put his hands into his pockets and faced the window to look out at nothing in particular.

"How did you sleep, Heald?"

He turned back but kept his gaze on his water.

"Not bad. Just fine."

The sound of the stream roiling within the coffee machine and the mechanism letting loose the hot liquid into various chambers filled the room. The machine grew steadily louder as the pressure built and the slow drip of the dark brown coffee began to flow into the pot. Heald looked up at his mother and saw that no part of her had moved and that her eyes were still fixed on his. He was desperate to turn the attention to anything else.

"Any word about Grandma?" he asked with an inflection of genuine concern.

His mother relaxed her stance and looked over to the two cups in front of her.

"Yes, she called," she said, finally grinning. "She said that she was in good spirits this morning. She had a relatively good night."

Head nodded and felt comforted.

"That's good."

Heald's father walked into the room and stopped, saying nothing until both Heald and his mother looked over at him nonchalantly.

"We were just wondering if you guys wanted to get something to eat. As in go out," he said, pointing back toward Heald's sister in the living room. "Everyone's gotta be hungry, and we could go to the Coney like we used to. If you want."

Heald nodded his approval.

"Sure. Mom and I were just going to have a quick cup of coffee and then I'm up for going."

His father looked at his mother.

"Another cup?" he said, pointing to the machine. "What, did you not sleep well? Did you get up in the night?"

* * *

The Coney Island diner was a small, family-owned restaurant that had been in the neighborhood since well before Heald's family had moved there from the city. It was a lackluster building attached to a long chain of stores within a strip mall—the kind of place you might miss if not for word of mouth or only frequent out of habit, like the Brown Family.

They walked through the double doors and Heald felt an instantaneous swell of nostalgia. There was still a large chalkboard near the door that had the day's specials listed on it, as there had been since he was a child. The same handwritten sign hung from the ceiling pointing toward the restrooms. A large, older waitress spotted them from behind a counter filled with people sitting and drinking coffee and munching on pastries. She waved at them and pointed toward a booth in the back.

The floor of the diner was unusual as it was carpeted, but it had been pressed flat with age and years of foot traffic. The family slid into the burgundy leather booth; Heald sat next to his father, the women on the other side.

His sister reached for the menus and counted out four from the stack pressed against the wall by a napkin dispenser and ketchup and mustard bottles. The menus were in a tri-folded plastic sheath, sealed around the edges with a dark red plastic border sewn shut with red thread. They were frayed and worn and the stitching had fallen loose at the corners over time. Nothing had really changed on the menu itself, save for the prices, which had been adjusted by placing little white stickers over the old ones. Even a place like this could still make a necessary change to survive, Heald thought.

The family browsed over the menus only half-interested, each already knowing what they would order, but unable to break the habit of just looking. A new, younger waitress came over to the table carrying four small glasses of ice water and placed them in front of them one by one. She asked if anyone would like any coffee and they all politely declined, instead asking for orange juice, except for Heald, who asked for a grapefruit juice. Heald's father said they were all ready to order. She pulled out her order pad and began to jot the items down. Each order was written down carefully, and the family had to repeat aspects of their order a few times as she apologized and continued to scribble. Heald wondered how new she was to this, and why she'd chosen to work in a diner normally frequented by older folks and blue-collar types. He also thought she was rather attractive. She thanked them, said she'd put their orders right in, and began to walk away, only to turn back with a smile.

"Oh, and if you guys need anything else, my name is Janice."

Heald's eyes opened wide while the others politely grinned and said thanks. His mother saw Heald's expression and began staring at him. His father collected the menus from the table and slid them back between the napkin dispenser and the wall.

"So, Heald," his father began, "how's the census going?"

Still lost in thought, Heald showed no reaction.

"Heald," his father said nudging him. All eyes were on Heald, including his mother's.

"Oh," Heald said, rousing himself. "Work? Work's good. Fine."

His sister took a sip of water and set her glass back down upon the paper doily.

"What do you do every day?" she asked. "You don't actually have to go out door-to-door and count everyone, right? You work in an office?"

Heald took a gulp of his water and placed his hands at his sides.

"No, no. Those are the enumerators. We hire them from census to census, and they go out into the fields and collect the data by doing the door-to-door thing. Yeah, I work in the Chicago Regional Census Center downtown, next to the Sears Tower. Or Willis Tower it's now called."

"Really?"

"Mm-hmm. Forty-ninth floor."

"*Woowww...*"

They had sometimes spoken about Heald's job before, but he tended to be vague, as if revealing any specifics might somehow put his position in jeopardy in some way.

"You know, we're very proud of you, Heald, for finding a job like that in this economy," his father said. "I know it couldn't have been easy."

"Thanks," Heald said taking another drink. He was still quite thirsty. "Really, thanks."

His mother was silent.

"So things are good, then?" asked his sister.

"Oh, yes, indeed," he replied while nodding and turning the base of his water glass in circles around the doily. "Well, actually...there's a situation going on in the office right now. It's pretty serious."

They all perked up and leaned in. Just then the waitress returned with their drinks.

"What?" his sister asked with a higher-pitched tone after the waitress had left. "Is everything okay?"

"Well, I don't know. You see, we seem—I say *we* as in someone from the office, the royal we—seem to have lost or misplaced some pretty confidential information."

"What does that mean?" his sister asked.

"TITLE 13."

"TITLE 13?" his father asked.

"Yes, TITLE 13. TITLE 13 is very good information. The highly classified, top-secret stuff. All hush hush and whatnot. The stuff of dreams, apparently." Heald smiled to himself as he recalled the lecture from Elina Flohard earlier in the week when she revealed her fanatical desire for TITLE 13 information. But thinking back now, he had difficulty remembering anything specific that she had said.

"And someone lost it?" his father asked. "*You* didn't lose it, did you?"

"No, dad, it wasn't me," Heald replied. "At least, I'm pretty sure it wasn't. I'll tell ya, though, it gets pretty screwy in there sometimes, and it can be hard to tell exactly what is going on."

His father looked confused.

"Really? You know, I worked in a government office for a short while when I was younger—state government—and I gotta say, it never seemed very screwy to me. Always by the book, which was fine."

Heald took a sip of grapefruit juice and shrugged.

"Maybe it's you who's screwy, Heel," his father added with a small chuckle. Everyone giggled except for his mother.

"Yeah," Heald said. "That does make more sense. Who knows."

Heald could see the waitress walking back toward their table with a large tray of food. He loved the fact that small Coney diners seemed to prepare their food faster than anyone else. As she approached, the tray wobbled a bit, and she stopped to balance it before continuing with two hands holding the tray. She placed their food in front of them, asked if they needed anything else, then returned to the kitchen. Heald looked at his omelet, and though he'd felt hungry when he first woke, he now had no appetite.

"So what happens now?" his sister asked. "The TITLE 13 information. Where is it? How much did you guys lose?"

"I'm not sure," Heald said, pushing the food around his plate. "We lost thirty-seven pages of it, I know that."

"Is that a lot?" his father asked.

"Not sure about that either. Maybe? They're making us turn the office upside down in hopes of finding it. They're even enacting all these strange rules and measures in an effort to bring the missing paperwork to light. They implemented a 'No Stumbling' policy and force people to stand and blindly point at anything that is suspected of being lost TITLE 13 information—civil servants everywhere standing like mannequins pointing at random things in the office." He laughed a bit. "In fact, I'm fairly certain that they may have even cubed...never mind."

"What?" his father said while chewing. "Cubed what? What do you mean 'cubed'?"

"It's nothing. Joke. I think."

His mother set her fork down on her plate and looked earnestly at Heald, seemingly wanting to say something of significance to her son. Instead, she looked at the glass of orange juice in front of her and picked up her fork again. Then she spoke for the first time since the family had sat down.

"Do you think it's serious, Heald?" she asked poking at her hash browns.

Heald lowered his head and stopped stirring his food. He didn't look at her face.

"I'm not sure," he replied. "But I suppose it could very well be."

* * *

Back at home, Heald retreated to his bedroom. His first thought was to borrow one of his parent's cars and head to the liquor store to buy another bottle, but the guilt was overwhelming. Scarcely had a Saturday gone by in as long as he could remember that he hadn't already started drinking by this point in the day, and now, just past noon, he was beginning to feel the trembling returning to his hands and the familiar dizzying sensation in his head. It was always hard for Heald to pull himself away from his family to sneak drinks and act secretive when all the while he knew how much they loved him. Instead he took their trust and mixed it into a bottle, drank it down, and flushed it away. His urge was to go out there and sit with them and talk with his hands outstretched in front of him, motionless, and with his eyes wide open and lost in theirs, but he couldn't deny that it was a battle he was no longer winning. Regardless, he told himself that he was determined not to give in and drink. He needed something to keep him physically occupied right now; something that could keep his hands busy and his mind from straying too far.

From the living room, Heald could hear his father tell his mother that he was heading outside to cut the grass. Heald's head jolted up. He had cut the grass for his family ever since he was a boy, doing so even on the weekends when he was home from college and when he lived there again briefly before moving to Chicago. It was the perfect distraction and a great way to be outside in the sun, sweating out whatever foul elements were dwelling inside of him. He went to talk to his father, while the growing sickness weighed on his body and mind.

In the mudroom he found his father putting on a pair of beat-up tennis shoes caked with flaky dead grass clippings and coated in a sheen of bright green.

"Hey, Dad. How about letting me give the grass a cut and you take it easy?" Heald stood meekly with his hands in his pockets as his father looked up from his shoelaces.

"Really?"

"Sure, why not?" Heald replied. "I'd like to think I can still earn my keep." Heald started to walk toward the closet door. "Are my old shoes still in here?"

"Oh, I doubt it. I think your mother probably threw those out a while back. But there's an old pair of mine in there that you can wear if you like." His father rose and put out a hand in protest. "But really, you don't have to do that. I don't expect you to cut the grass anymore." He paused for a moment. "I know it's not the greatest of circumstances that brought you home this weekend."

This gave Heald momentary pause.

"Maybe not, but I'd still like to help. I'll take care of the grass for you."

His father looked stern, then smiled. "I ain't an old man you know, Heald," his father said, still grinning. "I can still cut the grass just fine. Better than most. I'm not gonna hurt myself or anything."

With that, Heald looked at his father in a new light. Not just as the strong, consistent force he had grown up with, but rather as something new: a living and breathing human being, capable of his own degeneration. As he briefly looked him over, Heald realized that his father's hair was thin and almost completely gray, some of it gone altogether. He noticed how his once hardened physique seemed to be softer and more pronounced in spots, how the lines on his face had grown longer and just a bit wider. Heald was overcome with a strong sense of affection for his father.

"I just wanna help while I still can. While I'm here," Heald said. "Before I leave. That's all." He put his hands back into his pockets.

His father's stance loosened and his grin widened.

"Sure," he said. "Thanks, Heald. I think there's another pair of old shoes in there somewhere. While you're cutting the grass, I can trim the hedges and do the edging. Just don't walk back through the house once you put those old shoes on or you'll track grass everywhere and you mother will have a fit." He finished tightening his laces and stood back up.

"Yeah, trust me. I remember," Heald said. "Wouldn't you rather go sit down, though?"

His father continued in his motions. "Work to be done, Heally."

"Fair enough."

Heald began to rummage through the closet until he found the older pair of shoes that his father had been referring to. Heald stared down at the shoes, which were clearly larger than his own. He bent over, leaning his back against the wall of the small mudroom, and slipped his foot into his father's shoe with ease, noting that he hadn't even untied the laces. He did this with the other shoe and stood up straight, feeling a little dizzy. He took a few awkward steps, then walked over to the sliding door and watched as his father opened up the shed in the back, stepped into it, and emerged with the hedge trimmers, all the while appearing to make every move just a little more slowly and with a bit more care than Heald remembered.

And as Heald watched, he felt a tear come to his eye. He knew that though all humans are captives to time, to endlessly ticking clocks and mandated regimens, time also relies on humans; it depends on living things to press its influence upon, to make itself known. It pools in our bones and saturates our genes, mutating and rearranging our internal setup in an unwelcome feng shui. Time collects on our bodies and weighs us down like barnacles on a ship's hull, continually accumulating until the heft of it all finally pulls us down into the deep.

* * *

As he began cutting the grass, Heald was overcome with fatigue. The simple task of guiding the self-propelled lawn mower up and down in parallel rows and stopping to empty the clippings was completely draining him of his energy. In addition, his coordination was off and he began making mistakes. The whole ordeal began to alarm and frighten him, for not long ago, this was an activity that Heald not only completed regularly and with ease, but also one that he found rewarding after a time, too. When he was much younger and first tasked as family's groundskeeper, Heald loathed having to spend his weekends cutting the grass while other kids were playing. What he really wanted to do was run off and play in the woods. He would cut row after row while always keeping one eye on the long line of trees that separated the Browns' backyard from the hidden trove of untouched nature beyond. His sole focus was on finishing as fast as possible so he could drop everything and run off into the woods to get lost in some wild abandon, far from the then-perfectly manicured lawn. But over time, Heald began to take pride in the work that he was doing, looking up every so often as he got older to see his father standing by the sliding door of the house keeping an eye on him. Now, the task was more daunting than ever, and with each step, Heald could feel his strength, the little that he had, fading away. He slammed his hand down on the bin of grass clippings.

His father was busy trimming around the edges of a large bush on an island in the middle of the yard next to a great maple tree. He paused, looking over at Heald, and began to walk over toward his son. Standing silent for a moment, his father watched him and then began calling out something to Heald, pointing to an area behind him, but Heald could not hear him over the roar of the mower, so he switched it off.

"I said you missed a spot back there!" cried out his father, pointing to a small strip of uncut grass in the path behind Heald.

"I saw it! I'm gettin' to it!" Heald cried back, nodding, and gave his father a thumbs-up to show that his message had been received loud and clear.

"If you're gonna do a job, Heald, you should do it right," his father said loudly. "Anything worth doing might as well be done right." His father remained where he stood.

"I know. I know, dad."

His father turned back toward his work, and Heald reached for the mower's rip cord when he realized he was standing near the garden plaque marking the spot where the family had buried Alan's ashes. Heald bent down and cleared off the debris and grass trimmings from it and stared at the stone marker, thinking of the time when the puppy had destroyed all of his mother's tulips on this spot. Heald had chosen the location for the marker.

Chapter Nineteen

STEPPING INTO THE HOUSE, Heald could not help feeling defeated. He had finished cutting the grass, but the ordeal had left him drained both physically and mentally. As he watched his father continue to work in the backyard, Heald resigned himself to his deterioration and removed the shoes from his feet by easily kicking them off, though he was careful not to let any of the fresh clippings flutter any further into the house.

The palms of his hands were relatively smooth as he rubbed them together with soap. The tremor was evident as he rinsed and toweled them off. He started to make his way toward his bedroom when he nearly ran into his distracted mother, who had been coming from the other end of the hall. At first she looked concerned, then she smiled.

"I see you helped your dad with the grass," she said. "That was awful nice of you." She put her hand on Heald's shoulder.

"It was nothing," he said. "I just want to help. You guys have done so much for me."

She gave the shoulder a squeeze.

"It's mutual, Heally. We love you."

To this, Heald felt himself pull away just slightly. He looked down at the floor.

"I love you, too," he said.

His mother drew her hand back and clasped them together in front of her, as if in prayer. "Now what shall we do for dinner later? You wanna go out?"

Heald felt a sudden urge to hide; that familiar feeling of a repressed transgression welled up inside of him, and an underlying fear led him to make a split decision that he immediately regretted.

"Actually, I know it's probably not what you guys want to hear, but I think I ought to be getting back to Chicago." He looked up at his mother's face and regarded the instantaneous display of disappointment.

"Oh, but Heald," she began, sputtering her words, "W-why so soon? What about your grandma?"

The remorse flooded over him.

"I know, but I'm glad she's feeling better today. I wish I could stay here indefinitely right now, but I do need to get back either way." Saying the words felt just as rotten as they sounded, Heald thought. "And I can come back later should anything change."

"But I was hoping we could have some time to talk," she said. "We just want to make sure everything is going okay for you. We know so little about what's going on." She was kneading her fingers in her hands now.

"I'm fine," Heald said. "It's just this dang TITLE 13 stuff going on back at the office, and all kinds of stuff. I really should get back."

"I'm concerned about you, Heald," she said softly. "It's hard with you being so far away and us not being there with you."

"But I'm not really that far away, Mom."

"It does feel like it though, Heald. More so all the time."

Inside, a part of Heald wanted to cast the whole plan aside and commit completely to his family's wishes and stay with them for as long as they wanted. Perhaps he could even get help.

"I'm sorry," was all he could say. Then he walked down the hall and into his room, leaving what felt like little pieces of him scattered in his wake.

* * *

His body craved alcohol and his mind was fixated upon his next drink. He knew that it was closer since he had decided to head back to Chicago that evening. The ride back would be a long one without a drink, but Heald tried not to focus on that. Looking up the next departure times for the buses heading to Chicago from Detroit, he saw that one would be leaving in just over an hour—just enough time to have his parents and sister drop him off at the station and, more importantly, not enough to wallow in regret over the decision. He told his family the plan and they agreed, after a bit more hesitation on their part, that they would all go downtown together to see him off.

Once he had packed his bag and satchel in the family car, his parents waited outside while he went back into the house to say good-bye to Arnold. Heald sat on the floor next to the dog and he wagged his tail generously as Heald scooted closer and began to pet him, rubbing both his hands down the dog's back. He pushed his cheek against the dog's face and the dog licked his ear. Heald stood up and walked out the door. As he was about to close it behind him, he opened it back up slightly and eyed the dog, who perked his ears up as Heald softly said, "*Respice post te. Hominem te esse memento...Memento mori.*" Then Heald clicked his tongue and closed the door.

* * *

The car ride to the bus station was mostly silent. Heald attempted to fill the stillness by asking his sister questions about the wedding she and Richard were planning for the following year. Hearing about the ceremony and the meticulous care being taken concerning the preparations made him feel good. His sister talked about the reception and how they were looking to book the old marina's event hall at the same location that they had kept the family boat years back. Heald fondly remembered the boat and how he used to sit in the bow of the old Chris-Craft next to his sister while they passed other boats coming back into the harbor, his father navigating from the big mahogany wheel.

The reception would be an impressive one, she insisted, though due in most part to Richard's extensive Greek family. She went on about the food and flowers and music and more, all over a year away, and Heald's head began to swim. Making plans for anything further off than a few days into the future was a distant memory for him. Heald had felt a sense of accomplishment when he had made plans to meet with Janice at the Art Institute on Monday night and could barely fathom the idea of planning an event a year into the future. In fact, he thought, if he could make it to Monday night in one piece, he'd be quite proud of himself. Still, Lynn spoke now with a familiar gaiety and enthusiasm that sparked something deep within him. Heald didn't need to talk much at this point, happy to let the rest of the car ride be filled with her exhilarating plans for days to come.

When they pulled into the downtown station they still had twenty minutes to spare, but the bus was already waiting by the curb and the driver was helping a few passengers load their bags into the carriage below. His father had pulled the car into a nearby loading zone, and they gathered by the trunk to bid Heald farewell. His parents and sister lined together on one side, and as he stood facing them, Heald was suddenly despondent; something inside of him made him think that this might be the last time that he would cast his eyes upon this scene. He took a brief look up at the massive Detroit skyscrapers and then back toward his family. They were each smiling and so was he, but his smile felt false, like a wax casting, and looking at his mother, he sensed that hers was similar. A part of him thought about getting back into the car and telling them to head back home.

"Thanks again, Heald, for helping me out by cutting the grass," his father said. "It was kind of you, but you know I never expect for you to have to do that for me."

"I know, dad, but I wanted to do it. I was happy to do it, really."

The father and son stood awkwardly still for a moment before each of them made a quick twitching movement toward the other, then stopped and made the same movement again, at which point Heald committed and took the full step toward his father and brought one arm around his father's back to embrace him. His father held him tightly for a few seconds, then loosened his hold.

"Thanks," his father said.

"Happy to do it," Heald repeated.

Heald turned toward his sister as his father went to the car to close the trunk.

"Thanks for talking to me about the wedding, Heally,"

she said. "I didn't know you were looking forward to it so much. It makes me excited!" Still grinning, she looked over at his bus. "Oh, and you don't have to say anything now, and don't freak out or anything, but I think Richard is going to ask you something...about the wedding." She began to grin.

"It's fine," Heald said returning her smile. "Whatever it is, it's fine and I'm sure I'll be happy to do it."

She leaned in with a jolting movement and grabbed hold of her brother with both arms, pinning his arms to his sides, and kissed him on the cheek. He laughed.

"Good luck with all that TITLE 13 stuff," she added. "Sounds like a headache to me, but I know if anyone can figure it all out, it's you."

Heald nodded in appreciation and looked down at the cement in front of him, knowing that his mother was next. He pretended to focus on something on his shoe and lifted his foot a bit. His mother walked up to Heald and put her hand on the strap of his bag, which he was still holding, then turned to his father and sister.

"I'm going to help Heald get his stuff packed onto the bus. We'll be right back."

Within a flash, the warm sensation from his sister's farewell disappeared and was replaced by panic. His sister and father waved to him and turned to get back into the car though Heald kept his eyes intently on them, wanting to be sure he saw them for every second that he could until they escaped from view, cataloging every sober moment to memory, not wanting to ever lose it.

As his father opened the car door and moved to step in,

he stopped and turned to Heald.

"You know we love you, Heald," his father said.

Heald could feel his heart clench like someone was pushing down onto his chest with both of their hands.

"Yeah, I know, dad," he replied. "I love you, too."

"Okay then," his father said. "Just making sure."

His father climbed into the car and started the engine. Heald knew his mother was standing right in front of him, just a foot away, but he almost felt like he could not see her there.

They took a few steps toward the bus and his mother stopped him, turning him toward her.

"You know it's true, right?" she asked. "Do you know how much we really love you? What we would *do* for you? We would do anything for you, Heald. *Anything*."

"I know, Mom," he replied. "And I appreciate it. I love you, too."

"And you know how much your grandmother loves you."

Heald was silent.

"Her love is just like all our love for you. Your dad's, your sister's, and mine. We couldn't stand to see you hurt for anything, Heald. Not for anything."

"Yeah. You'll keep me updated on her condition, right? Let me know how she's doing?"

"I will, but we're basically just waiting now. I'm going over there tonight to stay with her."

"You are?" Heald's head perked up. "Could you just tell her how much I love her? And I'm sorry that I can't stay? She'll know, but could you tell her?"

"I'll tell her."

"I love you, too, Mom."

She looked at her son with that solemn mix of concern and care that only a mother possesses.

"Would you tell me if something was wrong, Heald?"

His reply was fast and rehearsed.

"Yes, of course I would. Mm-hmm."

"We love you, Heald."

"Mm-hmm. Me too."

She pulled her son close and hugged him with all her strength and didn't loosen her grasp.

"You can do anything, Heally. We're so proud of you. Just so very proud of you." She gradually let him go and took a measured step back, and Heald cold see there were tears in her eyes. "But no matter what, you can always, *always,* ask us for help. Or anyone. Your family will always be there to help you with whatever you need. Don't you ever be too proud to not ask for help. You let us be the proud ones for you...don't you let it get you."

"Don't let what get me?"

"Whatever it is that you're fighting, Heald."

* * *

Heald wished that he could have stayed right there on the corner of Cass and Michigan Avenue in downtown Detroit, content to share that real and ardent moment with his family for as long as it would last. He was desperate to reveal his devastating secret, just wishing to be done with the whole thing, wanting to toss his bags aside, fall to his knees in tears, and reach out his arms to grasp for some kind of help.

But he was entrenched in this calamity.

Always present in the back of his mind was his growing need, and at that moment the only way to be delivered from his physical suffering was to take that first step onto his ride home. As the bus began to pull away, Heald could see his family's car still waiting on the side of the road. He turned himself to face the car and wanted to wave, but he knew that they couldn't see him behind the tinted windows. Instead, he sat staring as the bus rolled down the avenue gaining speed among the enormous high-rises that had stood for nearly a century. He watched their car fade off into the distance until the bus eventually turned a corner.

Only once did Heald turn around and look to see the skyline as the bus left Detroit city limits. He could have watched it until it had completely disappeared, but instead he turned forward, knowing that it would be there for some time, standing unbroken and true—an unambiguous beacon for those who called it home.

Heald focused his thoughts on the facts now: the bus would be pulling into a truck stop in about an hour, somewhere west of Ann Arbor, and there he could buy more of the booze his body so desperately needed. Free from the sight and reach of his family, Heald's withdrawal symptoms overtook him and his hands began to shake uncontrollably. In the silence he could feel his heart thump violently. Despite the air-conditioning and the bus being quite cool, Heald had begun to sweat profusely. Closing his eyes, he felt like he was sinking underwater, his hearing muffled and the sea's pressure building upon him with a menacing momentum.

To counter this, he tried to concentrate on something else. He thought about Janice and her smile as he'd joked with her during their private lunch earlier that week, and he thought of her as she let her long hair down, the way it clung close to her body, covering her contours, and he thought of walking by her side outside their building, and soon he fell into a type of restless slumber, a fevered meditation, finally where no morose thought could ensnare him, if only for a short time.

When he opened his eyes, Heald's first thought was that he must have dozed off for hours, but looking out the window, he saw a mile marker along the side of the expressway that indicated they were about fifty miles past Ann Arbor, and Heald had not missed the rest area. His panic ebbed away, comforted by the knowledge that they would soon make the stop. He fiddled with the contents of his satchel until he could feel the bus change gears and move to the rightmost lane, slowing and making its way toward the exit ramp.

When the bus had come to a full stop, Heald tried to act nonchalant as the rest of the passengers slowly stirred from their huddled positions. But before he could give it a second thought, he found himself heading down the staircase from the bus's top deck to the back exit. Through the darkened windows of the bus he could see the neon lights above the truck stop beaming out the word *Liquor*. As the doors opened, the bus driver mentioned something about the passengers having only twenty minutes, but Heald was already out the door, knowing he wouldn't need that long.

Inside, Heald headed straight for the counter where many small and perfectly lined bottles lined the shelf under a fluorescent light. He was hoping to make his purchase quickly before any of the other riders followed him in. He'd brought his satchel in with him and was carrying it on his shoulder.

"One pint of that vodka, please," Heald said pointing to one of the plastic, cheap-looking bottles that sat on a lower shelf. He paused for a moment as the clerk turned to reach for the pint. "Actually, make that two."

The clerk turned back.

"Would you just like a fifth? It comes in fifths."

"No thank you," Heald responded. "Just the two. Please."

The clerk placed the two bottles on the counter and reached for his scanner gun to ring them up. Heald looked around and then at the door, watching. Satisfied, he took out his wallet and opened it over the counter. Heald's hands trembled and he struggled to pull out the credit card while clerk watched his hands intently and then brought his stare up to Heald's face. The clerk was inclined to speak, biting his lip and moving his head back, but said nothing and scratched his nose instead. He slid the card through the machine and grabbed two small paper bags, placing the bottles in them. Heald took them and brushed away what he thought was an offer of a receipt only to have the clerk insist for his signature. Heald scribbled with his unsteady hand upon the dotted line, thanked the clerk, and made his way outside.

The plan had already been set in his mind as he turned the corner of the storefront toward the side of the building. Hidden from plain sight, he cracked the top off of one of the bottles and heard the familiar sound that sent his heart fluttering with delight. Standing next to an out-of-service payphone, he took a final look around and brought the bottle up to his lips and took a long drink, reveling in its harsh, bitter sting. He took a quick breath, let it linger for just a second or two more, then gulped the rest of the bottle down with one full swallow. Even though the alcohol's effect would take a few minutes, the sense of relief itself was intoxicating. Heald tightened his fists, leaned his head all the way back, and looked at the cloudless blue sky above him. It was a beautiful day, he thought.

He peeked out toward the front of the store then walked over to a dumpster and tossed in the bottle. He thought briefly about opening the second bottle, but decided against it; he could use the bus's tiny restroom to drink more if he wanted to. But the second bottle was already in his hand, waiting to be opened. He had to make a conscious effort to return it to his bag and step out from his hidden spot.

There were still passengers waiting outside of the bus; some were on their phones while a few were puffing hastily on cigarettes, taking their last drags. Heald casually made his way back onto the bus. His belly felt warm with a dull burn that jostled around lightly as he made his way up the staircase to the top deck. He took his seat, packing in his satchel neatly between himself and the window, resting his forearm over it, and watched as the bus driver made his way back from the store and gave a small wave to those still standing outside to follow him into the vehicle. The doors closed and they headed out of the parking lot. The driver's voice came over the speaker system and he informed them that they would be traveling nonstop now and would be in Chicago in roughly three hours.

Heald could feel the alcohol taking effect—his hands

were still and his movements cool and composed. The bus continued down the highway, and somewhere in the west, deep behind the forward horizon, a shapeless mass of dark clouds was taking form.

* * *

When he opened his eyes the sky was opaque and gloomy and the windows of the bus were covered with shimmering broken ribbons of rainwater that streamed down reflecting the bright orange tint from the streetlights that lined the expressway. It reflected something else too: the color of fire. Heald adjusted his focus past the windows, and off in the distance he saw the tall, slender metal stacks that billowed a glowing, smokeless blaze into the air. They were traveling through Gary again.

Beyond the towers tipped with amber flames, Lake Michigan looked completely still, unaffected by the wind and weather. The purplish water and faded ruins lay in perfect harmony with one another, and he thought about how all the things on the land might yet slip silently under the cover of the lake, like a pile of dust being swept under a rug. But it was all still there, and the fires burned and would continue until some force, some broom, remembered its purpose and swept it all away, setting the course for something palmy and virgin.

Heald leaned back and opened his eyes, assessing his physical state. He still had a good buzz going and he held his hands out in front of him, palms flat and facing down. They were perfectly still, and he brought his index fingers together, forming one flat plane with his thumbs tucked underneath. He turned his palms up from the center, so his hands formed a bowl, like a beggar, and he held this pose for a moment before becoming self-conscious and bringing his hands back to his face to rub his eyes. He leaned forward, resting his elbows on his lap with his head still in his hands, and thought of his grandmother.

In about an hour he would be back in Chicago, he knew that, but he couldn't help wondering where his grandmother might be in the next hour. During their conversation the day before, Heald had been fascinated by her cavalier attitude toward knowing that her life could be over at any moment. She seemed so at peace, as if suddenly dying were no different than an unexpected need to use the bathroom.

Heald thought about his own mortality and reasoned that if he were to die at any moment, it would be no real tragedy. But Heald also knew the other thing he had told his grandmother was true: many young people do fear death, whether they admit it or not, because they have so little real-time experience with it. It's easy to say that dying doesn't matter, or that a city washing away into the waves is no lamentable thing, because there is a fundamental component missing to the shared existence of young people: the absence crucial relationships with the elements, places, and people of the world that give them true meaning and bind their fates to their surroundings.

When his grandmother said she had resigned herself to her own demise, it was not for lack of care for those connections that she had formed in her life, but rather because they had been played out; the narrative of her life had come full circle and the bonds that she held with this world had served their purpose—thus they must now unravel, her story concluded. It was not a heedless acceptance of death, but rather a welcome capitulation after a long life—the next turn on a journey never-ending.

When he looked back out the window, Gary was gone, only black water in view. Heald felt the front end of the bus rise steadily and saw that they were ascending the massive Skyway bridge over the Calumet River. Near the top, the aura of city light from Chicago filled the horizon, and from the shapeless plane of darkness rose the two enormous white spires from the top of the Sears Tower. Then, all at once, the rest of the scintillating skyline was there like an island of light situated at the center of a black sea, spreading out like a glowing spider web into the west.

The lakefront's border was sharp and defined at night, with bright lights cutting out the coastline. The bus dipped down the bridge to the lowered expressway, and the cityscape was gone, leaving only two large concrete walls lining each side of the road. Soon enough the Dan Ryan would wind north and he would be facing the monolithic Sears Tower head-on, back downtown—back to where he lived but could not call home.

Chapter Twenty

IT WAS LATE when Heald got to his apartment. He'd carried his bags from Union Station to the Red Line Jackson stop, nodding dopily at the Herald Washington Library along the way as if it weren't a building, but rather an old friend he'd spotted. Heald had spent a great deal of time in that library upon first moving to Chicago. Anxious to establish some form of residency that tied him to the city, he applied for a Chicago library card with proof of the first few bills sent to his new address. Once he received his card, he checked out as many books as he could, reading voraciously about the city's history. In truth, he was happy back then just to stroll around the old building with booze in his veins and a new sense of freedom that shot through him like a starting pistol.

One biography on Beethoven particularly interested him, and he became obsessed with the composer's Symphony no. 9, the "Ode to Joy." In particular, he was captivated by the chorale of the final movement in the piece, as it exemplified the enormity of what he first felt walking along the Riverwalk downtown. He gazed at the grandiose buildings, the rising and lowering bridges, and the plethora of people lining the water while in his head he heard the lush arrangements playing out. The books had never been returned to the library, and upon his last check, his late fees were staggering—and embarrassing.

Standing now at the front door of his apartment building and fumbling for his keys, Heald was terrified by the possibility of running into Alice heading in or out, though he wasn't quite sure why. Inside the lobby, he realized that he hadn't picked up his mail in days, but opted to disregard that for now.

The wood-paneled elevator had a mirror in it. Before he hit the button for his floor, he stood staring at his rumpled reflection; he looked run-down and downtrodden. His hair was mangled on one side and his face looked puffy, with dark bags hanging under each eye like mud-slung hammocks. The skin on his face was pale and appeared the color of weak urine and he was in dire need of a shave. Most of all, he looked exhausted, like he'd performed poorly in a long fight.

There had been no sign of Alice anywhere. He entered his stifling apartment and walked over to the two small windows to open them. He placed his bags on the futon and sent a quick text message to his mother and father to let them know that he had gotten back safely and that all was well. Opening his bags to take out his clothes, he found the empty bottle wrapped in a shirt. He studied it for a moment, then reached over into his satchel and took out the unopened pint of vodka he'd bought at the rest stop store. Opening the freezer, he placed the pint next to a cantaloupe that had been frozen solid (the reason for which he could not remember) and took out a nearly full half-gallon of vodka already in there. The little fruit flies that had been swarming around the sink all week had multiplied over the course of the last few hot and sticky days, and he quickly rinsed out a glass and set it on the counter, filling it to the brim with vodka. He drank it without hesitation and exhaled loudly when it was empty. Holding his breath, he opened the refrigerator and took out a plastic bottle of orange juice and took a long gulp, swallowing it hard. The room was still disgustingly hot, and his belly burned with a pleasing sting.

Heald thought about Janice and even considered sending her a message to see if she might be interested in a late-night drink, but decided against it, knowing he wasn't quite drunk or foolish enough to make such a bold move. He stepped toward the window and saw that the sky had cleared, and he decided to drink just a little bit more and go for a stroll down to Millennium Park to sit by the Bean and watch the Saturday evening tourists take pictures along Michigan Avenue before heading back to their hotels. Heald sometimes avoided the north side of the city late at night on the weekends due to the large crowds of young, loud partygoers, opting instead to stay near the Loop and downtown where crowds usually thinned out to nonexistence by midnight. He took a few more drinks and headed out to waste time and try to make sense of things.

* * *

The drunkenness came on strong. At first he thought he might have drunk too much before he left, but he reassured himself that it was fine because he was no longer by his apartment and near easy access to cheap booze. If need be, though, he could always stop in at any bar and order a quick double, even if it was overpriced.

He ambled up the tree-lined trail toward Cloud Gate on Michigan Avenue, still teeming with people, and spotted an open metal picnic table near the Bean where he took a seat. The view from this spot on a warm summer night rivaled any in the city. The Crain Communications

Building, with its unmistakable light-rimmed diamond top, overlooked the whole park. When he sat down hard on the seat, he knew he would have trouble standing if he needed to rise. He watched as groups young and old stood in front of the large bean-shaped sculpture and posed for pictures in the dark, the flashes from their cameras lighting up the area like bolts of lightning with no report. Then he surveyed the buildings around him again, feeling like Augustine of Hippo, and thought about how Chicago was not a city originally built for the young at heart.

St. Augustine held a belief about the cities of the world. Cities, he wrote, were a collection of people assembled together through their shared love of one object. Simply put, there are but two objects of true love within the realm of earth: God and self. Thus, there are only two types of cities: the City of God, built for the sole purpose of His glory and a community of charity, and the City of Man, where sin is abundant and each individual works against one another in favor of their own self-interest. The City of Man, as seen through Augustine's eyes, was Hell on earth.

The Windy City, much like Detroit and other Rust Belt cities, came to be by way of the hardworking people who laid the foundations and assembled the heavy building blocks of the town over a century prior. It was painstakingly put together piece by piece by men with broad shoulders who were bent on planting a stake in the earth that they could call their own during a turbulent time in a country defined by a domestic war, civil strife, and cultural upheaval. Their focus was not on repairing a divided nation pulled apart by conflict, but on establishing something for themselves through hard work. Many different bands of ethnicities bonded and battled over this process. Perhaps not realizing it at the time, they were laying down future roots—blueprints for the generations to come—as these clans would then claim a heritage to the city. Chicago, like other Midwestern towns that had a strong history of industry, had a defined and simple purpose that would serve as its charter into the future.

Sometime in the first half of the twentieth century, cities like Chicago and Detroit became not only places to work and live, but also to play. The business leaders and back-alley hustlers of the Windy City (who could very well have been one and the same) made sure that those who came to the city had every opportunity to stray into whatever fantasy their heart desired. Chicago would no longer just be the "Hog Butcher to the World."

Around midcentury, after decades of boom times in these urban epicenters, white flight gripped cities across the Midwest. Those in the Greatest Generation took their children out to the safety and promised homogeneity of the suburbs, coming back into the urban epicenters only for work and a bit of play on the weekends. As the baby boomers grew up in the second half of the century, they had children of their own, to whom they extolled the passed-down wisdom and celebrated virtues of wide lawns and home ownership, while warning them about the nefarious nature of the concrete jungle. But some of these restless children were not swayed; they saw the tall towers like those of the Second City breaching the horizon from the tops of their backyard jungle gyms and developed a longing to head out from their monotonous environs and into these strangely foreign and exotic oases.

The suburbs and rural areas were old and lackluster to these new generations, while places like Chicago were incapable of growing stagnant, adopting what appeared to be an evolve-or-die mentality. Education was no longer a luxury, and many of these young adults felt sophisticated, educated and worldly beyond the level of their parents and brave in their own right—not of issues concerning the heart, but in the curiosities of the mind.

Heald's head dipped drunkenly, and a small group of people that walked by watched him and whispered to one another. He began to roll over a question that had been stirring in his head since moving to Chicago: Are the relationships between urban and rural environments cyclical? He thought back to the stories his parents told about their decision to move out of Detroit and into the northern suburbia. At the time, the suburban areas offered something that had never been available before outside of rural areas. There was a sense of freedom and a plot of land to safely call your own, freedom from the dangers of a crumbling city like Detroit. But it was also something clean and untarnished, like a newborn child, and where better to raise a child than a newly-constructed suburb that all but had the price tags hanging off the gutters?

But after nearly two generations, the urban cores now seemed to be responding, calling people back. The cycle would continue to rotate as they have throughout history and one side would win out for a while, but people would grow older and needs would change. Heald wondered how long this wave would last.

There were still a lot of people walking up and down the Magnificent Mile at this late hour and Heald figured it must have been because most of them had stayed inside earlier during the rain. If you traveled to Chicago, you wanted your money's worth. He had left the park a few minutes earlier when it closed. He was staggering a bit and decided to make his way through the small crowds and head for the subway.

Heald was unable to shake the fear that he might accidentally run into Janice somewhere in the city, and though he didn't want her to see him as drunk and disheveled as he was, he told himself that she wasn't likely to be alone. Somewhere in the city she was probably walking arm in arm with Miłosz, and they were undoubtedly having a wonderfully sexy time. Then he figured that maybe it would be best to run into her in his current state so that he could face the truth without the shattering realities of sobriety. He would be forced to stomach it like a wild haymaker, and he could flash a toothless drunken grin, bid them a happy life, then walk off into the lake or fall down an open manhole. As he descended the steps down into the subway station, he contemplated a series of other equally hilarious and fitting ways in which he might deal with seeing the two of them.

A train pulled into the Lake station, and Heald decided to take it north to Wrigleyville, hoping to get lost in the sea of bodies for a while. When the train emerged from its subterranean tube and raised back into an elevated line, he could again see the well-lit city and the backs of row homes zip by the windows as he heard the familiar *clank-clank-ka-lank-clank-clank-ka-lank* of wheels spinning upon the track.

Soon the train was pulling into the Addison stop in the heart of Wrigleyville, and he stood, wobbling for a moment, walked over to the doors, and exited. As he stepped onto the raised wooden platform above the street, he thought that he might like to stop at a Cubs bar for a quick drink.

* * *

"Double whiskey," Heald said to no one because no one was listening to him. He thought he had caught the attention of the bartender, but the young man quickly looked away as he spoke. Heald raised his hand in a hailing motion, but to no avail. Perhaps I need to be louder, he thought.

"Double *whiskey*, please, God!"

The bartender looked up, and just as Heald realized that he'd caught his attention, he took a slight elbow to the side from the careless man seated at the bar next to him. The bartender stared as Heald held his side for dramatic effect and shouted once more. "Whiskey!" he yelled and, remembering that he had wanted a double, held up two fingers.

The bartender nodded and finished pouring a beer from the tap. Heald watched him move to the wall behind the counter pooled in the blue and red neon lights of Cubs and beer advertisements. The bartender grabbed a bottle of something fancy that looked expensive and might have even been sealed in wax at some point. He saw the bartender pick up two scotch glasses and set them side by side and began to fill one and then the other. Oh well, thought Heald.

"Here you go," said the man, setting the drinks in front of him. "Or wait, did you just want one? A *double*? Dammit, I thought you might have said double." The bartender had obviously realized that Heald was alone upon getting a closer look at him.

"This'll work just fine," said Heald.

The bartender shrugged.

"All right, it's twenty-one dollars."

"I hate this city," Heald said. He handed the man a five and a twenty.

"What?" asked the bartender, cupping his hand to his ear. Heald found the amount of effort needed to understand someone in a bar tantamount to riding a tandem bike, alone, against hurricane-force winds.

"Ain't it a *great* city!?" yelled Heald. "A *grrreat* city!" He drank both drinks quickly, exhaling loudly then slamming both palms onto the countertop.

"Sure," said the bartender unenthusiastically. "You want change?"

"Yes, I want *change*, but no, I don't need that change," Heald said smiling. "Well, I want that change too, but that's fine. Keep it."

"What?" said the bartender.

"I want *everything* and I want *nothing*, dammit!"

"What?" said the bartender.

"*Hivno*!" yelled Heald, ejecting the foreign word from his mouth with no small amount of spittle.

The bartender squinted at him.

"Good day, ol' bean-dick!" cried Heald as he turned on his heels to head for the door. On his way out, someone wearing a Cubs jersey bumped into Heald, spilling a glass of beer onto him and immediately apologizing, but Heald was already halfway out the door. Heald turned back and flashed a smile, gave a thumbs-up and quietly mumbled *hivno*, then winked at the man.

Heald was carefully jostling up the steps that led to the raised platform of the L station over Addison Street. He took a seat on a bench that gave him a splendid view facing east down Addison toward the lake. Large groups of people teemed on either side of the boulevard. The entire street near Wrigley Field was as bright as it was during the day thanks to all the lights. Heald could feel the warm burn from the whiskey as it settled comfortably into his recesses; it was top shelf stuff. If it weren't for all these people, this might not be a half-bad moment to be alive.

The numbers don't lie, Heald thought as he sat on that bench above Addison. During his time working at the CRCC, he'd learned an irrefutable fact above all others: the population of America was growing at an alarming rate. And it wasn't just in the big cities like Chicago that this was happening, it was happening everywhere—urban areas, rural areas, suburbs—all over. But in a town like Chicago, despite an already massive population, a place where you felt like just a few more couldn't possibly make a difference, you realized that it could.

And Heald Brown was a part of it, too.

When his office sent out the CCM enumerators into the field and they returned with data that proved that the decennial censuses were right, that the numbers were ballooning, no one else in the office seemed to have much of a reaction—not Martha Leifhat or Leeka Johnston or Gilbert Tabin (wherever he might be), and not even Ms. Elina Flohard, the deputy director. The numbers just kept growing and growing, compounding onto every decennial census that had ever taken place. The populations were increasing and the cities and towns around the country were swelling, pushing their very borders and building higher and higher into the skies to accommodate the augmentation.

To many, this might have been seen as a form of progress, as a natural evolution of mankind's relationship to the metropolises that he himself had created, and it very well might have been a harmless thing as such, but to Heald, something about it all felt a little unnatural. In response, he began to wonder just how could humanity, as a concept, flourish amid the density of the bodies in such tight quarters? Heald was a statistic himself, on both sides of the equation: in addition to being one more resident of Chicago, he was another young adult who had abandoned Detroit and added to that city's equally staggering population decline.

Gazing east along the busy street, Heald saw an intoxicated man stumble in front of a taxi barreling down the road. The man was narrowly missed at the last second by what looked to be the grace of some slip in conscious physical reality—as if the cab had simply gone through him. The man jumped back onto the sidewalk alongside his equally oblivious friends, unaware of the apparent phenomenon that had just taken place, and they continued walking toward the lake.

The reports from the field kept coming in day after day. Each morning a seemingly endless series of handcarts wheeled in a surfeit of tightly sealed and highly sensitive TITLE 13 information that was ready to be unbundled and prodded, dissected, and collated. Every afternoon he and his coworkers came to the same conclusion: more and more people were alive. There was also no way to be *absolutely* sure that they were counting them all in the first place, which in itself was a scary thought. Heald suddenly felt a burning desire to know more, to see every bit of TITLE 13 information. He wanted to hold it, pet it, and fan it with colorful plumage...

When he had accepted the job, Heald cared very little how many people were filing into Chicago, the Midwest, or any other part of the country; the natural evolution of a growing population seemed irrelevant. He figured that it was typical, which surely it was, for no more could you control the amount of rain that fell from the sky. And yet despite how much water fell from the sky, the oceans never rose and overtook the lands and floods never came to swallow up the world. Somehow the equilibrium was always maintained. Could the same be said for the proliferating nature of man? Would something down the line return a balance? Or would the country's megacities continue to swell and expand until everything was incorporated? If the relationship between the populations of urban and rural areas was truly a cyclical one, perhaps all of this was moot. But despite a lack of care for such issues when he first started at the census, Heald couldn't help but to be drawn in by it now. These questions took up more and more space in his mind as each new precious box of TITLE 13 information rolled in.

Heald was leaning back against a steel barrier on the platform. The whiskey had hit him hard, and he was fully inebriated. It was sometime in the early morning now and there was still an abundance of people around, but Heald was beginning to believe that this wasn't the only reason why he had started to think about population numbers and the census. There was the obvious thought of having to return to work on Monday, the unknown of that night with Janice and Miłosz the previous week, and how everything seemed to come to a head within the CCM office. It had felt like ages since he had been in that office, but in reality, it hadn't even been two days.

Heald knew that alcohol had been altering his perceptions of time for a while. The whole process was exhausting, and he felt much older than he should have. All he ever wanted when he was drunk was peace of mind, the grace to handle overwhelming anxieties, and the power to overcome insomnia, but with every drink the distance between him and those ambitions grew further apart. The cycle of everything held firm, unbent and unbroken.

The Addison platform was crowded with chatting people in high spirits, though Heald hadn't noticed when they arrived. It was as if they had materialized from some phantom train moments before. Only pockets of consciousness remained, and Heald was too drunk to keep the fabric of reality tightly woven, imagination and fantasy interlacing themselves without order.

Somewhere down the tracks from the north, a dull faint light appeared and gradually morphed into two bright small globes. A train was approaching, and Heald stumbled forward on the platform toward the tracks. Everyone around him kept their feet off the yellow warning strip at the edge of the platform, but Heald was standing on it. He turned and looked at the approaching train—it hadn't slowed down yet. He crept one foot closer toward the edge of the warning track, just before the drop onto the rails. His hands were tucked behind his back and he leaned his head ever so slightly forward. For a moment, he did nothing. Then the sound was deafening, and when he turned to face the train it was nearly upon him. Without another thought, he outstretched his arms behind him and pulled his head back as quickly as he could, and the train went speeding by. Heald took a few off-balance steps back and nearly fell, stopped only by a steel beam against his back. The train slowed to a halt, but his heart continued to race. Scanning the fuzzy faces of the people around him, Heald could recognize that everyone appeared shocked. The doors to the train car opened and people began to file in, one eye on him as they walked past.

* * *

One of the things that Heald valued about riding the L were the automated noises and announcements of the rail system. The regulated series of sounds pertaining to the whole experience gave him a comforting sense of procedure and regularity that he severely lacked in his personal life. Sometimes, when he was quite drunk, he was able to attain an ironic sense of being on a higher plane, somewhere sacred.

At every stop as the doors closed on each of the train cars, a calm and collected male voice announced, "Doors closing," preceded by two reassuring and measured chimes that could easily be mistaken for church bells. It felt good knowing that even from some great distance someone was ensuring that the doors on that car were closing, and this person's only concern was to make sure that the passengers were safe and aware of the closing doors. The entire occurrence, repeated over and over, stop after stop, ride after ride, had become a somewhat religious experience for Heald since moving to Chicago, or as close to one as he could have ever fathomed in his life. This concept was further enhanced by not-infrequent encounters with sacerdotal men in tattered clothes bellowing sermons for the masses about some oncoming doom—these priests of the parochial subway lines in their vestments of torn rags and weather-beaten Bears jackets, preaching to the multitudes who carried on, unwitting parishioners of the Church of the Closing Doors.

Chapter Twenty-One

SUNDAY IS A DAY for rest—a day for deity, divinity, and devotion—a day set aside for moral reflection. However, as Heald awoke that morning, stretched thin and tearing at the seams, he realized that his offering plate was empty. Thousands of Chicagoans would soon be making their way into churches and houses of worship, meanwhile Heald had already devoted much of himself to the tenets of his own life. His faith was unwavering and despite his best efforts, could not be broken.

Somewhere on the other side of the tiny apartment on top of a tall bookshelf, a digital clock showed the time, but Heald was not concerned with that; it didn't really matter what time it was. His only concern was making it to the freezer. He had not eaten since breakfast the day before with his family, but food was no longer on his mind. There was no bread in his Eucharist, only wine, and thus he made his way to the kitchen with great difficulty to take his communion. It would be a long day but it would not feel like it.

All around the city and throughout the world, people were surrounding themselves with the magnificent ambiance of tutelary forces while Heald haunted the space between the four walls of his sepulchral box.

Heald took no calls this day, nor ate any food, nor did he do anything other than make frequent trips between the freezer, the bathroom, and the futon. All thought was eliminated except for that of his hopeless veneration for the madness that swept him up like a babe in its arms, quiet as a setting sun, and carried him off somewhere outside his reality.

Chapter Twenty-Two

ON MONDAY MORNING, the alarm went off as always, and Heald leaped from the futon. His body was weak, and when he made it to his feet he reeled and fell back on the screen within the open window, bowing it out toward the street below. He regained his footing, sat on the sill, and clasped it with both hands. Before he could make it over to shut off the alarm clock, he paused midstride and turned toward the bathroom, lunging at the toilet but not quite making it, vomiting a thin orange liquid into a small pool on the floor. Using the toilet paper left on the roll, he wiped up what little he could and flushed it.

As he walked down the street just outside his apartment, the wind was strong and blowing with his direction, giving him a much-needed push. His legs felt like brittle, hollow twigs beneath him. He stopped briefly on his way to the subway to once again look at the large mural of a woman holding her hands over her eyes and heart. While he faced it, Heald put his own hand over his heart and he could feel it beating with a terrible ferocity. He ignored it and quickened his pace to the station.

During the ride on the subway, he could feel that his tie was too tight. There was nothing new about this, but what did alarm him was the amount of sweat already collecting at the top of his shirt collar, seeping down onto his neck and upper chest. It was hot, and the closed space of the subway car felt like a kiln, but his rate of perspiration was worse than usual. Heald figured that once he got off the train he could catch the cool morning breeze off the river for a few minutes to dry out.

The air off the Chicago River was cool and he stood in the shadow of an enormous skyscraper to escape the sunlight. His suit was damp and needed cleaning, but he hoped that any lingering scent of alcohol was carried off in the breeze. Throughout his time working for the Department of Commerce, Heald had never once called in sick due to his drinking, and he clung to that as a rare point of pride.

For one thing, he never wanted to miss a day that could be spent with Janice at the office—sharing time with her, trying to make her laugh, and just watching her do simple things like filing papers. So long as he still had the physical ability to get up each morning and make it in to see her sitting at her desk, he knew that there would always be some part of him willing to fight to maintain an element of control. Heald realized that they had not spoken since the message he sent about their plans to go out to the Art Institute that night—the thought of which made him stand up straight and loosen his tie just a bit. He wondered if she would be in the office this morning. Then he wondered if Miłosz would be there as well. Knowing that his present condition was not likely to improve, he headed toward the front of the Jomira Transportation Center.

* * *

The codes on the doors had been changed again. It was the first welcome sensation of helplessness that he had felt in some time. He thought about finding a pair of black aviator glasses and standing guard outside of the door, saying nothing to anyone, just watching people approach the door, but he knew that he would be unable to stand on his feet for very long. Plus, the stunt would probably get him cubed. Janice was likely on the other side of the door, and suddenly he wanted to get through without any further hesitation or thoughts of shenanigans. However, the fact remained that the codes had been changed, and he was stuck.

He heard the elevator doors open, and Martha emerged wearing her usual jovial expression. As she approached the door, she recognized Heald, and her mouth abruptly closed and formed into a frown. She walked toward him as one might uneasily approach the scene of an accident.

"Hello, Heald," she said, timidly looking him over. "Is everything all right? I mean, good morning and how are you, of course, but how is your grandmother?"

Heald had been wearing the same stupid smile that he regularly wore around the workplace, but at the mention of his grandmother, his defenses fell.

"Good morning, Martha. She's, um...well, she's not good, to be honest." He thought about how he must look. "I'm afraid I didn't sleep very well over the weekend."

"Oh, I'm so sorry," she said shaking her head.

"I'm also afraid I don't know the new door code," Heald said.

"Oh!" Martha cried moving past him toward the door. "Yes, they changed it again on Friday after you left. The TITLE 13 situation hasn't improved, and security is getting tighter. Everyone is a little on edge, you know?" She began punching the numbers into the coded metal door lock. "It's 3-2-1." She pushed the door open and held it for Heald.

"3-2-1?"

"Yes. I know..."

* * *

Janice was not at her desk, but upon closer inspection, Heald could see a purse on her chair, and his disappointment became elation. Looking over at Miłosz's desk, he could see no personal effects whatsoever. He was thrilled at the prospect of Janice being there and Miłosz not. The feeling was short-lived as he soon saw the short-cropped hair, pale skin, and defined forehead vein of the eastern European making his way into the CCM area. Miłosz was smiling and noticed Heald looking at him, so he waved and smiled some more. Heald grinned and squinted at him.

"I hope your grandmother gets better soon," said Martha behind him. "I'm sorry. I understand if you would rather not talk about it. Just wanted to let you know I was thinking about you."

Heald sat down in his chair.

"No, it's quite all right," he said. "I hope she feels better soon, too."

Martha began to shuffle through a few papers on her desk then reached down into her bag and took out a bagel wrapped in wax paper and placed it in front of her. Heald looked at it and suddenly felt nauseous.

"Is Gilbert back yet? Did he ever come back?"

Martha had picked up her bagel and looked as if she was pondering whether she had time to take a bite before responding. Her expression grew dim as she set it down.

"I'm afraid he's not back yet. It appears that Leeka has taken charge of the office for now."

"They haven't said anything?"

"Nothing is certain."

"Very strange."

"Very strange."

Janice appeared, and as Heald watched her walk to her desk, all his feeling of sickness washed away. For the first time in a long time, he felt at ease. He hoped that she would look over at him, but she did not. Instead, he thought he saw her shoot a glance over to Miłosz, but he wasn't sure. Miłosz was busy with something inside his fingernail. Doubt and unease washed over Heald just as simply as it had left moments before, and he cursed his failure to command even a minor sense of control over his emotions. Janice went right to work arranging files on her desk while Heald sat studying her movements, wishing he was someone else.

"Can you help me pull the Kenosha folders from the cabinet, Heald?" Martha said from behind him. "I think we should start sorting through that."

"Not a problem," Heald replied. He stood onto his weak legs and placed one hand on the desk to steady himself.

"Are you sure you're all right, Heald? Do you need something?"

"No, thank you. I'm fine," he said as he walked over to the cabinets lining the partitions.

* * *

His sense of time was still warped, but being at work, Heald at least felt some sense of routine. He realized, though, that hours must have passed, and he had not seen Janice or Miłosz since that morning. Being shut out gave him full license to fill the blank space with endless ribald details. It all seemed to be happening right there inside the office, and yet, he couldn't confirm what was *really* happening between the two of them. Or perhaps he did know *exactly* what was happening and refused to acknowledge it.

Heald had been poring over the Kenosha files for a while, going through the numbered sheets of TITLE 13 information trying to identify any missing documents. While there was certainly a part of him that wanted to be the one to locate the missing information, he also realized how important it was *not* to be the one to locate it, lest he somehow personally attach himself to this debacle and end up like Gilbert Tabin. If winning a fortune in the lottery was the best of luck and developing some form of inoperable cancer was the worst, then being the one to uncover the whereabouts of the TITLE 13 information had to fall somewhere in between—though with Ms. Flohard being the ultimate arbiter, it was impossible to tell where. It was probably closer to the cancer.

Heald needed water. The walk to the office break room was much more challenging than it should have been, and he was woozy on feet. On the Decennial side of the office, the atmosphere was just as chaotic as it had been the previous week.

At a corner workstation, a short man with a large girth sat at his desk with his white dress shirt sleeves rolled up to his elbows; he was meticulously folding what appeared to be a sheet of aluminum foil into a pyramid. The man looked up and noticed Heald eyeing him from across the open room, then he quickly opened a drawer in his desk and nonchalantly slid the foil object into it. The entire area where the man sat appeared to be suffused with the wavy, shimmering effect of a heat signature.

As if she had emerged from some trap door below him,

Leeka Johnston materialized right in front of Heald as he was watching the other man. She was dressed in a dark gray suit, and her hair appeared to be much larger than it had ever been before. As they crossed paths, Heald said hello, though she either didn't wish to respond or didn't recognize Heald, perhaps not having heard his weak greeting, and continued along her way back to the CCM area. After a couple of steps, Heald turned back to say something else, but she was gone, though there was nothing but open ground in front of her and a large copy machine against a wall. Looking closely, Heald could see that the copy machine appeared to have been moved slightly askew, away from the wall. He looked back toward the large man sitting at his desk, but now he was gone too, and yet Heald still saw the bottoms of two shiny black dress shoes underneath the desk between a small opening and the carpet.

As he entered the break room, Heald could hear Janice speaking. He clung tightly to the wall, back against it, and listened. The break room was separated into two sections: One side was a makeshift kitchen with two microwaves and a sink area, a few cabinets, and a refrigerator, and the other side, separated by a wall, consisted of a larger room with dining tables that Heald had sat at with Miłosz and Janice so many times during lunches. Between the two rooms there was a door, always open, and through that door came Janice's voice. Pressed against the wall, Heald couldn't make out what she was saying. A few words filtered through the jumbled speech: "Cicero...filter...salt... ear makeup ...grandmother." Then he heard her say "Institute."

Was she discussing her evening plans with someone? Or

were they perhaps discussing where they planned to send him after the men with white coats came and took him from his futon? Despite knowing that she was likely sitting alone at a table with Miłosz, Heald decided to enter the dining area and participate in the conversation, if only to understand what was being said.

When he stepped into the room, there was no one there. The tables were clean and empty, except for the one closest to him; upon it sat a single sad orange, long past its prime. Heald bent down to look under the tables and glanced around the corners of the room but found nothing else. The room was silent. He picked up the orange and held it in his trembling hand. He ran his thumb over the pores of the orange's flesh. He palmed it and walked out, refusing an urge to suddenly turn and look back.

Heald had not eaten in days, and his stomach felt tighter than a clenched fist, but as he walked back to the CCM area he found himself digging his thumb nail around the top of the orange, pulling away the peel.

He started to feel sick.

A woman sitting at her desk remarked loudly of the sweet smell of oranges in the air. Heald came to a standstill and turned toward her as she looked around for the source of the smell. When he approached she looked at his hands, noticing the half-peeled orange. She did not say anything else. Heald set the orange down by her hand and leaned against her desk, feeling nauseous. On her desk he noticed a small, unlit candle labeled *Morning Citrus*. Heald picked up the small glass container holding the candle and turned it upside down, letting the short cylinder of orange wax fall into his hand. He set the glass container down, put the sad orange into it, and then walked over to the massive window looking out at the Sears Tower. Putting one hand behind his back, he brought the candle up to his nose so he could smell it. After he had inhaled its aroma, he brought it to his mouth and took an enormous bite out of it, nearly fitting the whole thing into his mouth. He dropped what little remained into a wastebasket next to him.

* * *

Back at his desk, Heald looked over and saw that Janice and Miłosz were still gone. He tried to ignore it and threw himself back into the Kenosha files.

"Hey, Heald," said a voice next to him. Heald looked over the waist-high partition to see Bobert Roberts looking at him in earnest.

"Yes?"

"Were you just in the kitchen?"

"Yes."

"Are there any coffee cups in there still?"

"I don't know. I didn't look."

Bobert slumped back into his chair.

"Shoot. I think someone from the Decennial side must have took 'em all. Maybe knows we're shutting down or something."

"Mergers and acquisitions," Heald said as he turned back to the files and began to count the pages stacked in front of him.

* * *

It was late afternoon, well past lunch, though Heald

hardly noticed that he hadn't eaten because he had become so accustomed to eating with Janice and the others. Without them around, he had disregarded it, though he'd brought nothing to eat anyway. Wendy had been over in Bobert's department diligently working all day, and he'd nearly forgotten that she was a part of the office until he heard her curse out loud at a paper cut. Heald looked at the clock and began to wonder when Janice would be coming back to her desk; he knew she would have to return at some point to pick up her purse before she left.

Heald stood and looked over toward Janice's desk and was stunned to see that the purse was gone. When could she have come back and picked it up? Heald thought, panicked. Where was she? And where the hell was Miłosz? Heald wanted answers. He took out his phone to look for any missed messages, but there were none. He looked over at Wendy.

"Hey, Wendy, have you seen Janice or Miłosz? Did they take off for lunch or something?"

"No, haven't seen 'em," she replied without ever taking her eyes off her work.

Heald looked back at his phone and decided to send Janice a message.

HEALD: Hey there. Where have you been?

Heald sat staring at the phone while minutes went by. Finally, it buzzed.

JANICE: Hi. I've been working in another room with Milo.

HEALD: Just you and Milo?

JANICE: Yes.

HEALD: That's great. So, are we still on to meet tonight for the Art Institute? I'd really like to talk.

Another long pause without a response. Heald began to feel the familiar choking sensation in his throat.

JANICE: OK.

Relief!

HEALD: Great! Looking forward to it. Meet you by the Bean at 7:00?

JANICE: OK.

Chapter Twenty-Three

HEALD WAS TORN.

On the one hand, he desperately wanted to be honest with Janice when they met that night. He wanted to prove that she was more important to him than alcohol, though he doubted she had any real suspicion of his problem beyond their fuzzy night out the previous week. But really, he knew he was actually seeking to prove to himself that there were still things more important to him than drinking. With what willpower he could muster, he intended to focus on the little flames in his life that might be kindled back into purpose.

As he stood in his tiny apartment facing the open window, struggling to remove his tie with quivering hands, Heald could feel the sickness in every tendon of his body. His last drink had been the night before, and the ramifications could be felt all over. The frenetic feeling driven by his rapidly beating heart made his muscles twitch and sent waves of tension through his core. A numb lightheadedness descended from the crown of his head, and he felt like vomiting. Every faculty was compromised.

Heald tried to remember when he had crossed the line. He thought back to the years before his drinking had gotten out of control, trying to recall a point in time when alcohol was not a necessity. Of course, it was impossible to identify when he started to *need* it and not *want* it, for that happens progressively, with no announcement that the shift has been made. Just like a cancer, devoid of fanfare or warning, the sickness did not need an audience.

Bile rose in Heald's throat, choking him, and though he

knew he should eat something, he also knew it was futile to try. Whatever went in at this point would be back out just as fast. Even now, as he thought of Janice and walking through the Art Institute at her side, his mind cried out and pleaded for him to just take one drink—just one glass of vodka, which, if he could keep it down, would end his needless suffering.

There were two choices: fight what was happening and struggle with Janice while sober, or give in and drink to become the calm, relaxed Heald, free of physical and mental complications—a Heald worthy of love. The sunlight shone onto his floor through the window in an elongated square. It was bright on the old, poorly kept hardwood. He took a step toward the light and extended his hand into it like a waterfall of sunrays, casting his shadow onto the wood. There he watched the shadow of his hand tremble ever so slightly, not knowing what to do.

His phone buzzed and he picked it up. There was a message from Alice asking if he wanted to come up for drinks and a movie. As he struggled with his shaking fingers to hit the tiny buttons to write a response, another message simultaneously popped up on the screen. This one was from Janice.

JANICE: Heald, I have to be honest. I don't think it's a good idea for us to meet. Milo and I are together now. I enjoy working with you and you're a good friend, but I'm not interested in anything more than that. I'm only saying this now to avoid a potentially uncomfortable situation at the Institute, but if you'd like to meet just as friends, we can do that. I'm sorry but this is how I feel. I'm worried about you, Heald. Milo is too. If I can help, you know I will.

For a moment, Heald stopped shaking. His head cleared, the confusion dissipated, and all he could feel was the beating of his heart. Then he was outside of himself, hovering, watching from above as if in a dream—the nightmare that he'd had over and over. He tried to float down to see his face, wondering if perhaps it looked as he thought it would when he knew someone had seen through his mask. The Heald who drank to enter a world of plausible deniability left him in that moment. When he returned to himself, standing near that ray of light and holding the phone with Janice's message, he was the Heald he had been actively trying to avoid. It was clear to him then that this was the Heald he was meant to be—shunned, broken, and beaten.

He set the phone down and felt the sickness return. He tried to pinpoint where and when he might have fractured. He thought of his mother, his father, his sister, and his beloved grandmother. Even Alan, his old dog, whose love was so unconditional. How could they care for an abominable thing like Heald? How could so many fundamental elements be absent and still qualify this tainted being as loveable? It was a foolish question to ask, but one that he could not ignore any longer.

This somber line of questioning did make one thing clear: he was tired of it. He was tired of the inquisition, the wondering why, and battling with a faceless monster in his heart. If he was doomed to live within the life of his mind, then he would do so as only he knew how.

Heald was no longer torn. In a small way he was relieved, he told himself, for the decision had been made for him. All roads headed to the same cornered destination. Things were simple.

Heald took the bottle out of the freezer.

* * *

During their first few months with the Department of Commerce, Heald began to understand that there was a lot more to Janice than met the eye. He tried to be the lovable scamp with a sarcastic wit, and while Janice rarely discounted him and seemed to genuinely enjoy his company, no emotional connection developed. Their one-dimensional friendship had stalled over time and Heald had decided to try something new: sincerity. But with financial security, Heald's drinking worsened, and each day he found himself in a darker place, as if he were in a room filled with hundreds of lights that gradually burned out one by one.

While he tried to build the courage to tell Janice how he really felt, he took consolation in nightly drinking and began obsessing over his anxieties and depression. His conversations with Janice adopted a bleak and absurd character, and he watched her push away from him as he slipped further down his own rabbit hole.

Time marched on, and the department progressively descended into chaos as the 2010 Decennial Census operations commenced and extra staff were brought on (including Miłosz). Heald's life mirrored the situation in the office, and his own fate became inextricably tied to that of the census and the TITLE 13 information.

* * *

As he rode on the subway headed for the Art Institute,

Heald couldn't help wondering what his life in this city might have been like if he were not an alcoholic. How different might things have been? It was easy to think about now, since he was quite drunk and all thoughts came with ease, but there was really no conceivable way to answer the question. Drinking was perfect for pondering the difficult questions of life, but it was lousy at solving any of them. Nevertheless, Heald welcomed the barrage of contemplations as a distraction from his obsessive thoughts over Janice and the message she had sent.

Despite Janice canceling on him, Heald decided to go to the Art Institute alone, if only to fill his eyes with other beautiful things. Before leaving, he'd briefly considered heading up to Alice's apartment to accept her offer of drinks and a movie, but the thoughts of her subsequent interrogation and those goddamn cats crawling on his head had been enough to send him out. Art would provide him with all the distraction he needed.

Heald's grandmother was an artist. As a small child, he could remember walking through his parents' house and looking at her paintings, which his mother had hung throughout their home: beautiful landscapes with images of lush trees, mighty rivers, and autumnal forests. She never painted in front of other people, but she had a small art studio on the top floor of her condo that had been converted from an attic space. There she would spend countless solitary hours recreating scenes of nature from recollections of her travels.

Only on a few occasions did Heald ever dare to enter her studio, and it felt like sneaking into a barren church. Something sacred and spiritual happened in there and he knew it; the last thing he wanted was to somehow set askew the delicate energy flowing through that room.

At the same time, the connection that Heald drew between his grandmother and her painting instilled in him a greater respect for art itself. Though he had no artistic talent of his own, he came to appreciate it all the more. After those rare excursions into her studio, he would return home and stare at the paintings on his parents' walls and feel a sense of astonishment as he concentrated on the tiny brush strokes. Regular trips to art museums around Chicago had become a beloved pastime for him, and the Art Institute was his favorite. It was a thrill to get lost in the thought process of art, if only as a respite from his own cyclical depression.

Heald was drunk as he paid for his ticket at the entrance but was admitted without incident. He had become quite good at appearing sober and in command despite being intoxicated. He didn't need to drink to enjoy art, though at this point in his life, he could hardly imagine doing anything other than his job without the aid of booze.

Before visiting any of the galleries, he went up to the second floor, where a small café served hard cheeses, soft cheeses, crusty breads, and, of course, overpriced wine. He took a seat at the counter and ordered a glass of red wine and, as he was already drunk, decided to savor it and take tiny pretentious sips to match the ambiance. Heald drank slowly and thought about the last painting that he had seen of his grandmother's; it was of a spider's web weighed down by morning dew in a maple tree.

After a second glass, Heald thanked the bartender, pushed his seat back, and stood up, sliding his motionless hands into his pockets, and made his way toward the modern art exhibit. Modern art was easy for anyone to understand after a few drinks, he thought. He should have no trouble at all.

Modern art was easy to stomach—it could be processed and freely analyzed without too many preconceived notions as to the specifics of its creation—it just *was*. He loved the florid, curlicue landscapes of impressionists and the deep, robust Carpaccioesque work of the Italian Renaissance, but too often it drove him to be sentimental toward the work and thoughts of his grandmother. For now, he thought, it would be best to stick with the deceptively simple modernists.

Heald made his way from piece to piece through the modern exhibits, giving each just enough time to be superficially assessed before moving on to the next. There were two paintings that were part of the Art Institute's permanent collection that he made sure never to miss, though both could easily be considered "touristy." He didn't mind that, though, and gave himself over to them, hoping to find something new and hidden each time he visited.

The first was *Nighthawks* by Edward Hopper, and he found it with ease. Heald never bothered to read others' explanations of the piece. Instead, he opted to just see what he saw and draw his own conclusions. As he looked at the painting now, the lone man at the counter in a clean, fine-pressed suit and neat fedora seemed to be lightly eavesdropping on what the picturesque couple might have been saying to the attendant next to them. Perhaps the attendant was busy under the counter preparing something for them—maybe a single milkshake with two straws? As Heald studied the painting more closely, he put himself into the position of the solitary man sitting alone opposite the couple, listening to the man and woman describe how they first met, when they knew that they were right for each other, and what plans they held for the future. All the while, the man sat with nothing more than a cup of coffee, his own future plans consisting of nothing beyond the next hour.

Heald was done looking at this painting.

American Gothic, by outward appearances, was a simple painting much like *Nighthawks*. It was Grant Wood, a Midwesterner, who had created this seemingly unassuming slice of Americana that portrayed a man and woman in front of a rustic and equally unassuming farmhouse. But as Heald looked deeply at the painting, far into the unnamed man's eyes, it became clear to him that there was something more happening there. This was a man, Heald thought, who had want for nothing, and yet gave off the impression that somewhere along his path in life, something had gone awry, or had been left unsaid, and all that was left to do was settle with the consequences. A painting can mean something different to each person who sees it, but for Heald, this man—with his worn overalls and best country jacket, accompanied by his trustworthy pitchfork—had something to hide, something that lightly warned you to only take a quick glance and then softly step back and turn away, lest you come too close to whatever secret he was silently guarding.

Heald had to continually readjust his focus, blinking often, for his drunkenness had now gotten the better of him. His gaze was drawn back to the old man's eyes. Perhaps this Midwestern man was once like the solo Nighthawk—a city-dweller just hoping to find someone to share his life with, a man who gave it all up and abandoned that life to start something new on a farm with someone he thought was special. And perhaps once this man had all the things he thought his heart desired, he found there was still a part of him that hurt, that was left yearning, and he took that part of him and locked it away deep within a wooden box in the cellar of the home that stood behind him. Now he was forever on guard, always ready to turn away those who would come to investigate and discover his secret box, the sadness that was gradually killing him. The woman by his side, meanwhile, might mean nothing to him at all.

* * *

Heald was outside now and it was late. He looked around at the giant metal people locked in place around him in the dark. Dozens of them, perfectly still in midstride, towered over him, headless and hollow. Plenty of Chicagoans say that the *Agora* figures in Grant Park give them the creeps, but there was nothing actually menacing about them.

In a city full of real people, some with real intentions to hurt and maim and kill, the colossal men of this installation meant no harm. The fear that they sparked was meant to trigger a sense of agoraphobia, to make the individuals walking through them feel acutely aware of their unique and sometimes uncomfortable social setting in the city. They reminded people of the strangeness of being human.

Chapter Twenty-Four

HEALD SAT AT HIS DESK. On an average morning, he suffered minimal hangover symptoms from the previous night's drinking, something that heavy drinkers will tell you is one advantage to a body's acclimation to excess drinking...save for possible withdrawal, of course. But this was not an average morning.

Many of the physical ailments Heald now felt were caused by what he could only assume were the effects of chronic alcoholism. The lower half of his ribcage on his right side felt strange. That spot felt strange when he was sober, too. There was no pain, but definitely a feeling of something foreign within him, as if a surgeon had come one night after he passed out on his futon, opened him up, and placed a lump of clay inside him, perhaps just for a laugh, turning to the attendant beside him in the dark apartment, saying "Let's see what this bastard thinks of this" before they closed him up.

The shaking in his hands and extremities, the dizzy spells, the sudden choking sensations, and rapid heart rate all made him feel ready to leap from his chair at any moment. Heald knew that he hadn't been as aware as he might have wished while these symptoms had crept up over the past few years. Then again, he thought, it wasn't like hitting a light switch; evolution itself, as a model, takes millions of years to play out. The whole process of Heald's descent into alcoholism was not revolutionary, it was evolutionary. Each day, one slight mutation at a time, his body adapted to changes in an effort to help his mind survive the shifting ecosystems and perceived threats around him.

Janice was there somewhere, for Heald had seen her at her desk when he'd walked in that morning with a throbbing headache. She had watched him as he made his way to his desk, and her face appeared to display of concern, a pleading for absolution. More than anything, he figured she wanted him to let her know that everything was all right, that it was all fine, though Heald was unwilling to give that to her.

At first, he wondered if he was intentionally looking to make her suffer for his own satisfaction, taking joy in her concern, but he discovered that he took no such pleasure. Where a reservoir of emotion should have been within him, Heald instead felt nothing, and this unsettled him. Thus, Heald had avoided Janice most of that morning and kept to his desk, running through the motions of feigning solicitude for the still-missing TITLE 13 information.

It was Tuesday morning, nearly one week since Deputy Director Elina Flohard had announced to the office that thirty-seven pages of the highly classified material had disappeared. Though the office had been turned upside down, it appeared that no one was any closer to locating it. As the previous week had progressed, tensions had risen throughout the floor, but Heald had paid it little mind. Too much had been happening in his own life for him to care, though he had worked hard to move his thoughts away from his own personal concerns. They were still present somewhere in his mind, like the lump in his ribcage, a reminder of something yet to come, yet pushing those thoughts away opened a blank space, and there he actually began to focus on the TITLE 13 issue. He still didn't really *care* about it, but the more he considered it, the more he felt that *something* was there.

Every so often Heald would look up and see Janice looking at him. Each time, he insouciantly met her gaze and then went back to the item he was working on. Shortly before lunch, when he was feeling even worse physically, Heald went over to Ramone to ask him about one of the files that had come in for inspection from a region in northern Wisconsin. Ramone leaned back in his chair as far as it would allow, inserted his thumb into his belt by maneuvering it under his heavy paunch, and smiled. After Ramone faced him, Heald saw the man's smile promptly fade as Ramone assessed him up and down.

"Ramone?" said Heald. "I said, do you know which field office this file came back from? The line on the form is blank."

Ramone was not listening.

"Ramone."

Ramone didn't move, keeping his expression still. "Heald, you all right, son?"

Heald furrowed his brow. "Yes, I'm fine. Do you know which office this came from? Was it Superior?"

"Heald..."

"Yes?"

Ramone let a soundless moment pass between them as he kept his focus on Heald's face. Heald took a small step back, ready to return to his desk.

"Heald, normally I can turn at just about any time and look out that great big window there and see many strange things: shapes, colors, faces, whatnot, all on the buildings just out there, popping up all over downtown. But right now, that's not what happened. Right now...right now I'm seeing all the strangeness on you...on your face."

* * *

It was almost noon. Again Heald had not packed a lunch, for he had no appetite. Janice still seemed to be keeping a watchful eye upon him. He knew that at any moment, if things were to maintain some semblance of normalcy, Janice would head over to both him and Miłosz and ask them to break for lunch. Heald knew this was coming, and he dreaded the very thought of it.

Right as the clock ticked noon, Heald could feel his throat tighten. He watched as Janice reached down for her bag and walked casually away from her desk. Heald avoided eye contact and did not look over to Miłosz, who had been moving around the office in a flurry all day. Out of the corner of his eye, Heald could see that Janice had turned down his row and was making her way to his desk. The shapeless mound lodged at the top of his throat, and he was unable to swallow.

She stood directly in front of his desk, but he was too timid to look up, hoping she might just see this broken thing in front of her and turn away.

"Heald."

He looked up, pretending that he had just noticed her.

"Janice," he said, swallowing hard. "How are you?"

"I'm fine. Heald, can we talk?"

"Um, now? Sure."

"Can we go for a walk? We can eat downstairs or something and just talk," she said, holding her purse in front of her at her waist. "Did you pack a lunch?"

Heald looked at his desk.

"I forgot it," he said.

"Well, what are you going to eat?"

"I'm not hungry."

"If you want, we could go downstairs and get something to eat from the cafeteria."

"I'm all right. Big breakfast."

She rested her purse on the edge of his desk, still clutching it.

"Can we go talk now, Heald?"

"All right."

* * *

They didn't walk too closely, though it didn't appear that they were trying to keep their distance. They had taken the elevator down in silence and were strolling slowly along the second floor among the shops and restaurants. Heald thought back to making this same trek with Janice just a few days prior, in an entirely different world.

The crowd was generally a business-themed one. Among the many fast food joints and places to eat was a small bar whose main clientele were sports fans and business people who stopped in for a drink or two before boarding their train back home to the suburbs—one last taste of the city before heading out. Walking past the bar now with Janice, Heald had wondered how he had ever been able to ignore it for so long, never stopping there for a drink. As they pushed their way through the crowd of professionally dressed men and women, he wanted nothing more than to lose Janice among the sea of people and covertly sneak into the bar, hiding at the far end of its long, poorly lit counter.

"Let's go outside," Janice said.

Heald nodded.

It was warm but pleasant outside. The bright sun reflected off the Chicago river just outside the doors of the building's east exit. The red River Center building, with its bold white lettering at the top, resonated in the sun across Washington Boulevard. The loud noise from the people inside the Jomira Transportation Center was replaced by the general ambient noise of the city itself: cars honking, a musician playing a brass instrument on a corner somewhere, high notes reverberating through the building corridors, and always the sound of a police or fire siren off in the distance. If you didn't listen for it, though, Heald told himself, you might not hear it. If you live downtown long enough, the subtle sounds do become lost in contexture, a part of the city-living experience. He tried desperately to listen for any other sounds he might have become too accustomed to. Anything.

They were in the massive courtyard of a neighboring building now, just along the river. All around were benches surrounding small trees and centerpieces of little bushes and flowers, everything else straight, clean concrete. Some of the benches held people reading books or newspapers with sack lunches next to them. On other benches, couples sat and chatted, one sometimes laughing while the other smiled and leaned forward, others turned to face each other, one arm over the backrest of the bench, buried deep in a conversation. They walked a bit more and Janice turned toward an open bench, looking back to make sure that Heald was following her. They sat side by side without saying anything at first. Then Janice spoke while still looking forward.

"I'm sorry that I canceled on you last night."

Heald was also looking ahead.

"Oh, that's all right."

"Were you disappointed?"

"Not really. I ended up going anyway."

Janice didn't respond for a moment, then turned toward him.

"I don't even know why I asked that," she said. "Of course you were disappointed. I'm sorry if I made you feel bad, but I did what I felt I needed to. Sometimes it can be hard to just be honest with people."

"It's fine."

"I think it's clear you know how hard it can be to be honest with people."

"Sure."

"Heald..."

Heald paused.

"I wouldn't say it's any harder for me than it is for the next person," he said.

"Heald," Janice began, "I know it'd be easier to be honest if I had given you the answer that you wanted, but that doesn't mean that you need to shut down to me and the rest of the world. I know quite well that there are different sides to you, as there are to me, but I also know that behind that sarcastic and boyish exterior, even behind this quiet and reserved person that you're being right now, there is someone else in there, back in the recesses, who spends a lot of time in isolation, weighed down by a lot of cumbersome thoughts." She paused. "Am I right?"

Heald didn't say anything.

"Being honest isn't a curse, Heald. Holding the significant things back doesn't guarantee safety. In fact, it can often suffocate us and lock down these emotions and brick them up. You're not alone. You know that. I think you're smart enough to know that."

"I don't know about that, Janice," Heald said. "You'd be surprised. I have a machine that ties my shoes for me each morning before I go out the door."

Janice waved her hand at Heald.

"There. Right there," she said. "*Who* is that? Who just said that?"

"You know who said that."

"Sure, *I* know who said it, but do *you*?"

"I know who said it."

"Do you know why you said it?" she asked.

"I have a strong inclination, yes."

"And why is that?"

Heald didn't respond. Janice looked forward and leaned on her elbows.

"I often fear I'm going to end up alone, Heald," she said. "I can't tell you exactly why I feel most comfortable with Miłosz right now, because I'm not entirely sure I know. But when I'm with him, I feel good, and when we're together, I don't feel like there's something being left unsaid or some great unknown thing lurking around behind him. I'm not saying that I, or someone else, can't feel that same way with you, but with you being who you are at this point in your life, I can't convince myself that that isn't a valid concern.

I'm not saying you're a bad person or anything like that, just that those who really know you, which I'm guessing isn't too many people, might be alarmed by what they see if they're being perceptive. There's nothing inherently wrong with you, Heald, but for those who try to get close to you, you are an incredibly complicated person, and not in an appealing way. It's frustrating, really. Someone may want to be with you, and as soon as they draw near, they find that you've suddenly constructed a wall in their path after already lowering the gate." She paused again and turned her gaze back at Heald, who was looking down at the cement. "Does that make sense to you?"

"Yes. It does."

"Why does that happen?"

"Probably because I feel similar to the way you do about certain things."

"As in a fear of ending up alone?"

"More as...fear in general."

"Fear of what?"

"Everything. There's only two ways of dealing with fear. You allow it to become all-consuming, crippling and paralyzing you into submission, or you wander aimlessly through the minefield, laughing hysterically as you go while each step seems to come closer and closer to triggering an explosion."

"And which one is your plan?"

"I tend to dabble in both."

Janice let out a low, sighing laugh. "I *knew* you'd say that," she said.

"You seem to know a lot about me," Heald said, putting

his hands in his pockets and leaning back.

"Maybe. Maybe not," she said. "Tell me: how do you get away with subscribing to both methods? Seems like one would take precedence over the other at some point."

"I don't do it alone," he replied.

They sat as two pigeons walked near their feet, bobbing their heads forward and back in rhythm, pecking at the ground occasionally.

"The alcohol?" said Janice.

Heald closed his eyes and gripped his thighs through the lining in his pockets.

"I'm sorry if that's forward, Heald, it's just...my uncle was an alcoholic. He lived with my family for a while. It doesn't take long to know that someone is a problem drinker, though I knew about him before he moved in with us. I guess, actually, maybe because I knew beforehand, spotting the signs became routine. The shaking, the strange behavior, the deflection of personal conversation or reluctance to be honest. Of course, the smell, too. He was an angry drunk, yelling and throwing fits, but you don't seem like that. You're more of a sad drunk, aren't you? It makes you what you are."

The pigeons flew away and they were alone.

"That night last week when we all went out and I saw you drink, it finally clicked," she said. "Am I making you uncomfortable?"

Heald didn't speak, just kept his eyes closed and shrugged a bit.

"Well, I'm sorry if I am, but if we're going to be honest here, we might as well be honest."

"All right," Heald replied.

"Why do you drink? Is alcohol your safety net? Your guard against emotion?"

"I think it's my brick and mortar against reality."

"Does it protect you from getting too close to people?"

"I don't know, to be honest," he replied. "I didn't have a problem getting close to people until I got too close to myself at some point. Examine any structure too meticulously and you're sure to find some cracks in the foundation." He brought his hands out of his pockets and crossed his arms in front of his chest. "What's your crutch? Where do you hide?"

Janice didn't say anything for a moment and then looked up high, up toward the top of the Jomira Transportation Center.

"I think I seek out a relationship when I get too insecure. When the fear of being alone—of being alone *forever*—when that fear grows to be too much, I think I try to get involved with someone to let a little of that pressure off myself."

She looked over at Heald, and for the first time since they had sat down, the two looked at each other.

"Wow," Janice said, shaking her head. "It's weird when it all comes out simple like that, when you just decide to tell the truth. I can't believe I just said that." She smiled. Then her expression turned inquisitive. "Do you think Milo is a good guy?"

Heald exhaled loudly, slumping his shoulders, and put his palms on his knees.

"I do," he said. "A bit unusual, definitely a foreigner, but yeah. He seems like a good guy."

"Right," she said, smiling again. "Lots of foreign guy stuff."

"And that vein in his forehead," Heald said while pointing to his own forehead. "Don't forget about that thing. I'm worried about that thing."

"Yes," she said and chuckled. "That poor, poor thing."

Heald still had his hand by his forehead and they looked at it simultaneously, as it was trembling freely. Heald brought his hand down and put both back into his pockets.

"How bad is it, Heald?"

Heald turned his face away from Janice.

"It's not that bad," he said. "Please, really, don't worry about me. I'm fine."

"Honestly?"

"Honestly."

They sat quietly in the ambiance of the city. Heald still had his hands in his pockets. Through a short decorative gate, they could see the shimmering Chicago River flowing effortlessly along just on the other side. Looking down at the water, Heald could see a row of kayakers paddling by.

"Can I ask you something, Janice?"

"Sure," she replied.

"Can you tell me what happened to your uncle?"

She took her eyes off Heald and focused them on the river. Heald could tell through the subtle but increasingly steady movements in Janice's chest that her breathing was becoming more rapid. She kept her hands on the purse in her lap and gripped the cloth straps. She blinked a few times, and it was obvious that her eyes were becoming glassy. She continued to look away from Heald.

* * *

Back at his desk, Heald felt tired. When they had gotten back to the office, Janice had offered Heald some of her lunch, which she said she was just going to eat at her desk. Heald politely declined and realized that it was true: he wasn't hungry. Despite not having eaten for several days, all he felt was tight sensation in his stomach that he knew would not allow the passage of anything solid. A deep, resonating ache bloated from his core and met halfway with the foreign lump in his ribcage. The choking sensation had returned as well.

Heald felt weak all over, bathed in an incredible amount of sweat that was lining the tip of his collar.

"Heald?" He was startled by a voice from behind him. He turned around in his chair as he wiped his brow with a trembling hand, sweat dripping into his eye. Martha was looking at him from her workstation with a stern yet concerned expression.

"Is everything all right?" she asked.

"I think so," he replied. "Why do you ask?"

"Well," she said, looking back at her computer screen, "I just got the strangest email saying that you will be 'collected' and brought to have a private meeting with Ms. Flohard. Do you know anything about that?"

"Really?" Heald asked almost too casually, knowing that he should be alarmed. "No, I can't say that I know what it's about. I haven't heard anything. Does it say anything else?"

"I'm afraid not."

"Hmm."

"Do you have anything that you want to share with me?"

asked Martha.

Heald's eyebrows arched.

"I certainly wish I did, Ms. Leifhat." It was the first time that Heald had formally addressed his supervisor since his first day in the office when she'd assured him that it wasn't necessary.

The wind was blowing hard outside on the great windows lining the office now, and they were shuddering slightly with the pressure. Martha's gaze shifted to stare at something directly behind Heald, her eyes going wide. Heald heard nothing but knew there was someone standing there.

He turned.

In front of his desk was a large man in a black suit whom he had never seen before. The man's face and posture were devoid of emotion, though he seemed saturated with purpose. The man held his hands together in front of his waist, and where his mouth should have been, there seemed to be only a slight crease surrounded by a smooth and hairless surface, as if not a bit of stubble had ever grown there. The man looked straight ahead, out the window and over the city, despite now personally addressing Heald.

"Ms. Flohard is here to collect you for your private meeting with her in her office," said the man.

Heald looked around cautiously.

"She's here? Where?"

"To collect you," the man said again.

"She's here?" Held repeated.

"In her office," the man said.

Heald looked back at Martha and could see she was filled

with terror. His own expression was one of puzzlement.

"Is this really happening?" he said quietly to Martha, but there was no response. She didn't move. The window behind her rattled.

"All right," Heald said, turning back to the man. "Just one moment."

Heald reached toward the front of his desk and picked up the framed picture of his dog with the inscription written on the back. He removed the cardboard backing from the frame and took out the photo, folding it in half and slipping it into his inside jacket pocket. Then Heald stood up, and the man slowly began to lead him away.

Before he left, Heald turned back to Martha and leaned in close over her desk. The window rattled as he spoke.

"I have a feeling I'm about to get a lot smaller."

Chapter Twenty-Five

TRANSCRIPT OF MEETING BETWEEN MS. ELINA FLOHARD AND MR. HEALD BROWN

JULY 20, 2010

FLOHARD: Mr. Brown, thank you for coming in here today.

BROWN: I have to admit, I'm puzzled as to why I'm here.

FLOHARD: And why is that?

BROWN: Well, to be honest, I assume I'm here, or was brought here, to discuss the missing TITLE 13 information. I should tell you, though, I don't know where it could be. I'm just a clerk.

FLOHARD: I think that's a perfect reason for us to have a conversation.

BROWN: What is?

FLOHARD: You just being a clerk, of course.

BROWN: If anything, I believe that would only reinforce the fact that I don't have the type of clearance to know what might be going on, or where the missing TITLE 13 information could be.

FLOHARD: Oh, I know where the missing TITLE 13 information is.

BROWN: Oh good. So long, then.

FLOHARD: Have a seat, Mr. Brown. You see, the problem is not that I don't know where the TITLE 13 information is, it's that I don't have it.

BROWN: I see.

FLOHARD: Do you?

BROWN: I do.

FLOHARD: Do you?

BROWN: I do not.

FLOHARD: Perhaps you don't. Allow me to illuminate you. You see, the missing information is not here.

BROWN: Right.

FLOHARD: But it should be.

BROWN: But of course.

FLOHARD: So what we have here is a fundamental breakdown of the system.

BROWN: I would say that was obvious.

FLOHARD: Why would you say that?

BROWN: I don't know.

(PAUSE)

FLOHARD: Your hands are shaking, Mr. Brown.

BROWN: Hyperthyroidism.

FLOHARD: You're perspiring. Why are you perspiring, Mr. Brown?

BROWN: Salt. I must need sodium.

(PAUSE)

FLOHARD: Do you want to know what I think is going on here?

BROWN: I think I do.

FLOHARD: Thirty-seven pages of highly classified material have gone missing. At some point, I'm willing to bet that that information, or some of it, may have been in your hands. Show me your hands again. (PAUSE) Yes, those hands have touched TITLE 13. I think at some point that highly classified and secretive information somehow became a part of you. At some point, you yourself became TITLE 13 information.

BROWN: Of course.

FLOHARD: So you don't deny it?

BROWN: How could I deny it?

FLOHARD: And why would you?

BROWN: Precisely.

FLOHARD: So you see, I have a problem here. You are my nadir. My harbinger of doom. For myself, this office, and everything else, you are the apogee of destruction. You are the spark between two atoms that triggers the mushroom cloud. I'm going to need it back.

BROWN: Tell me, Ms. Flohard, is this real? Is this happening?

FLOHARD: The stars are not just for you.

BROWN: So I am death personified?

FLOHARD: Not entirely, for it goes on, but for you yourself, yes.

BROWN: I already knew that.

FLOHARD: But of course.

BROWN: I take it with me, don't I?

FLOHARD: Of course you do. Speaking of which...

BROWN: Right. Is it this door over here?

FLOHARD: That's the one.

(END OF TRANSCRIPT)

Chapter Twenty-Six

THE SUBWAY WAS SWELTERING. Heald could feel sweat cascading down him as if from a busted faucet. He reached into his jacket pocket to ensure that the photo of the dog was not getting wet, then he patted it through the outside of his suit jacket, as if to reassure himself that it was still there.

Heald accidentally bumped a man's arm when he reached for his pocket, and the man glared at him. Heald wanted to look away, but instead he returned the gaze with a concentrated intensity, contorting his face as much as he could, giving off a comically horrific expression. Normally, Heald might have assumed that the man was eyeballing him because of the government identification tag that regularly hung from his neck, but Heald was not wearing the tag. To the glaring man, and everyone else on the train, Heald was just another guy in a wet suit.

Heald's phone vibrated in his pocket.

It was a message from Janice, asking him what had happened and where he had gone. He did not know how to respond. Heald thought about what he felt had happened, but couldn't quite understand it, nor was he able to make any sense of it, so he left Janice's message alone and sent no response. Putting the phone back into his pocket proved to be a frustrating task, as his hands were shaking uncontrollably and the pocket seemed smaller than before. With each moment that passed, he felt increasingly dizzy and more bewildered. He was nauseated. Heald listened to the electronic bells chime over the speaker and heard a transcendent voice announce that his stop was next.

Walking up the steps to the street level at the Clark & Division stop, Heald marveled at how quickly the sky had changed. Before he had entered the train station, he thought he remembered a bright light above him, though he had no physical memory of any such thing. The air was unexpectedly cool and moist, and the ominous smell of rain was everywhere. Overhead, dark gray clouds amassed into one long, overstuffed group that looked like a giant ball of soiled cotton.

Gloomy weather always felt like good thinking weather to Heald—the dark atmosphere providing the perfect ambiance for avoiding distraction, allowing a person to focus on their thoughts. Sunshine and clear skies made it too easy to get lost in a simple idea.

The city itself could no longer be felt or experienced for what it was: a living and breathing entity. Heald only looked at it now like a painting and picked it apart for its positive and negative qualities. Instead of trying to explore its secrets, all his attention was trained upon what could be seen with a wide-angle lens, disregarding belief for what could be passed off as reason and reality. Chicago had defined life for Heald, but it was no longer the wild and exciting force that had drawn him there. Years ago, the thought of subway rides through a major urban thoroughfare felt like an exploration of culture, but now, looking at it sober, it was just a sticky, smelly way to get from Point A to Point B. The magic was gone, and Heald struggled with the thought of whether it had naturally eroded over time or he had willingly abandoned it. Somewhere over the lake the sky boomed.

Outside of his apartment building, the newspaper man Heald had become well acquainted with over the last few months stood teetering on both feet, calling out to those who passed him by. It had been a week since Heald last saw him working there on his usual corner.

"Boss man," the man said. "There's the Boss man. How you doin' today, Boss?"

Heald walked up to him with both hands in his pockets.

"I'm fine today, Charlie. How 'bout yourself?"

"Charlie? Sheee-it, man, I look like someone named Charlie to you?" He laughed with deep rasp.

"Do *I* really look like a boss man?"

"You sure does in those threads, my man. How 'bout you buy a paper?"

"Sure, Charlie," said Heald as he reached into his back pocket to pull out his wallet. He held out his hand with the cash to give to the man. His hand was shaking badly. Heald looked up at the man's face and could see he was no longer smiling. Heald pushed the money into the man's hand and took his paper.

"How's things in Boss Land, Boss man?"

"I can't lie to you, Charlie, things are strange."

"It's a bad world if you let it be, Boss man."

Heald opened up the paper and leafed through it. Thunder rolled through the chasm of the tall buildings and echoed down the streets.

"Anything in here about the weather?"

"Man, you don't need no paper to know what the sky's aiming to do." He pointed to his own eyes. "These the only weatherman you need."

Then the man looked up.

* * *

The apartment was boiling hot, so Heald opened the window to let the cool air in. After that, his next thought went to the freezer, but he diverted his attention to removing his suit. With his unsteady hand, Heald attempted to undo the knot of his tie, but after a minute or so of fumbling with it, he loosened the noose with a great tug of both hands and pulled it violently over his head, popping a button on his collar and ripping part of the shirt. Heald threw the tie into the open closet and began to remove his jacket with the same vigor when he felt the photo in the front breast pocket. He took it out and unfolded it, the inscription on the back now facing him: *Respice post te! Hominem te esse memento! Memento mori!* Heald turned the photo around and looked at the triumphant smile on the dog's face. He sat gazing at it, trying to steady his hands so he could hold the photo still. He placed it on the small end table near his futon to better look at it, dog and owner face-to-face.

When he was growing up and getting older as a teenager, heading off to college and accepting more responsibility, Heald sometimes thought about how Alan's only concern was to make sure that she gave as much love as she could. A dog only got hurt if its love was repudiated, intentional or not, though it never had long to feel true sorrow in response because it never held its love back, regardless of reciprocation; the dog just tried to love you more. No other distractions such as work, home, friendships, or lovers—just the insistence of undying and unwavering affection in the truest sense of the word—asking for only a fraction of what it gave.

It was an existence that Heald envied and admired, and it only weighed on him more when he considered the rare and undeniably questionable gift of knowing that he would die—that he was mortal. A dog could only embrace love absolutely, without hesitation, and could devote itself to it with complete and unabashed abandon, for the world was forever.

Heald lay on the futon, closed his eyes, and tried to think of anything through the dizziness and confusion that might distract him from his shaking and withdrawal, anything that would not remind him that what sat in the freezer just a few feet away could make it all go away.

* * *

The phone continued to buzz occasionally on the countertop in the kitchenette. He figured that Janice had been checking in on his whereabouts, but he didn't quite feel like responding or even inquiring into whatever it was, for he didn't feel obligated to. Instead, Heald had spent the last few hours lying quietly on his futon trying to distract himself from the incredibly powerful urge to walk over to his freezer and pour himself a drink. With just one, maybe two drinks, Heald told himself, his head would return to normal, and he'd be able to get a grasp on what was happening around him. With any luck, his insides might settle as well.

For these past few hours, Heald's head had throbbed with a pressure that felt like a zip cord had been tightened around his skull. There was a dizzying sensation that made looking around the room feel intensely nauseating. Closing his eyes produced the same horrible reaction, only more intensely and with a claustrophobic element to it, like being placed into a spinning sack and dropped into water. He focused on the exposed pipe in the top corner of the ceiling. The pipe had been painted over with the same cream-colored paint of the walls and ceiling and looked to be wrapped with what was some type of fire-retardant padding that was surely packed with hazardous materials. As he sat there looking at the pipe, he imagined the asbestos particles raining down on him and a lawyer somewhere far away adding his name to some mesothelioma class-action lawsuit.

Heald kept his left hand over the right side of his chest just at the bottom of his ribcage. Right behind those ribs, sat the clump of clayish doom, hardened and tough, as if it had been baked and allowed to cool inside him. It still didn't hurt, or even ache, just made itself known, a constant reminder that Heald was feeding something malicious inside of him, giving purpose to a thing whose sole animus was his destruction.

He wondered what it would be like to have mesothelioma, though he knew it was unlikely to ever happen. He tried closing one eye to see if that would help with the nausea. He lay there with one hand over his chest and one over his eye.

The pains in Heald's stomach were very real. He was well aware that he had not eaten in days. Though he felt no pang of hunger, he knew he'd be best served by trying to eat something.

Despite his near-comatose state, Heald's heart felt as if it were beating one thousand times per minute, pumping blood into the far reaches of his body and awakening every part of him with signals of alertness and desperation the likes of which he had not felt before. His brain commanded that he get up and take his medicine. His body was depleted of nutrients, and despite his desire to remain still, he began to rise utilizing very carefully orchestrated movements.

Before he had completely stood up straight, Heald felt violently ill. He flung himself onto the cracked tile floor at the foot of the toilet, heaving up empty pockets of foul air and globules of spit. After a few dry heaves, he actually felt better, a wave of relief flooding over him. When he was done hugging the porcelain seat, Heald decided that it was as good a time as any to try to get some food down. The orange-tinted spit and bile circled at the bottom of the bowl as he flushed.

He crouched and peered into the fridge, rejuvenated, perhaps even a little hungry. On the bottom shelf, near an unopened case of dark beer (he rarely drank beer by himself anymore), was a small, lunch-sized container of crackers, deli meat, and cheese. He took this out, along with an oft-ignored plastic bottle of mustard, and made his way back to the futon, collapsing with emphasis.

Heald peeled off the top plastic, picked up one of the crackers, and held it in his hands, watching it shake in his grasp, then reached into the container to peel off a piece of the pre-sliced cheese from the block. When the cheese was free, he placed it onto the cracker, though it was slightly askew. Heald tried to right the cheese, concentrating on his movements, but the one hand seemed to be unwilling to cooperate with the other, like two squabbling siblings. He reached for a small slice of meat and had similar problems.

Heald blinked, trying to clear his blurred vision. Frustrated, he dropped the tiny stack of food onto the table and picked up the mustard, popping open the cap to reveal a crust that Heald could not flick off, so he squirted it, crust and all, onto the tiny sandwich. He picked up the uneven stack of food and quickly pushed it into his mouth, smearing his lips with mustard.

Heald chewed, feeling the dry, brittle crunch of the cracker and the cold, slimy texture of the meat and cheese. Heald imagined chewing on an old, waterlogged piece of wood with a dead beetle on it might be similar. He swallowed and awaited the results. When nothing happened, he assembled and ate a few more.

Before he had even finished eating, he knew he would be sick again. Back at the foot of the toilet, he managed to get most of it out of him but felt too faint to stand after the second purge, so he crawled on his hands and knees out of the bathroom and back toward the futon. He rolled his body up onto it and onto his left side, careful not to disturb the clump of *thing* under his right ribs, and focused on the back cushion now facing him.

It was late and the sky outside was dark as a steady rain continued to fall across the city, interspersed with light cracks of thunder and strobes of lightning. He knew if he turned himself around and looked out his window, he would see light filling the apartments in the building across from his. The lights in his apartment were off, and would stay that way, as he needed to sleep.

* * *

Heald had been lying on the futon on the edge of sleep

for about an hour when the steady shaking gave way to periodic spasms that jolted him into full consciousness. The quick, sporadic movements startled him, and after a time, he turned onto his back so that he might stop staring at the cushion and instead look up at the ceiling; it appeared faintly red with the street light pouring in through the window from the world outside.

His mind raced while random thoughts buzzed around his head at a frenetic pace, and all the while he tried to think back to the last time that he had fallen asleep without the aid of alcohol. He couldn't remember, and he felt terribly ashamed.

A fear gripped him as yet another spasm sent a bolt of electricity down his spine that forced his fists to clench and caused his calf muscles and toes to tighten up. Heald was as flat as a board on his back and turned to curl into a fetal position, bringing his arms and hands up to his chest, when he realized that his jaw felt as if it had been bolted shut. He forced it open by trusting his tongue through the top and bottom rows of his teeth like an eel.

The longer that he lay there, the further away the possibility of sleep seemed. He felt like the dark room was pushing all his fears and anxieties right back onto him, left to pile up on his chest like leaves from a dying tree, everything around him spinning. He was coated with sweat and could feel the damp outline of his body on the cushions beneath him. He swallowed repeatedly, constantly trying to eradicate something from his throat that could not have been there. Every so often he stopped, unable to swallow, sensing the lump in his throat—some blockage that plagued him. He thought of something else. He looked at the pipe in the corner. He wasn't breathing. That's okay, he thought, look at the pipe. The tape around its fittings was falling loose. He could fix that. Swallow the lump first. His eyes darted around the room. He was perfectly still. Not breathing. The two halves of his brain thought of two different things. He stopped shaking for a moment.

SPASM.

He swallowed and his teeth gritted and clenched shut, and once the electricity had passed through him, he gasped loudly for air, wheezing, but did not sit up. He would not sit up. It would pass. Would this pass? He had to sleep.

He thought about his grandmother, lying on her deathbed back in Michigan—he couldn't remember where. Maybe she had died already. He wondered if she was sleeping at this moment. Where was her soul? He thought about his parents. How they were asleep and Arnold was probably at the foot of the bed, examining them without lifting his head. He wanted to be a young boy again, bursting into their room, crying out for help, pleading to be shielded from another night terror. He thought of the warmth of his parents' bed after his mother made room for him by her side. He thought about how Alan would come to the side of their bed after he had settled in and she would stick her nose under the covers and peek at him to make sure he was calm, the canopy of covers above them and then a dog's face right there. He remembered touching Alan on the nose, cold and wet, then pressing his lips on her snout and sensing the movement in the dog's back signaling a wagging tail.

SPASM.

Blind white. He was on fire, and the sweat beaded and dripped off him with regularity. The futon was soaked now. His shaking allowed the droplets of sweat to collect into pools all over him and roll off his body. He imagined a woman next to him on the futon trying to share the space with him in this state. He laughed as he thought about his arm shooting outward from a spastic movement and knocking into Janice, rousing her. He thought about her hair sticking to the wet pillow. He would reach over and cup her breast with his hand, giggling as her breast jiggled with his tremors. She would put one hand over his heart and the other on top of his head, brushing his wet hair back as she mouthed the soft words of a lullaby. He would close his eyes and smile through those gritted teeth.

All around him in any direction he was surrounded by people, so many thousands, yet never had he felt so alone. The bottle in the freezer could make it stop. The bottle in the freezer was filled with life, with ataractic bliss. She could get it for him. Bring him a tall glass. Help him sleep as he pulled her into his spoon in gratitude. Stop his shaking. Blow lightly on his ear. Make her smile as they drifted off to sleep, lying still. Both smiling. Still.

Heald had almost fallen asleep when a violent seizure flattened him out and shot his eyes wide open with a flash before them. After a moment, he could feel pain and then something warm spreading through the inside of his mouth that tasted bitter and metallic. It began to pool slowly at the back of his throat, and he swallowed it with a grimace.

He had bitten off the side of his tongue.

Chapter Twenty-Seven

WHEN HEALD OPENED his eyes he was unsure if he had ever slept. Sunlight reflected up onto his ceiling, but he couldn't convince himself that it hadn't always been there. He had opened his eyes in the midst of a thought and despite still being inside of it, he struggled to pin down exactly what it was he was thinking. He felt as if he'd just been dropped onto a moving train with no idea of where it was headed and no clue as to the cargo on board. He could feel the wheels striking the rails on the tracks and his body was shaking accordingly. Heald held his hand out in front of him and watched his fingers wiggle and his thumb contract randomly. His right hand was his left hand suddenly, and he couldn't remember when he had raised it to look at that one. There were six fingers on his left hand, he thought. One was hiding. Where did it go? he asked himself.

POP.

Heald sat up as quickly as he could and as he did, he felt some of the hair on the back of his head get pulled out. He reached back and felt a hard, crusty substance with some hair stuck to it. Feeling it out, he followed a thin, dry trail of the stuff that led under his ear to the corner of his mouth. He pulled his hand out in front of him and examined it, seeing that his index and middle fingers were coated with tiny red specks atop a faint reddish blush on his skin. Heald turned over and saw the dried red stain on the cushion where his head had rested. It terrified him, and when he went to touch it, he could not locate his hand, nor remember where it had gone.

POP.

The sound spun Heald's head around. In the small apartment, little could not be seen, yet he saw nothing that could have produced such a popping noise. It sounded like someone had stepped on a balloon. Looking over toward the bathroom, Heald thought he could see something orange on the floor, but wasn't sure. His head and his body were shaking, and the movement was distracting.

He placed both feet on the floor and raised himself, but almost instantly his feet tangled and he crumpled to the floor. His arms never reached out to break his fall, and he came down upon his shoulder, but felt no pain—only fear. He rolled onto his back and looked up at the ceiling and noted that the angles were all off—instead of having four lines intersect at their ends to make a four-sided square ceiling, there seemed to be a fifth line, a fifth side. Studying the ceiling as a whole, it was hidden, but focusing on each intersecting side joining with the wall and counting them, the mysterious fifth side became apparent. I'm in the Pentagon, he thought.

POP. POP.

Heald struggled to his feet, wobbly. His heart was racing and he could feel his chest rise and fall beneath his neck as he sucked in copious amounts of air. His right hand was over his lower ribcage, as if he were guarding it.

From somewhere close by he could hear the opening bass notes to the "Ode to Joy," but they didn't sound quite right. Not like they should sound. Or so he thought. He needed to make sure.

Dun-dun-da-dun-dun-da-da-da-dun-dun-da-dun-dun—dun-

dunn.

A fear was all over him, like something hatched inside him that had been aging, and was now mature and ready to emerge. The thing had grown up and looked him in the eye and professed its love and its gratitude for the nurturing shelter. *It* could smile.

Heald had had enough. He was terrified. The part of him that he had once felt was the dominant force, the will of control, the power over his weakness, he realized had left him long ago. He knew now that he was unable to stop himself from drinking. Despite his internal insistence that sobriety was always an option for him, it was clear that this was no longer the case, and the realization filled him with an intense feeling of dread and guilt.

Without a full awareness of it, Heald found himself with his hands around an ice-cold half-gallon jug of vodka from his freezer. The frost around the frozen glass of the clear bottle sent a shiver up his arm and down his back. He broke the seal off the top, and as he tipped the large container into his mouth, he felt a very real sensation of shame and failure enter him with the alcohol.

The sting of the liquid felt shocking and painful on the gnashed hole in the side of his tongue, and for a moment, there was a gripping agony, but it was soon replaced by the warm burn that he could feel all the way down his throat, settling into his stomach like a feather falling gently onto a pillow.

Like a man exhausted after running a marathon, he gasped, as he had drunk as much from that one pull as his body would allow. He set the bottle down hard onto the counter, shooting some of the liquid up through the top. The yin and yang of relief and guilt twisted through him like two ropes in a knot. It was short-lived though, for without warning, he leaned over the sink and vomited the burning liquid onto the dirty pots and pans with a terrific force.

Heald fell to the floor, grasping the bottle in his hand. His meager burst of energy had run its course. Looking out the window and across the street onto the red bricks of the adjacent building, he took a few long breaths and tilted the bottle back up to his mouth and drank. This time he did not stop, taking only short gasps of breath, until the large bottle was nearly empty. Heald closed his eyes and set the bottle down on its side next to him. It rolled for a moment and came to rest at the base of the refrigerator. Time began to pass slowly as Heald could still feel his heart racing within his chest and the jagged, spasmodic movements causing him to bump his elbow harmlessly against the counter behind him.

When he opened his eyes again, his heart felt like it had begun to beat normally. He looked around the room, and the delayed vision and lightheadedness let him know that the alcohol was taking effect. A euphoric calm came over him as he stuck out his hand in front of his face, relieved to see no shaking in his hands. Still, throughout this respite, his eyes watered with the preponderant senses of guilt and resignation. He suddenly felt like he had to know how his grandmother was. He closed his eyes. He wanted desperately to hear his mother's voice. Anything.

Though Heald felt better and could sense some strength returning to him, he also began to feel quite sluggish. He reached up above his head and grabbed his phone off the counter and, still disregarding the messages that were on there, dialed the number for his parents' house. It was difficult to do, as some of the text on the phone was fuzzy, and he had to bring the phone quite close to his face to make out the numbers. Heald put the phone to his ear and heard it ringing on the other end; he hoped he had dialed the right number.

"Hello? Heald?" a voice said. It sounded like his mother, he thought. He tried to say hello, but all he could manage was to plop a sound from his mouth onto the receiver.

"Momp," said Heald.

"Heald, is that you? Are you at work?"

He tried to respond, but could only manage more unintelligible sounds.

"What's wrong, Heally? I can't make out what you're saying. Are you okay? Heald?"

He wanted to tell her that he loved her. He wanted to tell his father and his sister that he loved them. He wanted one more chance to say good-bye to his grandmother.

"Heald, please tell me what's happening. Please. Are you okay? Your father is here listening, too. Tell us what's going on."

"Love," Heald managed to say, though he was no longer quite conscious of why he had said it.

"Did you say 'love'? Heald, did you say 'love'? It's so hard to understand you. Are you feeling all right?"

Then, after a brief pause, his mother's voice came back louder and more clearly, as if she had moved closer to the phone.

"Is it the drinking?" Another pause. "Oh, Heald...my boy."

Heald was no longer aware that he was on the phone, slipping now between being aware, and someplace else.

"Heald, please, we need you to respond. Heald, please." His mother's voice was growing frantic.

"Sick," Heald said out loud.

There was some commotion on the other end of the phone and both Heald's mother and father could be heard talking back and forth.

"We love you, Heald, just hold on. We're calling for..."

Heald's phone fell into his lap. The arm holding the phone fell limp to the floor. His eyes were open, and on the small table near the futon he could see the photo of the old dog. He looked at it for an eternity. The dog's smile. The light in its eyes. The matted fur he could smell. Pushing his nose hard into the dog's nape. Pulling the skin back on its cheeks so all its teeth were exposed into a grin. The dog's smile.

Outside the window, on the streets of Chicago below, a man sold newspapers and the sun was high and shining and there was not a cloud in the pale blue sky. In the distance, the wail of an ambulance siren could be heard growing louder. There was not a cloud in the pale blue sky.

Epilogue

THE WOMAN LOOKED out the window at the small lake. There was a short dock extending out onto the water with three children fishing off it. They laughed and pointed at something in the water, but the woman did not smile when she saw this.

She turned and looked around at the room with its easels standing erect and empty. There were large photographs pinned to the walls and little statues and clay molds of things on shelves throughout the studio. She walked carefully through the maze of boxes on the floor, all filled with her mother's paintings and framed canvases, and went over to a table. On it rested old bottles of paint, half-empty, and a number of dried leaves, stones, seashells, and other trinkets, all covered in a thick layer of dust.

She leaned down and picked up a cardboard box and delicately selected the paints one by one and put them into the box. Then she picked up the leaves and stones and shells and placed them on a bathroom towel and lightly folded the towel up, inserting it next to the paints. She carried the box out into the hallway toward the staircase.

The rest of the place was barren of furniture and anything else. The walls were bare. She walked through the kitchen, past her husband who stood at the counter filling out paperwork, concentrating on what he was writing.

She carried the box out the front door and turned toward her car and its open trunk. Past the driveway, just off in the woods, a deer watched silent and still, unseen, and a cardinal nestled under the eaves chirped brightly.

About the Author

Born and bred in Detroit, Michael A. Ferro holds a degree in creative writing from Michigan State University and won the Jim Cash Creative Writing Award for Fiction in 2008. Michael's fiction and essays have been featured in numerous online and print publications. *TITLE 13* is his first novel. Michael has lived, worked, and written throughout the Midwest; he currently resides in rural Ann Arbor, Michigan.

Additional information and writing can be found at:

www.michaelaferro.com

More books from Harvard Square Editions:

People and Peppers, Kelvin Christopher James

Gates of Eden, Charles Degelman

Love's Affliction, Fidelis Mkparu

Transoceanic Lights, S. Li

Close, Erika Raskin

Anomie, Jeff Lockwood

Living Treasures, Yang Huang

Nature's Confession, J.L. Morin

Love and Famine, Han-ping Chin

Dark Lady of Hollywood, Diane Haithman

How Fast Can You Run, Harriet Levin Millan

Appointment with ISIL, Joe Giordano

Never Summer, Tim Blaine

Parallel, Sharon Erby